FACE OF THE VOID

DESA KINCAID BOOK 3

R.S. PENNEY

Dedicated to Jori Vian, the person who made this possible.

PROLOGUE

The noonday sun beat down on a clearing surrounded by trees that Desa couldn't name. Skinny trees with trunks that rose fifty feet before sprouting a single branch, fat trees as large as a house with roots slithering into the earth like grasping tentacles: all of them growing green and strong. They were well south of the Borathorin, far beyond the borders of the *Al a Nari*. It was summer on this side of the world.

The clearing was about half a mile across, dominated by a rock-strewn hill that rose about fifteen feet into the air, and at its crest, the ruins of something that might once have been a temple stood solemn and forgotten.

Crouching at the base of the hill in brown trousers and a white blouse with the top buttons left open, her eyes shaded by the brim of a hat, Desa wiped the sweat from her brow. "This is it."

Kalia stood a few feet away, dressed in similar clothing, seemingly unbothered by the heat. The woman *had* grown up in a desert. A little scorching sunlight was nothing to her. "You're sure?"

"If I'm wrong, we'll know soon enough."

Rojan Von Aldono emerged from the forest with the strap of his knapsack slung over one shoulder, his face glistening with sweat. "My people have formed a perimeter," he said. "Are you certain you wish to enter that structure? If this is a place of the gods, there may be devices that we do not understand. Some may be dangerous."

Desa stood up, knuckling her back. "Mercy brought us here for a reason," she said. "There's something here that we need to see."

The ride south had taken the better part of two months. It would soon be mid-winter back in Aladar. Months in which Desa had left her people to fend for themselves against Adele. Against *Hanak Tuvar*. Mercy would appear now and then to point them in the right direction, but the goddess – or whatever she was – could only remain with them for a few moments before she was yanked back to the abandoned city in the desert. As such, they had been forced to make several course corrections.

Desa reached for Kalia and felt a moment of reassurance when the other woman took her hand. Together, they ascended the hillside until they reached the top. The temple was just a collection of stone slabs that had once formed the base of a building and pillars that no longer supported a roof, all with moss growing on them.

She saw nothing of note until her eyes fell upon a set of stairs that led down into a cavern of some kind. Or more likely the temple's basement. Desa wasn't sure, but the structure was definitely man-made. How old was this place? How could her primitive ancestors have managed such construction?

Drawing her pistol, Desa lifted it up in front of her face, its barrel pointed skyward, and cocked the hammer. "I'll go first."

Leaning one shoulder against a pillar, Kalia folded her arms and sighed. "Really?" she asked, eyebrows rising. "Are you expecting to find trouble down there?"

"I always expect trouble," Desa muttered. "And I am seldom disappointed."

She raised a hand, triggering the Light-Source in her ring to hold back the darkness. The walls of the tunnel were composed of a thick, gray stone that sparkled. Down she went, step by step, until she reached a large dome-shaped chamber.

Waving her hand back and forth, she searched for something, anything, that might make this long journey worthwhile. But there was nothing. Only mud and lumpy rocks that protruded from the floor. Maybe they had taken a wrong turn somewhere. Maybe this was not the place Mercy wanted them to find. What could-

Her light fell upon a stone arch in the middle of the chamber, a smooth doorway growing out of the floor with unmistakable glyphs on its surface. They weren't in any language that Desa recognized, but it was clearly a form of writing. What she wouldn't give to have Dalen with her on this expedition. She was willing to bet good money that there was a reference to this device – or something like it – in the *Vadir Scrolls*.

Pistol in hand, Desa crept forward and narrowed her eyes. "I think I've found it," she said. "This must be what Mercy wanted us to see."

As if the sound of her name summoned her, the goddess materialized right in front of Desa, blocking her path. Once upon a time, the sudden appearance of a hooded figure in black robes would have been terrifying, but now, it was almost blasé.

Mercy had her hands up in a forestalling gesture as if trying to warn Desa not to get too close to the arch. She kept shaking her head for emphasis.

"What is it?"

The air stirred when the goddess vanished and then reappeared next to the wall, pointing insistently at the ground under her feet.

"You want us to dig something up?"

Mercy was gone before she could answer, pulled back to her desert prison. That was always the way. Sometimes, she could stay for a few minutes, and sometimes for only a few seconds, but she always vanished when Desa was about to ask something pertinent.

Exhaling, Desa focused her thoughts and let the exasperation drain out of her. She cleared her mind, going through exercises that were so familiar they had become rote, and reached out to the Ether.

The cavern became a tempest of dancing particles. Even the light emanating from her ring had changed, now visible to her as tiny packets of energy expanding in all directions.

Kalia was a galaxy of molecules at the foot of the stairs, and yet, somehow, Desa could still sense the contours of her face. The other woman was frowning as she stared at the spot where Mercy had been standing. "What was that about?"

Unable to reply, Desa probed the ground with her mind. She found something she had not expected: a metal box buried about three feet deep. Now, wasn't that interesting?

The world snapped back to normal as Desa released the Ether. "Something's down there," she said. "Help me dig it up."

THE CRACKLING campfire sent motes of flame into the night sky along with a plume of smoke. Its flickering light reflected off the trunks of nearby trees. They had settled in for the night about a mile north of the ruined temple. Rojan's people were all curled up in their bedrolls or enjoying a second helping of a stew made from goat meat, carrots and celery.

Desa sat with her back against a log, the metal box resting in her lap. She traced the glyphs along its lid with one finger. What a strange device. It had a locking mechanism, but no keyhole. Who would design such a thing?

Standing just a few feet away, Kalia put one hand on her hip, cocked her head and flashed a smile. "Any luck?"

A grimace betrayed Desa's frustration. "No," she muttered, shaking her head. "I can't get it open. I've probed the device inside through the Ether, but it's like nothing I've ever seen before."

"What do you think it does?"

Falling back against the log, Desa covered her eyes with both hands. "I haven't the faintest idea," she said through a yawn. "A weapon, perhaps. Something that we can use against Adele."

Kalia turned her head to stare thoughtfully into the fire. She really was quite lovely. There were days when Desa wished that she could have met the other woman years ago, but then, things might have gone wrong if she had encountered Kalia Troval as a young woman. Or rather, they might have gone wrong sooner. Love always went wrong. It was the way of things.

"Hmm," Kalia murmured. "Maybe you should ask Mercy about it the next time she makes an appearance."

"I intend to."

"Still can't believe the ghost in the dead city was a goddess."

Desa crossed her arms, a frown tugging at the corners of her mouth. "I don't think Mercy *is* a goddess," she said. "Not really. She's powerful but fallible."

Kalia sank to her knees about five feet away, folding hands in her lap and breathing deeply. "Then what do you think she is?" she mumbled. "What else besides a god could survive for so many centuries."

"Perhaps she's a creature from beyond the stars."

"What?"

Turning her face up to the heavens, Desa squinted. "Is it really so unbelievable?" she asked. "We saw Vengeance fly off into the sky when she left us. My people believe that our world is only one of many in the cosmos."

Inspiration fell upon her like a tidal wave. She had the Ether in an instant, the world transforming before her eyes. Particles. Particles everywhere she looked. She could trace the contours of every object with her mind, every blade of grass, every rock, every tendril of smoke. It was all there for her: a world just begging to be explored.

The locking mechanism was a pair of switches *inside* the box. Switches with small, metal prongs directly across from them. At first, Desa had thought that an oddity. Why include such a useless feature that only took up valuable storage space? But now, she saw the solution.

She began a pair of Infusions, feeding strands of the Ether into the space between the molecules that made up those two prongs. It only took a few seconds to complete the work. She would only need a tiny amount of kinetic energy. Releasing the Ether, Desa triggered the Force-Sources she had created.

The lid popped open.

Kalia's jaw dropped, a soft gasp passing through her lips. "Almighty," she hissed, scooching closer. "You did it."

"Ingenious," Desa said. "Whoever created this wanted to make sure that only a Field Binder could open it."

Inside the box, she found a blue crystal with a brass cage around it. The whole thing was small enough to fit in the palm of her hand. But she still had no idea what it did.

Mercy appeared a moment later, standing before her in black robes that seemed to drink in the firelight. The darkness in that hood threatened to swallow her whole. Desa did not know how the goddess had been trapped in such a menacing form, but she was confident that Vengeance had a hand in it. A cruel joke. The goddess of benevolence cursed with a form that made everyone too afraid to accept her help.

"What is it?" Desa asked, communing with the Ether the

instant the words left her mouth. Once again, the world changed, and so did Mercy. No longer a shadowy wraith, she now appeared to Desa as a matronly woman in a blue dress. Black curls framed a face of dark-brown skin. Her eyes shone with the warmth of the sun. The Ether revealed the truth. Always.

"Technology," Mercy said. "You must power it with the Ether. The Infusions will have faded after ten thousand years, but they can be renewed. Take it back to the clearing where you found the temple, and activate it there."

What will I see?

"The truth."

And what was that archway in the cavern?

"The answers you seek are in the device. Do not go near the archway until you understand its purpose. Some dangers are best avoided."

Mercy bent over, placing one hand on Desa's head and the other on Kalia's A pleasant warmth passed through Desa. "So that you may understand the words of a tongue long dead," the goddess explained. "I cannot remain. Use the device. Learn the truth. And when you have your answers, seek me out. We have much work to do."

IT TOOK NEARLY two hours to Infuse the cage around the crystal with a suitable connection to the Ether. When Desa scanned it with her mind, she found something she had not expected: circuitry encased within the metal. Circuity far more advanced than anything she had seen in Aladar. Whoever had created this device was at least a century ahead of the Aladri. Probably more. All she could say was that this thing would draw a considerable amount of power.

The silver light of a full moon illuminated a narrow path that cut through the forest, providing just enough illumination for her to see clearly. A good thing too. She was tired after Infusing the device; she didn't want to have to replenish her ring as well.

"What I don't understand," Desa said, lifting a vine so she could duck underneath it, "is why Vengeance would want to curse her sister with the form of a wraith."

Kalia was right behind her, grumbling as she made her way over the uneven terrain. "Everyone who encounters the ghost sees something different," the other woman replied. "But it's never anything pleasant."

Pausing with one hand on a tree, Desa looked back over her shoulder. "Still, the question remains," she said. "What purpose could it serve other than cruelty?"

"Are you sure it was Vengeance?"

Desa felt wrinkles lining her brow. "As sure as I can be of anything," she muttered, starting forward again. The forest seemed to close in around her, and she was forced to wiggle through a gap so narrow bark brushed her arms.

"Well," Kalia said, grunting as she stepped through. "Her name *is* Vengeance. So, maybe it was just cruelty for cruelty's sake."

Closing her eyes, Desa shook her head forcefully. "No, I don't think so," she said, hopping over a large root. "Vengeance is harsh, and she might even take some pleasure in seeing people suffer. But there seems to be a lesson in her cruelty. She let us go when we demonstrated compassion."

"Well, you've got me," Kalia said. "I wouldn't presume to know the mind of a creature from beyond the stars."

The path opened into a clearing, and a cool breeze brought some relief from the night's muggy heat. Moonlight reflected off the rocks that jutted out of the hillside. At night, the ruined temple was an ominous shadow against the darkness, a setting right out of every ghost story Desa had ever heard.

She set the crystal down on a patch of dried mud.

Rising, Desa dusted her hands and strode deeper into the clearing. "That should do it." She spun around to face her partner. "Mercy gave us no specific instructions about where to use this thing. Here seems as good a place as any."

Kalia was standing at the tree line, her face barely visible in the moonlight. "Are you sure?" she asked. "Based on what you told me, I got the impression that Mercy wants us to use the device *inside* the temple."

"I think she would have told us if that were the case."

Kalia shrugged, stepping forward to glower at the small device at her feet. "I guess we won't know until we try," she mumbled. "We'd best get on with it then."

Desa triggered the Electric-Source she had created.

The crystal began to glow with a soft, blue light that expanded until it filled the entire clearing. Teal beams scanned back and forth, painting images that stood hundreds of feet tall, sketching the outlines of buildings. Desa felt her heart pounding, felt sweat on her palms. She had never dreamed that such a thing could be possible. Though her rational mind knew better, some small part of her believed that this could only be the technology of the gods.

Other colours filled the image, and soon she was surrounded by transparent spires of glass. They came in all shapes and sizes. One was a perfect cylinder that stood at least thirty stories high with a ring of windows on every floor. Another was shaped almost like a set of stairs but with grass and trees growing on the top of each step. More and more appeared all around her. Some of those structures seemed to be rising out of the forest, causing birds to squawk and animals to flee.

Kalia stared up at the ghostly city in wide-eyed wonder.

People appeared as well, men and women in fashions that Desa did not recognize, each one of them as transparent as the towers that surrounded them. And automobiles. Automobiles unlike any she had ever seen before.

One man walked right through Kalia, and she screamed, covering her mouth with one hand. "Ghosts!" she moaned. "This is a city of the dead!"

"Yes, it is," Desa agreed. "But they aren't ghosts." She waved her hand through the spectral image of an old woman who seemed to be hobbling across the street. "It's only sculpted light. No different from a painting, just much more advanced."

The front steps of a grand building appeared over the hill that led up to the temple. A fitting place, in Desa's estimation. The building itself was magnificent, round with a domed roof.

A man in this world's equivalent of a suit stood behind a podium at the foot of those stairs. "Thank you all for being with us on this momentous day," he said to an audience that had gathered around Desa and Kalia. "For many years now, our physicists have suspected that the Unifying Field expands beyond the confines of our world. Beyond the confines of our solar system."

Desa exchanged a glance with her partner.

"Now, at last, we have confirmation," the man went on. "Not only does the Unifying Field permeate every inch of space within this universe, it also connects to many others. Worlds so very much like our own but where history unfolded differently."

Desa strode forward, passing through ghostly figure after ghostly figure as she approached the stairs. "Other universes," she murmured. "I think I understand."

"That makes one of us," Kalia said.

The man at the podium smiled for the crowd. "The Unifying Field can bridge one universe with another," he said. "Our people will step into a new frontier, explore new worlds, create new possibilities."

He turned, gesturing to something on the stairs behind him.

Desa looked up to find two men in white coats on the top step. Scientists, she suspected. And standing between them was a metal doorway with glyphs on its surface. Metal. So, not the same device that she had discovered in the cavern. But a companion to it, perhaps.

The image faded away, buildings, people and cars all vanishing, but the crystal continued to emit soft, blue light. Enough to illuminate the entire clearing.

Kalia stepped forward with her mouth agape, shuddering as she drew in a breath. The poor woman was trying to make sense of what she had seen. "They were travelers from another universe? And they came here?"

"And settled."

"What?"

"They're our ancestors, my love," Desa said. "I'm sure of it."

Kalia grimaced, shaking her head. "How can that be?" she demanded. "Surely, we would know about it. There would be some legend or...*something!*"

Dirt scuffed under Desa's boots as she approached the other woman. "There are legends," she said. "My people's earliest myths are of Mercy and Vengeance leading us away from danger, to a new home."

"Away from danger?"

Turning her back on the other woman, Desa gazed up at the ruined temple, at the spot where the metal doorway had stood. "Away from *Hanak Tuvar*," she said. "Or at least, that is my guess."

She was about to say more, but the crystal began constructing another image, teal beams drawing the outline of a room. Colour bled into the walls and the furniture. Desa was surrounded by metal tables and some kind of equipment she didn't recognize, all sterile and white. And transparent.

A woman appeared from out of nowhere, marching across the room. She was about average height, slightly plump with a round face of dark-brown skin. Her curly hair was left to hang loose to her shoulders. A pair of spectacles sat on her nose.

Desa recognized her instantly.

Mercy.

"Daily log," the woman said. "Well, the chancellor made quite an impression today with his speech. Grand dreams of exploring other universes. A noble goal, I suppose, if pursued as a matter of scientific inquiry, though I suspect the Council of Twelve will insist upon colonization. Since any suitable world will likely have lifeforms comparable to our own, I shudder to think about what might happen if our expeditions should encounter any less advanced societies."

The woman paused at a counter that ran along one wall, hanging her head and letting out a sigh. "Still, we here at the Transcendentalist Project will continue our work," she went on. "Expanding outward to other universes is a remarkable achievement, but there are those among us who see greater value in looking inward. To become one with the Unifying Field itself..."

"Are you still recording?"

Another woman came through a door that must have led out to a hallway, this one tall and slim with pale skin and red hair tied up in a ponytail. Vengeance. She wore a uniform of some kind, most likely that of a military officer. "The general is growing impatient with the delays, Nari."

"The general's impatience does not concern me."

"He says that we're making very little progress."

Nari's high heels clicked on the floor tiles as she paced across the room. "That is because he asks the impossible!" she protested. "Direct Infusions into living tissue? It cannot be done, and we have told him as much."

"Listen-"

"The Field can be bound to inanimate objects," Nari pressed on. "Never to living tissue. Not even to something that had once been alive!"

Vengeance – or whatever her name was – put her fists on her hips, thrust out her chin and sniffed. "We have poured an enormous amount of funding into this project, Nari," she said. "Funding that could be diverted to more practical applications."

Baring her teeth, Nari hissed. She looked very much like a cat that wanted to claw something. "So that you can create a living weapon!" she spat. "You think I don't know your true purpose? I began this project to expand the limits of human consciousness, not to create yet another instrument of destruction. I will not-"

The image vanished, and the crystal went dark, its energy source depleted. Thick darkness settled over the clearing. It took a moment for Desa's eyes to adjust.

Kalia dropped to one knee, retrieving the small device, cradling it in the palm of her hand. "What does it mean?" she asked. "Everything we saw..."

Desa put her hands on the other woman's shoulders, dropping to her knees before her. She stared into Kalia's lovely, brown eyes. "It means we have work to do," she said. "Tomorrow morning, we start going north."

PART I

1

Consciousness crept into Desa's mind, and she rolled over to find Kalia sound asleep beside her. A light drizzle patterned against the window, and the gray light of an overcast morning streamed into the bedroom.

Two months.

Two more months in the saddle, making their way northward across some very rough terrain. They had crossed through scorching flatlands and dense swamps until they finally reached the *Al a Nari* city of Te'Alon. That was five days ago.

Desa had planned to set out again the very next morning – they had to get back to Eradia; that was where they would find Adele – but exhaustion had convinced her to remain for one more day. And then another. And then one more after that. Each night, she went to bed, promising herself that tomorrow, she would begin the long journey to her homeland, and each morning, she found another reason to stay.

Here, in the northern hemisphere, the winter rains had come. It was still warm this close to the equator – much warmer than it would be in Eradia, anyway – but the weather was still unpleasant, making the prospect of another journey even more unappealing.

Curled up on her side with the blankets pulled up to her neck, Desa blinked a few times. "Sweetie," she whispered. "It's time to wake up."

She kissed Kalia's nose, and the other woman opened her eyes, a slow smile blossoming on her face. "Are you sure?" Kalia murmured. "Couldn't we stay just a few more minutes?"

"We have to get moving," Desa lamented.

Mercy had appeared to her several times over the last week, always to ask when Desa would resume her trek northward. The goddess may have been mortal once, but she seemed to have forgotten the strain that travel put on a human body.

Sitting up with the covers held to her chest, Desa squinted at the wall across from her bed. "Come on," she said. "No more dawdling."

She was dressed in five minutes, having donned a pair of beige pants, a red blouse and a brown, leather jacket. A wide-brimmed hat completed the ensemble. She hurried out the door and down the stairs before Kalia could protest.

The small hostel where they had taken lodgings was a gray-stone building with a garden in its front yard. None of the plants were in bloom, sadly, leaving nothing but mud on either side of the narrow path that led down to the sidewalk. The paved road was slick with rainfall, and on the other side, several other buildings just like this one stood in neat, little rows.

A man in a brown coat rode past on a bicycle, slowing to offer a friendly wave before he continued down the street. Water sprayed into the air as he splashed through a puddle. Just another winter morning in Te'Alon.

Walking across the street with her hands in her coat pockets, Desa exhaled through her nose. "We've been here too long already," she mumbled. "Hot food and comfortable beds turn good women into layabouts."

Rain fell upon a gray building with black shingles on its gabled roof. Light spilled out from the two, rectangular windows on either side of the front door. When Desa went inside, she found a small café with round, wooden tables. There were a few patrons present, but with the workday starting soon, the place was quiet.

A copper-skinned woman in a red dress stood behind a wooden counter. She looked up when she heard the door open and flashed a smile. "Desa Nin Leean."

"Kadya Nin Pareem," Desa replied. "I see business is going well."

"Well enough. What can I get you?"

Folding her hands on the counter, Desa frowned as she considered the question. "Do you have any of that wonderful tea?" she said at last. "The one you served me a few days ago?"

Kadya turned around, scanning the top shelf with her index finger. "Let me check," she said. "I think I might-"

She was cut off by the sound of the door opening, and Desa whirled around to find Rojan stomping into the café. His hair was drenched, droplets of water trailing over his olive-skinned face. "You're here," he said. "Good."

"What's wrong?"

He shuffled up to Desa and leaned in close to whisper in her ear. "The scouts on the northern perimeter failed to report in." He cast a glance around the room to make sure no one was listening and then pressed on. "Something is amiss."

"You've never had scouts fail to report in?"

"It's part of the protocol," Rojan explained. "They carry radios. If the squad leader is in some way indisposed, someone else takes on the task. For the entire team to be out of contact for so long..."

"I understand."

Clearing his throat, Rojan glanced over his shoulder toward the window. Then his eyes fell upon her again. "You have proficiency with the more aggressive aspects of Field Binding." Did he have to put it that way? Desa would have felt better if he had simply said that she knew how to kill. The euphemism made it seem dirty somehow. "I was hoping you would come with me to see what went wrong."

Another delay. She had been hoping to start northward before noon. But the *Al a Nari* had shown her incredible kindness. She owed them. This small favour was not too much to ask. "Of course," she said. "Kalia should come as well. Her talents almost rival my own."

RAINDROPS SLID over the lenses of Desa's binoculars, distorting the image somewhat, but it wasn't hard to miss the black coats and blue trousers of Eradian soldiers, men who crept through the damp grass with rifles in hand. They moved slowly as if they expected trouble to jump out from the trees on either side of them, which it very well might. The *Al a Nari* preferred to ambush foreign invaders before they got too close to a city.

Desa hid behind a small outcropping of rocks with Kalia, Rojan and the rest of his team. From her position at the top of a hill, she could see the enemy clearly. "Eradians," she muttered under her breath.

Crouching on her left with one of those energy pistols in hand, Rojan snarled as the word passed through her lips. "The scouting team was six miles north of here when they last reported in," he spat. "Now, we know what happened."

Lowering the binoculars, Desa shook her head. "How could they have gotten past you?" she asked. "I remember the warm welcome you gave me and my friends."

Kalia was on her right, hands gripping the rock ledge as she ventured a peek over it. "Could they have slipped past the patrols?" she wondered aloud. "Your territory is vast. I can't imagine that you would be able to monitor every inch of the border."

"Their technology is at least a century behind ours," Rojan grumbled. "And they do not have access to the Ether. We can sense an approaching army before it gets anywhere near one of our settlements."

"Then maybe they had help," Desa muttered.

"What kind of help?"

She didn't answer him. Adele had demonstrated the ability to transport troops over great distances. Was this another raid? If so, then Desa was the cause of it. The attack on Aladar had been nothing but an elaborate scheme to kill her.

But why now?

Adele had been relentless in her attempts to kill Desa during those first few months after she gained her new powers, but Desa had not seen her since their fight outside the Temple of Vengeance. Four months of silence was, in her estimation, a very good sign. She had even started to entertain the notion that the other woman might have died from her wounds. But Mercy insisted that *Hanak Tuvar* was still a threat.

"Help or no help," Rojan growled. "It's time to put an end to this."

He hopped onto the rocks standing tall so that the Eradians below could see him. "Gentlemen!" he called out in their language. "I think it's time you turned around and went home."

Desa looked through the binoculars again and found *Al a Nari* scouts emerging from the trees on either side of the field. Every one of them carried one of those crescent-shaped pistols or a longer, tube-like device that would be the equivalent of a rifle. The latter weren't any more powerful than their smaller cousins – that size of an object had no bearing on how much energy it could store – but some people found the larger weapons easier to aim.

The Eradians lifted their rifles.

Rojan's team fired first.

Streaks of lightning converged on the enemy from all directions like spokes on a wheel meeting at a central point. Converged but never quite found their targets. They seemed to run up against an invisible dome that had sprung up around the Eradians. Desa had never seen anything like it.

The glare of all that electricity in one spot made her eyes smart. The dome crackled and hissed, raindrops evaporating the instant they made contact.

Adele was suddenly there, appearing from out of thin air and gathering all of that energy into the palm of her hand. Desa gasped at the sight of her. The other woman had changed considerably since their last encounter.

Her golden hair was now as black as pitch and as coarse as straw. The scales on her left hand had traveled up her forearm almost to the elbow. When she opened her mouth, Desa saw two pointed fangs. And her eyes. Orange with vertical slits where the pupils should be.

Instead of the flowing, white gown, the woman now wore a simple, black dress that left her shoulders bare, its flaring skirt nearly brushing the grass. Whatever human skin remained was now pale and sickly.

When she had collected all of the lightning, Adele screamed and sent it into the sky as a single jagged lance. The peel of thunder that followed made Desa's ears pop. Silence fell over the field as everyone stood dumbstruck.

Adele extended a scaly hand toward the *Al a Nari* on her left, closing her fist with a growl. The ground erupted with a spray of dirt, tossing bodies into the air. Before they landed, she stretched a pale hand toward the men and women on her right, and they too were tossed about like toys kicked by an angry child.

"Adele!" Desa screamed.

Rounding on her, the other woman flashed a smile that displayed her fangs. Her eyes shone with eagerness. "Ah, so *here* you are!"

Desa was over the rocks and charging down the hillside in an instant, drawing her pistol from its holster. She cocked the hammer, raised the weapon in one hand and fired. *CRACK! CRACK! CRACK!*

Bullets became wisps of smoke when they got within an inch of Adele. But they were nothing but a distraction. Sound and fury to draw the eye and addle the mind.

Sliding to a stop, Desa thrust her closed fist toward the other woman and triggered the Electric-Source within her ring. A blast of lightning shot across the field. Adele was forced to stagger backward, gathering the electricity between her two palms.

She spun to her right, ignoring Desa, and sent it hurtling toward an *Al a Nari* man as a single bolt that struck him right in the chest. The poor fellow was thrown backward into a tree, his scorched body falling to the ground.

The Eradians sprang into motion, firing at the men behind the rocks and the ones in the trees. They ignored Desa completely. And why not? If the Aladri witch wanted to challenge their goddess, it was no business of theirs.

Rage spiked within Desa, driving rational thought away. Before she realized it, she had a hand in her pocket. She fished out a small coin, threw it as hard as she could and triggered the Heat-Sink.

The coin came to a stop, hovering about an inch away from Adele's delicate nose. Mist formed around her body, but the other woman was unaffected by the sudden drop in temperature. Her cruel laughter felt like nails digging into Desa's brain.

With a quick pivot to her left, Adele concentrated all of the super-chilled air into one spot and released it as a thin stream that hit an *Al a Nari* woman as she ran through the trees. In seconds, the woman was frozen solid.

"That's two!" Adele shouted. "How many of your new friends do you intend to kill, Desa? I would have hoped that you might stop with Sebastian!"

Desa ignored her, slamming her gun back into its holster. She dashed through the grass in a headlong charge, heedless of any danger. If necessary, she would squeeze the life from her enemy with her own bare hands.

Adele stopped her with a dismissive flick of the wrist.

Some invisible force flung Desa sideways, to her left. Her shoulder hit the trunk of an oak, and she bounced off, pain surging through her body. No time to recover. She had to put an end to this.

When she turned, Adele was gliding toward her, feet barely touching the grass. The woman chuckled, shaking her head. "You never do learn, do you?" she purred. "Let me say it clearly: you cannot kill me."

She stretched a hand toward Desa.

The tree behind her cracked and split, groaning as it began to topple over. Desa leaped out of the way at the last second, thirteen hundred pounds of wood hitting the ground with a rumble.

Wincing as tears slid over her cheeks, Desa gave her head a shake. Her shoulder was dislocated; she could feel it. It took everything she had to stay on her feet, to fight through the pain.

Adele just kept coming.

Spinning to face her, Desa backed up into the thicket. "Come on!" she panted. "If you're so powerful, why can't you kill one insignificant woman?"

A scream ripped its way out of Adele's throat.

Triggering her Gravity-Sink, Desa jumped and back-flipped mere moments before the ground exploded with a deafening roar. Dirt fountained into the air. Some of it pelted her, sending new jolts of pain through her body.

She landed with a grunt, then jumped and back-flipped again. Another explosion followed half a second later. At this rate, the entire valley would be a wasteland in a matter of hours.

A burst of kinetic energy hit Desa like a punch to the chest, pinning her against the trunk of a tree. She was trapped, unable to move, barely able to breathe. Maybe her luck had finally run out.

Adele strode across the craters that she had made, her face red, her eyes wild with feral hatred. "Impudent, little primate," she seethed. "You really think your pitiful powers are a match for mine?"

Desa laughed.

"Bravado in the face of death," Adele said. "Well, at least that's something. What's so funny, Desa?"

"You stepped right into the trap."

The other woman opened her mouth to speak, but she was cut off when the blade of a dagger punched through her chest, right between her breasts. Adele looked down at herself in confusion. "Perhaps we're unclear on the concept of immortality," she said. "Is this supposed to stop me?"

"No," Desa replied. *"This* is."

She found the Ether with no effort, and the world became a sea of dancing particles. The trees, the dirt, the clothes on her body: all clusters of molecules. Except Adele. She was nothing but a black pit of emptiness.

Emptiness that could be filled.

Desa forced the Ether into the gap, temporarily severing Adele from the source of her power. She expected to hear a scream or a whimper, but there was nothing of the sort. Only a soft, gurgling sound. The force holding Desa in place vanished, and she released the Ether as she fell.

Adele was hunched over, blood spilling from her mouth as she choked. Her eyes were blue again. Blue and full of terror. She fell to her knees, revealing Kalia, who stood right behind her.

A snarl twisted the sheriff's face into a mask of hatred. "That," Kalia seethed, "was for betraying the woman I love." She yanked the dagger out, producing a squeak from Adele as blood fountained from the wound. Grabbing a fistful of black hair, Kalia tilted the other woman's head back to expose her neck. "This..."

"Protect the weapon!" an Eradian shouted.

He came running into the thicket with a rifle clutched in both hands.

Responding to the noise, Kalia spun to face him and raised a hand to shield herself. The man lifted his rifle and fired with a thunderous roar. His bullet jerked to an abrupt halt, hanging in midair.

Drawing her pistol with her good hand, Desa spun it around her index finger and then cocked the hammer. She fired a single shot, releasing a bullet that landed at the soldier's feet.

The ground exploded when she triggered the Force-Source, sending the poor man flying. He crashed right through the hanging branch of an ash tree, causing it to snap, and then fell to land some fifty feet away.

Adele looked up, her eyes becoming orange again, round pupils transforming into vertical slits. She hissed, displaying those sharp fangs.

Two seconds later, she vanished.

Desa tossed her head back, squeezing her eyes shut and trembling with impotent rage. "No!" she groaned. "Not again!"

The Eradians were fleeing. Without their goddess, they were no match for Rojan and his team. *Al a Nari* scouts fired blasts of lightning that sent them running.

"We had her," Kalia lamented. "The plan worked perfectly."

"Except she still escaped!" Desa kicked a rock, sending it skittering through the dirt until it hit a tree. "And good people died."

With the immediate danger gone, the pain in her arm became too much to ignore. Eight hours in the saddle was not something that she looked forward to, but there was no getting around it. They couldn't afford to delay another day. Not after what they had just seen. They needed a permanent solution to the problem, and Mercy was the only person who had one. Desa would just have to spend some time in the Ether's embrace.

"Come back to the city," Rojan said. "Let's regroup."

AN ELECTRIC BULB in the ceiling cast light down on the wooden table in the hostel's dining room. Raindrops hit the window with a steady drumbeat. Not a good day to begin a journey. Especially if you were recovering from a nasty wound.

Desa sat in a wooden chair, rubbing her upper arm and wincing from the pain. "I am sorry," she said. "Your people are dead because of me. It's a debt that I can never repay."

Rojan had reset her shoulder. Now, it was just a matter of time before the Ether healed her. What she wouldn't give for some time alone. She had had none since the end of the battle.

Pacing around the table with his chin clasped in one hand, Rojan grunted at her apology. "I fail to see how any of this is your fault, Desa Nin Leean," he said. "You did not kill my people."

"I gave Adele the means to kill them."

The man spun to face her, leaning forward with his hands on the table. His brow furrowed. "From what I saw, she was perfectly capable of dealing out death without any help from you," he growled. "She redirected the energy you used against her because she knew you would blame yourself. I suggest that you don't play her game."

Kalia sat with one leg crossed over the other, her mouth a thin line as she worked through something in her head. "What I want to know," she said, "is why that soldier called Adele 'the weapon.' Seems an odd name for an entity that you revere."

Desa slumped over, covering her face with one hand, massaging her eyelids. "It doesn't matter," she groaned. "The plan failed."

"It almost succeeded."

"Almost isn't good enough."

"She will be back," Rojan lamented. "We've received messages by telegraph. The Eradians have attacked four of our outposts, and your Adele was present in every one of those engagements. Each time, our forces managed to repel the invaders until – and I quote – 'the black-haired demoness arrived and called lightning down from the sky.'"

Desa stood up, exhaling slowly, and nodded once. "She will be back," she agreed. "Which means we can't stay here."

"We could use your assistance, Desa."

"And I would gladly offer it." The thought of leaving these people after they had shown her such kindness was like a knife to the chest. Once again, Desa Kincaid failed those who needed her most. "But you saw the power that Adele wields. Brute force will not defeat her. We need to know her weaknesses, and Mercy is the only one who can tell us what to do."

Rojan studied her with obvious skepticism in his brown eyes. "Can she not impart such knowledge during one of her frequent visits?" he inquired. "It should be a simple matter for a goddess."

"I've asked," Desa replied. "Mercy can only appear for a few moments at a time. Not the easiest way to teach someone about the abstract concepts of metaphysics. We need to know what she knows."

Rojan sighed.

Moving around the table, Desa put herself right in front of him. She looked up into his eyes. "Two more Field Binders won't save your people," she said. "If Adele isn't stopped, your nation will fall in a matter of months. I can do much more for you if I find a way to end this threat once and for all."

"Then go with our blessing, Desa Nin Leean," he said. "And come back soon."

THE WEAVER REAPPEARED in her cell, shivering as she dropped to her knees. She could feel her organs healing, changing. With each use of her powers, the humanity drained out of her. Soon, she would be as monstrous as Benny.

Her uncle Timothy stepped into the doorway, scowling at the sight of her. "What happened?" He strode into the cell, seized her chin with one hand and turned her face up to him. "You were injured."

The Weaver said nothing.

"This should not be possible," Timothy said. "No one should be able to harm you in this way. Who did this?"

"Desa Kincaid."

Timothy backed away, resting one hand on the stone wall. His head drooped as if he had been the one to fight a harrowing battle. "I've heard the name," he barked. "She's a bounty hunter from the northern towns, is she not? What's she doing in Ithanar?"

Laughing maliciously, the Weaver felt a grin coming on. "Looking for ways to kill *me,*" she said. "She has a rather singular focus."

"And she was able to harm you?"

The Weaver tried to rise, but the pain forced her back to her knees. She pressed a hand to her chest instinctively. "It wasn't the first time," she muttered. "I had hoped that this vessel might last for years, but Desa has removed that possibility."

Seating himself on a wooden stool, Timothy folded his hands in his lap. His mouth was tight with disapproval. "If she can harm you," he began, "this woman may prove to be an impediment to our plans."

"Such incisive observations," the Weaver murmured. "I can see why they made you mayor."

"You will go back and destroy the savages."

"I will do no such thing."

Reaching into his coat, Timothy retrieved a black crystal from its inner pocket. He held it up to the light so that she could look upon its shimmering surface. The sight of it made her want to claw his eyes out. "Need I remind you which of us is in control?"

Crawling on hands and knees, the Weaver made her way toward him. She looked up and flashed a devilish smile. "You can compel me to fight," she said. "But this body will not survive. And do you know what happens then?"

She forced herself to stand.

Timothy tried to rise as well, but she clamped a hand onto his shoulder and pushed him back down onto the stool. She traced a scaly finger along his cheek, lightly scratching him with the claw. "Back to the void I go," she cooed. "To the prison they made for me."

Straddling him, the Weaver sat in his lap and seized his face with both hands. "Painful as it is to admit," she said. "This bag of meat and bones is the only way I can survive in your universe. Human bodies are such disgusting things, aren't they? Always secreting their fluids all over the place."

Her tongue darted out to glide over his cheek, causing him to wince and recoil. "No, dear Uncle," she purred. "You won't give up your weapon so easily. You'll let me heal the vessel before sending it back into battle."

"Get off me!" Timothy snapped, throwing her to the floor.

"What's the matter, Uncle?" she said through a fit of giggles. "You always said you wanted me to show an interest in men! Is it so horrible that I should start with you?"

He stood up, shivering, and then walked out of the cell without another word. Her maniacal laughter followed him.

2

The blue sky of a clear, winter morning allowed sunlight to filter through the skeletal trees to a muddy slope. Hebar's Hill, it was called, a lump in the earth that stood twenty feet high at best. The surrounding area was dominated by a stagnant swamp, making it less than ideal for a campsite, but it did provide some privacy.

Miri slipped between two trees with a hand resting on her holstered pistol, pursing her lips as she inspected her students. "Careful now," she said. "All of you."

Zoe was a tiny slip of a girl in workman's clothes that seemed to hang off her body. She couldn't be more than sixteen years old, and the freckles on her pale cheeks made her look even younger. Freckles and blue eyes with flecks of green, hair as red as a flameu. At first glance, you might think she had grown up in Tommy's village.

The girl held a revolver in trembling hands. The weapon had not been loaded – you didn't give live ammunition to someone who couldn't even touch a gun without quaking in terror – but you might have thought the weapon was a hissing snake by the way Zoe held it.

Stepping up to the girl, Miri gently pushed her hands up to aim a little higher. "Like that," she said. "Feet apart, knees bent. Squeeze the trigger, don't pull."

Sweat glistened on Zoe's face.

"Go ahead."

The gun clicked when Zoe did as she was told. It was hard to say without an actual shot, but Miri was fairly certain the girl would have hit the target she had painted on a tree. "Keep practicing."

She moved on to Ken, a short and wiry man with a fringe of dark stubble around the back of his otherwise bald head. This one had the perfect shooting stance. You could see it in his eye: that intense focus as he took aim.

Crossing her arms, Miri looked him up and down. "Very good," she said, nodding. "Take the shot."

CRACK!

A hole appeared in the tree trunk, on the red spot that Miri had painted. He almost hit the bullseye. Zoe flinched at the sound, nearly dropping her gun. They would have to find her a different weapon. Guns were not safe in that girl's hands. In truth, they had no intention of letting her get anywhere near a battlefield. There were all sorts of jobs that needed doing, and Zoe had a deft hand when it came to needle and thread. But Tommy insisted that everyone in the camp should receive basic weapons training, and he had the right of it.

Next in line was Shawn, a gangly young man with a dark complexion and a strong chin that could have been chiseled on a statue. He had a haunted look. As a slave, he had been forced to work in a munitions factory until she and Tommy had liberated him two weeks ago. She suspected that he had been mistreated.

They had not yet had the opportunity to remove the brand from his cheek. It could be done with the crystals they had taken from the Temple of Vengeance, but Miri remained adamant that those should be reserved for treating grievous injuries. The Ether's healing power would eventually remove the mark if Shawn learned to commune with it. A handful of those they had liberated had found a measure of success on that score, but most were still struggling. Miri could sympathize. She had given up trying to find the Ether years ago.

"What's wrong, Shawn?" she asked.

The young man gave her a sidelong glance. "Are you sure we should be doing this?" he muttered. "Guns make a lot of noise. I'd rather not draw the attention of any merchant who happens to be riding past."

"We're a day's ride from Hedrovan," Miri countered. "There aren't many people out this way."

"Still..."

"And," she pressed. "We have Sonic-Sinks around the camp. No one will hear your gunshot, I promise you."

He turned his head to glare at her. She could see it in his eyes. Now that he was free, he just wanted to slip away and hide rather than lead a revolution to liberate those who were still in chains. Honestly, she couldn't blame him. But they needed all the people they could get. "Those things you mentioned," Shawn began. "The...The..."

"Sonic-Sinks."

He stiffened as if the word left a bad taste in his mouth. "Right. Won't they prevent us from hearing an enemy's approach?"

"That's why we also have people on lookout," Miri replied. "Shawn, I know you're scared, but truly, this is the safest place that you could be."

"If you say so."

Miri clapped him on the shoulder, producing a grunt from the young man. "Keep practicing," she urged him. "If nothing else, you'll be able to defend yourself should the need arise."

Target practice went on for another twenty minutes before

she dismissed her students and allowed three others to take their place. This was her life now. When she wasn't teaching someone how to handle firearms, she was going through hand-to-hand drills or reviewing basic tactics. The latter was somewhat difficult for her. Miri could fight on her own, but the finer points of strategy had never been her forte. She was a spy, not a general.

Their camp was a series of colourful tents in the middle of the hilltop. With the trees surrounding them, it was unlikely that they would draw any unwanted attention from anyone who happened to be passing by. Counting those who had fled the *Golden Sunset* along with those they had liberated from nearby factories and farms, they had over four dozen ex-slaves living here. Their food supplies were stretched thin. Tommy had raided the inn's larders, and they had done the same for several other high-end establishments in Hedrovan, but the fact remained that they couldn't remain here. She had visited the city on her own several times, and everyone was talking about the band of outlaws preying on innocent, hard-working merchants.

It was time to move on.

Miri saw people moving through the streets between the tents. A young man with red hair and a pointed chin carried a basket of laundry to the nearby stream that fed into the swamplands. Another fellow carried a buck he had shot toward the cookfires. So, they would eat well tonight.

She opened a tent flap and peeked inside to find Tommy and a group of his students sitting cross legged in a circle. They all had their eyes closed, deep in concentration. Miri felt a burst of pride when she looked upon her love.

Tommy now had a thick, golden beard that made him look at least five years older. His face had filled out a little, no longer quite so gaunt-cheeked. "Let your mind drift," he said. "Don't try to find the Ether. Let it come to you."

Letting the tent flap fall, Miri strode away, shaking her head. "They're never gonna pick it up," she muttered. "Not in time to be of any use, anyway. Most of them will go years without finding the Ether."

A large, maroon tent stood at the end of the street, nestled under the bare branches of a towering oak. She could already hear Dalen puttering about inside. What exactly had her other love discovered?

When she went in, she found the young man standing with his back turned and talking to himself. His books were strewn over the floor so that there wasn't a clear inch of space to set foot on. Even her bedroll was covered with ancient volumes of Aladri and Eradian writing. He had "borrowed" some of those from Hedrovan's grand library.

"Still looking for a legal remedy to our problems?" she asked.

Dalen tensed up, only just realizing that she was present. He turned and greeted her with a sheepish grin. "I may have something. Seventy years ago, a farmer near Fengen's Wake was ordered to free his slaves after it was discovered that he was essentially starving them."

"Is that so?"

Dalen tripped over one of his books as he strode toward her, nearly falling flat on his face. Righting himself with a grunt, he waggled his finger like a professor giving a lecture. "That set a precedent that a master is responsible for the well-being of his slaves."

Cocking her head to one side, Miri raised an eyebrow. "And you believe that you can use this...precedent to what? Compel the Eradian troops to stop hunting us?"

"A cursory inspection of the living conditions at *The Golden Sunset* ought to reveal something that we can use. Some failure by Sirilla Althari to properly care for her slaves. At which point-"

"And who will conduct this inspection?"

Dalen blinked.

"Well?"

He stood before her with his eyes downcast, shifting his weight from one foot to the other. "I suppose," he mumbled. "A magistrate."

Miri sniffed derisively. "Yes, I suppose that could work," she said. "We'll just go to the magistrate's office and politely ask him to-"

Dalen raised his hands to forestall her, backing off and stumbling over another book. "All right," he said. "The point is made. It's just...Tommy has the Ether; you are proficient in just about every weapon known to man, and I have books. Books that seem to be of little use out here."

"Are you feeling useless, love?"

"A little."

Miri stepped forward, grabbing his shirt and pulling him close. She kissed him softly on the lips. "Don't."

His face was beet-red, his eyes fluttering as he tried to catch his breath. "Right," he said, nodding. "I'll just...stop feeling useless."

"Excellent."

The tent flaps parted, allowing a copper-skinned girl with long, dark hair to poke her head inside. Mikala was barely fifteen years old, scrawny with a dimpled chin. *The Seaside Jewel* had been using her to wait tables when Miri and Tommy liberated her. Given that place's reputation, they would probably have used her for other less reputable services when she got a little older. "They're calling a meeting," the girl said.

Miri stepped out into the open, holding her coat closed with one hand as the chilly wind assaulted her. "A meeting," she muttered. Already, she could see that many of the camp's other residents were moving toward the tent where Tommy taught his classes.

Dalen followed her out, hopping to keep up. He looked this way and that with obvious anxiety on his face. "Oh, this isn't good," he muttered. "Look at them. They're quite unhappy."

He wasn't wrong.

The sour expressions she saw on pretty much every former slave she passed told her that this would not be a pleasant meeting. People only looked like that when they had a grievance to share, and for so many to look so dissatisfied...Yes, they had been talking behind her back. And behind Tommy's as well, she suspected.

The large, blue tent was packed with bodies when she entered. Everyone stood in three tight circles, pressed so close together there was barely space enough to breathe let alone move. No one wanted to be out in the cold. She had to see what was going on. Thankfully, people shuffled aside to let her enter the innermost ring.

Brian Hanson, a tall man with a barrel chest, pale skin and a dark beard stood with his arms folded. The brand on his cheek was still plainly visible. He had not yet found the Ether.

Tommy stepped forward with his hands clasped behind his back, greeting the other man without a hint of anxiety. "What's the trouble, Brian?"

"We want to leave," Brian replied.

Closing his eyes, Tommy let out a breath. "You're free to go at any time," he said. "You know that. But there's very little food to be had out there, and you'll probably run afoul of some Eradian patrol."

Brian sneered, baring his teeth. "We know the risks," he spat. "And we want out. We want nothing to do with you."

"You're safer here."

In two quick strides, Brian was toe to toe with Tommy. He reached out to seize Tommy's shirt, but Miri caught his wrist and twisted it just enough to make him hiss. The man gave her a threatening glare.

She smiled.

Cowed by that, Brian pulled his hand free and took control of himself. Good. That one had been trouble since the day he arrived. Best that he remember who he was dealing with.

"Your revolution is no concern of ours," Brian said calmly. "We're free now. And we're not going to risk being recaptured. Some of us want to get as far away from here as possible."

"Well, I regret your choice," Tommy said. "But I won't stop you."

Miri saw a dangerous glint in Brian's eye. The man was about to push his luck; she knew it. "We want you to heal our brands," he said. "So that we can leave this camp and pursue work as free men."

Tommy looked up into the other man's eyes. To his credit, he never flinched. "The best way to remove those marks would be to commune with the Ether," he said. "If you stay, I can teach you."

"No!" Brian growled. "No more lessons! No more promises of magic that we will never possess. You think we don't see through your charade? You have the crystals. We have seen what they can do. You can use them to heal all of us now."

"The crystals are for treating severe injuries," Miri insisted.

Brian turned his gaze upon her, every last scrap of fear gone. "And who decides that?" he barked. "You? If we stay here, we're as good as dead."

"No one is stopping you."

Pointing at the mark on his cheek. Brian snarled at her. "And if I leave with this, I'm *still* as good as dead! Did you free us just to turn us into soldiers in your little war?"

"Brian," Tommy said. "Those of us who put ourselves at risk to free the slaves of Hedrovan *will* eventually be injured. We need those crystals to keep ourselves alive. You are free now. Don't you want the same for your brothers and sisters?"

"Piss on that," Brian spat. "I'm free, and I won't go back. Those who are still in the city can fend for themselves."

"Charming," Miri murmured.

Brian ignored her, stepping forward to tower over Tommy. "The real question is," he began, "will you live by your word? Are we free? Or will you use these brands to coerce us into obeying you like the masters did."

Heaving out a sigh, Tommy looked down at the floor. He licked his lips, trying to decide what to do. "I'll give you five crystals," he answered in a rasping voice. "Five to share with anyone else who wants to leave. That should be enough. You'll only need a small fragment to remove a brand."

"That will do."

"I DON'T THINK you should have given up those crystals," Dalen said. He knelt behind Tommy, who sat on the floor of their tent, gently massaging the other man's shoulders. Miri watched them silently. Her instincts said that Dalen was correct, but if her boys were about to have a spat, she wanted no part of it.

Tommy winced, groaning in frustration. "I'm not going to force people to stay here," he replied. "They're free now. They're not obligated to fight for our cause."

"And we're not obligated to give aid to those who don't fight for our cause," Dalen countered. "We're gonna lose people this way. And I don't just mean those who intend to walk away. Once the fighting starts, those of us who stay will die without those crystals."

Tommy shut his eyes and let his head fall back against the other man's chest. "We still have ten of the shards the *Al a Nari* gave us," he said. "That'll be enough for now. Once we have liberated all the slaves in Hedrovan, it will be time to move on."

Miri had serious misgivings about that plan. They had survived thus far because Field Binding and Ka'adri training gave them a clear advantage. But the Eradians would not sit still while Tommy "stole their property." They would step up security. Guns were dangerous, even to Field Binders. And she suspected they would eventually come up with something to counter that advantage as well.

The crystals were such odd things. A clean cut with a knife only segmented them into smaller fragments, but crushing them released the power within. Why that should matter was beyond her. When you broke a crystal, it was broken! Why should the method make a difference? It was almost as if these things were alive. As if they had intent.

"We'll just have to see what happens tomorrow," Tommy muttered.

THEY DID INDEED FIND out the next morning. Miri walked through a camp of empty tents, silent and desolate under the gray, winter sky. Not a soul in sight, not a sound to be heard. She wandered for nearly five minutes before she found Zoe standing outside of her tent.

The girl was hugging herself, rubbing her arms and shivering. She looked up when she heard Miri drawing near. "They're gone," she said. "Most of them anyway. Run off with Brian. A few of us stayed behind."

Head hanging, Miri touched fingertips to her forehead. A groan escaped her. "How many?"

"There are ten," Zoe answered. "Ken is still here, and my mother. And Jeff as well. Kaylee and Victor and Michael. Old Mrs. Potts and her two boys. And Sarah. I wasn't able to find anyone else. We...We still believe in the cause, ma'am."

Perhaps they did, but thirteen people weren't much use against an army even if one of them could Field Bind. It seemed the revolution was over.

3

A crackling campfire sent tiny flickers of flame up to an over-cast sky. The night was cool, but at least it wasn't raining. Desa felt exposed, sitting in the middle of an open field with no one but Kalia and Midnight for company. The stallion waited patiently at the edge of the firelight with their packhorse. At first glance, he almost seemed eager to press on, but Desa knew that he would appreciate the rest. They had been traveling hard for the last six days. Soon, they would reach the northern shores of Ithanar.

Desa knelt in the grass with her coat off and the sleeves of her blouse rolled up, heat from the flames leaving sweat on her brow. "We'll make an early start tomorrow," she said. "If all goes well, we'll reach the Halitha in a few days."

Kalia stood on the other side of the fire with her back turned, peering off into the distance. The woman said nothing, lost in her own thoughts. Not a good sign. Desa had come to know her well enough to realize that silence almost always meant that Kalia was trying to decide how to bring up a diffi-cult subject.

"After that, we press north," she went on. "North and west.

42

We should be able to reach the desert's southeastern border in about two weeks. Assuming no major setbacks, of course. We'll have to pass through Pikeman's Gorge. Not an easy trip. Bandits like to take refuge in the caves. But you and I can handle-"

"Tommy and the others might still be at Hedrovan," Kalia cut in. "We should try to find them."

Desa wrinkled her nose in distaste. "No," she insisted. "Kalia, we *don't* have time. We have to get to Mercy as quickly as possible."

The other woman turned, looking over her shoulder, watching Desa out of the corner of one eye. "With every passing day, you grow more desperate," she said. "Will a day's delay make that much difference? The others may need our help."

Desa stood up with a sigh, reaching up to thread fingers through her short hair. She blinked a few times. "The world needs us more," she said. "You saw what Adele did."

"I did."

That should put an end to any further discussion on the matter. Any delay, no matter how small, put more lives at risk. Adele would attack the *Al a Nari* again. It was only a matter of time before their defenses fell. Desa had to find a way to thwart the other woman's power before that happened. If Mercy had the answer...

She ignored the niggling thought that had been plaguing her for days. What if Mercy *didn't* have the answer? If the goddess knew something, wouldn't she have shared it by now? Instead, she sent Desa and Kalia on a quest to recover artifacts that had been buried under the earth for millennia. Artifacts that told the secret history of her people.

Desa had activated the strange crystal a few times on their journey back to Te'Alon. She would have combed through it for every last scrap of knowledge she could find, but the device required a great deal of power, and she was often too tired after a day in the saddle to Reinfuse it. Still, she had pieced a few things together.

Mercy had once been a human woman, a scientist who specialized in expanding her people's knowledge of Field Binding. They seemed to have been trying to Infuse living tissue with a direct connection to the Ether. Just as Bendarian had. Was that what had roused the *Hanak Tuvar*? She would have to watch more of Mercy's diary.

"Are we going to talk about it?" Kalia asked.

Nudging a rock with the toe of her boot, Desa clamped a hand onto the back of her neck. "Talk about what?" She had no idea what her lover was getting at, but she was sure that it would be a most difficult conversation.

The fire cast flickering shadows over Kalia's face, but her eyes were like daggers, trying to pierce through Desa's armour. "Your growing desperation," she said. "I hear you talking in your sleep some nights."

"You do?"

"You blame yourself for what happened at Te'Alon."

Clenching her teeth, Desa turned her face away from the other woman. "I gave Adele the lightning that she used to kill those people," she said. "I didn't think. I just attacked. Threw everything I had at her in pure desperation."

Kalia seated herself on a rock, folding hands in her lap. She looked up at Desa. "And that's not like you," she noted. "For as long as I've known you, you've been careful, methodical. There's only one thing that sends you running headlong into danger without considering your options."

Desa arched an eyebrow.

"Guilt," Kalia explained.

"You're exaggerating."

"No, I'm not," Kalia breathed. "Eleven years ago, you blamed yourself for teaching Bendarian Field Binding. So, you left everything you knew behind and chased him into the wild, nearly getting yourself killed in the process. You felt guilty for killing Tommy's lover; so, you took off again, racing into the desert for a final showdown with Bendarian. No doubt you expected to die."

"All right," Desa said. "Your point is made."

"You can't let guilt drive you, Desa," Kalia pressed. "If you do, you're going to make the same mistakes. So, tell me, why do you feel guilty?"

A single tear slid down Desa's cheek. She closed her eyes, trying to steady herself. "It doesn't matter," she croaked. "Just another failure in a long list of failures."

Sighing softly, Kalia stood up and made her way around the fire. She put her hands on Desa's shoulders, leaning in close to kiss her forehead. "Don't run from it, my love," she murmured. "Tell me what happened."

"It's my fault."

"What is?"

"Adele," Desa growled. "I trusted her, and I shouldn't have. If not for me, she would have never gotten anywhere near that pyramid. She would have never become whatever it is that she is now."

"Trust is not a sin."

Desa backed away from the other woman, shaking her head in disgust. "It is when you know better," she said. "Something about her seemed off from the very beginning. But she was so insistent."

"Is that why you took her with you?"

"No," Desa muttered. "We took her with us because she said that she could track Bendarian."

Sucking on her lower lip, Kalia looked down at the ground under her feet. "And stopping Bendarian came before every-thing else," she sighed. "Desa, you weren't blinded by Adele. You were blinded by your obsession with Bendarian."

"I created him. I had to stop him."

"No!" Kalia insisted. "You helped a man in need by teaching him a valuable skill. That he went on to abuse the knowledge you gave him is not your fault. The real problem here is that you went against the customs of your people by teaching Bendarian how to commune with the Ether. You decided that the philosophies of Aladar were misguided; so, you rejected them. And when that resulted in disaster, you were humiliated. You've been living with the shame of it ever since. It consumes you."

Shutting her eyes tight, Desa buried her face in her hand. "What do you want me to do?"

When she looked up, Kalia was watching her with such sincerity. "I want you to forgive yourself," the other woman said simply. "To let go of the shame."

"And if I can't?"

"Then you're going to make more mistakes," Kalia replied. "And people will die."

ANOTHER DAY of travel brought them a little closer to their goal. Desa kept expecting to see the Sapphire Sea, but it never came. She did, however, recognize the outcroppings of rock that protruded from the grass as the land sloped gently downward to the water's edge. The trees that sprouted here and there were all bare, but she remembered when they had been lush with foliage. This was the way they had come five months ago.

So much had changed in such a short time: Marcus gone, their hopes for defeating Adele dashed. Now, the Eradians were marching south. That fact alone slowed her down considerably.

Desa tried to avoid the simple paths that an army would use. That forced them to travel over some very difficult terrain. As they neared the sea, she began to suspect that she needn't have bothered. There should have been some sign of an enemy force making its way into Ithanar, but the land was barren, empty. Which meant that Adele must have been transporting them to their destination. Such extensive use of her powers was ravaging her body.

Night came early at this time of year, the sun dipping under the horizon to make way for a dark sky where the stars twinkled faintly. It was cool here but not bitter cold, and once again, she blessed her good fortune. There was no sign of rain. That would make it easier to sleep. The tiny tent Rojan had given them would be enough to keep out the night's chill.

Desa found herself lying on her back with hands folded over her chest, staring thoughtfully into the darkness. Was Kalia right? Was it guilt that drove her to make poor decision after poor decision?

The other woman was curled up on her side with her back turned, breathing slow and steady. So beautiful. What would a goddess like that want with Desa Kincaid?

Rolling onto her side, Desa wrapped an arm around her lover's tummy. She kissed Kalia's cheek, waking her.

The other woman turned, looking up at her through fluttering eyes. "It's not your fault," Kalia whispered.

"What do you-"

"You know what I mean."

Kalia seized her face with both hands, kissing her hard on the lips. The next thing Desa knew, she was being pushed down onto her back. Deft hands undid the buttons of her shirt. Soft lips found her neck, her collarbone, the smooth skin of her tummy.

Piece by piece, their clothing fell away until she was alone and vulnerable with the most magnificent creature to ever draw breath in this benighted world. Kalia kissed her, and she melted into the other woman's embrace.

Squeezing her eyes shut, Desa arched her back and shuddered.

Enough was enough. She had never been the sort to remain passive in such moments. She rolled Kalia onto her back and kissed every inch of her. Every delicious inch.

She couldn't say how long it lasted – hours or minutes; Time seemed to blend when she was lost in the dreamy haze of lust – but it wasn't long before Kalia was curled up, sound asleep with her head on Desa's chest.

Desa, however, was wide awake.

With the moment past, the niggling guilt returned, creeping into her mind despite her efforts to keep it away. She had defied her people. She had taught Bendarian the basics of Field Binding. In a way, that one decision had set all of this in motion. Would *Hanak Tuvar* have been released if not for Bendarian's twisted experiments? Would the world be facing destruction if not for Desa Kincaid?

Unable to sleep, she rolled Kalia over – the other woman didn't wake – and dressed as quietly as she could. Her legs wanted to move.

Out in the night, she found nothing but grass and rock and the odd tree that sighed in the gentle wind. After the warmth of her lover's arms, it was painfully chilly. But the cold was good for her.

Desa marched over the uneven ground with arms swinging, shaking her head. "Let go of the guilt, she says," she muttered. "By the Eyes of Vengeance, how am I supposed to do that?"

She fished the blue crystal in its brass cage from her coat pocket, setting it down on a rock. "Let's see what secrets you have to tell."

Backing away with her hands in her pockets, Desa closed her eyes and nodded once. A thought was all it took to trigger the Electric-Source that she had Infused into the metal.

The crystal began to glow with cerulean light, thin beams fanning out in all directions, drawing the outline of the room. Colour entered the image a moment later: white walls and white cupboards, tables loaded up with equipment that she couldn't even begin to describe.

Then Mercy appeared.

The woman wore heeled boots, black pants and a white coat that fell halfway down her thighs. Her black hair was done up with a clip. And of course, she wore a pair of thin spectacles.

The goddess turned her head so that she seemed to be looking directly at Desa. "Now, where were we?" she mumbled. "Ah, yes. Attempts to use the gateway have been met with setbacks. Despite Kiaz's familiarity with the Unifying Field, he has been unable to send a manned expedition through to another universe. Even the automated probes have failed to offer much hope. It seems most universes operate under laws entirely different from our own. The probes simply cease to function on the other side. And any living beings who went through would almost certainly perish."

Mercy used her index finger to push her glasses up her nose.

Clearing her throat, she began to pace across the length of her laboratory, looking back toward the device that recorded her journal. "None of which has anything to do with my project," she added. "Except that Kiaz's misfortune might be my gain. I received a notice this morning indicating that the Council of Twelve is reevaluating the budget, and they are now willing to provide us with greater funding.

"Access to the particle synthesis technology will be key. The Field cannot be bound to living tissue or to anything that had once been alive. But what is living tissue but a specific configuration of molecules? The same matter in a different configuration might be a rock or a piece of metal. The technology that allows us to break down industrial waste into its constituent elements will be crucial. If one were to achieve communion with the Field at the moment disintegration...Of course, the price of failure would be immediate death. So, you can imagine why I lack for volunteers."

She cut off when a siren started wailing, turning to look out a window. Her posture was rigid, stiff. The sound had small animals scampering through the field to get away.

Kalia emerged from the tent a moment later, still doing up the final buttons of her shirt. She stopped dead when she found herself in the middle of Mercy's laboratory, her eyes widening.

Mercy spun to face Desa, breathing hard. "Something is wrong," she panted. "Something is very-"

The image flickered several times and then vanished completely, leaving her in darkness. Silence fell over the field, broken only by the soft rustle of squirrels running through the grass.

"What happened?" Kalia asked.

Closing her eyes, Desa drew a deep breath through her nose. "I think," she said, "that we just witnessed their first encounter with *Hanak Tuvar*."

TWO DAYS LATER, they were well into their journey across the Halitha. The grass was yellow under Midnight's hooves, and an overcast sky seemed to press down on them. Desa remembered crossing the land bridge in the summer. Even then, with a plethora of worries hanging like a stone around her neck, the journey had been much more pleasant. It was amazing what green grass and blue sky could do.

Kalia sat behind her with her arms wrapped around Desa's waist and her chin resting on Desa's shoulder. By the sound of her steady breathing, she was about two inches away from falling asleep.

The packhorse with their supplies shuffled along behind them.

Pursing her lips, Desa stared directly ahead. *How much longer?* she wondered, her brow furrowing. *We should be seeing it soon.*

There was nothing before her but grass and hills that ran all the way to the horizon, but that would change soon enough. She knew from her previous journey that they would soon come up against an impenetrable barrier.

The forest.

Last time, they had been forced to walk along the beach to go around it. She didn't relish the thought of doing so again, especially when the sand would almost certainly be a thick muck after all the recent rainfall. Come to think of it, Midnight probably wasn't thrilled about the prospect of wading through that either. But there was no choice. And muck was the least of their worries.

She shivered when she remembered the shrill cry of the creature that lived in that forest. They had no name for it except "the man-bat." Would it show itself again? She couldn't help but think that if it had wanted to attack her group, it would have done so. But that didn't make it benign.

Either way, there was no turning back. Their food supply was growing thin. They had enough to make it to Hedrovan but not enough to return to the *Al a Nari.*

"How much further?" Kalia murmured, voicing her thoughts.

Squinting into the distance, Desa shook her head. "I don't know," she answered. "A few hours. Maybe half a day."

Her initial estimate was correct. By mid-afternoon, they were confronted with a line of towering trees that grew larger and larger as they drew near. Just the sight of that forest made her skin crawl.

But there was something else.

At first, she thought she was imagining it, but once they got close enough, she knew her eyes had not deceived her. Something was different from the last time she had been here. There was now a path leading directly into the forest and presumably through to the other side.

She and Kalia dismounted, approaching with caution. Shivers ran down Desa's spine. She wanted nothing more than to be as far away from here as possible, but she needed a closer look.

The trees stood at least a hundred feet high with naked branches crisscrossing in an impenetrable bramble. A human might be able to maneuver around those gnarled trunks and exposed roots, but horses? No, it was impossible.

And yet, the path was blessedly free of obstacles: no roots, no rocks, no twigs. Just a narrow corridor that cut through the forest so cleanly it might have been done with a knife. "Could we have missed it the last time?" Desa asked.

Stepping up to the edge of the forest, Kalia rested her hand on a tree. Her eyes were wide with alarm. "No," she murmured. "Tommy and I scouted the area for miles in each direction. There were no pathways through."

"And yet this one appears right where we need it," Desa growled. "I don't believe in coincidences."

"Me neither."

Desa looked up to the treetops, blinking several times as she considered her options. "I am no hare to be led to the trap," she said, spinning around and striding back to Midnight. "We'll take the beach. Like last time."

So, they turned to their right and began making their way eastward through the soggy grass. It was slow going: a dreary, unpleasant trek that had her struggling to ignore her growing sense of unease. She led Midnight by his bridle, and Kalia did the same for the packhorse. The air was cool and damp, and moisture seemed to cling to her skin.

Desa couldn't shake the feeling that she was being watched. On several occasions, she tried to work up the nerve to say so, but the words always died on the tip of her tongue. Kalia was equally silent, and the animals plodded along almost mechanically, never complaining.

Evening was coming on when the ground sloped gently downward to a muddy beach. The waters of the Sapphire Sea washed up on the shore, and gulls swooped low over the waves. But any hope they had of an uneventful journey died before they took even one step.

The trees spilled down the hillside and over the narrow strip of land where the beach should have been. If she had to guess, she would say that the forest extended at least half a mile into the water. That had *not* been the case on their last visit.

Kalia's mouth dropped open when she took in the sight. "That's not possible," she whispered. "Forests don't grow like that."

"I feel as though I'm being herded," Desa grumbled. Toward what, she couldn't say, but she didn't like it one bit. No, not one bit.

She stooped to pick up a rock and then threw it into the trees, listening to the clatter it made as it bounced off trunk after trunk. "Hey!" she screamed. "I know you're in there! Come out and show yourself!"

Nothing happened.

Desa took Midnight's bridle in one hand, guiding him back up the hill. "Come on," she said. "There's no point in remaining here."

"Where are we going?" Kalia asked.

"Our host – whatever it is – has made the rules of this game clear. If we want to go through, we must do so on its terms. Well, I see no reason to delay. Let's get this over with, shall we?"

At the top of the hill, she waited for Kalia to bring the packhorse up. The other woman gave her a skeptical stare. "Are you sure that's wise?"

"It's the only way through," Desa insisted. "We survived Vengeance's traps. We can survive this too."

So, they set off toward the spot where they had seen the path, but they had only traveled half the distance when it became too dark to see. There was nothing to do but set up camp on the eaves of the forest.

FINDING sleep was difficult for Desa even with a tent to shut out the cold and the damp. A Heat-Source coin under her bedroll provided more than sufficient warmth, but she just couldn't rest. Not knowing where they were.

Kalia was sound asleep, which left her feeling both envious and mystified. Try as she might, Desa just couldn't let her guard down. Every rustle of wind through the nearby branches jolted her back to full alertness.

She sat up, hunched over with fingertips pressed into her forehead. The beginnings of a headache had settled behind her eyes. In another hour, she would be in a great deal of pain. And grumpy to boot.

Something snapped in the distance like twigs crunching underfoot. The sound made her jump and reach for the pistol she had left next to her bedroll. But of course, nothing came of it.

Restless, Desa threw on her coat. Kalia murmured at the sudden motion, but she did not wake. Good. One of them should get some sleep.

Taking her pistol in hand, Desa crawled out of the tent and stood up. She looked around, scanning her surroundings for any sign of trouble.

The forest was a mass of shadow before her, the twisted branches of trees black against a starry sky. A crescent moon hung overhead, providing just enough illumination for her to notice the contrast.

She crept forward, staying low, listening for any sound no matter how faint. The damp air left a film of moisture on her skin. She hated it.

When she got within arm's reach of the trees, Desa stood up straight. She thrust out her chin to look down her nose at whatever might be watching her from the darkness. "I know you're there."

Nothing happened.

"Show yourself!"

Still nothing.

She turned around, shuffling back to the tent and heaving out a sigh. Head hanging, she scraped a knuckle across her brow. "What am I doing?"

A branch snapped behind her.

Spinning around, Desa pointed her gun into the forest. Sure enough, she saw a pair of glowing, green eyes watching her from within the gap between two trees. The man-bat was here. Perhaps it had been here all along. Maybe it was taunting her. "What are you?" Desa demanded. The eyes receded into the darkness, fading away.

Unable to help herself, Desa raised her free hand and triggered the Light-Source in her ring. Radiance washed over her, illuminating the yellow grass underneath her feet. The packhorse whinnied, but Midnight soothed him.

When she peered into the forest, she saw only twisted tree trunks and drooping branches. There was no sign of the creature. She got the impression that it was trying to lure her in. She would not be taking that bait.

The tent flaps parted as Kalia emerged, brushing dark hair out of her face. The poor woman blinked, her eyes adjusting to the light. "What happened?"

"It's here."

"The man-bat?"

Desa nodded grimly. "It's been watching us," she said,

striding toward the trees with her hand aloft to hold back the gloom. "I suspect that it wanted us to know it's been watching us."

"Why would it want that?"

"Because this particular hunter likes to play with its food," Desa growled. "It knows that we will be entering its domain. So, it wants to taunt us."

"Well," Kalia grumbled. "So much for sleep."

By MID-MORNING, they found the pathway through the forest in the same place it had been the day before. The sky above was still gray and dreary, shutting out the warmth of the sun. A perfect day to enter the lair of a predator.

The packhorse resisted as Kalia led him to the edge of the forest, trying to pull away and bolt. He almost reared more than once, but Kalia managed to quiet him with a few soothing whispers.

Midnight was as calm as a tranquil river, waiting patiently beside Desa. He turned his head to nuzzle her shoulder, a gentle reminder that he would be with her to the bitter end. She could not have asked for a better steed.

"Are you sure about this?" Kalia muttered.

"I see no other option."

"No...Neither do I."

Desa had to work up the nerve to take that first step forward, but when danger failed to leap out from every shadow, she breathed a sigh of relief. It was just a forest: old and ugly but no different from any other she had seen. And positively tame compared to what she had experienced in the Borathorin.

The path was quite wide. More of a dirt road, really. It provided ample space for both horses to walk abreast. Desa searched for ditches or roots or anything that might trip one of the animals, but the ground was smooth.

They had been walking in silence for almost ten minutes when she put a name to the fear that had been nagging at her from the moment that she had entered these woods. The trees on either side of her: they were too neat.

She had no other way to describe it. All of their branches grew on the side facing away from the path, leaving the way clear for Desa and Kalia. That couldn't be natural. But then nothing about this place felt natural. If she journeyed eastward, would she still find the forest extending into the sea? Or had that been some trick of the man-bat's?

Something about that felt very similar to what Vengeance had done to them in the Borathorin. Perhaps this creature could manipulate geometry in some way. Bend what should have been straight.

Walking quickly with the packhorse's bridle in hand, Kalia peered into the thicket. "How long?" she asked. "Until we reach the other side?"

"It took more than a day for us to cross the forest last time," Desa replied. "I should think this journey will be much the same."

"Meaning we have to spend the night in here."

"Indeed."

It was well past midday when Desa finally decided to stop for a light meal. Bread and cheese and raisins: hardly a feast, but it filled the belly just the same. The horses had grazed yesterday when they made camp, and they would have a chance to do so again tomorrow. For now, some oats and carrots kept them happy.

Kalia was leaning against a tree, munching the last few bites of her sandwich. She licked her fingers one by one and then sighed. "Something that bothers me," she said. "We haven't seen any animals."

On the other side of the path, Desa stood with arms folded, nodding along with that assessment. "We should have seen something," she agreed. "A squirrel or a rabbit at the very least."

"What do you think it means?"

Tilting her head back, Desa narrowed her eyes. "If I had to guess," she began, "I'd say it means most animals are smart enough to avoid this place."

"And what does that say about us?"

"That we're desperate, my love."

With bellies full, they pressed on, continuing their sombre march northward. The path meandered somewhat, curving slightly to the east and then slightly to the west, but it was always unnervingly free of obstacles.

The hours passed in silence, and the gray clouds overhead began to darken, a touch of twilight blue creeping in. The air grew chilly and damp. Desa knew it was unrealistic, but she kept hoping to see an open field around the next bend. Maybe they overestimated the size of this place. They had been forced to walk along the beach last time, and that slowed down the horses.

She kept hoping, but there was only more forest.

As the light began to fade, she was confronted with the revelation that they would have to make camp in these woods. Even with Light-Sources, traveling by night was a bad idea. She didn't trust this place not to throw a ditch in their path, and if one of the horses broke a leg...

She was just working up the nerve to voice her thoughts when the sound of a crackling fire made her pause. Another traveler? Could she be imagining it? The scent of smoke put paid to that idea.

They rounded another bend and found a campfire in the middle of the road, complete with a black stew pot that sent steam wafting up to the treetops. The aroma of chicken soup greeted Desa and made her mouth water.

A man in a poncho and wide-brimmed hat stood with his

back turned, stirring the pot with a wooden spoon. "Don't be alarmed," he said without so much as glancing in their direction. "Come. Join me."

"Who are you?" Desa inquired.

The stranger turned around, and she had to resist the urge to jump back. His face was unusually pale, but that was hardly his most striking feature. No, it was his unearthly, rictus grin that set her nerves on edge, a grin that stretched from ear to ear. "Just a fellow traveler," he said. "It would be most unwise to go any further tonight."

Kalia had one hand on her pistol, ready to draw. Her eyes were fixed upon the man, sizing him up. "You never answered her question," she said. "Who are you?"

The packhorse was snorting, trying to back away, but Kalia held its bridle in a tight grip. The animal sensed something amiss, and Desa had to concur.

Cocking his head, the stranger regarded Kalia for a long moment. His grin never faded, never even twitched. It was almost as if he were a manikin come to life. "Heldrid," he said. "You may call me Heldrid."

Suddenly, there was a wooden bowl in his hand. Had that been there a moment earlier? He spooned soup into it. "Come," he said. "You must be hungry."

His footsteps were almost inaudible. The sight of him coming toward her made Desa want to reach for a weapon, but she resisted that inclination. Whatever this thing was, she did not want to provoke it.

Heldrid offered her the bowl.

Desa looked down into it, her mouth tight with anxiety. She raised an eyebrow but said nothing.

The stranger tossed his head back with a rich, belly laugh, a laugh that sounded like the buzzing of bees. All the while, that hideous grin never wavered. "If I wanted to kill you, Desa Kincaid, I could do it easily."

Perhaps she should have been unnerved by the fact that he knew her name, but it only made her angry. "Don't be so sure about that."

"True, you are more dangerous than others of your kind."

"What are you?"

He shoved the bowl into her hands, then turned around and sauntered back to the fire. "Once I was a wanderer," he said, spooning soup into a second bowl that she could swear had not existed mere moments ago. "But I have wandered long enough. I like it here. I would prefer to stay."

Desa was certain that if she tried to flee, this Heldrid would only find a way to trap her. Perhaps the path would suddenly end in an impenetrable thicket. Or perhaps she and Kalia would walk for hours only to find themselves right back here. The same tricks that Vengeance had employed.

Defeating the goddess had been a matter of wits, not of strength. She suspected that it was much the same now. If she wanted to get past Heldrid, she would have to play his game. For now.

Gesturing for Kalia to follow, she cautiously approached the fire. "I'm curious," she said. "If you are content to remain here, what is preventing you from doing so?"

Heldrid offered her a spoon that seemed to come from out of nowhere, and she used it to stir her soup. It was actually more of a thick stew with peas, carrots and tender chicken meat. Hesitantly, she tasted it. It was wonderful!

Heldrid gave the second bowl to Kalia and then bowed low like a servant at court. He chuckled and then returned his attention to Desa. "Why, you are, of course!"

Pausing with the spoon raised halfway to her mouth, Desa scrutinized him. "Dear me," she said. "It sounds as if I've been a dreadful inconvenience. What precisely am I doing to make you leave this place?"

"Well, it's not so much what you're doing as what you've done."

"Meaning?"

"Hanak Tuvar."

Desa shoved a spoonful of chicken into her mouth, then shut her eyes and chewed thoroughly. After a week of dried bread and cheese, it was the most delicious thing that she had ever tasted. "I see."

Heldrid moved with serpentine grace, his grin insinuating things that she would rather not think about. "If *Hanak Tuvar* is left unchecked," he began. "This world will no longer be safe for a lowly wanderer like me. Frankly, Desa, I need you to clean up your mess."

"Then why have you delayed me?"

"Because you haven't the faintest idea of how to begin," he replied. "And neither does that aberration in the desert. Don't you think she tried? The best that she could do was imprison it, wrap it up in what you call the Ether. A prison as fragile wet cloth. All it took was for one of you little monkeys to pull on the wrong string, and..."

"So, how do I kill it?"

"Eat your soup," Heldrid muttered. "We'll talk."

He slipped between two trees, and when she tried to follow him, he was just gone. There was nothing to do but wait; so, she ate. Kalia seemed to be enjoying the soup immensely. "Best meal I've had since we left Te'Alon," she murmured.

An hour passed, and the last traces of sunlight vanished from the sky. Midnight waited at the edge of the firelight with the very skittish packhorse. She had hobbled him with thick rope to prevent him from bolting, but the poor dear was frightened.

Desa was beginning to grow impatient. Where was Heldrid? The man...or entity...or whatever he was had said he wanted to talk. But then he just disappeared? Perhaps he had to go tend to the man-bat.

After two hours, Kalia began to pace around the campfire, rubbing her hands together for warmth. "Should we leave?" she asked. "I don't think he's coming back."

Leaning one shoulder against a tree trunk, Desa grunted as she considered her next move. "I don't believe he would go to all this trouble just to exchange pleasantries," she said. "We should make camp."

"Here?"

"We already have a fire."

Kalia pressed a fist to her mouth, clearing her throat forcefully. "No offense, love," she said, striding toward Desa. "But I don't fancy going to sleep when I know that thing is lurking in these woods."

"If he was going to kill us, he would have tried already," Desa said. "I don't know what his game is, but if he has information that can-"

She was cut off by the shrill cry of the man-bat and the sound of wings flapping overhead. The packhorse whinnied. If not for the ropes around his legs, he would have fled in terror.

Before she even realized it, Desa had her pistol out and pointed at the treetops. But there was nothing to see. The firelight made it impossible to distinguish one shadow from another.

The next cry seemed to come from miles away, from somewhere well to the north of here. Perhaps it had gone to terrorize the farms near Hedrovan. Desa had come to realize that there was a reason no one would settle too close to the Halitha.

Kalia was crouching by the fire, her face turned up to the sky. "I was wondering when it would show up," she muttered. "What's Heldrid's relationship to that thing?"

"He might be its keeper."

"And what? It hunts for him?"

Squeezing her eyes shut, Desa shook her head. "Nothing about this place makes sense," she said. "Any attempt to understand these creatures is doomed to fail from the outset. I suggest we get some rest."

The other woman was reluctant to take that advice, but in the end, Kalia concurred that making camp was their best option. Trying to leave might anger Heldrid, and then the man-bat might be hunting *them*. Still, they couldn't stay forever. If the stranger did not return by morning, she would set out northward.

The packhorse required quite a bit of soothing. Some gentle brushing from Kalia and nuzzles from Midnight calmed him enough to let him sleep. After that, it was a simple matter of setting up the tent.

Desa's exhaustion was so intense that she fell asleep within minutes of curling up in her bedroll. The last thought she had as consciousness drifted away was that she felt oddly safe here. It wasn't so much that she trusted Heldrid, but the knowledge that he wanted her alive suggested that no harm would come to her. If there were other predators in these woods, the grinning stranger would keep them away.

She woke a few hours later, feeling somewhat rested, dimly aware of Kalia's soft breathing. And of soft footsteps just outside the tent. Instead of getting up to investigate, Desa made use of a much more powerful tool.

She made herself one with the Ether.

Her mind stretched out through the fabric of the tent, sweeping over every inch of the campsite. The fire was out. She sensed neither heat nor light from the small pile of charred wood a few paces away. The trees on either side of the path were just as they had been: twisted branches growing on only one side of their weather-worn trunks.

But there was something else.

Not a man, not a bat, but a distortion. A wrinkle in the

fabric of reality that moved around the tent. At last, she began to understand.

Dismissing the Ether, Desa threw off her blankets and climbed out of the tent. She stood up slowly, arching her back as she stretched. And when she turned around, it was right there in front of her.

With a thought, she triggered the Light-Source in her ring, and then she was looking at Heldrid's hideous face. That rictus smile promised all sorts of unspeakable things. "You're not from this universe, are you?" Desa whispered.

"Clever, clever girl."

"You came here with my ancestors," she went on. "No doubt they visited your realm on one of their many expeditions, and you decided to follow them. Eventually, they led you here."

"Very good."

Craning her neck to stare up at him, Desa narrowed her eyes. "No more games," she said. "How do I defeat *Hanak Tuvar?*"

Seizing her by the shoulders, Heldrid leaned in close to whisper in her ear. "It will try to impose its will upon the world," he said. "You must not let it."

"That's it? That's all you have for me?"

He tilted her chin up with two clammy fingers. She wanted to cringe, but she refused to give this thing the satisfaction of knowing that it had unnerved her. "Good luck to you, Field Binder," Heldrid said. "I will be gone when you wake up in the morning. Do not be here when I get back."

4

The spyglass gave Tommy a good view of the black-coats. He estimated at least eight dozen camped just beyond the swamp at the base of Hebar's Hill. They were setting up tents in neat, little rows. If he wasn't mistaken, several of those men wore epaulettes that marked them as officers. This looked like a campaign.

Lowering the spyglass, Tommy squinted into the distance. "Trouble," he muttered, shaking his head. "Big, big trouble."

Miri stood at his side on the hilltop, clasping her chin as she assessed the situation. "Big, big trouble," she agreed. "They showed up an hour ago and made camp."

"Is there any chance they aren't here for us?" Zoe asked. She was stooped under a tree branch, watching the distant army like a cornered cat. "Maybe they're on their way to Hedrovan or something."

"And why might they be on their way to Hedrovan?" Miri countered.

"Don't panic," Tommy urged. He was amazed by the steadiness of his voice. Guilt warred with fear for his attention – guilt over having led these people to disaster, fear of what that army might do to his people – but he couldn't show any of it. They needed him now. "They have to cross through a quarter-mile of swamp to get to us. And we set up traps, remember?"

Michael, a copper-skinned man with black hair that he wore parted to one side, approached the edge with caution. "We're all assuming they'll come from the west," he said. "What if they hit us from the east?"

"To do that, they'd have to cross through three miles of swamp," Miri replied. "No, they'll come this way."

Tommy exhaled, his face crumpling at the realization that he had failed to anticipate that possibility. He mopped a hand over his face. "Well, just the same. I should check the traps on that side of the hill."

They didn't require much checking; he could feel them as little knots of awareness in the back of his mind, Force-Sources that he had Infused into rocks and scattered across the hillside. Anyone trying to attack this camp would be in for an unpleasant surprise. Still, he had grown so accustomed to those little knots of awareness that he might not have noticed if one was moved by wind or rain. He would have to do the work himself. The others would have no idea what to look for.

"We should break camp," Miri suggested. "We've been meaning to do it for the last few days. Now is as good a time as any."

"We're light on supplies," Tommy said. "If we're going to undertake a long journey, I'd rather have food." That had been the reason for their delay. Well, that and the fading hope that he could free the last remaining slaves in Hedrovan with one more raid on the city. The Banker's Guild was still using some of them as clerks. Their security was tight; he had not been able to devise a workable plan even with Field Binding at his disposal. Tommy hated the thought of leaving anyone behind, but this revolution was dead.

"Besides," Zoe added, "they've blocked the easiest way out

of here. Unless you want to wade through three miles of swamp yourself, escape isn't an option."

Miri turned her head to fix the younger woman with an icy glare. "Better the swamp than the guns and cannons we'll be facing soon enough." A moment of cold silence passed, and then her face hardened. "Spread the word to everyone in the camp. Gather your things and saddle the horses. We're leaving."

Tommy could have argued with her. Neither one of them was in command, per se, but the others needed guidance, and they generally looked to either him or Miri. But in this case, he suspected that Miri had the right of it. It was time to abandon this place and move on. Some small part of him had been hoping that Desa and Kalia would come north before they were forced to depart, but it was a fool's hope.

Quickly, they ran back to the camp, to the tiny city of empty tents in the middle of Hebar's Hill. Tommy remembered the mission that he, Miri and Dalen had undertaken to get those supplies. After returning north from Ithanar, they had come upon a regiment of Eradian soldiers about two days north of Hedrovan. A little creative Field Binding had convinced those idiots that the Almighty himself had come down upon them in a fit of wrath, and then it was just a matter of grabbing whatever they could find.

At the time, Tommy had been expecting at least four or five dozen freed slaves to join his cause. He had even entertained ideas of seizing Hedrovan itself. Foolish notions. Just the daydreams of a bumpkin from a northern town that no one had ever heard of. He had never truly believed that taking the city was possible, but he *had* expected things to go better than this.

Slipping into the tent that he shared with Miri and Dalen, he began packing up the other man's books. Dalen would, of course, be livid that Tommy had displaced his belongings, but there was no time to waste.

The tent flaps parted, and Dalen came in, opening his mouth to protest. He thought better of it and decided to help Tommy instead.

"Miri found you?" Tommy asked.

Dropping to one knee, Dalen began shoving books into a leather satchel. A scowl twisted his face into a haggard expression. "I heard," he grumbled. "We're leaving. Well, I suppose it's about time."

Somehow, even in what was essentially a military camp, Dalen still managed to look like a librarian. His beige pants and white shirt were clean and free of wrinkles; his brown hair was neatly combed.

Standing up, Tommy slung the strap of a bag over his shoulder. He nodded once to the other man. "I'll go see to the horses."

When he stepped outside, he found himself on an empty street lined with many other tents. Sunlight filtered through the cracks in the ceiling of clouds. The camp should have been bustling, but it was as silent as a tomb.

Well, except for Petra.

Zoe's mother was a handsome woman with her hair tied up in an iron-gray bun. The brand had not yet been removed from her cheek. "Mr. Smith," she said. "I've set Victor and Jimmy Potts to the task of gathering up our food supplies."

"Very good."

"Should we take down the tents?"

Tommy hesitated. Should they? It would take the better part of the afternoon to take them all down, and there was no telling when those Eradians would make their move. On the other hand, leaving them here would be a clear indication that someone had used this place as a campground. And there was always a chance, however remote, that the soldiers would find some clue as to where Tommy and his people had fled to. Tommy couldn't say how since he had yet to pick a destination, but betting on misfortune was always a good move.

Anxiety began to well up within him. Why, oh, why had he ever thought that he could survive in a position of authority? "Only those we need for shelter," he said. It was as good an answer as any other. "Leave the rest."

"Very good, sir," Petra replied.

Now, what he been planning to…Right, the horses! He was on his way to check on them when Sarah came running toward him from the outskirts of the camp. The girl was barely twelve years old and far too pale. "Mr. Smith, come quick!"

"What is it?"

"Where is Miss Nin Valia?"

Miri emerged from a nearby tent, removing her wide-brimmed hat and blinking in confusion. "Sweet Mercy," she muttered. "What is it, girl?"

"I think we're in trouble."

They followed Sarah to the eastern side of the hilltop, into the thicket of trees that surrounded the camp. By the time they arrived, the girl was huffing and puffing, and Tommy was a tad winded himself.

Bent over with her hands on her knees, Sarah drew in a breath. "Look," she panted, pointing into the distance. "Out there."

Tommy took the spyglass from his coat pocket and lifted it to his eye. At first, he saw only a stagnant swamp that he could smell from up here, but it wasn't long before the source of Sarah's alarm became clear to him. There, on the edge of the marshlands. Another group of tents with black-coated men scurrying about like ants. The Eradians had boxed them in on both sides. There would be no getting out that way. They probably had encampments to the north and south as well.

"What is it?" Miri asked.

Tommy passed the spyglass to her. What had he done? How

many innocents had he condemned to death? He had to stifle a laugh. What a silly question! The answer was ten. Assuming, of course, that the others hadn't been captured after they fled his camp. Death or slavery: he had made that choice himself once. Better to die than to live your life in chains. He just hoped his friends felt the same way. "Gather our people," he said. "Tell them to prepare for battle."

"THAT ONE," Desa said, pointing to a fine revolver in a glass-fronted display case. The shopkeeper, a short and spindly man in a white shirt and black vest, replied with an eager smile. He was a jittery fellow with a large nose that held up a pair of spectacles. "Very good, miss," he said.

The shop wasn't much to look at: wooden walls and wooden floorboards, a large counter where the tiny man sat cleaning his many guns. Large windows on either side of the door looked out on a muddy street where people hurried back and forth.

Hobbling over to the wall, the shopkeeper bent over and lifted a key in a trembling hand. He shoved it into the lock and jiggled it a few times. "Apologies, miss," he went on. "I used to have help, but..."

In a brown coat and wide-brimmed hat, Desa leaned against the wall with her arms crossed. "Something happened?" she asked, raising an eyebrow. "They quit?"

"They were stolen."

"I wasn't aware that people could be stolen."

The shopkeeper opened the case and reached inside to retrieve the revolver Desa had selected. "Not people, miss," he clarified. "Slaves. But that bandit...He freed almost every slave in this city."

"Some would say he performed a service."

The old man turned his head to give her a dangerous look. Satisfied that she would say no more on this subject, he returned to the task at hand. "Yes, the Lessenger is quite the weapon," he said. "Hardly ever jambs up."

Desa sauntered across the room, reaching into her pocket to pull out a handful of bills. She slapped them down on the counter. "Can't say it's ever happened to me," she muttered. "Though I did have one melt on me once."

"Melt?" the old man asked, returning to his place behind the counter.

A sly smile was Desa's only reply to that. "No need to worry about it," she assured him. "You might say it happened under extraordinary circumstances."

The man took her money, tucking it away inside a drawer, and then offered her a few copper coins as change. He went through all the standard pleasantries, thanking her for her patronage, assuring her that he could acquire almost any firearm she could want, pointing out the low price of his ammunition. Desa took him up on that last one, buying two boxes. She was running low on bullets.

A bell jingled when the door opened, and then Kalia slipped into the shop, casting a glance back over her shoulder. "People out there are in a fury," she muttered.

"It's the bandit," the shopkeeper explained. "Most businesses in the city have lost at least half their workforce."

Kalia opened her mouth to argue, but Desa caught the other woman's eye. She shook her head slowly. Upsetting the man with her own thoughtless comment had been foolish, and she didn't need Kalia compounding her error. The people of Hedrovan had some repulsive beliefs, but this city was just a brief stop on their journey to the desert.

If things had been different, she would have gladly joined Tommy on his quest to free the slaves, but with the fate of the world in the balance, stopping Adele had to be her first priority. She had no time for anything else. Besides, her young protégé seemed to be doing quite well without her.

The floorboards creaked as Kalia shuffled across the room and frowned at the gun Desa had purchased. "You really need another one?"

"You can never be too careful."

"Isn't that the truth?" the shopkeeper put in.

Her plan was to carry two pistols on her person, one with Infused ammunition and one with ordinary ammunition. That should make it easier to switch between them. She would explain as much to Kalia at another time. The people of this city were quivering with rage and fear. Everyone kept talking about the bandit who used black magic to free the slaves. Exposing herself as a practitioner of Field Binding would be most unwise.

Heaving out a sigh, Kalia turned her face up to the ceiling. "Well, if your business here is concluded," she huffed. "Perhaps we could be on our way?"

"Yes, I think it's past time," Desa agreed.

The gun shop was a blocky, stone building on a street lined with blocky, stone buildings. Carriages rolled past, their wheels leaving trails in the ever-present mud that coated every road in Hedrovan. It was even worse in winter.

Kalia pulled her into a nearby alley.

The woman was frantic, looking around as if she expected to find the City Watch closing in on her. "I did a little scouting while you were busy," she whispered. "There are soldiers staying at the *Golden Sunset* and the *Seaside Jewel.* A man down at the fish market tells me they're here to deal with the bandit."

Closing her eyes, Desa let out a shuddering breath. "Tommy," she mumbled. "Sweet Mercy, they're going to kill him."

"Desa, we have to help him."

A wince came on as Desa shook her head. "We can't," she protested. "Kalia, we don't have time for this. We have to get to the desert."

The other woman's eyes were a pair of augers piercing

Desa's soul. "You would leave him to die?" Kalia hissed. "After everything we've been through together?"

"I have no choice!" Desa growled. "It's a handful of lives versus millions. Every passing day puts more people in jeopardy. How long will the *Al a Nari* hold out if we don't stop Adele? And what about my people? Or those living on the other side of the ocean. The Eradians plan to spread their empire to every corner of the globe, and if they've found a way to control Adele's power, then nothing stands in their way!"

"You really think one day will make that much difference?"

"I think we have to be practical."

Backing away, Kalia rested one hand on the alley wall. She blew air through puckered lips. "Practical," she murmured. "Somehow, I knew you would say that. You can go to the desert, Desa. You can leave today if you're so inclined. But if you do, you will be going alone. I'm going to help my friends."

Desa shoved her way past the other woman, striding to the mouth of the alley. She paused there, trying to stuff her anger down into the pit of her stomach. "If that's how you feel," she croaked. "Then I respect your decision. Good luck."

"There is one other thing."

When she turned around, Kalia had one shoulder propped against the wall. The poor woman looked as if someone had punched her in the stomach. "I overheard a couple soldiers chatting down by the pier," she said. "One of them was afraid. There are a lot of rumours going around. Seems the bandit has been using Aladri magic to win his battles."

"And?"

"And," Kalia said, marching forward with grim determination on her face. "The other one said he had nothing to fear. Because their commander found a new weapon. Something even more powerful than Aladri magic."

Desa felt her jaw tighten, a shiver passing through her. "All right," she whispered. "Let's go find Tommy."

. . .

ANOTHER DAY IN THE CELL. Four walls of stone, a stool for sitting. The Weaver was quite certain that if she were still human, her back would be terribly sore. But a little back pain was nothing compared to what this body had endured.

She sat upon the stool in a sleek, black dress, raven hair falling over her shoulders. The fingers on her right hand traced the rough scales on her left. What an odd sensation. Humans perceived the world in such a limited way. It was a wonder they were able to accomplish anything of use.

The power within her surged. Not at her command. It just flared to life, and reality twisted around her, her surroundings blurring and split apart. She was transported against her will to someplace she did not know.

It appeared to be a tent of some kind, a tent where her uncle sat at a small table, eating steak. By the sounds of people shouting outside, she suspected that she was in a military camp. The exact location was not important. Only one thing mattered.

Her eyes were drawn to the black crystal sitting idly next to her uncle Timothy's plate. Somehow, her uncle had managed to calcify a fragment of the Ether that had been used to confine her for ten millennia. He literally carried a piece of her prison around with him. And since part of her essence was still trapped within that prison, so long as he had the crystal, she would be forced to obey him.

Timothy cut his meat with gusto, stabbing a small piece of it and shoving it into his mouth. He grunted, nodding with satisfaction. "Thank you for joining me, my dear."

Spreading her skirts, the Weaver offered a deep curtsy. "My pleasure, uncle," she said. "I take it you have need of my services."

"I do indeed."

She claimed the chair across from him, crossing one leg over the other and placing her hands on the armrests. Her predatory smile made Timothy pause. Good. Best that he remembered he held a captive wolf, one who might slip the leash at any time. "And who shall I slaughter for you today?"

"There has been a rebellion."

The Weaver arched an eyebrow. "A testament to your skilled leadership, I'm sure."

Leaning back with hands folded over his stomach, Timothy regarded her. "It seems the slaves of Hedrovan have decided to revolt," he explained. "About a month ago, a stranger came to the city and freed them using Aladri sorcery."

The Weaver bent forward, setting her elbows on the table and resting her chin atop laced fingers. "Interesting," she said. "Tell me, why do you even care? Isn't slavery illegal throughout most of the Empire?"

"Most but not all," he confirmed. "Calvor Province still permits the practice."

"Well, you will forgive a foolish, young woman for commenting on your policies, but this seems to be a waste of resources. Surely, my efforts would be better spent expanding the Empire's reach. And you can return to your new post as a Member of Parliament."

Timothy dabbed at this mouth with a napkin, his eyes shut tight as he formulated a response to her objection. "Lawlessness cannot be tolerated," he said. "If these rebels are not brought to heel, it will encourage others to rise up."

He lifted the crystal between his thumb and forefinger, its black surface catching the light of the nearby kerosene lanterns. "I am here because I am the one who discovered the means to control *Hanak Tuvar*."

"Very well," the Weaver sighed. "Let's get on with it then."

"Patience, my dear."

She waited for him to finish his meal. If she tried to leave, he would only use the crystal to force her back into the chair. Patience *was* necessary. She could be patient if she had to. Yes, she could.

Rising from his chair, Timothy gestured to the tent's entrance. "Shall we go?"

He led her out to a large camp where soldiers in black coats scurried about. Some of them ventured a glance at her as she passed, but none let their eyes linger too long. The part of her that was still human was mortified. For them to see her in this condition...Ugly and scarred. Were any of these the same men she had used to attack Aladar?

The sky was gray with only a few shafts of sunlight piercing through the clouds. Everyone gave her a wide berth, and well for them that they did. Timothy took her to the edge of the camp, to a swamp that stank.

Here and there, twisted trees rose out of the dark waters, but there was little to see except a high hill less than a mile away. Thicker trees on the hilltop blocked her view, but she was certain that was where the rebels had made their camp.

"Very well, then," the Weaver muttered. "Let's get on with it."

She raised her hands, intending to call lightning down from the heavens, but nothing happened. The power within her would not budge. A glance to her right revealed her uncle standing by the water's edge with the crystal in hand. It was glowing with faint, purple light. "Not so fast," he said. "I prefer to keep you in reserve for the time being. No need to tip our hand to the enemy."

"Why bother? I could destroy them for you in a matter of minutes."

"I don't want them destroyed," Timothy answered. "I want them broken. I want tales of this battle to spread far and wide. I want them to know that even Aladri sorcery cannot stand up to the Empire's might."

She noticed that he had several cannons in a line, all pointed at the distant hill. The Weaver knew little of warfare, but unless she missed her guess, those cannons would fire six-pound balls. Light artillery.

"We're ready," Timothy said. "Begin the attack."

5

Tommy watched the Eradians through his spyglass, watched them lining up those cannons for a long-range shot. Men in black coats lit the fuses. He imagined that he could hear the soft hiss. "Steady," Miri said. She was observing the battlefield through a spyglass of her own. "Nobody, panic. We're in no danger."

The cannons went off with a fearsome roar, each one flashing as it spat a ball at Hebar's Hill. The recoil had them each rolling back a few feet. Tommy looked up to see those three balls rushing over his head to descend upon the camp behind him. Tents collapsed as they were struck.

"Steady," Miri said again.

Most of his remaining followers had joined him on the western side of the hilltop. He had posted a few as lookouts on the east side, just in case the Eradians tried to sneak around.

Mrs. Potts was wrapped up in a warm blanket. Zoe was down on her knees, checking and rechecking every pistol and rifle they had brought to make sure they were loaded with ammo. Jim Potts stood beside Tommy with a bow in hand, as did Victor Wyatt. And then there was Dalen. The poor man knew that he was useless in a fight. So, he busied himself with checking the horse lines and supply carts. If they survived this, they would be leaving as quickly as possible.

Jim was tall, pale and lean with a thin nose and a mop of sandy-blonde hair. He did an admirable job of keeping his fear under control, but Tommy could tell he was nervous. And who wouldn't be?

Victor was a few inches shorter, tanned with almond-shaped eyes and hair that he kept shaved. That one kept plucking the string of his bow, eager to be doing something. Anything!

Perched upon a rock with the spyglass pressed to her eye, Miri grunted. "Lommy," she said. "I do believe it's time for you to strike some fear into them."

Tommy planted himself at the edge of the hilltop and triggered the Sonic-Source in one of his pendants. It would amplify the sound of his voice in one direction. Toward the enemy. "You cannot harm us!" His voice boomed over the swamp. "Your pitiful attacks are meaningless. Leave now, and we will spare your lives."

He killed the Source.

The Eradians knew almost nothing about Field Binding. They had to be wondering how he could project his voice with such volume. If they feared Aladri magic, perhaps it would be enough to make them turn away.

"They're coming for us!" Miri growled.

Then again...

Another glance through the spyglass showed him at least two dozen men in black coats marching into the swamp, wading through knee-deep water as they approached the base of the hill. Every one of those soldiers carried a rifle. If they reached the hilltop...

Miri drew herself up to full height, gesturing toward the battlefield. "Archers!" she bellowed. "Blue feathers!"

Tommy selected an arrow from his quiver, one that was marked with bright, blue fletchings. At Miri's command, he nocked and drew back the string. Jim and Victor did the same on either side of him.

"Loose!" Miri shouted.

Bow-strings snapped and arrows flew, each one landing in the swamp, disappearing into the water. Every one of those arrowheads was a Heat-Sink. Tommy triggered all of them with a single thought.

The water froze with a creaking sound, solidifying around the legs of every soldier. Some of those men cried out in shock. A few of them fainted as the heat was drained from their bodies.

"Rifles!" Miri yelled.

Ken, Kaylee and Billy Potts approached the edge, each lifting their rifle to peer through the sights. They lined up shots and fired, thunder filling the air and making Tommy's ears ring.

Bullets ripped through Eradian bodies with a spray of blood. Unable to fall over, many of those men just flailed. A few of them tried to lift their weapons and return fire, but with their legs trapped by the ice – not to mention the frigid cold that addled their brains – they couldn't get a clean shot.

Miri shot a glance toward him, her eyes wild with urgency. "Lommy," she barked. "Take out those cannons."

Even without the spyglass, he could see that the gunners were adjusting the inclination of their artillery and loading balls for a second volley. They knew now that their enemy had gathered at the edge of the hill and that firing on the camp was useless.

Without looking, Tommy seized an arrow with white feathers, nocked it and drew back the string. Compensating for the mild, southward wind, he loosed. He didn't need his eyes to tell him that the arrow landed true about two feet in front of the cannons.

Tommy triggered the Force-Source.

A blast of kinetic energy hurled chunks of dirt into the air, and the cannons rolled backwards, nearly running over the gunners who leaped out of the way. One of them fell over onto its side. Not good enough. He would have to disincentivize them from going anywhere near those heavy weapons.

Tommy chose another arrow. Nock, draw and loose. The shaft planted itself in the dirt next to the first one he had fired, and he triggered the Electric-Sink he had Infused into the arrowhead.

The first gunner to get to close went rigid as if he had been taken by the paralyzing venom of a snake. A few seconds later, his muscles went limp, and he fell to the ground, dead. The others had no idea what had happened, but they were wise enough to steer clear of cannons.

"Stand together!" Miri shouted. "This is just beginning!"

THE WEAVER HAD to resist the urge to laugh. Barely five minutes into this battle and her uncle had already lost about a tenth of the force he had brought with him. She would have helped, but Timothy had to have his grand story of heroic soldiers triumphing over the rebels and their black magic.

She stood next to a tent with her arms folded, smiling impishly as she watched the scene play out. "Oh, uncle!" she called. "A moment of your time."

Another platoon of men tried to charge across the swamp, but within seconds, they were slipping and sliding on the ice. Many fell flat on their faces only to be struck down by bullets from the distant hilltop.

Standing well back from the water's edge, Timothy twisted around to glare at her. "What is it?" he snarled.

"I think I know the identity of their Field Binder."

"Their what?"

Shutting her eyes, the Weaver sighed in frustration. "The one using black magic," she said in tones that parents usually reserved for unruly toddlers. "His name is Tommy Smith. He likes to Infuse his arrows with all sorts of nasty surprises. Are you ready for me to step in yet?"

"Thaw the water," Timothy commanded.

Raising her human hand, the Weaver curled her fingers, channeling heat into the swamp. Within seconds, the ice melted, becoming stagnant water once again. Soldiers were splashing through the reek, trying to reach the base of the hill.

"Very good," Timothy said. "Now, teach them a lesson."

Spreading her arms wide, the Weaver threw back her head in exultation, grinning like a little girl with a new toy. Now, she would have a little fun.

SOMETHING WAS WRONG. The water should not have melted that quickly. Tommy reached out to the Ether – the crystal atop Vengeance's temple had granted him the ability to find it in seconds – and the world changed before his eyes. Particles swirled all around him, billions of them. Trillions!

His first instinct was to scan the enemy camp with his thoughts, but something got his attention, something he would never have noticed without the Ether. A build-up of electrostatic energy in the atmosphere. But that could only mean...

Releasing the Ether, Tommy turned and dove for Victor. "Everybody, get away!" he shouted, tackling the other man to the ground. They rolled partway down the hillside, stopping when they collided with a tree.

He caught a brief glimpse of the others scattering.

Then a jagged bolt of lightning struck the hilltop. The flash was bright enough to blind him. His ears popped from the peel of thunder, and tears streamed over his cheek.

The purple afterimage faded just enough for him to see the

blurry trees and mud all around him. There was motion on the hilltop, but he couldn't tell who had survived the blast. His head felt like it had been stuffed with cotton.

Reaching into his pocket, he found the tiniest shard of crystal and crushed it in the palm of his hand. A rainbow spread over him, red to orange to yellow to green. It faded away before turning blue, but that brief moment of healing was enough to restore his vision and clear the fog out of his brain.

Adele. It had to be her.

He communed with the Ether, letting his mind drift over the swamp, ignoring the black-coated men who converged on the hill. Within seconds, he was mapping the enemy camp with his thoughts. It didn't take long to find the dark pit of emptiness that must have been Adele.

She turned her head toward him, sensing his attention.

He had caught her in the middle of preparing something vicious. Perhaps another lightning bolt. What was it Desa had said about severing her connection to her power? Tommy forced the Ether into that emptiness. He could feel Adele's scream even from this distance.

Dismissing the Ether, Tommy scrambled up the hill with his bow in hand, huffing and puffing until he reached the top. "It's Adele!" he yelled. "I've incapacitated her for now, but she'll regain her power in a few-"

He cut off when he saw the scorched bodies lying in the mud. It took a second for him to recognize them as Billy and Kaylee. They had taken the brunt of the lightning strike. "Almighty protect us."

Jim ran along the ledge, scanning the swamp below. "They've almost reached the hill!" he said. "We're about to be overrun!"

Miri stepped out from behind a tree with her teeth bared. A gash in her forehead dripped blood onto her cheek. "Red feathers," she panted.

Obeying her order, Tommy and Jim raised their bows, firing the appropriate arrows into the water. The men at the base of the hill hopped back, trying to avoid each projectile that came their way, but sharp steel was the least of their worries.

Tommy triggered the Heat-Sources he had created weeks ago.

The water began to bubble, steam rising from the swamp as the frightened soldiers retreated. One fellow managed to get his rifle up and fire a single shot that left a ringing in Tommy's ears.

The bullet pierced Jim's stomach, causing him to fall to his knees. He clutched at the wound as if trying to hold his guts inside.

"He needs a crystal!" Tommy shouted. "He needs-"

A thought occurred to him, diverting his attention away from his injured comrade. Ducking out of sight behind a tree, he made himself one with the Ether and directed his thoughts toward the enemy.

Adele had indeed regained her power; he could feel her manipulating air molecules. To what end, he could not say. Once again, he tried to force the Ether into the darkness that suffused her body from head to toe. But this time, she was too quick for him. As he gathered his will for an attack, Adele simply disappeared. He searched for her, letting his mind fly over the enemy camp and the hilltop, but she was just gone.

One of the black-coats came charging out of the boiling water, racing up the steep slope. Some of them were smart enough to realize that pressing on was wiser than trying to go back to their camp. Or rather, it would be if hot water was all they had to worry about. Tommy triggered the Force-Source he had Infused into a rock.

The ground exploded under the young soldier's feet, hurling him backward into the bubbling stew. He screamed as his body was submerged.

The others were dancing about. Many of them had

dropped their rifles; a few had retreated to a safe distance. The heat that Tommy had unleashed would soon dissipate throughout the swamp. In a minute or two, the water would be cool again.

Miri rushed to Jim, dropping to one knee beside him. She pressed a crystal into the palm of his hand and then crushed it. Tommy felt the Ether surging, healing the other man's wounds. He could sense damaged organs repairing themselves, sense the growth of new cells.

"He's weak," Miri said. "He'll survive. but he needs rest."

Adele's sudden reappearance in the Eradian camp drew Tommy's attention like an iron filing to a magnet. He sensed her among the enemy troops, a cloud of darkness in the shape of a woman.

Gathering the Ether, Tommy prepared to attack, but once again, she was too quick for him. She vanished before he could cut her off from the source of her power, taking a dozen black-coats with her.

They materialized on the hilltop, only fifty feet away. Tommy was so shocked that he lost the Ether. The sea of spinning particles became a world of solid objects, and he was confronted by a raven-haired Adele who smiled at him, her orange eyes alight with anticipation. "Here we are, boys!" she said. "Enjoy!"

Then she was gone again, disappearing to the Almighty knows where.

Black-clad soldiers raised their rifles.

Tommy got up and charged toward the enemy, triggering his Force-Sink pendant. Their guns flashed as they opened fire, and bullets slammed to a stop in front of him, hovering in the air.

One of the soldiers flailed as Miri shot him in the chest; another went down when Victor's arrow took him right between the eyes, but the rest fanned out. They had Tommy and his followers pinned. Enemies before them, a steep slope behind.

Mrs. Potts jumped on one man before he could take aim, tackling him and striking him repeatedly with her fist. Petra did much the same, whacking one of the soldiers with her broomstick. She hit several times before the man turned and ran her through with his bayonet. "No!" Tommy screamed.

He was dimly aware of Miri using those fancy holds she knew to disarm one man and send him careening into a tree. But there were just too many. He could already see an Eradian pointing a rifle at him. His Force-Sink was used up.

It was over.

Lightning shot out of the sky, thin blue streams that struck the ground and flung rocks into the air. Frightened by this new development, the soldiers turned around to see what was happening. And then bullets rained down on them. Men howled as their bodies were pierced.

Tommy looked up to see a tiny figure in brown descending from the overcast sky. No, it couldn't be! He laughed despite himself. Of course, it could! The newcomer extended her hand toward the ground, slowing her approach with a Force-Sink.

Desa landed in a crouch with her arms spread wide, her eyes wide with feral hatred. She was a mother bear protecting her young. Rising in one fluid motion, she snarled.

And the remaining soldiers backed up instinctively.

"Get down!" Desa barked.

Tommy didn't have to be told twice. He threw himself to the ground just in time to see her thrust her hands out with fingers splayed, releasing waves of kinetic energy from her rings. Men were hurled backward like leaves kicked up by an angry wind. One by one, they went over the cliff.

Tommy was caught in the blast as well, sent rolling toward the edge. He grabbed an exposed root at the last second, his legs dangling over the muddy hillside. Hopefully, no one else had been hurt.

He looked up to find Desa standing over him and shaking her head in exasperation. "I can't leave you alone for five minutes," she said, offering her hand.

He took it, letting her pull him to his feet. "Five minutes," he grumbled. "Begging your pardon, ma'am, but it was more like five months. How did you fly like that?"

Desa removed her spent bracelet, slipping it into her pocket, and then immediately drew out another one just like it. She slapped that one on her wrist. "A little trick with Force and Gravity-Sources," she said. "I'll teach you when we have a moment."

"Good to have you back, Mrs. Kincaid."

She looked up at him with large, brown eyes, perhaps wondering how much he had grown in her absence. "Are you ready to end this?"

"Just try and stop me."

Miri approached the cliff edge, wiping the sweat off her face and blinking the dust out of her eyes. She seemed to notice Desa for the first time and greeted the other woman with a smile. "Excellent timing."

"You still have ammo?" Desa asked.

"We do."

"Keep them off my back. Watch for Kalia. She'll be approaching from the south."

Tommy braced a hand against a tree, his head hanging with fatigue. "Adele's here," he breathed. "She's supporting the Eradians."

"I know." Drawing her pistol, Desa popped open the cylinder and loaded it with six new bullets. "Let's go to work."

. . .

THEY WERE COMING up the hill: Eradians in their black coats, each man carrying a rifle, trying not to slip and slide on the mucky ground. Snarling faces looked up at her with hatred in their eyes. Some of them were the very men she had knocked down moments earlier. The nearest one was almost to the top.

Desa reached into her coat pocket, pulling out a handful of black-pepper powder. She flung it at him and used a burst of kinetic energy from her ring to send it right into his eyes. The man stumbled, doubling over in a fit of sneezes.

Desa charged down the hill.

She jumped, planting one foot on the man's back and pushed off to launch herself at the next soldier in line. That one tried to get his weapon up, but his feet struggled for purchase on the soft earth.

Spreading her legs like scissor blades, Desa brought them together and trapped his head between her knees. Her momentum forced him down onto his back, and she landed perched atop the fool.

A punch to the face knocked him senseless.

Without even looking, Desa drew a throwing knife and tossed it off to her left. When she heard a yelp, she ventured a glance and saw that the blade had sunk into the arm of a soldier who had been trying to point a rifle at her. That fellow dropped his gun, sliding down the muddy slope.

A pair of black-coats at the bottom of the hill stopped in their tracks, both taking aim.

In a heartbeat, Desa had her left hand up to shield herself, triggering the Force-Sink in her bracelet. Thunder split the air, and two bullets appeared right in front of her, stilled by the power of the Ether.

She quickly rolled aside, taking refuge behind a tree. Bullets sped past her, rushing up the hillside toward Tommy and his people. She would do what she could to protect them, but she was just one woman, Field Binding or no Field Binding.

Desa drew her left-hand pistol, the one she had loaded with Infused bullets, and cocked the hammer. Carefully, she aimed around the tree trunk, firing a single round that landed at the feet of three men in black.

She triggered the Force-Source.

Mud sprayed into the air along with several bodies that were thrown backward. One by one, they landed in the swamp, water splashing around them as they broke the surface. And still, more came scrambling up the hill.

Shoving her left-hand pistol back into its holster, Desa drew the one on her right hip. This one carried ordinary ammunition.

She aimed around the tree and fired.

An Eradian flailed when her shot went through his chest, dropping to his knees and landing face-down on the hillside. One of the others swung his rifle around, trying to target her.

Desa ducked behind the tree, crouching down and crossing her forearms in front of her face. Gunfire rang in her ears. A massive bullet punched through the tree and flew right over her head.

Ripping off her necklace, Desa threw it into the cluster of men who were charging up the hill. And then she triggered the Light-Sink. A patch of darkness consumed them, voices crying out in alarm as the black-coats tripped and fell.

She fired blindly into the gloom.

CRACK! CRACK! CRACK!

Wounded soldiers cried out in pain. Bodies slid down the muddy slope, emerging into the light and leaving trails of blood in their wake. Arrows hit them from above, and men shrieked as they were stung.

Desa took the opportunity to load her pistol with fresh ammunition. More enemies were coming. The Eradian commander had at least a hundred men at his disposal. She had to end this quickly. Find Adele and put a bullet through her head. If the Eradians lost their greatest weapon, they might back off.

REALITY TWISTED around the Weaver as she was yanked back to her uncle's camp. She had been trying to keep her distance. The outcome of this battle was of no concern to her. She was certainly not going to put herself in danger just to prove the might of the Eradian Empire or some such nonsense.

The blurriness faded, and she found her uncle standing in front of a large tent with the glowing crystal in hand. By the look in his eyes, he was ready to skin her alive. "And where have you been?" he demanded. "You delivered those men to the hilltop almost five minutes ago! You should have come back here!"

"I take it the battle isn't going well?"

"See for yourself."

She ventured a glance around the tent and realized that her assessment had been a serious understatement. Men in black coats raced up the hill only to be met with gunfire and explosions. Over a dozen bodies floated in the swamp, blood pooling around them. There were wounded as well.

She saw men at the medical tent whose feet were nothing but a mass of red blisters. Others were crawling back to the camp, unable to stand after wading through the scalding water. Some had turned tail and run in any direction, as long as it was away from that hill. They would not be returning here. They knew the price of desertion.

"Do something!" Timothy demanded.

Rounding on him, the Weaver clasped her hands together behind her back. She tilted her head to one side with a sweet smile. "And put myself at risk?" she asked. "You saw what happened the last time. Tommy cut me off from my power."

Timothy flinched at the sound of a distant explosion,

gasping for breath. Perhaps he had learned to fear Aladri magic. "Your power is no good to me if you will not use it," he growled. "Do something."

"As you wish, uncle."

A BREAK in the shooting gave Desa an opportunity. She peeked out from behind the tree and found that most of the black-coats were lying on their bellies at the base of the hill. A few were starting to rise. Just the distraction she needed.

An instant later, Desa was on her feet and charging down the slope, heedless of the slippery mud beneath her. A few of those soldiers looked up, their jaws dropping in shock when they saw her.

Desa leaped, grabbing the drooping branch of a nearby tree. She swung her body like a pendulum, slamming her feet into the chest of a man who noticed her a second too late. The poor bastard fell onto his ass.

Releasing the branch, Desa back-flipped through the air, dropping like a pin to land in ankle-deep water. The others wasted absolutely no time surrounding her. At least six of them closed in.

One came up behind her.

Bending her knees, Desa drove her elbow into the oaf's stomach, producing a sharp wheeze. She brought her hand up to strike his nose with the back of her fist. And then he toppled over.

A large, pale man with a thick mustache towered over her, drawing his belt knife. His breath stank of whiskey.

Her hand flew out toward him, tossing another pinch of black pepper powder, and with the Force-Source in her ring, she propelled it right into his face. The man sneezed, dropping his weapon and covering his face with both hands.

She turned to her right just in time to see a lanky fellow

with hollow cheeks and ropey arms coming her way. He was bent double, charging like a bull.

Desa jumped, using her Gravity-Sink for extra height, and rolled like a log over his back. She made a large splash as she dropped back into the water. When she looked up, a brute with a scraggly beard stood right in front of her.

He threw a punch.

Ducking low, Desa let his fist pass over her head. She sent a pair of jabs into his belly and then followed that with an open palm to the chest, augmenting the blow with a burst of kinetic energy.

The bearded man went flying backwards, screaming as he crashed into a tree. He fell to the ground a moment later, landing face-down in the swamp.

She turned around to find the others staring at her in wide-eyed horror. One of them was holding a knife; another had a rifle with a nasty bayonet, but they were all afraid to attack. No one wanted to fight the demon woman with her black magic.

The rifleman threw down his weapon and fled, kicking up water as he sprinted away from the hill. It took the others all of five seconds to decide they wanted to follow him. Desa snorted as she watched them go.

Now, where was Adele?

It occurred to her that the Eradians must have been control-ling the other woman somehow. Adele Delarac was much too self-absorbed to dedicate herself to a cause. She would only fight for the Empire if she had no other choice. If Desa could get her hands on whatever it was they used to restrain her...

She was about to reach for the Ether, to search the battle-field for her enemy, when a hissing sound made her look up. Fireballs streaked out of the heavens like comets, igniting the trees they struck. In seconds, half the hillside was burning.

Desa's first instinct was to go find the others – she could put out those fires with Heat-Sinks – but that would be a tactical error. Tommy could snuff out those flames as easily as she could, and Kalia would lend her support as soon as she got here. They didn't need a third Field Binder.

But if she put down Adele once and for all…

Desa took off through the swamp, bolting for the enemy camp. Some of the black-coats gasped when they saw her coming, but no one tried to stop her. They were wise not to try. She had only one goal.

And nothing would stand in her way.

KALIA SCREAMED as she watched the ground rushing up to meet her. Why had she let Desa talk her into this insane method of travel? Human beings were not meant to fly! She could feel the Sink in her belt buckle feasting on gravitational energy. It was the only thing preventing her from breaking every bone in her body in a devastating crash.

She saw a collection of haphazardly-placed tents sprawled out across the hilltop. Some of them had been flattened by cannonballs. It dawned on her that she didn't have a good place to land.

Stretching her hand toward the ground, Kalia triggered the Force-Sink in her bracelet. It would not take energy from Kalia's body except in cases where she was hurtling toward a much larger object. Motion was relative. In a way, the bracelet was slowing the Earth as it approached *her*. Sadly, she had activated it a second too late.

Kalia hit the ground and bounced along it like a stone skipping across the water. A string of curses escaped her as she rolled through the narrow space between two lines of tents. "I am going to kill you, Desa Kincaid!"

Eventually, she skidded to a stop.

She looked up to find Miri standing nearby with a rifle in

hand. The other woman shook her head in amusement. "Haven't got the hang of it, huh?"

Kalia sat up, touching fingertips to the side of her head. She grimaced at the aches and pains throughout her body. "Shut up."

The trees at the edge of the hilltop were burning! How had she failed to notice that? For that matter, how could she have been oblivious to the fireballs raining down on them from above?

Kalia forced herself to stand.

Tilting her head back, she blinked as she took in the sight. "Adele?" she asked. "This is her doing?"

Miri shrugged and then turned her head, staring off in the direction of the Eradian camp. "She seems to be holding a grudge," she said. "We could use your help."

"Of course."

Miri took off down a crossing street, and Kalia made to follow, drawing her pistol. She had learned more about Field Binding in the last few months than she had in the previous five years, but a good six-shooter would always be a sheriff's best friend. If Adele decided to make an appearance, a well-placed bullet would do her in as well as anything else. Which was to say not very well at all. The bitch just refused to die.

Gun in hand, Kalia crept around the corner and saw that Miri was gone. She was alone on a long street between two rows of tents. And she couldn't shake the feeling that danger might come rushing out of any one of them.

Where had Miri gone?

Without warning, Adele appeared in front of her, about fifty feet away. The woman cocked her head and smiled. "Oh, it's you," she said. "I was hoping for...Well, I suppose killing you will suffice. I never could abide another woman taking what's mine."

Adele extended her scaly hand, a stream of fire flying from her fingertips.

Kalia threw herself to the ground, rolling across the width of the street. She flopped onto her belly, raised the gun in one hand and fired.

The other woman vanished an instant before the bullet went through the space where her head had been. Now, where could she have gone to? Kalia muttered a few more curses. How did you fight someone who could be miles away in the blink of an eye? She forced herself to get up.

A sudden whoosh of air made her turn around, and she found Adele standing in the intersection between this street and the other one. The woman raised her hand, but Kalia was quicker.

CRACK! CRACK! CRACK!

Every bullet became a puff of smoke before it got within an inch of Adele's body, but the evil woman still danced backward as if she were afraid of them. As well she might. This was just a distraction. Adjusting her aim, Kalia fired a single shot into the ground at Adele's feet.

And then she triggered the Force-Source.

The ground exploded. Adele was thrown backward by the blast, somersaulting in the air. She landed with a grunt, breathing hard, and when she looked up, there was murder in her eyes. "This no longer amuses."

She tried to shoo Kalia away with a dismissive flick of her wrist.

Raising her left hand, Kalia triggered the Force-Sink in her bracelet, and the kinetic wave that should have hurled her sideways into a tent was absorbed by the Ether. "Nice try," she said. "But I've watched you fight. And I know your tricks."

"Do you?"

Adele raised her scaly hand, fingers curled as if she held an invisible ball in her palm. Something changed. Kalia felt as though she had lead weights strapped to her arms and legs. She couldn't breathe! Her body was so heavy.

Fighting her way through the panic, Kalia focused her thoughts and triggered the Gravity-Sink in her belt buckle. Just like that, the crushing weight was gone. She wasted no time getting to her feet.

Kalia leaped, intending to tackle Adele from above, but the other woman stretched her hand out, and Kalia was suddenly suspended in midair, held aloft by invisible strings. One of those ropes coiled around her neck. She felt it squeezing. Her vision went dark, silver flecks dancing before her eyes. What a fool she had been to think she could win against this creature.

Abruptly, Miri stepped out from between two tents, raising her rifle and pointing it at Adele. Kalia could only see her as a blurry figure, but she heard the roar of the rifle's discharge. Those invisible ropes vanished.

Kalia landed on her knees, clutching at her neck.

Striding forward, Miri worked the rifle's lever to eject the spent shell casing. And then she fired again. The second shot went through Adele's chest, causing the woman to stumble.

Adele doubled up, pressing a hand to the wound as if trying to hold her guts inside her body. She looked up at them with anguish on her face.

Then she vanished.

"Are you all right?" Miri asked, offering her hand.

Kalia took it, allowing the other woman to pull her up. "Yes, I'm fine." It came out as a croak, but ten minutes in the Ether's embrace would sort that out. Assuming that she survived long enough to get ten minutes alone.

The trees were burning; she could smell the smoke, feel it burning her eyes. "The fires," she panted. "We have to put them out."

"Yes," Miri agreed. "We need Heat-Sinks. Please tell me you have some."

Kalia nodded.

"Good. Come with me."

CREEPING through the enemy camp with her gun in hand, Desa peeked around the corner of a tent. She found black-coated soldiers scurrying about, some running, others hobbling. Her heart broke at the sight of the men who had been wounded. Some would lose their feet to severe burns or frostbite. She was half tempted to give away the last of the crystals she had taken from the Temple of Vengeance.

This had to end.

She stepped out into the open.

Men looked up, but instead of fighting, they fled at the sight of her. One or two of them even screamed. That twisted her guts in knots. The last thing she wanted was to be a figure who struck terror in the hearts of ordinary people. Wealthy and powerful people on the other hand...

It wasn't hard to find the commander. He was a tall man, dark of hair, with flecks of gray in his mustache. He was standing outside a tent when she spotted him, staring off to the distant hill. Strangely, he didn't wear a uniform. For a moment, she wondered if she had the wrong man, but she knew authority when she saw it.

Lifting her gun in one hand, Desa squinted at him. "Well now," she said, striding forward. "Somehow, I get the impression that you're in charge."

The man turned his head and flinched when his eyes fell upon her. "How did you get in here?" he growled. "Why hasn't anyone stopped this woman?"

"Who are you?" Desa demanded.

"Who am *I*? Who are you?"

Reaching up with her free hand, Desa tipped her hat to

him. "The avenging spirit of Ithanar," she said. "Here to collect a debt."

"Kill her!" the man bellowed. "Kill her, you fools!"

The soldiers who hurried through the camp stopped in their tracks, trying to decide if they wanted to obey that order. One man tentatively reached for his sidearm, but he did not draw it. Desa almost pitied them. She counted about two dozen. Together, they could have overwhelmed her – at the very least, they could force her to flee – but they didn't know that.

They knew only that many of their comrades had suffered injuries that might leave them unable to walk, that someone had boiled the swamp. Desa recognized a few of those faces. Some of them had been on the hilltop when she hurled lightning at them from above. Others had tussled with her in the water. For all they knew, she was as powerful as Adele. And they were afraid.

"Kill her!" the commander shouted.

Desa stretched her hand toward the open sky, releasing a bolt of lightning from her ring. The men who surrounded her backed away. "You are welcome to try," she said. "But you won't like the results."

No sooner did she finish speaking than Adele appeared next to the commander. The other woman was bent double with a hand on her chest, gasping for breath. She didn't even seem to notice Desa.

"About time!" the commander snapped. "Kill her!"

Adele looked up, her eyes widening when she saw Desa. "Perhaps you failed to notice, Uncle," she began. "But I'm in no condition to fight anyone." She put her hand on his shoulder, and they both vanished, leaving their men in the lurch.

Uncle.

So, the commander was Timothy Delarac. That explained a few things. Desa still didn't know how he was able to control Adele, but at least she had a target. When she was finished learning whatever it was Mercy intended to teach her, she would go to Ofalla and settle this once and for all.

The Eradians stared at her in bewilderment, wondering what to do next. No one wanted to attack her, and well for her that they didn't. She had used up most of her Sinks and Sources in the fight.

Sliding her pistol back into its holster, Desa heaved out a sigh. "Run," she said in a rasping voice. "If you value your lives, throw down your weapons and leave this place. Your days as soldiers of the Empire are over."

She was pleased when most of them heeded her advice.

6

Desa sat alone in one of the abandoned tents, resting. She had spent the last half hour Infusing new bullets along with her rings, bracelets and belt buckle. All in all, she had come out of this battle ahead. No major injuries, only a few scrapes and bruises. The Ether's healing touch had made short work of those, but she was still tired.

Tired and reluctant to see the others. She couldn't quite put her finger on why, but something made her want to stay out of sight. Maybe it was the fact that she would be leaving in the morning. Tearful good-byes would only make that harder.

Grunting and cursing, Kalia ducked into the tent and knelt on the soft rug. The woman looked as if she had been riding hard for three days without sleep. "So," she said. "Are we going to talk about it?"

"Talk about what?"

"Your decision to go after Adele instead of helping your friends."

And there it was: the reason Desa had opted for seclusion. On some level, she had known this conversation was inevitable.

She had been trying to keep her mind off of it, to busy herself with other things.

Tilting her head to one side, Desa raised an eyebrow. "Some would say I *did* help them," she countered. "If not for me, the Eradian commander might have sent another wave of soldiers up that slope, and who knows what Adele would have done?"

"Perhaps."

"Are you saying I was wrong to go?"

"No, I'm not," Kalia answered. "I don't know if you made the right choice. Maybe if you had stayed, we would all be dead now. But I do know you're still fixated on Adele."

Desa narrowed her eyes. "Adele is a threat to the world itself," she said. "I love you and Tommy and the others, but I have a duty to mankind."

"Are you sure it's duty that motivates you?"

Something about that question irked Desa. She wasn't in the mood for another lecture about letting guilt choose her path. Quite frankly, she had good reason to feel guilty. None of this would have happened if not for her.

Kalia stood up, heaving out a sigh, and then looked down at her. "Adele was here," she said. "You went charging off to find her, and she decided to come to you. Miri and I fought her."

"Are you all right?" Desa breathed.

"Took a few bumps and bruises," the other woman grumbled. "Nothing the Ether can't fix. But the fact that you didn't even know proves my point. When Adele left, we spent an hour putting out those fires, and where were you?"

"Scouting the Eradian camps," Desa growled. "Making sure they had no plans to attack again. They've departed, by the way. Even the ones on the far side of the swamp."

Kalia folded her arms, her mouth twisting in disgust. "You didn't even think to check in with us," she said. "Miri can scout just as well as you. But you have Heat-Sinks that would have been of use to us. We could have decided as a group who should perform what task."

Raising her hands defensively, Desa grunted. "Your point is made," she said. "I will endeavour to be more considerate in the future."

"Well, it's a start," Kalia muttered. "Miri and the others are burying the dead. It would mean a lot if you joined us."

As much as she would have preferred to be alone, Desa couldn't say no to that request. Not in good conscience anyway. She followed her love through the camp to the south side of the hill.

For the first time, she noticed the extent of the damage. The trees here were all charred black, broken branches hanging limply. Some of the tents had been scorched, others flattened. One was nothing but a pile of rags.

Tommy, Dalen and Miri stood in a line, holding hands, their heads bowed in mourning. Desa noted the three shrouded bodies atop three piles of wood.

There were others present as well: a young woman with red hair who couldn't stop crying, a bald man who stared dejectedly at nothing at all, a girl who could not have been more than twelve. And four others that she could not name. She had not had the chance to introduce herself to any of them. Perhaps it was best if it stayed that way.

Tommy placed himself in front of the bodies, drawing in a breath. There was a quiet serenity about him. Where was the stammering boy that she had befriended a year ago? Much had changed in five short months. "We come here to honour those friends who gave their lives today," he said. "Petra Arneli, Billy Potts, Kaylee Dualo. They stood bravely against those who would put them in chains. We are standing here because of their sacrifice."

Two young men – one pale, one dark – came forward with

burning sticks. One by one, they ignited the three piles of wood.

And Miri began to sing.

Desa recognized the tune; it was an old Aladri funeral dirge. Something on Miri's face made her think the other woman was remembering her brother. Poor Marcus. True, he had forced Miri's hand, but it wasn't entirely his fault. Daresina had charged him with recovering the Spear of Vengeance, and Marcus would never refuse an order from his Prelate. One day, Desa would return home.

And then she would settle a few scores.

A GLOWING ROCK on the old, brown rug illuminated the blue walls of Desa's tent. It gave off light but not heat. She had been practicing Field Binding for twenty years, and she still wasn't used to that. Her mind insisted that anything that glowed must be warm to the touch, but if she threw that stone into a snow-bank, it would be ice cold in seconds.

The night's chill was held at bay by a Heat-Source coin that she had placed on top of the rock. It offered just enough warmth to let her take off her coat without freezing. She would have to renew its connection to the Ether before she went to sleep.

"Desa?" Tommy called to her from outside. "May I come in?"

"By all means."

The man who entered her tent was not the youth that she had taken from a sleepy village almost a year ago. Tall and lean, he stood before her in unrelieved black. She had to admit she was having a hard time getting used to the beard. "The rest of us are trying to plan," he said. "We can't stay here."

Kneeling on the floor about an inch away from the glowing rock, Desa lowered her eyes. She couldn't bring herself to look at him. Her shame at leaving the others to fend for themselves while she chased Adele was too great. "No, you can't," she agreed. "Do you know where you'll be going next?"

"We were hoping you might help with that."

Desa stood up, knuckling her back. A woman of thirty-one was hardly a crone, but she was already starting to notice aches and pains that lingered a little longer than they should have. Sleeping on the ground often left her feeling stiff when she woke. "I will be leaving in the morning," she said. "I really can't say what the rest of you should do. You will have to decide for yourselves."

Tommy approached her with his arms crossed, frowning at her. "You know, it's funny," he began. "This tent belonged to Brian Hanson."

"Friend of yours?"

Tossing his head back with a grin, Tommy rolled his eyes. "Hardly," he replied. "The man was a constant thorn in my side. He eventually demanded that I give him crystals so that his followers could remove their brands. I did, and they left."

Desa raised an eyebrow. "You gave away five crystals?" she asked. "Tommy, if you had kept them, your friends might not have died today."

He raised a hand to silence her, a snarl betraying his anger before he smothered it. "Miri said the same thing," he admitted. "But you can't free a slave and then use their branded flesh to coerce them into working for you. We had to give them a choice. They chose to leave."

"I'm glad to see you're still an idealist."

"And you're even more of a grump," he shot back. "Why are you avoiding us, Desa?"

The bottom fell out of her stomach, but she managed to keep her voice even. Barely. Had her former protégé become more perceptive? Or had Kalia been telling him about the journey north from Ithanar? "I'm not avoiding you," she lied.

"But I will be setting out on a long journey tomorrow, and I need rest."

He turned his back on her, ducking as he passed through the tent flaps. He paused there, half in, half out. "You know," he began. "Even if you won't be coming with us, you can still help us plan."

Exasperated, Desa threw on her coat and followed him into the cold night. It didn't quite get down to freezing on the southern coast of Eradia, but in winter, it got pretty damn close.

Tommy's tent was on the eastern edge of the camp. She could already hear people talking inside as she drew near. What was she doing? She had no business taking part in any of this. But if she tried to slip away, someone would come along to collect her. So, she steeled herself and went in.

The entire camp had gathered here.

Dalen stood over a small, wooden table with one hand clasping his chin, studying a map. Several young men had gathered around him. She could see it on their faces: they were afraid and trying to hide it. Boys of that age often tried to project confidence when they were overwhelmed by doubt.

Miri stood with her arms around the redheaded girl. The child kept sobbing while Miri whispered comforting things. Some of the others were milling about. And then there was Kalia; she stood in the corner and barely looked up when Desa came in.

"All right then," Tommy said, approaching the table to stand across from Dalen. Desa waited near the entrance. "We're all here. We need to plan our next move."

An old woman with curly, gray hair stepped forward, wiping tears off her cheeks. "Begging your pardon, Thomas," she said. "But I don't think there is a next move. We should scatter."

"It'll be hard to get by on your own," Tommy countered.

"Maybe so," the woman replied. "But if we go anywhere together, they will hunt us down."

One of the young men next to Dalen perked up at that. "Well, Mum," he said. "Maybe we need to go after the hunters."

"We can't take on the entire army."

"Maybe we don't have to," Tommy replied. He spun around, regarding Desa with that inquisitive stare she recognized from their first days together. Something told her that she was not going to like what happened next. "What can you tell us about the Eradian commander?"

Shutting her eyes, Desa heaved out a breath. "It's Adele's uncle," she said. "Timothy Delarac: the mayor of Ofalla."

"Former mayor," Dalen corrected, never taking his eyes off the map; this was just an academic conversation to him. Factual errors ought to be rectified as a matter of principle, and that was all there was to it. "I reviewed the records in the Hedrovan library. The thirty-third Eradian parliament took office last fall, and Timothy Delarac was elected to a seat. The latest reports say that Prime Minister Sharro has made him the Minister of Defense."

"Well," Desa said. "That explains a few things."

"I don't see how," Miri muttered.

Striding over to the table, Desa folded her hands behind her back and looked up at Tommy. "We encountered Eradian soldiers in Ithanar," she explained. "They were trying to conquer the *Al a Nari.*"

"Sweet Mercy," Miri whispered.

"Eradia's borders have been fixed for almost a century," Desa went on. "They've learned the hard way not to threaten Aladar. They've never moved further west than the Molarin Mountains, and we all know the legends about Ithanar. This expansionist policy is new."

"And you think Timothy Delarac is its architect," Tommy said.

"I'm sure of it," Desa growled through clenched teeth. She took a moment to collect herself; anger would accomplish nothing. "Somehow, he has discovered a way to control Adele's power."

Tommy nodded slowly as if that made perfect sense. "So, if we capture him..."

"We get her as well."

Turning his back on her, Tommy bent over the map and began running his finger over it. "Dalen, you said he's a member of parliament now," he said. "That means the best place to find him would be-"

"New Beloran," the other man confirmed.

Tommy stood up straight, looking to each of his followers. "Well," he said. "It seems we have a destination. I'll understand if anyone doesn't want to come with me. In fact, I think some of you shouldn't."

He turned to the old woman, placing a hand over his heart and bowing low. "Mrs. Potts," he said. "We still have some of the money we took when we raided the army for supplies. I'm giving it to you."

The woman blinked, stunned by this declaration. "But-"

"I want you to take Sarah, Jeff and anyone who wants to go with you," Tommy went on. "Where you go doesn't matter. As long as it's somewhere far away from here. Look for somewhere safe to settle down."

"Yes, sir."

"The rest of us will be going to New Beloran."

Working up her courage, Desa cleared her throat. Tommy turned around, and she could see the disappointment in his eyes. He knew what she was going to say, but that didn't make it any easier to get the words out. "I won't be going with you. I have to go back to the abandoned city. To find Mercy."

"Not sure we can do this without you, Desa."

She answered that with a small smile. "Of course, you can," she said. "You've come a long way, Tommy. All of you have."

He didn't protest. He just gave her a hug that almost had her tearing up. Now, that wouldn't do at all. The others gathered around her, each offering a fond farewell. For a little while, they talked amicably, sharing stories, enjoying each other's company. But the night wore on, and good-byes only got harder when they were prolonged. Desa forced herself to say good night before she started crying.

And then she made her way back to her tent.

AN HOUR LATER, she was lying in her bedroll, the Heat-Source coin keeping her warm. It was dark and eerily quiet. Idly, she wondered how long it would take her to fall asleep. She kept rehearsing a speech that she knew she would have to give in the morning. She hated good-byes. This was why she had traveled alone for so many years.

A soft, rustling sound announced the arrival of Kalia who muttered as she slipped into the tent. Desa sighed. It seemed she would be giving that speech sooner than she had expected.

Kalia dropped to her knees in the darkness, pawing at the floor until she found a blanket. "So, when do we leave tomorrow?" she asked. "I assume you'll want an early start."

"Not we," Desa lamented. "Just me."

A heavy silence hung over them for what felt like several minutes. In reality, it was probably less than one, but time always seemed to stretch during those difficult, painful conversations. "I see," Kalia said at last. "Does that mean it's over?"

Sitting up, Desa bent forward and massaged her eyelids with the tips of her fingers. "Of course not," she said. "I adore you. But you can't come with me on this journey."

"Why not?" Kalia protested. "Desa, you need me."

Taking her love by the shoulders, Desa pressed her lips to

Kalia's forehead. "The others need you more," she murmured. "They're in way over their heads, and we both know it. They need another Field Binder."

"I don't want to leave you."

Desa licked her lips, shutting her eyes as she worked up the courage to say what she needed to say. "You won't be," she promised. "You will be with me every day. As soon as I'm finished in the desert, I will ride for New Beloran. With any luck, I'll find you there. Please, Kalia, take care of my friends."

Kalia sniffled but nodded reluctantly. "All right," she whispered. "But I expect you to keep your word. As soon as you're finished-"

"I'll set out for New Beloran."

Her sadness evaporated when Kalia kissed her. Conscious thought drifted away as they snuggled under the covers. For a few precious moments, Desa was able to forget about the cold.

7

The train car window gave Tommy a view of endless fields under an overcast sky. Now and then, he spotted a tree or an outcropping of rock, but it was mostly just yellow grass as far as the eye could see. Winter was finally releasing its grip on this land. Maybe the snows will have melted when they reached New Beloran. He certainly hoped so. A winter of drizzle and damp air had given him an appreciation of southern weather.

They had boarded this northbound train yesterday in the town of Albraem. Tommy had wanted to go to Colman's Gate – the small city was only a day's ride from Hebar's Hill – but Miri had been opposed to that plan. "The Bandit will be on every wanted poster from here to Pikeman's Gorge," she insisted. "The last thing we need is for some Eradian soldier to recognize us."

So, they had ridden for over a week through cold rain and dense fog, crossing some remarkably difficult terrain. There were easy paths that ran parallel to the train tracks, but Miri had been unwilling to risk being seen. Someone might wonder why Tommy and his friends were riding for several days instead of getting on at the first available station.

They had crossed through Colman's Forest and the Aldridge Downs, a maze of meandering paths that skirted around grassy hills. Finding a good place to make camp in that mess was no easy task. The ground was covered in rock. Hardly ideal for sleeping. Miri had been worried about the possibility of thieves lurking around every corner. Tommy had assured her that he could sense no one when he communed with the Ether, but she never let her guard down. She was beginning to take on some of her brother's more abrasive qualities.

Jim, Zoe and Victor had come with them on their journey. The rest had gone with Mrs. Potts. Whereto, Tommy could not say. He had forbidden Mrs. Potts from telling him her destination. If things went according to plan, Tommy and his crew would soon be the most wanted criminals in all Eradia. If they were captured, they would almost certainly be tortured. He couldn't reveal what he did not know.

On their second night in the Downs, Jim had suggested climbing one of the hills to make camp there. His first attempt had him sliding down the muddy slope and landing hard on his bottom.

Tommy had decided that the climb would be easier with Gravity-Sinks; so, he and Kalia spent an hour making enough for everyone. He had no idea why the former sheriff had chosen to come with him instead of going west with Desa, and he was not foolish enough to ask. A wise man learned to keep his nose out of women's business.

The plan had worked, allowing them to set up their tents on the hilltop, but that only meant more exposure to the wind and the rain. If not for Heat-Sources, they would have been shivering in their tents. By the time they reached Albraem, Tommy was aching for a warm bed and a hot meal.

"You've been staring out that window for an hour."

The sound of Dalen's voice drew Tommy out of his reverie. He found the other man standing in the aisle that ran between the benches on either side of the train car. "Whatever you see out there can't be that interesting."

"I was just thinking," Tommy replied. "Sit with me?"

Accepting the invitation, Dalen sat down beside him and cuddled up with his head on Tommy's shoulder. Tommy's first impulse was to discourage such affection while they were in public, but he ignored that inclination. In Aladar men pursued relationships with other men, and no one batted an eye. Dalen wouldn't understand.

Closing his eyes, Tommy touched his nose to the other man's forehead. "You know that I love you, right?" he whispered. "That you mean the world to me?"

A slow smile blossomed on Dalen's face. His eyes fluttered open, and he gazed adoringly up at Tommy. "Of course, I know that."

"Good."

Tommy was about to say more, but the warmth of the other man's hand on his cheek made him pause. The next thing he knew Dalen's lips were pressed against his. Panic welled up – what if someone walked in on them? – but it was overwhelmed by a haze of lust and heat.

Heat that vanished like a flame snuffed by a strong wind when he heard the train car's door opening. At first, he thought it might be one of the crew. Explanations flew through his mind, things he might say to prevent the newcomer from revealing what he had seen to anyone, but they flitted away before he could grasp them. He ripped himself away from Dalen, causing the other man to grunt.

Luckily, it was only Miri.

In dungarees and a long, brown coat, she walked through the aisle with a huge smile on her face. "Was I interrupting something?" she cooed, claiming the seat in front of Tommy.

Red-faced, Tommy heaved out a breath. He scrubbed the

back of one hand across his brow. "Nothing of consequence," he whispered. "Did you need something?"

"The train's clear," Miri reported. "I don't think anyone is paying much attention to us. I was thinking we could meet in my cabin and review the plan."

She departed without another word. Tommy knew the protocol; he would wait a few minutes and then follow. Everything had to look casual. There was no reason why anyone should care about the comings and goings of a few travelers from the country, but a man and a woman slipping into one of the sleeping compartments in the middle of the day might elicit gossip. And gossip had a way of spreading.

He was so lost in his reverie that he barely noticed Dalen in the corner of his eye. The other man was glaring at him.

"What?" Tommy muttered.

"Are you that ashamed to be seen with me?"

Wincing, Tommy turned his face away from the other man. "Of course not," he said. "But if anyone saw us, they would be scandalized. I guarantee you they would remember our faces."

Dalen sat back with his arms folded, a frown tightening his mouth. "Scandalized because they saw two men in love," he grumbled. "No one seems to mind when it's a man and a woman. I see couples holding hands all the time."

"Holding hands and kissing are two very different things."

"That's not the point, and you know it."

"This isn't Aladar!" Tommy hissed. "Maybe you've forgotten, but I was thrown into a cell and nearly executed because my own brother caught me kissing another man! I would love to strike a blow for fairness and justice, but right now, we have a mission!"

He took that opportunity to end the conversation and make his way to the back of the train. Dalen would follow in a minute or two. A little time apart would do them good. Tommy was livid. He understood his lover's pain; he understood better than

Dalen might imagine. The shame of having to hide who you were and the rage that shame inspired. None of that was Dalen's fault, but it wasn't Tommy's fault either.

He found Miri's compartment in one of the sleeping cars. A soft knock at the door gained him entrance. It was a cramped space with two bunks. Kalia was stretched out on the top one while Miri sat on the bottom.

"Dalen will be along in a moment."

The other man appeared as soon as Tommy finished speaking, shouldering his way inside and claiming a spot in the corner. He said nothing, gave no sign that he was in any way upset, which was probably for the best. But it left Tommy on edge.

"Sonic-Sinks," Miri muttered.

With a thought, Tommy triggered the Infusions that he had placed in the walls of her compartment. He had worked on them for half an hour last night. They represented some of the best Field Binding he had ever done. The Sinks he had created would dampen sound in one direction, creating a box of silence around this tiny room. No one outside would hear anything that was said within these walls. The trade-off was that they would have no warning if anyone decided to barge in. "It's done," Tommy said.

"Grand," Miri replied. "So, how do we locate Timothy Delarac once we arrive in New Beloran?" They had discussed this issue on the ride northward. Thus far, they had failed to create a viable plan.

Dalen perked up, grinning as if he had just come up with a grand idea. Which, he probably had. "I was thinking about it," he said. "If we can get into the Hall of Records, we might be able to find his address. From there-"

Miri snorted, rolling her eyes. "You boys insist on doing everything the hard way," she said. "If you go poking around in the Hall of Records, someone will demand to know who you are. And then word will get back to Mr. Delarac."

"So, what do you suggest?" Tommy inquired.

Miri studied him for a very long moment, her eyebrows slowly climbing up her forehead. "Didn't you tell me you can feel the Sinks and Sources you create?" she asked. "That you always know exactly where they are?"

"That is how it works, yes," Kalia confirmed.

"So, all we have to do is get Timothy Delarac to take one of Tommy's Infusions back to his home, and then we'll know where he lives."

Pressing a fist to his mouth, Dalen cleared his throat. "Pardon the interruption," he said. "But your plan seems like something of a paradox. To plant a Sink or Source on Mr. Delarac's person, we would first have to know where he is."

Hunching over with an elbow on her thigh, Miri rested her chin on the back of her hand. Her wicked grin made it clear that she had anticipated this objection. "Sweetheart, you're forgetting that we already know where Mr. Delarac will be for eight hours a day, four days a week."

"The Parliament Building," Kalia observed.

"Indeed."

"Then why not just capture him there?" Dalen asked.

Heaving out a sigh, Miri shook her head in dismay. "Too public," she said. "We try it, and the City Watch will be on top of us before we can breathe. We need time to interrogate him so that we can find out how he's controlling Adele."

Drumming his fingers on the wall behind him, Tommy looked up at the ceiling. "So, let me see if I understand this," he said. "You want to corner Mr. Delarac on the Parliament Building steps so that you can slip an Infused coin into his pocket?"

"Who said anything about an Infused coin?" she scoffed.

"Once again, you boys do *everything* the hard way. Tommy, how long does it take you to create an Infusion?"

"It depends on how strong you need it to be."

"Does the strength affect your ability to track it?"

"No," he answered quickly. "I can track my Infusions even if they're down to their last trickle of energy. Why do you ask?"

Miri was beaming at him. He had seen that particular smile before, and he knew that she had come up with something truly devilish. "Because we're going to be spending a lot of time outside the Parliament Building," she said. "We'll come up with some excuse. Maybe we're selling pastries or taking donations for the poor. When we see Mr. Delarac's carriage pull up, you'll Infuse it-"

"And then all we have to do is wait for the driver to take him home," Tommy whispered. "Genius!"

Retrieving a slip of paper from her bag, Miri unfolded it to reveal a charcoal sketch of a man with a thick mustache and long sideburns. The detail was exquisite: the wrinkles on his forehead, the prominent nose. "Dalen, you are a remarkable artist."

He nodded curtly, accepting the compliment. "Desa described him for me," he said. "I just followed her instructions."

"We wait for him to come out of the Parliament Building," Miri said. "We see which carriage picks him up, and then Tommy Infuses it."

"Well then," Dalen said. "Since that's settled, I think I'll get some lunch."

Tommy was about to ask if he wanted company, but the other man just stormed out. His heart sank. He had hoped that Dalen's anger might have abated. Maybe they could talk about it tonight in their cabin. "Excuse me," Tommy murmured. "I seem to be a bit peckish myself."

. . .

Two days later, they arrived at New Beloran Station. Tommy was jostled by several impatient people as he exited the train. The throng of bodies pulled him along like a leaf caught in the flow of a river.

When the crowd dispersed, leaving him on the long, stone platform, he got his first breath of fresh air since boarding the train at Albream. The noonday sun was shining bright in a cloudless sky, but the wind was sharp with a tinge of winter's chill lingering.

He stood on the platform in a simple, brown duster and a wide-brimmed hat pulled low over his eyes, gnawing on a toothpick. His suitcase was heavy, and the added weight of Miri's bag left a slight ache between his shoulder blades.

"You don't have to carry that, you know," Miri said, stepping up beside him. She was radiant in an old pair of trousers and a work shirt with its collar left open. When he tried to tell her that, she only snorted. "You think I look radiant in everything."

"That's because you do."

"Are you going to let me carry my bag?"

Forcing a smile, Tommy bowed his head to her, "No, ma'am, I don't think I will," he said. "I know you're quite capable of it, but being this close to home leaves me with a longing for the traditions I grew up with."

Miri squinted at him, and he got the impression that she was trying to decide if she approved. A moment later, she flashed a grin and then kissed him on the cheek. "Well, if you insist."

The others joined them in short order, Jim and Victor carrying Zoe's suitcase while the young woman stared in wide-eyed wonder at everything. She had never left Hedrovan until the night Tommy had taken her from the barracks behind the *Golden Sunset*. And he was willing to bet that she hadn't seen much of that city. A serving girl didn't need to leave the hotel.

Even from here, Tommy could see that the nation's capital

was nothing at all like Hedrovan. The train station was at least two miles away from the outermost buildings, connected to the city by a cobblestone road with lamps on either side. Several carriages were parked along the roadside, their drivers offering rides to anyone willing to pay for the convenience. He could smell the horses.

Kalia sauntered up with her hands in her pockets, the strap of her bag slung over one shoulder. She still wore the sheriff's hat that she'd had ever since Dry Gulch. "Shall we get going?"

Tommy nodded.

They had traveled less than a hundred feet before one of those drivers – a towering man with a thick, brown beard – called out to them. "Fancy a ride into the city, sir? Only ten cents! Cheapest rates in town!"

Miri looked up and greeted the fellow with a winning smile. "I think we'll walk!" she said, "But thank you!"

Tommy was beginning to wonder if offering to carry her belongings had been a good idea. And that devilish glint in her eye! She knew exactly what he was thinking! Serves him right for being chivalrous.

The air was cool but not frigid, and a good walk was enough to drive the chill away. He could have used a Heat-Source coin in his breast pocket, but there was no need. Best to save it for colder nights. With any luck, spring would be here in another week.

As he drew near the city, he got a better look at the architecture. The streets were lined with tall buildings of red brick with brown shingles on their gabled roofs. Each one had a large, bay window next to the front entrance. He saw a cobbler hard at work through one, a tailor taking measurements through another. The tales he had heard about Ofalla and High Falls as a boy had left him believing that large cities were wondrous places, full of magic. But they were really just several small towns crammed together.

A sigh from Dalen drew him out of his reverie, and he looked around in search of what had upset the other man. It didn't take long to find it.

Zoe and Victor were walking hand in hand, taking in the sights. Now, when had that happened? Tommy hadn't noticed them getting closer on the journey to Albraem. "Did you know about this?" he whispered to Miri.

She gave him a sidelong glance. "You didn't?"

They turned down a larger street lined with large buildings of gray brick, each with a columned front entrance. These were townhomes, Tommy realized. The cost to rent one – or to own one, for that matter – must have been astronomical. They followed a gentle slope northward until Tommy was greeted by a familiar sight.

Sunlight glinted off the dark waters of the Vinrella like a thousand diamonds strewn over a black canvas. He saw nothing but fields and thin patches of woodland on the other side. Unlike Ofalla, New Beloran only occupied the south bank.

Those meadows of yellow grass left him with a longing for his homeland. All he had to do was take a ferry across and ride for ten days...He remembered the way, and he was willing to bet that if he followed that dirt road that ran over the rolling hills, it would eventually join the one that led to his village.

Well...first, he would need to acquire a horse. He already missed the gelding that Marcus had purchased for him in Hedrovan. They had sold their animals in Albraem. It was the only way to make enough money for seven train tickets. Luckily, they had some left over. Enough for a week's rent, he suspected, but he wouldn't be buying a horse anytime soon. Besides, if he went home, the people that he had called friends all his life would put a noose around his neck.

All those sombre thoughts reminded him of their dismal financial situation. He would have to find a job if he intended to stay in New Beloran for any length of time. They all would.

"This way," Miri said. "I know a place where we can stay."

"Well," Mrs. Carmichael remarked, "you are a motley group, aren't you?" She was a woman of average height, slightly plump with tanned skin and gray hair done up in a braided tail. Her frown deepened as her gaze settled onto each of them.

Tommy and Dalen stood on her front step with Zoe, Jim, Victor and Kalia on the sidewalk behind them. Miri was on the porch with her hands clasped behind herself, smiling demurely at her shoes. "I do meet some interesting people."

"You do indeed, Miss Williams," Mrs. Carmichael agreed. "If you don't mind my asking, where is your brother?"

"He is...traveling along the southern coast."

Tommy wanted nothing more than to put his arms around Miri and hold her. So many nights, she had cried over what she had done to Marcus. It had been necessary, but reminding her of that fact did nothing to stem the flow of tears. No one could kill their own brother without dying a little bit inside. Such an act left a hole in your soul. At times like this, Tommy wondered how Lenny could have been so comfortable condemning him to execution.

Mrs. Carmichael offered a curt nod of respect. "I see," she muttered, running her gaze over the lot of them one more time. "And will you all be staying in the same apartment then?"

"Yes, we will," Miri confirmed.

"Well it's no business of mine," the old woman huffed. "As long as the rent is paid on time."

She led them to an apartment on the second floor. The living room was rather posh by Tommy's standards. White wainscot lined the green walls, and the large, rectangular window allowed plenty of sunlight to fall upon the sofa and the wooden cabinets. It even had a fireplace. But there were only two bedrooms. Some of them would have to sleep on the floor.

Zoe was gaping at everything she saw. No doubt this was a palace compared to what she was used to. If Tommy had not seen what life was like in Aladar, he would have been just as transfixed. Victor took her hand and whispered something in her ear.

Mrs. Carmichael stood in the doorway, frowning as she observed them. "The rent is due by noon on the first day of each week," she said. "I trust you'll all be finding some form of gainful employment?"

"About that," Zoe said. "Do you know if anyone might be hiring a maid? You might say I have some experience in that regard."

"It just so happens that I'm in need of one," Mrs. Carmichael replied. "For this property and the one across the street. Come downstairs after lunch, and I'll introduce you to Mr. Black. If you can make a room presentable after he's through with it, then you've got the job."

Dalen was halfway through the act of removing his coat when he looked up and blinked. He seemed to have only just realized what the two women were discussing. "And will you be needing a clerk as well?"

Mrs. Carmichael sniffed. "No, but I'm friends with the man who does my books," she said. "He owns a business just a few blocks away. I'd be happy to introduce you."

She left them to get settled in, a process that took all of thirty seconds. Jim took a seat at the wooden table, and Victor plopped himself down on the couch. Tommy was content to stand by the window.

"So," Jim mumbled. "What becomes of the rest of us?"

Finding jobs should not be hard for them. Tommy had used the last of the crystals to remove their brands. No one would ever know that they had once been slaves. "Take whatever work you can get," Miri said. "But be ready to move at a moment's notice. Because we're going after Delarac at the first opportunity."

TRAPPED IN HER CELL, the Weaver was lying face-up on a bed of nothing but air, hands folded on her chest as she stared at the ceiling. She had been counting the holes in the stone. The crystals that kept her bound to this room were pulsing. She could feel them.

Her uncle Timothy stepped into the doorway, grunting derisively when he saw her. "Defying gravity, are we?" he spat. "I take it then that you've healed from your encounter with the rebels."

The Weaver sat up, her musical laughter causing his face to darken. "Well, that's a matter of perspective, Uncle," she purred. "Each time I heal myself, my body changes."

She floated down, slippered feet touching the floor, black dress clinging to her body as she paced across the room. Timothy recoiled when she reached for him with her scaly hand. "Were you hoping to enlist my help? Are more of your little soldiers in trouble?"

"Without your power," Timothy growled, "our men cannot repel the savages' magic. Our forces are in retreat."

Pursing her lips, the Weaver tilted her head to one side, her eyebrows slowly rising. "Quite the shame," she murmured. "But I'm afraid I've lost interest in helping you with your little war."

"You'll do as you're told."

"Or what?" she scoffed. "You'll leave me down here to starve? I wonder, does Auntie Danielle know that you're keeping her favourite niece in the basement of an abandoned vineyard?"

Backing away from her, Timothy hissed. He reached into his jacket, producing a black crystal that began to glow when he pinched it between his thumb and forefinger. "You will do as you're told!"

The Weaver was forced to retreat, compelled to sit on the wooden stool. She didn't choose it; her legs moved of their own accord. "Yes," she conceded. "You can exert a measure of control over this body. But can you do the same for my power? Go ahead, Uncle. Produce a bolt of lightning, a gust of wind."

"What are you saying?" he breathed. "That you will refuse to fight? I will force you onto the battlefield anyway. If you do not fight, the savages will destroy your vessel."

"I would merely be exchanging one prison for another," she replied. "It might take another ten millennia, but I will be free again. And I will have the thought of your misery to comfort me. I can't tell you the joy it brings me to imagine how you will react when all of your ambitions turn to ash."

Timothy was trembling with fury that he failed to contain. His face was red, his eyes wild with raw hatred. He strode into the cell and struck her across the cheek with the back of his hand. Pain flared hot and bright. She nearly blacked out from the dizziness, but she could see him through the stars that filled her vision. "You will not speak to me in that tone ever again! Do you under-"

Her scaly hand shot up, fingers closing around his throat, producing a gurgling sound. Her other hand snatched the crystal out of his grip. "Now, now, Uncle. I think it's time we reevaluated the terms of our relationship."

Standing up, she easily lifted him off the floor, the top of his head nearly brushing the ceiling. His legs kicked feebly. He seized her wrist with both hands, trying to free himself, but it was no use.

The Weaver lifted the crystal, allowing him to look upon it one last time. Then she closed her fist around it, crushing it to dust. Black flakes fell to the floor. "You see," she said. "I grow stronger every day."

His cheeks were puffed up, his eyes watering.

"I could kill you," the Weaver murmured. "But I want you to understand the depth of your defeat. The scope of your humiliation."

She dropped him, and he fell to his knees before her, gasping for breath. Hunched over, he massaged his tender throat.

Touching the claw of a scaly finger to his forehead, the Weaver released a trickle of her power. Black veins spread over his brow, dipping into his eyes, which became pools of darkness for a few seconds before returning to their natural shade of brown.

"You work for me now," the Weaver said. "And we're going to have some fun."

8

The blue crystal began to glow, rays of light drawing the image of a woman who floated in the middle of an empty field. Just the outline at first, but colour filled the image a few seconds later. The sight of a goddess on her knees was so unnerving to Desa that she barely noticed the fact that Mercy was hovering about three feet off the ground. Gods knelt to no one. But then Mercy wasn't a god. Her real name was Nari, and whatever she was now, she had once been as mortal and fallible as Desa.

Those turquoise beams expanded, drawing a bed under Nari along with walls and a chest of drawers. Desa breathed a sigh of relief when she realized that the other woman wasn't actually floating. A bedroom then? Strange that Nari would choose to record her message here of all places. And stranger still, it wasn't even her bedroom.

Desa could not say how she had reached that conclusion. Perhaps it was the lack of personal effects. She would have expected to see knickknacks atop the dresser. Jewelry, bottles of perfume, *something!* She could have been wrong – maybe Nari wasn't the sort of woman who cared about such things – but this place felt remarkably impersonal to her. A hotel room? Did that mean that Nari was on the run?

She was just starting to wonder about the strange, rectangular device that had been bolted to the wall when Nari sprang into motion. The woman twisted around, looking over her shoulder at the door. Was she afraid that someone might walk in on her?

"Something went wrong," Nari gasped. "The...the Gateway Project. They brought something back with them."

Standing at the foot of the bed, Desa covered her mouth with one hand. Her brow furrowed as she considered the implications.

"It destroyed Ulonsia in a matter of minutes," Nari went on. "Devastation for miles. I barely got out."

Hanak Tuvar! That had to be it. It must have taken possession of someone as it did Adele. It could wreak all sorts of havoc once it claimed a host. But something felt off about that. These people knew how to Field Bind. Nari's previous entries made that perfectly clear. They should have been able to put up *some* resistance.

Touching her fingertips to her temples, Nari forced her eyes shut as if she had a terrible headache. "I tried to record it," she panted. "Something...Something went wrong with the equipment. I-"

She was cut off by a knock at the door.

Nari was on her feet in an instant, pacing across the room and rising up on tiptoes to look through the peephole. She unbolted the door when she was satisfied that she was in no danger, pulling it open to reveal the same redheaded woman that Desa had seen in a previous recording.

Vengeance strode into the room, shouldering Nari out of the way. "We have to go forward with the project," she declared. "You're expected to report to General Lanson first thing tomorrow."

"It's too dangerous!" Nari protested.

Vengeance rounded on her, a scowl exposing her rage. It was the same scowl that Desa had seen in the Borahorin. "In case you haven't noticed, we're out of options. You saw what it did to the capital."

"Driala, listen to me!" Nari exclaimed.

Unmoved by her pleas, Driala shoved her finger in the other woman's face. "Seven O'clock," she said. "Don't be late."

And then the image vanished.

ANOTHER DAY in the saddle brought Desa and Midnight further north and west across the Plains of Kalai. They had been traveling for ten days across the empty countryside, encountering very few human settlements. Two days ago, they had crossed the Mira, a narrow river that ran south from Lake Paula to the Emerald Sea.

If Kalia had not insisted on stopping at Hedrovan, Desa would have turned west after crossing the Halitha, following the coast to the town of Solsmar. From there, she would have been able to book passage upriver. But there was no point in fretting about what might have been. Her friends were still alive. At least something good had come out of their detour.

She had purchased supplies in Beck's Landing, a village on the eastern bank of the river. She had filled a knapsack and several saddlebags with bread, pork jerky, white cheese and raisins. From there, she had taken the Ford of Keltana across and continued her journey north and west. If she was careful, she would have enough food to last another two weeks. That would get her past Pikeman's Gorge and halfway to the southeastern corner of the Gatharan Desert.

It was what came after that worried her.

If she had read the maps correctly, she would have to make a hard right three days after passing through the gorge. She intended to skirt the desert's eastern border. Going that way would add at least a week to her trip, but it couldn't be helped. Sticking to the grasslands was the only way to make sure that Midnight had enough to eat.

She put those worries aside, choosing to focus on the moment. There were plenty of obstacles between now and then. These lands might appear desolate, but five long years of wandering the wilderness alone had taught her to keep her guard up. You never knew who you might run into out here.

And she was riding into danger.

Pikeman's Gorge was the only way through the Avaline Escarpment. There were trails that would lead her up the rock-face and down the other side, but almost every one of those involved some amount of climbing, making them impassable for horses. The gorge was the preferred route for most travelers, which was why it had developed quite a reputation. Bandits sometimes hid there, waiting for some unsuspecting trader to come stumbling through.

She had come this way once, a very long time ago. With Martin. They had been pursuing a man who had killed three people in the city of Carthinas. Martin had gotten a tip that he was heading south in search of a ship that would take him across the Sapphire Sea to Ithanar. They never did find him, but they did encounter a pair of sisters who had been passing through the gorge on their way to the southern coast.

When they first met Emily and Annie, the pair had run afoul of some highwaymen. A trio of louts who thought they could rob two helpless women. A few well-placed shots from Martin and some mischief with a Gravity-Sink had been enough to send those men running for the hills, leaving Desa and her husband alone with two very grateful sisters, one of whom happened to prefer women.

They spent nearly a week with Emily and Annie, and by the time they parted ways, both sisters insisted that Desa and

Martin were the strangest married couple they had ever met. Those were good days.

Sometimes, she missed that innocence. Back then, her biggest problem had been a single man who misused Field Binding. And now...Best not to think about that.

Her heart ached for Kalia.

Whenever that longing started to nip at her, she soothed it by reminding herself that sending Kalia to protect the others had been necessary. They needed a skilled Field Binder. Tommy had come a long way in one year, but he still had much to learn.

So, the miles wore on with nothing to look at but grass and the odd tree. The sky had been a mass of gray clouds for the last three days, and sometimes – when fate was feeling particularly cruel – it let loose a cold drizzle.

On one afternoon, she saw a farm, which was a good sign. It meant that there was another settlement nearby. The farmer was a barrel-chested man in a flannel shirt whose beard was coarse enough to scrape the rust off iron. She offered to split his firewood in exchange for a hot meal and a night in his barn. At first, the man laughed, but he shut his mouth right and proper when she turned up at his door an hour later with a wheelbarrow full of split logs. A night in a hayloft was hardly ideal, but it kept her out of the rain.

The next morning, she visited the village of Holbrook. She could not recall having seen the town listed on any of the maps she had studied, but here it was! Not much to look at in Desa's estimation – just two concentric circles of log cabins around a central well – but it gave her a chance to resupply.

Her days were spent in quiet solitude with no one to talk to but Midnight. It was perfect! As much as she missed Kalia, she had forgotten the simple pleasures of traveling alone. Sadly, those pleasures were short-lived.

.   .   .

A FULL MOON hung over the eastern horizon as twilight set in. The clouds had finally dispersed, allowing her to see the first stars twinkling in the deep, blue sky. Fourteen days had passed since she had set out from Hebar's Hill. She was starting to feel the first hint of spring creeping into the land.

Desa sat in the saddle with the reins in hand, closing her eyes as the wind caressed her face. "It's a misnomer," she said. "Both of them are actually."

Midnight flicked an ear toward her, urging her to elaborate. The stallion was always happy to listen to her prattling on about whatever passed through her head.

"The Sapphire Sea and the Emerald Sea," she explained. "They're not seas at all; they're gulfs, each one extending to the Caliad and Anrael oceans respectively. One might hope that cartographers would take that into consideration, but I suppose the name 'Sapphire Gulf' just doesn't sound as good."

Midnight plodded along without comment.

Desa wrinkled her nose in distaste. "Well, what do you know?" she muttered, gently scratching the back of his neck. "It's not as if you pay much attention to-"

She cut off when Midnight crested a hill, and she saw the cliffs of Avaline like two shadows against the twilight sky. They had arrived at last at Pikeman's Gorge.

She brought Midnight to a halt, then swung her leg over his flanks and dropped to the ground beside him. Sighing softly, she stood upon the hilltop with her fists on her hips. "This is as far as we want to go tonight," she said. "We'll press on tomorrow."

The gorge was about sixty miles from end to end. Midnight could not cover that much ground in one day, which meant that she would be forced to spend at least one night between those towering cliffs. And given the place's reputation, she would rather keep it to just one night. Starting after dawn would be wisest.

With nothing else to do, she ate a small meal of hard bread and pork jerky and then crawled into her bedroll.

THE NEXT MORNING, she set out bright and early. Pikeman's Gorge wasn't quite so intimidating in the light of day. With the sun still hovering over the eastern horizon, the interior was bathed in gloom, but she traveled for several hours without encountering another living soul.

The gorge had been carved many thousands of years ago by a mighty river. What remained of that river was now a narrow stream of brown water with tufts of ricegrass sprouting from the mud on either side. The cliffs were made of some kind of beige rock. Desa had been told once that it was limestone, but she couldn't say whether that was true.

Leading Midnight by his bridle, she looked up at the blue sky with her lips pursed. "See?" she murmured. "It's not so bad."

Step by step, they continued their journey northward, keeping to the easy terrain near the stream. The ground was lumpy near the base of each cliff with dense thickets of pine trees, some growing over two hundred feet high.

By mid-morning, they had crossed paths with a family that was going south on the other side of the narrow river. A mother and father with several children and two brown horses pulling a covered wagon. Desa waved to them, but they refused to acknowledge her. She couldn't blame them.

Metal wheels and tarp over a wagon box: that was their method of transit. What would these people think if they ever saw an automobile? Or one of the *Al a Nari's* lightning pistols? Technology was sparse here on the fringes of the Empire. Most of the villages she had passed through had not seen a tax collector in decades. Some might not even know who their Member of Parliament was.

It was well past midday when she decided to stop for a quick lunch. More bread and dried meat. Midnight nibbled on some of the tall grass. All the while, Desa kept her eyes on those pine trees. If any troublemakers were lurking in this canyon, that was where they would hide.

An uneventful afternoon led into a quiet evening, and the shadows lengthened as the sun dipped toward the horizon. Dusk came on fast, making it too dark to press on. Desa could have used the Light-Source in her ring, but that might draw the wrong kind of attention. Better to get a good night's sleep and complete their trip through the gorge tomorrow.

Desa led her horse up the muddy slope to the pine trees under the eastern cliff. As she suspected, all that foliage had kept the ground dry despite the recent rainfall. A good place to get some sleep. She ate a quiet dinner and then curled up in her bedroll, trying to fall asleep. Under normal circumstances, it would be far too early for that, but she was tired. Finding sleep wasn't hard.

She awoke several hours later to the sound of laughter.

Sitting up, Desa tossed off her blanket and then ran a hand through her hair. She blinked a few times. "What time is it?"

All she could say was that sunrise was a long way off. It was dark, but her eyes had adjusted enough for her to see Midnight as a silhouette against the blackness. The stallion stood over her, but he wasn't the least bit interested in Desa.

It didn't take long to find out why.

When she crept out of the trees, she noticed the flickering glow of a campfire on the other side of the stream. Three people sat around it, enjoying a late dinner. They were rather loud – foolishly so, in her estimation – but at this distance, she could not make out what they were saying.

"It's no business of ours anyway," she murmured to Midnight. "We'll just stay nice and quiet. They won't even know we're here."

Everyone knew that the best way to cross through Pikeman's Gorge unscathed was to avoid drawing attention to yourself. Why these idiots insisted on ignoring that rule was beyond her, but if they wanted to risk an encounter with some bandits, it was no concern of Desa Kincaid's.

She snuggled back into her bedroll, curling up on her side with her back to the fire. She tried to drift off again, but that brief nap had left her with an abundance of energy. It was going to be a long night.

On several occasions, she came within an inch of falling asleep only to have some noise jolt her back to full alertness. More often than not, it was laughter from those louts around the campfire. She wanted to scream at them. But that would be unwise.

Perhaps she could make a Sonic-Sink.

Tommy had shown her the method, but she had little experience with that kind of Field Binding. More to the point, trapping herself in a pocket of silence might leave her vulnerable if someone decided to sneak up on her. She would just have to put up with the nuisance. Those fools had to be turning in soon.

She told herself as much every time they did something loud and obnoxious, but commonsense aside, those idiots seemed determined to stay awake all night. They were still going an hour later. Well, it wouldn't be a trip through Pikeman's Gorge without-

Her reverie was interrupted by a shill scream.

Desa didn't bother getting up to see what had happened. Instead, she made herself one with the Ether. The world changed before her eyes, and her consciousness swept through the canyon, noting every rock, every bump in the ground.

She sensed three clusters of molecules around a fountain of light that her mind identified as the campfire. Two men who might have been father and son and a woman who couldn't be much older than seventeen. The younger fellow had his arms around the girl's waist. She squirmed, legs kicking as she tried to free herself from his grip. Had the lass been fool enough to get involved with a pair of highwaymen?

It didn't matter.

The Ether fled as Desa threw off her blanket and got to her feet. She fetched her pistols from the saddlebags and slid them into their holsters. With any luck, the sight of an armed stranger would be enough to dissuade the two men from whatever it was they were planning.

Desa ran out into the open.

Triggering the Gravity-Sink in her belt buckle, she jumped and flew straight up into the air. She retrieved a coin from her coat pocket, a special coin that would apply kinetic energy to her body and nothing else. She had discovered the means of creating such a thing in Ithanar; it was a simple inversion of the lattice she used to exempt herself from a Sink or a Source. This particular Infusion exempted everything *but* her.

Tossing the coin out behind herself, Desa triggered it and used the wave of kinetic energy to propel herself over the stream. Then she stretched her hand out and activated the ring around her pinky. A Gravity-Source that would only pull on one thing.

The coin slammed into her palm, and she closed her fingers around it.

She let gravity reassert itself for only an instant. That was enough to put her on a downward trajectory. She saw the dark ground and the distant fire rushing up to meet her. Extending her hand, Desa triggered the Force-Sink in her bracelet, using it to decelerate.

She landed in a crouch at the edge of the firelight, then stood up and began a slow march forward. "All right," she said. "That's quite enough. Let her go."

The three of them stared at her bug-eyed. Whatever they

might have heard about Pikeman's Gorge, they had not been expecting a woman who swooped down from the heavens like a hawk on the hunt.

The young man licked his lips, then averted his gaze. He released the girl, but she didn't run or try to get away from him. "We um...We were just having a little fun."

"Jonas is my betrothed," the young woman explained.

"Betrothed?"

Heaving out a sigh, the girl stepped forward and smoothed her skirts. She was quite pretty: tall and slim with a round face and brown hair that she wore in a braid. "We're to be married in the spring. He likes to tease me."

The older fellow had long, gray hair and a beard to match. His clothes were worn from many long days of travel, but he carried no weapons that Desa could see. She was beginning to think that she might have misread this situation. "Forgive my son and future daughter in law," he pleaded. "They sometimes get carried away."

Folding her arms, Desa frowned at them. "A poor place for it," she said. "Any number of unsavoury people pass through Pikeman's Gorge. If I had wanted to rob you..."

Raising a hand to forestall her, the old man shut his eyes and nodded. "Your point is well taken," he said. "I was just about to insist that we turn in."

"I think that might be wise."

Desa slipped back into the darkness, moving as quietly as she could to make it that much harder for them to track her. She didn't want them to see her using a Gravity-Sink to go back across the tiny river. They had already seen too much. Her goal was to pass through this region without incident. She had no desire to set tongues wagging about a woman who could fly. Maybe those fools were headed south, or maybe north. But if they showed up in a village where she had stopped for the night, it could mean trouble.

It took almost ten minutes for her to make her way back to Midnight. She had to take hold of the Ether twice to find her way in the darkness, but doing so gave her a chance to look in on the three travelers. They had indeed climbed into their bedrolls and put out their fire. Desa prayed to Mercy that no one dangerous was lurking in the canyon tonight. If so, she had exposed herself to even more unwelcome attention.

She fell asleep only moments after laying down.

THE CRUNCH of rocks under shoes woke her, and she had to suppress the urge to sigh. Better if whoever was out there thought that she was still asleep. Maybe they would slink past without troubling her. She almost laughed. Since when was her luck that good?

"Are you sure she went this way?" Jonas whispered.

"Quiet!" his father hissed.

"We shouldn't be doing this," the young woman protested. "You saw what she did. There are other targets."

With the utmost care, Desa slid out of her bedroll and stood up, hiding between the trunks of two tall pine trees. She removed the ring from her third finger and tossed it down into the muck.

Then she listened.

Midnight was perfectly still, not making a sound. She could feel him looking at her. He wanted to know what he ought to do. *Just sit tight,* she thought at him. *I'll handle this.*

The seconds passed like hours, and then she heard the scuff of boots nearby. One of those idiots was right in front of her; she could smell him. Unless she missed her guess, it was the younger man. He was breathing hard, clearly agitated. She heard a soft *click* when he cocked the hammer of his pistol.

With a thought, Desa triggered the Light-Source in her ring, causing it to glow. Jonas raised a hand to shield himself from the glare. That momentary distraction gave her time to march forward.

The young fool tried to point his weapon at her.

Twisting out of the way, Desa caught his forearm with both hands. She wrenched his wrist hard enough to make him drop the gun, sending a jolt of pain through his body. She stepped on his foot, producing a yelp, then elbowed him in the face.

Jonas fell hard on his backside.

Footsteps nearby.

Desa stooped to retrieve the fallen pistol, then spun around and pointed it into the thicket. The young woman emerged from the darkness with a knife in hand, freezing in her tracks when she saw the gun.

"Drop it," Desa ordered.

Steel clattered to the ground; the child was wise enough to do as she was told. Which only left the old man. That one had to be skulking around here somewhere. She listened for him but heard nothing.

"Over there!" Desa growled, gesturing with her pistol. "Sit with your beloved." The girl hopped to obey, scooting over to Jonas and kneeling in the mud next to him. Two down. Now, where was-

"You're a clever one, aren't you?"

She turned around to find the old coot standing at the edge of the light with a revolver pointed at Midnight's head. His mouth cracked, revealing yellow teeth, and his eyes shone with the thrill of triumph. "But I suspect this beast means more to you than you're willing to let on."

Desa held his gaze, suppressing the anger that compelled her to act. Anger and humiliation. It had been a long time since anyone had gotten the drop on her. "You don't want to hurt that horse."

The old man chuckled. "Yes, I'm inclined to agree," he said.

"So, if you'll just give us your money and your supplies, we'll be on our way."

"You want money? It's in the saddlebags."

Like a greedy squirrel digging for nuts, he began rifling through her bags, checking every pocket. It took him all of thirty seconds to find a small pouch that jingled. "Now, what might this be?"

Fishing out a copper penny, he held it between his thumb and forefinger, squinting as he tried to read the Aladri script. "Never seen currency like this before. But I reckon it spends as well as any other."

He tossed the coin up with a chuckle and then caught it in his closed fist. "Thank you, madam. You've been most obliging."

Desa triggered the Heat-Source she had Infused into the metal.

The old man gasped, dropping the coin and his pistol as well. Reluctantly, he lifted a trembling hand and whimpered at the sight of blisters on his palm.

Desa charged forward.

She kicked his knee, forcing him to bend over, and then slugged him square in the nose. The poor fool staggered, trying his darndest to stay on his feet.

Desa spun for a hook-kick, her heel striking the old man's cheek. Thrown to the ground, he landed on his side and raised a hand to shield himself, terrified of the pummeling he expected to receive.

Desa knelt beside him.

Pressing the barrel of her gun to his forehead, she let her finger curl around the trigger. "I trust I've made my point," she said. "You'll behave yourself?"

He nodded enthusiastically.

"Good," she murmured. "Never threaten my horse again."

. . .

HALF AN HOUR LATER, she had the three of them kneeling by the riverbank with ropes binding their wrists and ankles. Young Jonas kept struggling against his restraints, but the other two had been chastened. They refused to look up.

A glowing coin on the ground let her keep an eye on them while she checked each of her saddlebags to make sure that nothing had been taken. She could feel her Sinks and Sources as little bundles of awareness in the back of her mind, and she knew they were all accounted for. The food she had purchased over the last few days was right where she had left it. No harm done then.

Patting Midnight with a gentle hand, Desa cast a glance over her shoulder. Her mouth twisted in distaste when she saw the three thieves kneeling before her. Jonas was cursing under his breath.

"That's enough of that?" she snapped.

The old man looked up at her with horror in his eyes. "What..." He cleared his throat and began again. "What are you going to do with us?"

Desa strode toward him, shaking her head. "First off," she began, "I'm going to take some of your food. It's the least you can do to repay me for my trouble."

"And then?"

Dropping to a crouch, Desa stared into his eyes for a few seconds. "Nothing," she said at last. "I'm going to leave you right here, unharmed. I'm quite certain that you'll be able to free yourselves in a day or so."

The young woman sneered at her, seething with impotent rage. "You're going to leave us here?" she spat. "Helpless and bound! A prize for any thief or who happens to come this way!"

"Poetic, isn't it?"

"You can't do this to us!"

Standing up slowly, Desa replied with a smile. "I think I just did." She turned away from them, making her way back to

Midnight, and began loading up her bags with some of the food she had pilfered from their camp. Tough bread, cheese wrapped in cloth, dried and salted meats: she took as much as she could fit inside the knapsack and several of the larger saddlebags.

DESA ESCAPED the canyon without any further difficulties and continued northward for three days. She turned east when she saw the first sign that the grass was beginning to thin. Entering the desert from this point would be suicide.

Her provisions lasted another week – though she had been forced to hunt rabbits on two occasions – and that was a lucky thing because she found no signs of civilization. No villages, no farms. Nothing but empty grassland as far as the eye could see. At least, the danger was minimal. No signs of human habitation meant little chance of crossing paths with someone who might want to steal from her.

She was almost out of food when she came upon a small town of wooden houses with black-tiled roofs. The people were lively, though somewhat suspicious of a stranger riding into their midst.

The first person she spoke to was an olive-skinned girl in a brown skirt and white blouse with laces. Long, brown hair framed a round face with a delicate nose. By the look in her eyes, Desa wondered if this child had ever met an outsider before.

She sat in Midnight's saddle with the reins in hand, favouring the lass with a smile. "Hello," she said. "I was wondering if I might be able to purchase some food."

The girl said nothing.

"I'm on a long journey, you see."

Shying back as if she feared that Desa might attack her, the girl kept her head down. Her only response was a shrug and a hastily muttered, "We don't have very much to spare."

"I'm willing to pay."

The girl pointed to the town's square. Taking her cue, Desa guided Midnight deeper into the village. Some of the people gave her wary looks while others ignored her outright. She noticed an old man in overalls and a straw hat who sat upon the porch of his tiny house. He looked up just long enough to notice Desa and then turned his face away.

This place reminded her of Tommy's village. The people there had also greeted her with a mix of wonder and suspicion. Small-town folk weren't at all used to dealing with outsiders.

Three apple trees stood in the middle of the town square, each with branches still bare despite the warming weather. A man in a black vest carried a basket full of turnips. Two boys followed him with another.

"You came to buy food?"

Turning Midnight around, Desa found herself confronted by a heavyset man with a neat, gray beard. A wide-brimmed hat sat atop the fellow's head, shading his eyes from the sunlight. "I'm the mayor of this town," he explained. "Marshall Collins."

"Desa Kincaid," she replied.

"I wish that we could sell you what you need," Mr. Collins said. "But you see, our stores are nearly depleted after a long winter. It will be several weeks at least before we have much to spare."

Closing her eyes, Desa nodded slowly. "I understand," she said. "But I might be able to offer something that will make it worth your while."

Mr. Collins removed his hat, holding it against his chest, and stared up at her in bewilderment. "I can't imagine what that might be," he said. "There are few things more precious than food when you live in these parts."

Pulling the ring off her third finger, Desa tossed it to him.

The old man caught it with a deft hand and cocked his head. "It's iron," he said. "A simple band. No stone. Not worth very much, I'm afraid."

"Don't panic."

Despite her warning, the poor fellow jumped when the ring began to glow. He took a few shaky steps backward and dropped it as if he thought it might burn his hand. When he found his flesh unblemished, he stooped to retrieve the ring again. "It's not even warm," he whispered. "How is this possible?"

"It's just a trinket," Desa said. "A small sample of what I have to offer. Imagine coins that can hold back the night's chill or keep a cellar cool for days. Rings that can offer more light than a hundred candles. I'll make as many as you like. All I'm asking is for enough food and water to last me six days."

"And where will you be in six days?"

Dropping out of the saddle, Desa strode toward him with a hard expression. "In the desert," she answered. "That's where I'm going."

The old man stood there with his mouth hanging open, staring at her as if she had just declared her intention to thrust a knife through her heart. "It's almost four hundred miles to the Molarin Mountains!" he exclaimed. "You won't cover that distance in just six days."

"I'm not going that far."

He made a face, clearly troubled by her foolhardy plan, and then gave his head a shake. "All right," he said. "Why don't you show me what some of these trinkets of yours can do?"

The town had no inn; she had to sleep in the hayloft of a barn, but compared to the hard ground she had grown used to, it was heavenly. She spent several hours making Sinks and Sources for every man or woman who wanted one. Most of the Infusions she created were attuned to heat. She created a Light-Source for a bespectacled boy who loved to read and another for a young man who insisted that raccoons kept digging up his garden at night. She gave each one a physical trigger and taught the townsfolk how to use them. It gave her such pleasure to see the enthusiasm in their eyes.

Perhaps she should have stayed in Aladar and taught Field Binding at the Academy. But if she had done that, Bendarian might have released *Hanak Tuvar* without opposition. And the world would have been unprepared for the carnage that followed. Perhaps some good had come out of her choices.

Well, how about that?

Maybe it wasn't all Desa Kincaid's fault.

Of course, Daresina might argue that if she had never taught Bendarian the basics of Field Binding, none of this would have happened. But looking out on these people who were so eager to learn, she couldn't make herself believe that. Field Binding was a treasure. It must be shared with the world. Her instincts had been correct all those years ago.

By sunset, she was exhausted and the townsfolk had at least three dozen Infusions that they could use to keep their food chilled or warm their houses. She stayed another day, making more. It was the least she could do if she was going to take even a small amount of their food. In truth, she would have liked to have stayed another week, to rest and recover. But she couldn't.

The desert called.

It was time for the final leg of her journey.

DUST SWEPT OVER HARD, red clay. The sun was an orange ball on the horizon, painting the western sky a deep red. It was cooler than Desa would have expected. She had always pictured deserts as places of painful, scorching heat – and that had certainly been the case when she came here last summer – but in early spring, the days were only warm, and the nights were almost frigid.

Desa sat cross legged on the clay with her hands on her knees, her eyes closed as she let go of the Ether. She had just finished Infusing the Electric-Sources in the metal cage around the blue crystal.

Though she couldn't see it, she knew that the strange device was only five feet away, sitting on a small lump in the ground. She was tired. Sweet Mercy, she was tired. Two days of crafting Infusion after Infusion and then three more in the saddle had left her worn out. Her throat was dry, but she didn't dare drink any more water today.

She opened her eyes.

A thought was all it took to trigger the Electric-Source, and then the crystal began to glow with soft, blue light. It cast those strange beams in all directions, drawing object after object.

One of them appeared to be a table or a slab that had been inclined at a steep angle, a suspicion that was confirmed when colour entered the image. It was indeed a slab with a woman held by metal cuffs around her wrists and ankles. A tall woman with wavy, red hair and a haughty expression. Desa recognized Vengeance. Or Driala as she had been called before her ascension.

The woman turned her head, snarling at someone that Desa couldn't see. "Get on with it then!" she barked. "We don't have much time!"

Nari walked into view with a clipboard in hand, watching Driala through the lenses of her spectacles. "I must protest this," she said. "The last three attempts ended in failure. I see now that this project was doomed from the outset."

Baring her teeth, Driala stared up at her. "They were weak and unprepared," she insisted. "I am not!"

"But our initial hypothesis was flawed," Nari protested. "Simply communing with the Unifying Field at the moment of molecular disintegration is not sufficient. Brin, Colm and

Athon were all in direct contact with the Field, and they died anyway."

Driala tried to sit up, but the restraints held her in place. Her body trembled for a brief moment, but she took control of herself. "And we don't have a choice," she said. "You have seen what the enemy can do."

"Yes."

"No weapon that we have devised can stop it!" Driala went on. "We were ill-prepared for what came through that gateway, and if we want to survive, we *must* embrace new tactics."

Nari seated herself on a nearby chair, clutching the clipboard to her chest. Her face was a mask of anguish. "Dri, this project was never meant to create a weapon," she said. "It was meant to-"

"Expand the limits of human consciousness," Driala cut in. "Yes, yes. I've heard it all before. Turn on the damn machine, Nari."

She must have been referring to the large, red device that was pointed at the slab. Desa had no idea what it did, but it looked like a gigantic gun. No doubt this was the moment when Driala became Vengeance, but Desa couldn't even begin to guess how that might have been accomplished.

"Power up the *glanashti*," Nari said.

Desa had experienced this several times before. Mercy had given her the ability to comprehend the ancient language of her people, but sometimes, they used words for which there was no Aladri or Eradian equivalent. Words for concepts that did not exist in the Aladri or Eradian lexica.

"Subject has made contact with the Unifying Field," Nari reported.

Driala had her eyes closed, but Desa couldn't feel anything. That didn't really surprise her, but she had wondered if the sensation of someone communing with the Ether had been captured by this device.

Nari stepped in front of her, blocking her view. "Dri, what are you doing?" A brief moment of silence passed. Was Nari communing with the Ether as well? She seemed to be deep in concentration. "The subject is trying to create an Infusion within her own body. The lattice will not form."

"Now," Driala croaked.

"What?"

"Now!"

Turning away from the slab, Nari paced across the room, passing right through Desa. "Begin," she said. "Full power. There's no point in holding back."

The strange, red device began to hum. It was a cannon with a barrel twice as long as Desa's arm, and it fired a pulse of light that hit Driala and transformed her into a being of pure radiance. The change lasted for only a moment, and then Driala broke apart into a thousand motes of light that scattered.

Nari shuffled up to the slab with her head down, a soft sigh escaping her. "Failure," she said. "As expected, the process induced complete molecular disintegration. The initial theory behind the Transcendentalist Project has proved to be-"

She cut off when those tiny flecks of light began to coalesce, swirling together in a cyclone that hovered over the slab.

Desa gasped.

She was tense with anticipation, eager to see the birth of Vengeance. Not that she had much admiration for the being she had met six months ago in the Borathorin Forest, but how many people could say they had witnessed something like this?

Her hopes were dashed when the image vanished and the crystal went dark. It was all she could do not to get up and kick the damn thing. A bad idea if ever she'd had one. She was fairly certain that the crystal wasn't fragile – it had survived for months in her saddlebags, after all – but violent outbursts would accomplish nothing.

"Come on, Midnight," she whispered. "Let's get some sleep."

SHE HAD BEEN in the desert for five days. Her food was almost gone, and she was down to her last few mouthfuls of water. The townsfolk had given her three canteens full, and now those were all but spent. As was the supply she had taken from a small oasis that she had passed two days ago.

The sun hovered in the blue sky, baking the red clay under Midnight's hooves. That was all she saw. Red clay in every direction. Nothing but an endless expanse of harsh, unforgiving terrain. Now and then, she passed a cactus. Yesterday, she had split one open to replenish her water supply. The plant was actually quite tasty once you removed all the spines. Almost like a cucumber.

That had given her enough hope to press on, but hope was a fleeting thing in this place. Last time, she'd had Bendarian to lead her. This time, it was just Desa and her horse. She reached out to the Ether frequently, and so did Midnight. But she never sensed any sign of the ancient city.

There were no obvious land markers. She saw rocks everywhere she looked, but they offered no clue as to where she should go. North and west: that was all she knew. But that could mean anything. If her angle was off by just a few degrees, she might miss the city by miles.

She didn't want to die alone in this wasteland.

What a fool she had been to send Kalia away. Amazing how the spectre of death clarified things. She loved Kalia. She loved the other woman more than she had ever loved anyone in her life. And the others...Mercy protect them all.

At least she had kept striving, kept pressing on until her very last breath. In the end, that was all anyone could ask. She had tried. She had journeyed from one end of this world to the other, faced dangers no human had ever dreamed of. Maybe all of this was bound to happen no matter what she did.

If Timothy Delarac possessed the means to control Adele, then it stood to reason that he knew about *Hanak Tuvar*. Which meant the knowledge was more widespread than she had realized. Which meant that sooner or later, someone would have been tempted by the power. Someone would have freed *Hanak Tuvar*.

All of this would have happened even if Desa Kincaid had never left Aladar. It would have happened even if she had never taught Bendarian how to find the Ether. And if that was the case, then...

Then it wasn't her fault.

Slumped over in the saddle, she started laughing hysterically. She mopped damp hair off her forehead. "I see it now," she mumbled. "All of it."

A pity that this understanding should only come to her now, in the desert, when she was alone. Unable to make use of her new insight, unable to change anything. The world was not cruel; it was simply indifferent, but sometimes the one felt very much like the other. She was going to die.

Exhaustion crept over her. If she could just close her eyes for a few moments. Just a short rest: that was all she needed. In those quiet moments, with her thoughts drifting away into a dreamy haze, she felt it.

A pulse.

Like a thrum in the air washing over her. At first, she thought she had imagined it but then she felt another. And another. Midnight nickered to get her attention. He felt it too; she was sure of it.

Forcing herself to look up, Desa blinked to moisten bleary eyes. "It can't be."

Midnight was already galloping in the direction of the pulses.

She drifted in and out of awareness, watching the red clay rushing past beneath her. The pulses were growing stronger. She could feel them like a beacon calling her. How much further? Ten miles? Twenty?

She got her answer when she saw a faint twinkle on the northern horizon. The crystal atop Mercy's pyramid. Just the sight of it was enough to start her laughing again. She wrapped herself in the Ether, bathing in its warmth. Perhaps she was just imagining it, but that comforting presence soothed the aches and pains out of her muscles. She held on for a little while, long enough to partially reverse the effects of sunstroke and dehydration, but exhaustion eventually got the better of her, and she had to let go.

Midnight pressed on, ignoring his own fatigue. It wasn't long before she saw the outbuildings of the abandoned city, dilapidated structures of stone that looked as though a strong wind might blow them away. It was the most beautiful thing she had ever seen.

Well, except for Kalia.

But this was a close second.

She must have dozed off because the next thing she knew, those buildings were right in front of her. They had made it! After nearly a month in the saddle, enduring cold, hunger and blazing sunlight, they had made it!

And there she was, standing between two ruined buildings like a vision of death: a ghostly figure in a black hood. Mercy came forward almost reluctantly, reaching for Desa.

With a great deal of effort, Desa forced herself to sit up. Her vision was blurred; her arms and legs felt as if they had turned to jelly. Even with the Ether's help, she was still a wreck, but she had dreamed of meeting Mercy ever since she was a little girl. This was a special moment.

The goddess seemed to be examining her. Perhaps she was wondering whether Desa was up to the challenge of whatever she had in store. Well, best to allay those fears right away. They had work to do, and there was no time to waste.

"So," Desa rasped. "What is the first lesson?"

She fell out of the saddle, landing on her side, and passed out right there on that ancient street.

9

When Desa opened her eyes, she saw an electric bulb glowing on the ceiling. This despite the ample daylight that came through the window on her right. She was lying on a soft bed, wrapped in a light blanket.

Slowly, she tried to take in her surroundings.

That window offered a fine view of tall buildings made from red and white brick. She knew of only one place in the world with such architecture. Somehow, she had been taken back to Aladar.

Her bed was rather small. The metal headboard and footboard suggested that she might be in a hospital. Which would make sense if she had been unconscious when she arrived in the city. The walls of her room were painted a soft, pastel green, and she noted a small vase of roses on the shelf.

Desa tried to sit up, but fatigue made her slump over. She pressed her fingertips into her forehead and tried to massage away the throbbing pain that was building inside her skull.

As if sensing that she was awake, a nurse in a white uniform came through the door. He was a tall fellow, lean and fit with tanned skin and thick, brown hair. "Easy there," he said, hurrying to her side.

"How did I get here?"

The man hesitated, exhaling roughly as he tried to formulate an answer. "We were hoping that you could tell us," he said at last. "They found you lying in the middle of Baker Street. A car almost ran you over."

"I was in the desert."

"The desert?"

Brushing damp hair off her forehead with the back of one hand, Desa groaned as she tried to get her bearings. She felt as though she had been pummeled with clubs for several hours straight. Maybe the nurse was mistaken. Maybe that car *had* run her over. "The Gatharan Desert."

"That's almost two thousand miles from here."

"And I need to get back there."

She tried to rise, but a gentle hand on her shoulder restrained her. When she looked up, she saw concern in the young man's brown eyes. "Miss, when we found you, you were severely dehydrated," he said. "You looked as though you hadn't eaten in days. We had a hard time getting some broth into you."

"I need to go..."

"You're in no condition to go anywhere."

She was about to protest, but another wave of fatigue forced her to lie down. Her eyelids felt so heavy. If she could just rest for a little while...Midnight? If she had been brought here, then where was Midnight? Was he still in the desert? Or had he been taken to a stable in the city?

She knew that she had to stay awake – at the very least, she should try to find out what had happened to her horse – but the siren song of sleep was impossible to ignore. If she just rested for a little while...Everything would be all right if she just rested for a few hours. "What's your name, Miss?" the nurse asked her.

"Desa," she mumbled before sinking into unconsciousness.

"I think she's coming around."

"Mercy be praised."

It was hard to open her eyes. The tiniest crack brought with it the painful assault of bright light. Her head felt like a drum that had been pounded. But the fog in her brain was starting to recede. Slowly,

Her vision came into focus, a whirlpool of colours resolving into the face of her mother. Leean was smiling. "She's all right."

Sitting up slowly, Desa pressed the heel of her hand to her forehead. She moaned at the sudden onset of dizziness. "Mom?"

"I'm here, little one," Leean assured her. "Where are your friends?"

"With any luck, they're in New Beloran."

"Why did you come home without them?"

Desa threw the blankets off and hopped out of bed, grunting when her bare feet hit the tiles. She was forced to bend double as a wave of vertigo hit her, prompting the nurse to rush to her side.

With a great deal of effort, she was able to stand, bracing her hands on the mattress for support. "I didn't," she answered. "The last thing I remember, I was in the Gatharan Desert. And I need to get back there."

"I'm afraid that will have to wait." a gruff voice said.

She turned around to find a man in yellow robes standing in the doorway. One of the Elite Guardians. Somehow, she had failed to notice him until now. By the Eyes of Vengeance, she *was* tired.

He was a tall fellow with a round face of dark, brown skin and a perfectly smooth head. "The Prelate wants to see you," he said, stepping into the room. "As soon as you're well enough."

Pressing her hands down on the mattress, Desa hung her head. A soft sigh escaped her. "Does she now? Well, I'm afraid I don't much care what Daresina wants."

"That has always been painfully obvious."

Leean rose from her chair on the other side of the bed. "Couldn't you stay for just a few days?" she asked. "Surely, you need rest."

"You will not be permitted to leave the city," the Guardian stated with all the fervour of a man reading off the items on a shopping list. "The Prelate has questions for you, and you *will* answer them."

Forcing herself to look up, Desa narrowed her eyes. "Fine," she hissed. "Then let's get this over with."

"Impossible," the nurse interjected. "You're in no condition-"

She silenced him with a look and felt a swell of satisfaction when the man backed away from her. Even in her weakened state, Desa Kincaid could intimidate fools with a glance. She took a strange amount of pride in that.

Leean rounded the foot of the bed, nudging the nurse aside so that she could wrap her arms around Desa. "Little one," she murmured. "You will do no good for anyone if you push yourself to your breaking point. Can't you just rest for a little while?"

"No, Mom," Desa murmured. "I can't."

They took her by car to the Prelate's office.

The whole way, Desa kept thinking about what she would have to do to escape. An elbow to the face would knock out the Guardian. Then all she would have to do was open the door and throw herself out of a car that was traveling at thirty miles per hour.

No. No good would come of that. Better to face Daresina and then escape the city when an opportunity presented itself. They couldn't watch her every waking second. Was Midnight here? If Desa had been transported to Aladar, was her horse here as well?

She noticed that her Sinks and Sources were miles away, somewhere to the east. Of course, they would disarm her. She didn't ask what they had done with her guns or her belt. Everything they had taken from her was probably in a vault in the basement of some police station. They were determined to keep her here, and they knew what a danger she was with a full arsenal of Infusions.

They led her through the columned reception area where she had fought several of Adele's loyal soldiers last year. She was pleased to see that the bullet holes had been repaired.

The receptionist behind the crescent-shaped desk went pale when she saw Desa coming. "I'll tell the Prelate that you're here."

Striding across the room with hands clasped behind her back, Desa smiled and nodded. "Thank you," she said. "And while you're in there, feel free to remind her about the time I fought eight men in this very room to keep her alive."

The young woman got up and scooted out of the room before she could say another word. Well for her that she did. Desa's tolerance for pointless pleasantries was at an all-time low. How did she get here? Surely Mercy wouldn't have sent her back to Aladar.

She noticed the small jar of marbles on the receptionist's desk. Perhaps she could Infuse a few while she waited. No. That Elite Guardian was right behind her. He would know the instant she made contact with the Ether.

Snatching a marble out of the jar, Desa held it pinched between her thumb and forefinger. "Such a tiny thing," she mumbled.

"What are you on about?" the Guardian demanded.

When she turned around, he was standing between the first two pillars, his yellow robes a sharp contrast to the red walls.

His mouth was a thin line, his brows drawn together. "Talking to yourself. When did you pick up that nasty habit?"

"I was just noting that sometimes those things that seem tiny and inconsequential to us can change the world."

"Philosophize on your own time."

Desa raised an eyebrow, and when that failed to produce a reaction, she sighed. "Do you have a name, Guardian?"

"Audrin," he answered. "Why?"

"Curiosity."

The door swung open, and the receptionist hurried out, breathing hard. She paused for a moment to collect herself and then put on a warm, inviting smile. "You may go in."

The Prelate's office was exactly as Desa remembered it. Soft, red carpet stretched from one crimson wall to another. A large, wooden desk sat in the daylight that came in through a massive window with brown muntin that segmented the glass into individual panes about the size of her hand.

She noticed another jar of marbles atop the wooden bookshelf and an ornate vase that contained no flowers. A strange choice, that; why keep the thing if you were not going to use it for its intended purpose?

A second Elite Guardian stepped out from behind the door. Desa had met this one before; his name was Tolan. He wore the same yellow robes that she had seen on every other member of his order, but unlike Audrin, he was pale with short, brown hair.

The pair of them flanked Desa on either side, never letting her get out of arm's reach. The message was clear; if she tried to run, she wouldn't get halfway to the door before they put her down.

Daresina Nin Drialla stood behind her desk in a purple dress with sleeves that flared at the wrist. Her olive-skinned face was marked by a small liver spot on her right cheek, and as always, her iron-gray hair was tied up with a clip.

The Prelate's attention seemed to be focused on the Lessenger 22 that sat atop her desk. Desa recognized the pistol as one of her own, the one without Infused ammunition, sadly. The Elite Guardians were not fools; they would have examined everything they had confiscated before letting the Prelate get within two miles of anything that Desa Nin Leean had carried on her person.

"Fine craftsmanship," Desa remarked. "Wouldn't you agree?"

The Prelate spared a glance over the gold rims of her glasses. "I am not so easily impressed," she said. "Where is the Spear, Desa?"

Folding her arms, Desa felt another smile coming on. She couldn't suppress the burst of laughter that bubbled out of her. "I should have known," she muttered. "I guess it was too much to hope that your first concern might be the lives of the people you sent on that mission."

"My first concern is the safety of Aladar."

Tilting her head back, Desa shut her eyes and exhaled slowly. "No," she replied. "Your first concern is expanding your sphere of influence. You wanted the Spear so that you could begin annexing territory from the mainland."

Daresina removed her glasses, cleaning each lens with a handkerchief. Casual as you please. You might have thought they were discussing a recipe for peach pie. "Marcus told you?" she inquired.

"He told Miri."

"Well...That one was always soft."

Desa had to resist the urge to scoff. If Marcus was soft, she didn't want to know what hard was. And yet this woman disparaged him with such indifference. Marcus had dedicated his life to Aladar, had chosen patriotism over friendship, family and even his sense of self-respect. To hear Daresina dismissing him like that was intolerable.

"He was a good man," Desa hissed.

The Prelate sat down in her chair, setting her elbows on the armrests and steepling her fingers. "And where is he?" she asked. "Did you kill him?"

A single tear threatened to slide down Desa's cheek. "Miri killed him," she whispered. "After he tried to take the Spear. He was going to leave us there in the forest and bring it back to you."

"Miri killed a Field Binder," Daresina breathed. "Well, well, well. I didn't think she had it in her. Of course, she will have to be executed when she returns."

"You have no right!"

"I have every right," Daresina countered. "I'm Prelate. Take her to a cell. We can execute her once she stands trial" Her tone implied that the outcome of such a trial was a foregone conclusion. Desa felt the rage rising within her. After everything she had done for this wretched woman...

Tolan came up behind her.

Desa stepped on his foot, eliciting a yelp, then elbowed him in the face. The fool went stumbling, crying out as he fell on his backside.

She rounded on Audrin.

That one was tense like a bull about to charge, his nostrils flaring with every breath. She recognized that glint in his eye. She had seen it before in the gaze of every man she had brought to justice. Audrin wanted to kill her; he was just waiting for an excuse.

Desa threw the marble as hard as she could.

It smacked him right in the groin, forcing him to bend double and clutch his pelvis with both hands. A sharp squeal escaped him. If he had wanted to kill her before, that desire was now doubly strong.

Turning on her heel, Desa ran for the Prelate. She threw

herself into a dive and rolled across the surface of the desk, snatching up the pistol.

Landing on the other side, she raised the gun in both hands, pointing it at Daresina. "Nobody moves." The hammer made a distinctive *click* when she pulled it back. "And if I feel even the slightest twitch in the Ether…"

Daresina backed away with her hands in the air. The woman's face was ashen, her confidence gone. "Think this through, Desa," she gasped. "You can't hope to get past two Field Binders. Not when we took away your Sinks and Sources."

"No," Desa agreed, watching the two men out of the corner of her eye. Tolan kept rubbing his nose while Audrin grunted and forced himself to stand up straight. Neither one made any move toward her. "But they can't stop me from killing you."

"And what will that accomplish?" Daresina countered. "You will die soon after."

Desa felt her lips pulling back from clenched teeth. Her heart was pounding, her body tense.. "Justice will have been served."

"Justice?" the Prelate exclaimed, her eyes widening. "But what of your great cause? Who will stop *Hanak Tuvar* if you are dead?"

"You're going to kill me anyway," Desa growled. "So, I don't see that there's much of a difference."

It shocked her when Daresina fell to her knees, raising clasped hands in supplication. The woman was trembling. "Please, Desa. You can't do this!"

Striding forward, Desa pressed the barrel of her gun against the Prelate's forehead. "You ordered Marcus to betray us," she hissed. "Because of you, Miri had to kill her own brother. You put your ambitions over the fate of the world."

"I'm sorry," Daresina croaked.

"Remorse?" Desa scoffed. "You're not capable of it."

"Please! Please!"

The rage was surging, demanding satisfaction. This woman had brought nothing but misery and pain to everyone Desa cared about. She deserved to die. Sweet Mercy, the world would be better for it. Daresina was every bit as dangerous as Timothy Delarac. If she had her way, Aladri soldiers would pour forth from the island and conquer everything in their path.

It was logical; it was ethical. So much suffering could be stopped if Desa just pulled that trigger. Her hands trembled. She could end the pain right here. End all of it with a twitch of her finger.

Instead, she uncocked the hammer.

Turning her face away from the other woman, Desa squeezed her eyes shut. Tears welled up as she sniffled. "Damn you," she whispered. "I will never forgive you as long as I live."

Everything went black.

HER EYES SNAPPED OPEN, but the blackness remained. She was lying on a rough, stone slab with nothing but her duster for a pillow. The air was musty, stale and painfully dry. Every breath she took scraped its way past her parched throat.

She was keenly aware of every Sink and Source that she had created, and they were all right where they were supposed to be. Her Infused bullets were loaded into a gun that sat on a nearby shelf. Her Light-Sink pendant was tucked safely into her shirt, her rings still snug around her fingers.

Desa triggered the Light-Source, illuminating the interior of a small hut with stone walls. Walls that looked as if they might collapse under the onslaught of a strong wind. She gasped when she saw the robed figure standing over her. Mercy offered a comforting hand, smoothing the hair off Desa's forehead.

"It was an illusion?"

Mercy nodded.

Sitting up despite her exhaustion, Desa glared at the goddess. "Why?" It came out as a hoarse whisper. "What could you possibly hope to gain from this farce?"

Mercy didn't answer. It took a moment for Desa to remember that the other woman could not speak in this form.

Clearing her mind enough to find the Ether was difficult even with the crystal's assistance, but when she did, the world changed before her eyes. Mercy became an angelic being wrapped in a halo of pure, white light.

She was a motherly woman of average height, slightly plump with a round face of dark-brown skin. She smiled when she sensed that Desa had made contact with the Ether. "Thank you," she said. "This makes things easier."

My question?

Mercy closed her eyes, breathing deeply. "It was a test," she said. "To see if you are ready to learn what I have to teach."

I assume I passed.

"You did. The days ahead will be difficult, Desa. You must put aside your need for retribution and embrace a larger view of the world. You cannot overpower *Hanak Tuvar* with brute force. Together, we will find a new way."

Turning away from Desa, the goddess shuffled over to the door. She paused there, looking back. "I've left you water," she said. "Make sure you drink it. You are still very dehydrated. When you feel up to it, I've prepared some vegetables from my garden. It's not much, but it will serve."

Thank you.

The Ether fled the moment she stopped trying to hold on. She was too tired to remain in contact. She found a copper bucket full of crisp, clean water and drank most of its contents before lying down. The stone shelf was hardly comfortable, but Desa didn't care. She snuggled up with her head on her folded coat and fell asleep in seconds.

. . .

WHEN SHE WOKE, sunlight was coming through the doorway. It was already starting to warm up. Her body was aching, but she felt as if she had come through the worst of it. And she was hungry. Sweet Mercy, she was hungry!

Sore and stiff, Desa sat up with a grunt. She winced, pain flaring through her body. "Sleep on stone," she muttered. "And wake up miserable."

Standing required some effort, but she was able to hobble over to the door. The harsh glare made her eyes smart, but the pain passed in a few seconds, and she found herself looking at the small orchard she had seen last year.

The water collector – a thick pole that stood taller than any of the ruined buildings – shimmered in the morning light. Copper tubes extended from it like tentacles, each one filling a bucket. The peach trees had not yet flowered, but they were growing strong and healthy. A tiny slice of paradise here in the desert.

Of all the things she had seen in her travels, the strangest by far was the shrouded figure of Mercy lifting a bucket for Midnight so that he could drink his fill. The goddess turned her head when she heard Desa's approach.

That hood offered nothing but a glimpse into a pit of darkness, but there was no malevolence in Mercy's stare. Once, Desa would have been terrified, but every scrap of fear had evaporated long ago. What could have happened to Mercy to trap her in this form? She was reminded of Vengeance – a withered crone in the heart of a rainforest. Left alone for centuries.

Somehow, Desa got the impression that they had done this to each other, each woman cursing the other with a form that she would find intolerable. For Vengeance, that was impotence. The woman that Desa had seen in the blue crystal's recordings was hard and relentless. Marcus would have liked her. The one thing that Driala could not abide was helplessness.

And as for Mercy...

If Nari had been the sort of woman who wanted to help people, then trapping her in a form that inspired terror would be the worst thing you could do to her. What could have possessed them to turn on each other like that?

Desa strode up to the other woman, craning her neck to peer into that hood. "Stay still," she said. "I want to help you."

She found the Ether with almost no effort, and Mercy transformed into the beautiful woman she had seen last night. Extending her awareness, Desa searched for a clue, some sign that something was amiss.

She found nothing.

The halo around Mercy was overwhelming. Pure, perfect light. Almost as if the woman were made from the Ether itself. Rojan had said something to that effect once; he had told Desa that the *Al a Nari* believed the crystals to be physical manifestations of the gods. The bones of the goddess, he had called them.

The crystals were calcified shards of the Ether, and when shattered, they released its healing power. Some of the *Al a Nari* believed that they were conscious. Which would make sense if they really were pieces of Mercy and Vengeance. So, if Mercy was formed from the Ether...

Desa focused on the halo.

At first, she found nothing wrong – just warmth and light – but she refused to give up. There had to be something! Gathering all of her willpower, she delved deeper. The nimbus that surrounded Mercy was so thin a speck of dust could not fit within it, and yet, when Desa directed her thoughts into that light, it was as vast as an eternity. She searched and searched. And there it was.

Emptiness.

The Ether that comprised Mercy's body had been cut off from the Ether that existed everywhere else. The gap was thinner than the width of a particle, but it may as well have been a mile across. A chasm of darkness exactly like what she saw every time she looked at Adele with True Sight. Desa couldn't just force the Ether into that gap. That might hurt Mercy. This was going to require some delicacy.

She let go of the Ether.

The world became a place of solid objects, and Mercy was once again a robed phantom in a black hood. She could tell that the goddess was intrigued. Had no one ever tried to help her before today? "I'm sorry," Desa said. "But I can't think of any other way to do this."

She stood on her toes, reaching into the hood to seize the other woman's face. She kissed Mercy's lips. And in that moment of connection, she found the Ether once again.

Its warmth flowed through her, suffusing every molecule of her. She gathered that heat, focused it and then gently guided it into the gap. A torrent of power surged through her like water from a burst dam. After only a second, she was forced to let go.

Desa fell on her backside, raising a hand to shield herself. Cautiously, she looked up to peek through splayed fingers.

Mercy stumbled backward, her black robes brushing the grass. Golden light spread from her chest, washing over her arms, her legs, her hood. The goddess threw her head back with a cry of delight.

And radiance exploded from her.

She was like a woman made of sunlight, blazing bright, banishing every shadow. Midnight whinnied, backing away, but Mercy soothed him with the gentle caress of a glowing hand.

When the moment passed, she was the woman that Desa remembered: plump with rich, dark skin and ringlets of hair framing her face. Her smile was nothing short of beatific. "Thank you."

"Um...My pleasure," Desa mumbled.

"This will make things much easier."

Mercy rose into the sky, spreading her arms wide and transforming into a figure made of crystal. The same crystal that glittered atop the pyramid.

The pieces of stone that littered the streets began to move, gathering together and assembling themselves into the buildings that had once stood tall and proud in this city. Light seeped through the cracks between individual pieces, and when it faded, those fissures were gone, leaving one solid structure.

Mercy floated over the city in a delicate dance, and every time her crystalline hand passed over a pile of rubble, it reformed into a house or a chapel or a library. It was a glorious thing to behold.

Grass sprouted around each building, growing lush and green. Flowers emerged in small gardens. It was like watching time run backwards, the city's decay reversed by the gentle touch of a goddess. Desa knew that Mercy wasn't truly divine – she had been a mortal woman who had been changed somehow – but for the first time since learning the truth, she almost believed. Almost.

Sunlight glinted off Mercy's crystal skin as she landed on the grass. A flash of light made Desa look away, and when it passed, Mercy was human in appearance once again. "There," she said. "It's a start. Come, my child. We have much work to do."

10

The tip of Dalen's pen scrawled a few numbers onto the yellow page of his ledger. He looked up to see half a dozen book-keepers sitting at slanted desks very much like his own. One of those was Jim Potts.

The young man seemed to be perfectly happy working away for Harmon Brothers' Bookkeeping for twenty cents an hour. But then his previous job had involved mucking out stables with no compensation other than room and board. And poor lodgings at that.

"And how are we doing in here?" Mr. Harmon asked.

A barrel-chested fellow in a white shirt and black vest, he strode through the aisle between the desks with a jovial smile, pausing to clap each man on the shoulder. He was handsome for a fellow in his middle years, tanned with a cleft chin and thick, dark hair that showed only a few threads of gray. "Excellent. Excellent."

The windows to Dalen's left offered plenty of daylight, but Harmon still kept a small lamp burning atop his desk. The scent of oil filled the air. The others didn't seem to notice, but

Dalen had grown used to electric lights. This all felt very... primitive to him.

Dipping his pen in the ink jar, Dalen licked his lips and wrote out the next line of a page on fur exports. *Mother always wondered why I learned to read Eradian,* he mused. *"What use could it possibly be, Dalen?"*

He almost started laughing.

Between his salary, Jim's salary and the money Zoe brought in as a maid, they had enough to cover Mrs. Carmichael's rent with plenty left over for food. As such, Miri and Tommy had given up on finding work, opting instead to go forward with the plan. For the last five days, they had been skulking around the Parliament Building, hoping to catch a glimpse of Timothy Delarac so that they could Infuse his carriage. Dalen had little to do with that. He was content to play his small part.

Besides, he was still angry with Tommy.

Well...Perhaps "angry" was too strong a word. It irked him that the other man was willing to stand up for the rights of slaves but not for their love. Tommy already had a target painted on his back after everything that had happened in Hedrovan. What was one more crime after all that?

Standing before them all, Mr. Harmon flashed another smile. "Well," he said, glancing out the window. "It seems we're nearing the end of the day. Best to pack up then."

"Sir?" one of the men questioned.

"We're ahead of schedule," Harmon explained. "Ten extra minutes won't make that much of a difference. But be ready for an early start tomorrow."

"Yes, sir!"

It took about ten minutes to put the ledgers and supplies away in any event. Really, they were just leaving at the appropriate time. The street outside was lined with squat buildings made of brown bricks. Horse-drawn carriages rolled along the cobblestones, their drivers sometimes slowing to offer the tip of a hat.

Dalen shuffled along the sidewalk with his hands in his coat pockets, his mouth tight with misgivings. Sometimes, he wondered how he had gotten mixed up in all of this. Which was foolish. He knew exactly how he had gotten involved in all of this; he had fallen in love with a wonderful man and an amazing woman.

And yet, there were moments when he felt like excess baggage. What had he contributed to the cause thus far? A little abstract knowledge about the Borathorin Forest? Moral support?

Money.

Revolutions were all well and good, but they had a habit of dying if you couldn't pay the bills. It wasn't glorious, but Dalen had something to offer.

Jim fell in beside him, walking with a spring in his step. The young man wore a smile that could drive away the darkest clouds. "Such a lovely day," he noted. "Why don't we walk through Calver Park?"

Dalen gave him a sidelong glance. "Because that route would take twenty extra minutes?"

"Twenty minutes of fresh air in the warm, spring weather," Jim said with a shrug. "Sounds positively dreadful."

In the end, Dalen took the offer. It was nice to just walk and talk with someone. So much of his life over the past year had been death and danger. He had grown so used to it that he had forgotten what it was like to not be in a hurry.

They followed a cobblestone walkway that cut through the grass with pine trees growing on either side of it. The air was cool and crisp, but the warmth of the westering sun made that quite pleasant.

For the most part, they were alone. Twice they passed a man in a suit who was headed in the opposite direction, but very few people had decided to cut through the park this evening. So few that Jim started to feel confident discussing topics that would otherwise be reserved for the privacy of their apartment.

"What's it like?" he asked. "Aladar, I mean."

Plodding along with his arms crossed, Dalen sighed. "I think you'd like it," he said, casting a glance over his shoulder. "For one thing, it's easier to get around."

"Oh?"

"We have devices that have replaced horse-drawn carriages."

Jim's face lit up at the mention of automobiles. "Yes," he whispered. "Tommy told me about them."

The mention of his love put Dalen in a sour mood. At this very moment, Tommy and Miri were waiting outside the Parliament Building for Delarac to emerge. Those two had been spending a great deal of time together. While Dalen was forgotten once again. "Thomas was quite smitten with Aladar."

Lifting the low-hanging branch of a pine, Jim ducked underneath it. He paused on the other side, staring down the path to the busy street at its end. Carriages were rumbling down Brahe Lane. "Maybe I'll go someday."

"You'd be happier there than here."

Jim rubbed his chin with the back of one hand, then wrinkled his nose as he worked through something in his head. "Something I don't get," he said. "If you have all these wonderful things – medicines that can cure disease, machines that can do back-breaking work – why don't you share them with the rest of the world?"

Dalen opened his mouth, intending to offer an answer, but none came to mind. Truth be told, he had never thought about it. "Perhaps we should," was all he could say on the matter.

Their walk home was pleasant; Jim was kind enough to avoid such difficult topics for the duration of the journey. He was a fine, young man. Dalen felt a little uncomfortable applying the adjective. Jim wasn't *that* much younger than he was. Only a year or two. Perhaps, one day, when they all returned to Aladar, Jim could come along.

A ROUND FOUNTAIN in the middle of Bowman Plaza sprayed water into the air, each drop catching the light of the sinking sun. People hurried about on the cobblestones, headed in all directions, some bumping into each other. There were at least a hundred. A year ago, Tommy would have never imagined that so many people could be gathered in one place, but after Aladar, large crowds were somewhat blasé. And they were not what he had come here to see.

On the other side of the narrow street, stone steps led up to a massive building of brown bricks, a building with framed windows on each of its three stories. Gabled roofs over both the east and west wings rose to a peak where flags stood in a line. Each one displayed the symbol of the Eradian Empire: a golden laurel on a field of green. The Parliament Building was nothing short of majestic.

Sitting on a bench with his hands on his knees, Tommy chewed on a toothpick as he watched the distant building for any sign of his prey. He had donned the fine coat and trousers that were common to men in this part of town – Miri's sugges-tion – but he would not give up toothpicks. He had to do some-thing with all that nervous energy.

Victor stood beside him, fidgeting. The young man was even more jittery than Tommy. Twice now, he had started to pace only to stop abruptly when he realized that it would draw too much attention.

"It's been four days," Victor muttered.

Tommy nodded.

"If he hasn't shown up yet..."

Catching the toothpick between two fingers, Tommy pulled it out of his mouth. He shot a glance toward the other man and blinked. "It's a shame you never got to train with Mrs. Kincaid," he murmured. "She could teach you the value of patience."

Victor took a few plodding steps forward, then spun around to face him. "I'm just saying we should be *doing* something," he insisted. "Four days of waiting and watching haven't accomplished very much."

"Take it easy."

"This plan isn't working."

With a heavy sigh, Tommy stood up and approached the other man. "If you want to go back to the boarding house, you can," he muttered. "But if you're going to stay, I will have to insist that you keep your voice down."

"I think I'll stay. Mrs. Carmichael is serving pork."

"You don't enjoy her cooking?"

"Everything is much too salty."

Tommy forced an awkward smile, nodding his reluctant agreement. "She is a bit too liberal with the salt," he said. "Tell you what: the next time we're on the road, I will take on the cooking duties. I'm sure I can come up with something more to your liking."

It dawned on him that he had started to emulate Desa's way of speaking. Now, when had that happened? A year ago, he spoke like most of the good folk in his little village. Perhaps it was the pressure of leadership, always feeling as though he had to inspire confidence in those around him. He suspected, though, that it started long before he was in a position where anyone listened to him.

"Doesn't it feel odd to you?" Victor asked.

"Hmm?"

Standing before him with a sheepish grin, Victor lowered his eyes. A touch of crimson blossomed in the man's cheeks. "A man cooking dinner," he clarified. "I'm still not used to it."

"In Aladar, men and women share the chores equally," Tommy said. "The same is true among the *Al a Nari*. I hope that, wherever the two of you settle, you don't expect Zoe to do all the cooking."

"Well," Victor replied. "A few months ago, I could never have believed that a slave might fight for his freedom. I suppose I can get used to this too."

Tommy clapped the other man on the shoulder, offering a nod of approval. "That's the spirit!" he exclaimed. "You're going to find that a lot of what you heard growing up is wrong."

He was about to say more, but a sudden movement in the corner of his eye made him stop. Miri strolled around the fountain in a modest, purple frock and matching hat with lace. She halted when she caught his eye and inclined her head ever so slightly toward the Parliament Building.

A man in his middle years was hurrying down the steps, a handsome man with dark hair and a thick mustache. Going by the sketches that Dalen had provided, this had to be Timothy Delarac.

"Shoot him," Victor whispered.

"What?"

"Why don't you just shoot him? He's right there."

Tommy raised a hand to silence the other man. Even in hushed voices, this was not the place for that kind of talk. Only a fool would open fire in the middle of a crowded plaza. There was every chance that an innocent bystander would be hurt. And if anyone overheard Victor's suggestion...

Clearing his mind, Tommy reached for the Ether.

Delarac climbed into a coach that was waiting for him on the curb. Once he was inside, the driver set the horses moving at a quick trot. Not much time. The further he got, the harder it would be to Infuse the metal.

Working quickly, Tommy began a simple lattice for a Light-Sink, working it into the carriage frame. He gave up after a few seconds. The Infusion he had created would barely dim the glow of a candle, but it didn't have to be strong. It only had to point him in the direction of Delarac's home.

The coach went around the corner.

And Tommy broke contact with the Ether.

Heaving out a sigh, he shut his eyes and slumped over, the tension draining out of him. "It's done," he said in a rasping voice. "We'll be able to track him."

Miri shuffled up beside him, gently patting his arm. "Excellent," she murmured. "Then it's time to move on to the next part of the plan."

"I DON'T SEE why you didn't just kill him then and there," Victor said. Thankfully, he was wise enough to keep his voice down even within the confines of their apartment. The young man sat on the sofa with Zoe beside him, holding his arm.

Miri wasn't listening to their conversation. She was much too busy buttoning up her blouse, checking the knives in her ankle holster and those on her belt as well. One look in the bedroom's stand mirror and she was satisfied. Unrelieved black wasn't exactly flattering, but it would serve.

"Because," Dalen said. "We need him alive."

"Why?" Victor demanded. "If he's starting all these wars-"

"He's not the only one starting them," Jim cut in. "Someone else would just take his place."

Miri stepped into the sitting room and found the lot of them gathered around the sofa. Tommy had claimed a wooden stool while Dalen sat in the large, cushioned chair. Jim was in the corner, leaning against the wall.

Victor looked dejected, sitting with his knees apart and his head hanging. It was clear that he didn't like being the odd man out, and he would like it even less once she was through with him. When a man spoke foolishness, a little shame was definitely in order. It might dissuade him from repeating such sentiments in the future.

Drawing herself up to full height, Miri glowered at the young man. "Perhaps you've forgotten," she began. "But we need Delarac alive so he can tell us how he's controlling Adele."

Striding across the room, her feet sinking into the soft carpet, she towered over Victor. The dolt looked up at her with fearful eyes. "And," Miri pressed on. "We do not put innocent people at risk."

"Yes, ma'am."

A sudden draft of air made her turn around in time to see Kalia coming through the door. Without a sound. Tommy must have activated the Sonic-Sinks when Victor started blathering like an idiot. She could kiss him for that.

The former sheriff removed her hat and began to speak, grimacing when she failed to hear her own words. A few steps brought her into the middle of the living room, and then she sighed audibly.

"Were we planning something?" Kalia asked.

"Teaching," Miri clarified.

"Well, the street is all but empty with the dinner hour upon us," Kalia said. "If we are going to do this, now is as good a time as any. Though I suppose we'll want to wait until Tommy is finished."

Miri raised an eyebrow.

"He's been in contact with the Ether for almost twenty minutes," Kalia said. "I suspect he's Infusing some of your accoutrements."

Pawing at herself, Miri gasped. Field Binding didn't scare her, but if Tommy was doing something to her shirt or her belt, she should have felt it? Shouldn't she? He could have Infused every button for all that she could tell. It was unsettling to think that he could kill her with a thought, and she would never be the wiser until it was too late.

Tommy just sat there with a vacant expression, lost in his own world. Sometimes, she wondered what it would be like to experience the Ether. Maybe she should have tried harder to learn. Her mother would have preferred that. And if she'd had Sources and Sinks at her disposal, she might have been able to stop Marcus without-

No!

She would not think of that now!

Tommy flinched, coming back to reality, and then stood up. "There," he said breathily. "It's done."

"*What* is done?" she asked.

"Tap your belt buckle twice in quick succession."

Miri did so and felt her stomach lurch as she was overcome by a sudden sense of weightlessness. She pushed off the floor with the lightest touch and floated up to the ceiling, where she caught herself.

Tommy stared up at her with a big, stupid grin, his blue eyes sparkling with glee. "Doing the same a second time will kill the Sink," he explained. "Here, let me help you down before you do it."

Ignoring his offer, Miri pressed her hands against the ceiling and pushed herself down. Her feet hit the floor with a soft *thump,* and then she tapped her buckle twice in quick succession to restore gravity's natural pull.

"With the field kept tight around your body," Tommy went on. "The Sink should last for about an hour. But I would still advise you to use it sparingly. Your second button is a Sonic-Sink; tap it twice and you'll be as quiet as a whisper. Your fourth button will stop bullets."

Miri felt her cheeks burning. She was not used to the idea of someone going to that much effort to keep her safe. "All right then," she said. "Just in case we're not entirely clear, tonight is about reconnaissance. Nothing else. We learn the layout of the house and what kind of security – if any – we're up against."

Tommy and Kalia nodded.

"If you happen to see what looks like a tempting opportunity," Miri said. "Maybe you catch Delarac taking a moonlit stroll in the garden. Ignore it. Our goal is to get him out of that house with no one the wiser. Which means we do not take any direct action until we know every last juicy tidbit of information we can learn. We don't make a move against him until we can walk the corridors of that house blindfolded."

"But if you happen to catch him out alone-" Victor protested.

Miri rounded on the boy, her lips parting as she drew air through her teeth. "We don't know if he's really alone," she explained. "He might have guards nearby that we didn't see because they were lurking around a corner."

Victor went pale, his eyes widening as he considered that. "I see," he whispered. "I'm sorry."

"Dalen, Zoe, Victor, Jim," Miri said. "I'm sure you all have a long day tomorrow. Turn in; get some rest. Tommy, Kalia, you're with me. Let's go."

THE WEAVER MATERIALIZED in a basement with walls of stone, a room lit only by a lantern that hung from a peg. Dust littered the floor. A wooden barrel in the corner looked as though it hadn't been touched in ages.

This room was located in a small village called Marva, a town on the coast of the Sapphire Sea, about two days east of Hedrovan. If you traveled by horse, that was. It was the latest of several places that she had searched.

She had been forced to disguise herself when speaking to the villagers: gloves to hide her scaly hand, a hood to conceal her orange eyes. It galled her. Once, she had been beautiful, worthy of worship, but Desa and her pitiful uncle had robbed her of that. Still, this vessel had served its purpose.

Soon, she thought. *Very soon now.*

She heard the scuff of boots on the floor an instant before someone came up behind her and pressed a knife to her throat. "Brave of you," the stranger whispered in her ear. "Sneaking into my home. Brave and foolish."

The Weaver allowed herself a smile. "Well, I was looking for you," she purred. "To present you with an opportunity."

"Not interested."

"Oh, come now! We both know that's not true."

"How did you find me?"

Puckering her lips as she stared up at the ceiling, the Weaver whistled a jaunty tune. "I went to village after village," she said. "It's not hard to locate someone like you if you know what questions to ask."

A hard shove sent the Weaver stumbling toward the wall. She steadied herself at the last second, barely avoiding a collision. "Speak!" the stranger growled.

When she turned, she was confronted by a woman dressed in red from head to toe. Soft boots, thin pants, a tunic and hood: all red. Naturally, the stranger hid her face. That was to be expected.

Bobbing a curtsy, the Weaver bowed her head to the other woman. "I thought you might like to have some fun."

"Fun?"

"Yes! A little mayhem. That *is* your forte, is it not?"

"Why would I want to help you with anything?"

"Because," the Weaver said with a playful smile. "We're going to be slaughtering a bunch of wealthy aristocrats."

11

The sinking sun left a tinge of blue in the darkening sky. To Miri's eyes, the vast mansion across the way and the wall that surrounded it were just shadows. Kerosene lamps on either side of the cobblestone street cast puddles of light, but it was easy to hide in the gloom.

She stood with her back pressed against a brick wall that surrounded yet another mansion. There were several in this neighbourhood. Her thin blouse and trousers were no match for the chill of an early-spring evening, but bulky coats would not do. "This is the place?" she asked, gesturing to the house across the street.

A shiver went through Tommy – whether from fear or cold, she could not say – but he took control of himself and nodded. "The carriage is behind that wall," he said. "It has been for the last two hours."

Clothed in black from head to toe, Kalia wore her long hair in a ponytail. Her face was grim. "I communed with the Ether and searched the property," she said. "It's big. I couldn't see all of it. But none of the servants are in the front yard."

"Then we should get a move on," Miri barked. "You know

the plan. Kalia, you take the north side. Tommy, you take the south. I'll take the centre. Start by counting the windows. I want to know how many rooms we're dealing with on the upper floors. If you can get inside without making too much noise, do it. But do *not* let yourself be seen? Are there any questions?"

They shook their heads.

"Let's go."

With a grunt, Kalia rushed across the street and then jumped, gaining incredible height. She flew right over the wall and slipped out of sight on the other side. Not once did she tap a buckle or give any other indication that she was activating a Gravity-Sink. Miri had never cared much for Field Binding, but today, she envied the other woman.

"That's twice," Tommy said.

Miri rounded on him.

He was just a silhouette to her eyes, but she could tell that he was uneasy. And she was fairly certain that he was blushing. "You called me Tommy," he said. "That means you're scared."

Crossing her arms, Miri sniffed disdainfully. "You're damn right I'm scared," she said. "I'd be fool if I wasn't."

"We can do this."

"I didn't say we couldn't," Miri snapped. "Shall we get on with it?"

Sighing softly, Tommy started across the street. She caught a glimpse of him as he brushed the edge of the lamplight, but then he was gone. Her heart sank. She didn't mean to be so terse, but he was still her Lommy. He had come far in less than a year, but she still felt protective of him.

Miri sprinted across the road. When she neared the curb, she tapped her belt twice and jumped, easily cresting the wall. Four more taps allowed gravity to reassert itself for a fraction of a second.

She landed in the grass and killed the Sink.

The property was huge; by her estimate, it was almost a

tenth of a mile from the house to the wall. The mansion had two wings with six framed, arch-shaped windows on either side. Light spilled out from the ones on the first floor, but curtains made it difficult to see the interior. Which also decreased the risk that anyone inside might have seen her. She was well beyond the range of the lamplight, but some people had sharp eyes.

Staying low, Miri crept through the grass under the fence, making her way around the perimeter. You didn't approach a house like that head-on. You looked for a spot where you wouldn't be noticed.

It took a few minutes to reach the corner and begin her trek along the next section of wall. Where was Tommy? She had gone southward, which meant he should be around here somewhere. He couldn't have reached the house already.

A flicker of movement in a nearby window made her freeze. She looked, but it was only one of the liveried servants passing by. Nothing to worry about. Unless that fellow had the eyes of a hawk.

Bracing one hand against the wall, Miri shook her head in dismay. "Why do I keep getting mixed up in these ridiculous plans?"

She moved in a crouch, following the south wall toward the back of the house. The cold wind cut right through her thin shirt. Couldn't Tommy have given her a Heat-Source? She had plenty of buttons to spare.

The house was a shadow on her right, but the last gasp of twilight allowed her to see windows on the first and second floors. Both were dark. Unless Delarac was prone to a particularly maudlin form of moping, there was no one in those rooms.

This was as good a place as any.

Double-tapping her second button, Miri ran through the grass with nary a sound, moving like a ghost on the wind. It was so strange to not hear her breath or the pounding of her heart.

She charged right up to the side of the house, then tapped her buckle and jumped. Dark bricks and windows scrolled past as she rose into the air. Within seconds, she had reached the roof.

Miri caught the black shingles to stop her ascent, planting her feet against the wall. "How does Desa do this?" Her mouth formed the words, but she heard nothing. Which was incredibly unnerving.

She climbed up onto the gambrel roof, leaning against its inclined surface. After a moment of rest, she killed her Gravity-Sink and continued up to the peak, where the slope was much less steep. And thank Mercy for that.

Miri wrinkled her nose in distaste. She had never liked heights.

Cautiously, she stood up and walked toward the centre of the house. She kept worrying that the roof would collapse beneath her. If it did, she would have no warning, no creak of straining wood or crunch of broken shingles.

Motion in the corner of her eye.

She reached for a throwing knife, but it was only Tommy perched on the ledge that overlooked the backyard. He twisted around, having sensed her presence somehow, and raised a single finger to his lips. Now, what was that about? Surely, he knew that her Sonic-Sink was active. Was he telling her to leave it on?

Creeping closer, Miri knelt beside him. Bent forward with her hands on her thighs, she squinted into the yard below.

Two lamps cast soft light over the grass, revealing a pair of men in livery who stood on the edge of a large, stone patio. One of them was gesticulating quite forcefully.

What she wouldn't give to hear what they were saying. But if their voices were loud enough to make it up this far, the sound would be swallowed up by her Sonic-Sink. Maybe she should turn it off?

One of the servants spared her the trouble.

He turned on his heel and walked back to the house, passing out of sight. The other one remained on the patio, shuffling about while he puffed on a cigarette. How long was she supposed to sit here?

She didn't feel comfortable moving around with that numbskull down there, but her Sonic-Sink was growing weaker by the second. An hour: that was what Tommy had said, right? No, wait, that was for the Gravity-Sink. How long would the Sonic-Sink last?

Tossing his cigarette down on the ground, the young servant put it out with his foot and then shuffled back to the house.

The explosion of noise when she tapped her button made Miri flinch. It wasn't loud per se, but compared to the total silence she had been experiencing, it was quite intense. The whistle of the wind, the barking of a dog in a nearby yard, even her own heartbeat: they all came roaring back.

"How long were they there?" Miri whispered.

"A few minutes."

She pressed her lips together, nodding slowly as she considered that. "Keep an eye on things up here," she muttered. "I'm going to look for an open window."

Working up her courage took a great deal of effort. She hated heights. By the Eyes of Vengeance, she hated heights! With a great deal of reluctance, she triggered the Gravity-Sink and let her legs dangle over the edge. Except they didn't dangle. They just floated. She twisted around, lying on her stomach, and then backed off the roof inch by torturous inch.

Tommy cocked his head. It was too dark to see his face, but she knew without a doubt that he was grinning. "Takes some getting used to, doesn't it?"

"Shut up."

Miri forced herself to let go.

Panic welled up inside her and faded when she didn't immediately fall. She wasn't still – the changing air currents had her flitting about – but she didn't plummet to an ugly death, and that was enough. Two taps on her button reactivated the Sonic-Sink.

Gripping the ledge once again, Miri pressed her feet against the wall. She began to shuffle sideways, searching for a window. The nearest one was about ten feet to her left.

She began to climb down the wall, using the bricks of hand-holds, resting her feet on the windowsill. Crouching, she peered through the glass and found only blackness staring back at her.

She tried to open it, but it was shut tight.

On to the next one!

Within a few minutes, her fear faded away, and she began to enjoy this bizarre kind of burglary. She moved from one window to the next and then the next, trying to break in. Each time, she was met with failure, but then she came across one that had been left open. Just a crack, but it was enough for her to slip her fingers inside. It had been warmer this afternoon. Perhaps the room's owner had wanted a little fresh air.

Gently, she swung the pane outward. Her first thought was that a creak might alert someone to her presence, but she needn't have worried with the Sonic-Sink swallowing every noise.

She pulled herself up and crawled through the opening, floating in the darkened bedroom. Two taps on her belt restored gravity's power, and she landed hard on the carpet. *Idiot!* she scolded herself. *If anyone downstairs heard that!*

Except there was nothing to hear.

After a moment's hesitation, she tapped her button. She expected to hear breathing – perhaps someone had gone to bed early – but there was nothing. She decided to leave the Sink inactive. It could be as much a hindrance as a help. The ka'adri had been trained to use all of their senses, not just their eyes, but ears were useless when you were wrapped in a pocket of silence. Someone might sneak up behind her, and she would never know it.

With the utmost care, she made her way out of the room.

KALIA CLUNG to the wall on the north side of the house, listening to the sounds of merriment drifting through a nearby window. Her back was pressed against the bricks, her hands and feet as well. She felt very much like a spider.

The Gravity-Sink in her belt buckle was slowly filling itself with energy. She had made three in preparation for this mission. If necessary, she could hang here for the better part of two hours. Hopefully, it wouldn't take that long to hear something useful.

If only she could hear clearly.

The Delarac family had been enjoying a pleasant evening in their parlour. She had listened to several songs on the piano. The Drunken Mule, the Woman by the River, Old Man Chester: she knew the melody to every single one, but the words she had learned were different.

People started talking in the gaps between songs, but their voices were too muffled for her to pick up anything specific. She had an idea, a way to amplify their voices, but it was risky. She had created a Sonic-Source with directional modifiers for exactly this purpose. In theory, if she placed it on the windowsill, it would project sound outward, away from the house. She could eavesdrop and no one would be the wiser. In theory.

The truth was that sound was tricky. Even with directional modifiers, it was hard to control. The amplified sonic energy might bounce off a tree and reflect back toward the house. She could mitigate the risk by refining just how much energy the coin released, but it was still a danger. And what's more, she would have to put herself right in front of that window to hear anything. Anyone could look out and see her. A Light-Sink might help with that, assuming, of course, that no one wondered why it was *too dark* outside.

Well, it was either this or try to sneak inside.

Turning her face up to the sky, Kalia narrowed her eyes. "You told me to take care of them, Desa," she whispered. "Can't blame me if it gets me killed."

She flipped onto her stomach, shuffled around and began to crawl down the wall, approaching the window from above. When she drew near, she carefully maneuvered around it.

Her hand darted out, leaving a coin on the windowsill.

Kalia dove for the ground, killing her Gravity-Sink just before she hit, and somersaulted through the grass She came up on one knee and triggered her Light-Sink. Darkness shrouded her, concealing her from prying eyes. Hidden, she moved in front of the window. They were still playing the piano. There was no point in using the coin now.

She would wait.

WITH HER BACK against the wood-paneled wall, Miri inched sideways toward the door. It was so dark; she kept worrying that she might bump something, but her training had taught her to move carefully even in places with poor visibility.

Retrieving a pair of gloves from her pocket, she slipped them on and then reached for the door handle. No need to leave fingerprints. From what she knew about Eradian law enforcement, they had not yet established the practice of searching for such clues, but the contingency you didn't plan for was the one that destroyed you.

The door made very little noise as it swung inward.

Miri stepped into a dark hallway that ran the length of the south wing. The only light came from a balcony at the end of the corridor, much of it streaming up from the first floor. It was enough for her to make out the tables that had been positioned along the walls between every pair of doors. She could hear a piano and people singing somewhere downstairs. With any luck, they would stay there while she learned the layout of the mansion.

Turning away from the balcony, Miri went deeper into the south wing. She counted the doors on each wall. Four on her left. Four on her right. If the north wing was a mirror of this one, that meant sixteen rooms. They couldn't all be bedrooms. She suspected that some were used for other purposes. A library or a study, perhaps.

There was quite a bit of space between the last door on her right and its nearest neighbour. The master bedroom? Only one way to find out.

With a careful hand, she opened the door and poked her head through the crack. Lamplight coming through windows that looked out on the backyard allowed her to see a huge, four-post bed with curtains drawn. There was no doubt about it: this was Delarac's room. When Miri's eyes adjusted, she saw a vase on a table next to the window and another across from the foot of the bed. She listened for any sign that she might not be alone, but thankfully, she heard nothing. "Last room of the south wing," she whispered. "Backside of the house."

Gently, she closed the door.

Now, all she had to do was find an escape route, a way to get Delarac out of here unnoticed. It was no easy task, to be sure. Bringing him downstairs risked running into a servant. They might be able to take him out a window with Gravity-Sinks, but which window? She would need to locate a guest room. Or perhaps the man's study would do. With Sonic-Sinks to muffle the noise, no one would hear their escape. She was halfway back to the balcony when she heard footsteps on the stairs.

Miri spun, pressing her back against the wall and squeezing her eyes shut. She was deep enough in the shadows; if she stayed quiet, whoever was out there would not notice her. She hoped.

"Well?" someone asked in a thick New Beloran accent. "Did you put the comforter back on Miss Callie's bed?"

"Aye," another voice replied. "Though I don't know what to do with that one. She had me put it away two days ago."

"Well, this weather has been frightfully unpredictable," the first woman said. "Cold one day, warm the next."

Two maids stepped onto the balcony, both in gray dresses and white aprons, each wearing a bonnet in her hair. One was a fair bit older than the other: a stately woman with a pale complexion. The other couldn't have been more than twenty. Short and plump with dark skin, she carried a lit candle in one hand.

The younger woman put her hand on the railing, smiling at her companion. "Well, with this party coming..."

Closing her eyes, the older maid drew in a shuddering breath. "Don't remind me," she said. "Mr. Delarac insists on bringing half of his colleagues to this house. Mr. Phillips will find fault with something."

"Aye. Because he always finds fault with something."

"And then *we'll* take the blame."

What was this? Delarac was planning a social gathering? Miri was willing to bet that this Mr. Phillips was none other than Anthony Phillips, the representative for East Colton. And one of the most hawkish men in the House. Over the past month, Miri had requested the minutes from several sessions of Parliament from the Hall of Records. Dalen wasn't the only one who could read.

Phillips was one of the most strident voices in pushing for

military expansion, arguing in favour of securing more loans from just about every bank in the country to support the war effort. He seemed to think that there was great wealth to be found in Ithanar. If Phillips was on the guestlist for Delarac's party, then who else might be coming?

"Well," the older maid said. "Best you see to Miss Callie's room. They'll be heading to bed soon enough."

The younger woman did as she was told, stalking across the balcony and slipping into the darkness of the north wing. The other one went back down the stairs, muttering to herself.

Leaning against the wall, Miri shut let out a slow breath. So, Delarac was having a party. If her guess was right, he would be inviting more of his war-hawk friends. Which might present an opportunity.

But that could wait.

For the moment, the original plan was still in effect. She continued her search for a viable escape route. One way or another, Delarac would get what was coming to him.

KALIA SAT in the bubble of darkness that surrounded her. The window into Timothy Delarac's parlour was so dim she could barely see it. Her Light-Sink drained energy slowly. Not enough for total darkness – that might be conspicuous to anyone who looked out the window – but enough to conceal her in shadow.

One advantage of mental triggers over physical triggers was that you could control the rate of energy flow and the area of effect. The former directly influenced the latter. Her cloud of gloom became unnoticeable a few inches away from the house. So long as she didn't move too much, no one would spot her. So, she waited for the piano music to stop. And then she triggered her Sonic-Source.

Muffled voices became louder and more distinct. The coin amplified the distortion caused by the window pane, but Kalia was able to make out the words. She adjusted the rate of energy flow to manage the volume. She didn't know what she would hear. Hopefully not another conversation about taxes. She had listened to several of those already.

"And you've had no sign of her?" Robert Delarac asked. Kalia strained to listen. His voice competed with those of Danielle Delarac and her sister-in-law. The two women were quietly discussing a servant whose performance had been unsatisfactory. Of course, they would be closer to the window.

"We've searched, Robert," Timothy said. "But I'm afraid we've had no luck. We don't know what happened to Adele."

Kalia perked up.

"She wouldn't just leave!" Robert protested. "Not like that! Adele was always willful, but she had sense enough to-"

"Robert," Timothy cut in. "We will find her."

So, Timothy was hiding the fact that he had already located Adele. Which raised the question of where he was keeping her imprisoned. It had to be that. He wouldn't just let her run loose if he intended to make use of her powers. Adele was unstable. She might burn down a village just to ease her boredom. That kind of thing drew notice. So, where was he keeping her?

Not here, Kalia suspected. A house like this would be teeming with servants and family members stopping in to visit. It was far too likely that one of them would stumble upon something they weren't supposed to see.

"I'm sure we will," Robert said, though it was clear he didn't mean it. "I had hoped that you might have something. I'm afraid I'm not long for this city."

"You won't be staying for the party?"

"Another week in New Beloran? I find the idea frightful."

A gathering in one week, Kalia mused. *Miri will love to hear about that.*

It dawned on her that she was supposed to be mapping the house, but she was fairly certain that Miri would find the information she gathered here to be of greater use. She stayed for a few more minutes, but when the Delaracs failed to discuss anything of interest, she decided it was time to go.

DALEN KNEW that he should go to bed. It was his turn to sleep on the sofa tonight, and he was aching for some soft pillows after spending two nights sleeping on the floor. The men rotated between the living room and one of the bedrooms while the three women shared the other.

He knew that he should just get ready for bed, but he couldn't. His legs were filled with restless energy. He had to walk. So, he had left the apartment shortly after dinner, and he hadn't been back since.

The lamps on each sidewalk illuminated the tall, gray town-houses on either side of Halper Street. Most of the windows were dark. He caught a flicker of light now and then, but most people had turned in. A quarter moon hung in the sky, surrounded by stars.

In brown pants and a matching coat that fell to his knees, Dalen shuffled along with his hands in his pockets. He grew flustered, thinking about what Tommy and Miri might have been up to.

If Delarac had caught them...

Pausing, Dalen tilted his head back, and a cool breeze ruffled his hair. "There's no reason to think that," he muttered. "They've both faced down enemies that were far more dangerous than Timothy Delarac."

Soldiers, Field Binders, the walking dead: Tommy and Miri had gone up against them all and survived. That was the prob-lem. He was in love with two people who had shared the kind of epic adventures that belonged in a storybook. What could Dalen offer in comparison to that?

Tommy and Miri stood together on a battlefield while

Dalen Von Sasorin hid in a tent and prayed for the guns to stop. Tommy and Miri ran off to scout the enemy's house while Dalen sat down at Mrs. Carmichael's table and ate salted pork. It would be one thing if he could be out there with them. At least then he would have a modicum of control. But this sitting and waiting...

"You're worried about them, aren't you?"

Dalen shrieked.

Clamping a hand over his mouth to silence himself, he spun around, and his eyes widened. "Don't sneak up on me like that!" he yelped. "You scared me half to death!"

Jim stood under the light of a nearby lamp, backing away with his hands raised defensively. The poor man was mortified. "I...I'm sorry," he stammered. "I just thought that...Maybe I should go."

Heaving out a breath, Dalen strode forward with his head down. "No," he said. "I could use the company."

"Are you worried about..." Jim hesitated, no doubt trying to decide how much he wanted to say aloud. "Our friends?"

"Very much so."

Dalen jerked his head toward the nearest intersection, urging the other man to follow. He turned around and began marching up the sidewalk at a brisk pace. He wanted to be far away before anyone came outside to see what all the commotion was about.

They rounded a corner onto a street very much like the one they had left behind: a narrow lane sandwiched between townhouses that stood three stories high. An old, gray cat came skulking out of the shadows, but other than that, he saw no one. He supposed it was safe enough to speak his mind.

Dusting his hands to ease his anxiety, Dalen kept his eyes fixed on the ground under his feet. "I should be with them," he said at last.

Jim gave him a sidelong glance. "What would you do?"

"Nothing useful."

"Then why-"

Gritting his teeth, Dalen forced his eyes shut. "I don't know," he growled. "I just hate being left behind. It's a constant reminder that I am useless."

He was surprised to feel Jim's hand on his shoulder. The other man was looking at him with such sincerity. "You are *not* useless," Jim insisted. "I was there, Dalen. You practically ran that camp."

"I hid in a tent while you fought the enemy."

"You managed our food," Jim said. "Our supplies. It may not be glamorous, but we would have accomplished nothing without you."

Dalen searched for a retort, but nothing came to mind. Perhaps Jim was right. He had felt like luggage from the day they had left Aladar. Sure, he offered the odd nugget of information, but when it came to fighting, he was beyond useless. More of a liability than anything else.

He remembered the way Marcus used to glare at him. That man could shoot with precision, craft powerful Infusions and take down an enemy with his bare hands. But what did Dalen do when trouble showed up?

He hid.

"Not everyone is a fighter," Jim went on. "You can't build a world with nothing but fighters. You need clerks and librarians, doctors and philosophers. Playwrights! Rather than fret about the talents you don't have, celebrate the ones you *do* have."

Only then did Dalen realize that he had been muttering his thoughts aloud. Chagrin swept over him in a wave, nearly drowning out what the other man had said. Dalen took a moment to consider it. Jim knew about his shortcomings, but instead of reacting with disgust, he saw something worthwhile in Dalen.

"Thank you."

"Happy to help."

Without warning, the other man stepped forward and kissed Dalen's lips. He pulled back all too quickly, his face flushed with embarrassment. "I'm sorry," Jim whispered. "I shouldn't have done that."

Dalen was unable to suppress a smile. "At least you were willing to do that," he said softly. "Some people are too afraid of what others might think."

"Don't be too hard on Tommy. He doesn't always show it, but I can tell he feels responsible for what happened on Hebar's Hill. He's not spending all this time with Miri because he doesn't love you. He's doing it because he feels like he let us down."

Squinting at the other man, Dalen grunted. "You're a strange one," he said. "First you kiss me, then you urge me to make up with my partner."

Jim shrugged, then turned his head to stare up the street toward Mrs. Carmichael's building. "I never wanted to come between you and Tommy," he said. "I promised myself that I was going to keep those feelings buried. But sometimes things slip out."

"Sometimes they do."

"Shall we go back?"

"Yes," Dalen said with a curt nod. "I think that would be wise."

When they returned, Miri was sitting on the couch with hands folded in her lap. She had her eyes closed, breathing slowly as if she might fall asleep. Dalen was afraid to say anything. Perhaps it was best to let her rest and find out what had happened tomorrow.

Tommy stood with his hands braced against the wall on either side of the window, staring out at the darkness. "You're sure about this?" he asked. "You really think that it's our best option?"

"I am," Miri replied.

Hanging his coat on the rack, Dalen stalked into the living room with a soft sigh. "Do either of you plan to elaborate?" he inquired. "Or will you be speaking in code for the remainder of the evening?"

Kalia was seated on the small, wooden table, wrapped in the folds of her coat. She shivered. And no wonder! Out in that chill with nothing but a thin shirt for protection against the elements? It was a wonder that she hadn't caught her death. "Delarac is hosting a party in one week," she explained.

"I see..."

"We're going to raid it," Miri said simply.

Spinning around to face her, Dalen waggled a finger as he strode across the living room. "Now, let me be certain I understand the situation," he began. "The original plan was to capture Delarac and find out how he has been controlling Adele. But we are now eschewing that in favour of..."

Miri sat forward with her hands on her knees, glaring at him. "Many of his war-hawk friends are going to be there," she said. "The very architects of the campaign against the *Al a Nari.*"

"And you hope to accomplish what?"

"The architects of the war gathered in one place," Miri said. "If a few of them die, it'll be a strong message to the rest."

Dalen just stood there, slack-jawed and trying to think of something to say. "You're talking about murder," he managed at last.

Miri looked up at him, her eyes blazing with quiet fury. "And what do you call it when politicians send young soldiers off to die?" she asked. "When they order soldiers to kill people who have never posed a threat to anyone?"

Dalen scrunched up his face. This whole conversation was tying his stomach in knots. "I'm not saying that-"

Miri was on her feet in an instant, striding forward and forcing him to retreat. "This isn't a debate," she said. "This is happening. They thought the revolution died on Hebar's Hill. They were wrong. I suggest you get used to that reality because, in one week's time, we are putting an end to this war."

12

The noonday sun shone down from a clear, blue sky, casting silver rays upon the ancient city. In just a few short days, the place had changed from the ruin that Desa had found a year ago.

The buildings were now as strong and sturdy as they had ever been. Instead of empty holes, they all had windows in ornate frames. Paved streets ran between the lush, green lawns that surrounded every home. Flowers in every imaginable colour grew in quaint, little gardens. At this rate, Desa would not be surprised if Mercy started creating furniture. It was as if she expected the people who had once lived here to return.

"Very good," Mercy said.

Desa sat crosslegged on nothing at all, floating above a small house on the north side of the city. Her eyes were shut, her mind drifting through the exercises that allowed a Field Binder to contact the Ether.

"Yes, I'd say you've got it."

She opened her eyes to find Mercy hovering over the street in her crystalline form. The goddess sparkled, light refracting as it passed through her body. "You have a very disciplined mind, my dear."

"Well, I should hope so," Desa replied.

She killed her Gravity-Sink and dropped to the rooftop, landing crouched upon the building. Slowly, she rose and paced to the ledge. "When I came here, I was hoping to do more than repeat the exercises I learned as a girl."

Mercy descended to stand upon the roof. Her form changed with a flash of light, and then she was an ordinary woman with dark-brown skin and curly hair. "I'm sensing a little impatience."

"My friends need me," Desa said.

"Yes, that is the problem."

"I don't understand."

With a soft sigh, Mercy stepped forward and reached out to press her finger against Desa's forehead. "Perhaps it's time for your next lesson."

JUST LIKE THAT, Desa was somewhere else, in a room with walls that had been painted a soothing pastel-blue. Morning sunlight streamed through skinny, rectangular windows with brown muntin. She recognized the city on the other side of that glass.

Aladar.

Lifting her hands, Desa was surprised to see the smooth, delicate skin instead of the calluses that she had grown used to. Her body had changed as well. She was now a slip of a girl, just barely into adolescence.

"Desa Nin Leean!" someone barked.

She spun around to find five people seated behind a wooden table. The speaker was Rael Von Casian, a short and compact man with olive skin and rough stubble over his jaw. His face was lined with creases. And his eyes...Large, brown and full of scorn.

A woman sat on either side of him: one tall and dark with short, gray hair, the other plump and tanned with a string of pearls around her neck. Desa knew them both: Adria Nin Shaleen and Mavoni Nin Tarese. This was the Academy's Council Chamber. She had not seen this place in-

"Do you have anything to say for yourself?" Rael demanded.

Desa opened her mouth, but no words came to mind. Her brow furrowed as she tried to figure out what was going on. "How did I get here?"

Leaning forward with his hands on the table, Rael fumed. His glare threatened to slice her into little pieces. "Don't trifle with me, girl!" he snapped. "You know perfectly well what you did to end up here!"

"You revealed our secrets to an outsider," Adria put in.

"Treason!" Rael spat.

Clasping her hands together behind her back, Desa forced herself to stand tall, forced herself to look him in the eye. "Field Binding is not ours to hoard." She knew the words by rote. "If learning the Great Art can ease Radharal's pain-"

Rael's fist came down on the table, producing a loud *thump* that made Desa flinch. "Foolish child!" he thundered. "Do you have any idea what you've unleashed upon the world?"

Desa froze.

That wasn't how this was supposed to go. When she had lived this day eleven years ago, Rael had been angry but not feral. He had delivered a scathing lecture, canceled her academic credits and sent her home in disgrace. That was not what she saw in the man who now stood before her. This version of Rael wanted to tear her limb from limb.

Come to think of it, she didn't recall him ever saying anything about what she had unleashed upon the world. Rael's only concern back then had been the security of Aladar. Field Binding was the only thing that kept the mainlanders at bay. If Bendarian taught what he had learned to someone else...

She gasped when she noticed the blue walls fading to a dark, sombre gray. The floor changed as well and the table. Colour drained out of Rael's face as he snarled at her like an enraged beast. "This is what you have done!"

Backing away from him, Desa felt her mouth drop open. "No," she rasped, shaking her head. "It wasn't me."

She turned away to escape the ghastly scene playing out before her only to find that she was no longer in the Council Chamber. She stood upon a gray field under a blue sky, dressed in an old, brown duster and carrying a dagger in each hand.

A colourless man in ratty clothing stood only a few yards away. Gray from head to toe, he studied her with dead, black eyes, sizing her up with the intelligence of *Hanak Tuvar*.

He charged for her in a mad dash.

Desa leaped, pulsing her Gravity-Sink, and flipped upside-down over his head. Her blade sliced cleanly through his skull, and then she landed in the dry grass, scanning her surroundings.

A gray woman in an apron rushed toward her.

Tossing one dagger up, Desa caught the tip and then threw it as hard as she could. Her knife tumbled end or end, landing in the dead woman's chest, causing her to fall onto her backside.

"This is what you've done!" Rael boomed.

"No!" Desa whimpered.

Two more gray men dragged Tommy toward the wooden fence at the edge of the property. Her young protégé was clawing at the ground, searching for something to hold. He reached for her with an outstretched hand. "Mrs. Kincaid!" he pleaded. "Help me!"

Desa turned her back on him, intending to run – none of this was real – but she was confronted by a furious Miri who blocked her path. A gash dripped blood onto the other woman's forehead. "This is your fault," Miri hissed. "Your fault!"

"No, it isn't!"

Seizing Desa's shirt, Miri pulled her close. "You made me do it!" she wailed. "You made me kill him!"

A hard shove sent Desa staggering backward until she collided with a big man. She didn't have to look to know who it was. Marcus grabbed her shoulders. "If you had just done what you were told..."

She pulled free of his grip, running for the gray farmhouse, but the sound of his footsteps pursued her. "Why couldn't you just do as you were told?" Marcus groaned. "Why do you always think you know better than everyone else?" Reluctantly, she forced herself to turn around.

Marcus shambled toward her with his head down, his face hidden by the wide brim of his hat. "Why?" he asked. "Why can't you just listen?" Step by laborious step, he closed in on her.

At long last, he looked up, and Desa gasped. The skin on his face was rotting away; his eyes were shriveled up and yellow. "Two thousand years of tradition!" he wheezed. "But Desa knows better."

"We never would have gone to Ithanar," Miri lamented. "There would have been no need. If you had just done what you were told, you would have lived a fulfilling life in Aladar."

"You might have been head of the Academy," Marcus panted.

Rage flared hot within Desa. She refused to suffer through any more of this charade. "Enough!" she screamed at the top of her lungs.

The vision ended.

She was back on the rooftop with a mildly amused Mercy. The goddess sat upon a wooden chair that seemed to have come from out of nowhere, greeting Desa with a smile. "A difficult journey."

Striding toward the other woman, Desa bared her teeth in a snarl. Her heart was pounding. "That's all you have to say?" she exclaimed. "'A difficult journey?' I didn't come here to be tortured!"

Mercy nodded her agreement. "Quite right," she said. "Perhaps I should make amends."

She lifted her hand, and a ball of light appeared over her palm, growing brighter and brighter until the radiance consumed her. When it faded, Mercy had a piece of pie on a small plate. "A fair approximation of your mother's recipe," she said.

Dumbfounded, Desa took the plate. She was about to mention the lack of any utensils, but Mercy stretched out her hand, and another flash of light produced a fork. Was this what it had been like to live in this city under the care of a benevolent goddess?

"Sit," Mercy said.

A wooden chair materialized behind Desa, and she accepted the other woman's offer. She couldn't resist the urge to taste the pie. The tart flavour of strawberries exploded on her tongue along with a hint of sweetness.

Shutting her eyes, Desa moaned with satisfaction as she chewed. "You did it," she said, nodding. "It's exactly like the kind my mother used to make when I was little."

"Well, I had to work backwards from your memory." Mercy gave her a moment to finish eating before pressing on. "Shall we talk about what you saw in your vision?"

"My friends blaming me for teaching Bendarian how to Field Bind," Desa replied. "For setting all of this in motion. All of them jeering at me in ways that were completely out of character, even for Marcus. To be honest, the whole thing felt a little on the nose."

Covering a smile with one hand, Mercy chuckled. "The vision was a manifestation of your deepest fears," she replied. "The ones you shove into the back of your mind and try not to think about. If the presentation was unrealistic, perhaps you should consider what that says about the fears themselves."

Pausing with a forkful of pie halfway to her mouth, Desa eyed the other woman. "Thank you," she muttered.

"My pleasure."

SUNLIGHT MADE the massive crystal sparkle, casting patterns of colour onto the stone walls of the pyramid's central chamber. The air was stuffy and a little too warm, but that wasn't the source of Desa's discomfort. She had avoided this place since arriving in the ancient city. The place where she had fought Bendarian, where Adele had betrayed her.

The strange red light caused by *Hanak Tuvar's* intrusion into this world was gone. The stone was once again pale, the sky blue. Desa breathed a sigh of relief about that. She wasn't sure whether the change had been natural – the world healing itself – or a result of something Mercy had done. Either way, she was grateful for it.

Mercy floated up to the raised floor, alighting on its surface. She grunted, shaking her head in disapproval. "No, this won't do at all."

Desa climbed the steep, stone steps, joining the other woman beneath the crystal. Being here brought back a flood of memories. The anger, the exhaustion, the horror of Bendarian's serpentine face. She had shot him, stabbed him, frozen him with a Heat-Sink, but the man refused to die. "What won't do?" she mumbled.

Mercy gestured to a scorch mark on the wall, a black smudge on the pale stone. It was quite the blemish.

A flush set Desa's face on fire. "Sorry," she muttered. "I tried to blast him with lightning."

"Yes, I recall."

"You saw?"

Turning slowly on the spot, Mercy examined the room with a critical eye. "I witnessed some of it," she said absently. "But I'm afraid that I was much too busy trying to maintain my molecular integrity to have seen much."

Desa wasn't sure she wanted to know what that meant. It sounded as if Mercy was saying that she had been having trouble keeping herself together. Granted, she had been in a weakened state then, but the thought of a goddess falling apart was not one that she wanted to contemplate. *Mercy is not a goddess,* she reminded herself.

It did no good. She knew perfectly well that the woman who stood before her had once been a scientist named Nari, but that did nothing to settle her unease. Mercy may not have been divine, but she was powerful. For her to have been on the verge of disintegration...

Planting her fists on her hips, Desa looked up at the crystal. Colourful light fell upon her. "Is this where you lived?" she asked. "A grand temple to your magnificence?"

Mercy spared her a glance, then snorted and returned to her inspection of the scarred walls. "This place was a school," she said. "I built it to teach your ancestors how to Bind the Unifying Field. Children would sit on this floor and meditate. Come."

Without warning, Mercy flew up toward a hole in the wall that led into a tunnel, disappearing into the darkness. Desa had no desire to follow. She had fought Bendarian in those narrow passageways. But this might be part of the lesson.

Desa ran across the raised floor, then pulsed her Gravity-Sink and leaped. She somersaulted through the air and landed in the tunnel with a grunt.

Mercy stood with one hand against the corridor wall, a wry smile on her face. "A tad flamboyant," she said. "But you have an intuitive grasp of gravity. Quite impressive. For many people, that is the most difficult energy form to master."

"Why are there no stairs?" Desa asked. "If this was a school, how could anyone be expected to get up here without stairs?"

"The same way you did," Mercy replied. "This section of the pyramid was dedicated to the study of gravity. Students were required to show a mastery of the basic principles before progressing to more advanced lessons."

It took less than a minute to find a place where Desa had fired several shots into the wall while trying to hit Bendarian. She remembered that fight, the way he would appear and disappear, always trying to sneak up on her.

"I do hate it when my guests make a mess," Mercy whispered.

She pressed her palm against the stone. Crystal spread from her fingertips, over the back of her hand and all the way up to her elbow. Her arm began to glow, and when the light faded, it was covered in smooth, brown skin once again.

The bullet holes were gone.

Spinning on her heel, Mercy proceeded down a second tunnel that branched off from the main one. The luminous stones that Desa had shattered were still lying on the floor, and somehow, they were still Infused.

The goddess set to work, clearing out the rubble, repairing the damage. A year ago, Desa had wondered why this stubby, little corridor had come to such an abrupt dead end. It turned out that it had once been much longer.

The huge rock that Desa had mistaken for a wall was actually a part of the ceiling that had collapsed centuries ago. A wave of Mercy's radiant hand had it rising and fitting itself back into place.

When she was finished the hallway extended for another

hundred feet, ending in a window that looked out on the blue sky. Daylight made the place feel more cheerful, but it was the doors in each wall that filled Desa with a sense of wonder. Each one led into a small, empty room. Quite unremarkable, really, but she was certain that she could guess their purpose. "This is where the students took their lessons?"

Mercy nodded.

"I'm confused."

"What troubles you, my child?"

"When you brought me here," Desa began, coming up behind the other woman. "I thought you were going to teach me about Field Binding. Show me something that I can use against Adele."

Mercy turned around, arching a thin, dark eyebrow. "You already know as much about Binding the Field as any human could hope to learn," she said. "That technique you used to restore my power...I have taught thousands of students over the centuries, but only a handful of them could have done that."

"Then why am I here?"

Mercy poked her nose with a plump finger, causing Desa to flinch. "To learn about you," she said. "To become the person you need to be. The one who can defeat *Hanak Tuvar*."

FROM HER PERCH upon the roof of a small house, Desa admired the evening sky. The sun was a red ball hovering over the horizon, its light striking the enormous crystal at just the right angle to create a shower of sparkles. Like rubies spilling from a bag. A gentle breeze carried with it the scent of flowers. Mercy's doing, no doubt.

The goddess sat in her wooden chair with her eyes closed, bathed in the crimson glow. She kept drumming her fingers on her thigh, humming a tune that Desa had never heard before. She almost looked tired.

It was a very human moment: satisfaction after a hard day's work. Whatever Mercy may have become, the core of who she was remained.

Sitting by the ledge with her legs curled up, her arms wrapped around her knees, Desa drew in a breath. "So," she began. "You really think I should forgive myself?"

"I think you should accept that there is nothing to forgive."

"The Synod would not agree."

Stretching out her legs, Mercy sat back with her hands folded over her stomach She seemed to be searching for something in the twilight sky. "Tell me something, Desa," she said at last. "Why did you teach Bendarian the art of Field Binding?"

"Because the Synod is wrong," Desa replied all too quickly. "The knowledge of Field Binding does not belong to Aladar. And because, when he came to us, he was a broken man. I thought it might give him something to live for."

"So, it was an act of kindness."

Desa's answer to that was a shrug. "I suppose," she muttered under her breath. "That was certainly how I intended it."

"Then allow me to ask you this," Mercy countered. "You've saved many people over the years. What if one of them goes on to become a murderer?"

A frown tugged at the corners of Desa's mouth. She grunted, shaking her head. "It's not the same," she replied. "The Academy had strict rules about not teaching the Great Art to outsiders. They said it was because hostile, war-like cultures would only abuse the power of Field Binding."

A tear spilled over her cheek. She wiped it away with the back of her hand. "I thought those rules were foolish," Desa went on. "Chauvinistic. But my decision to disobey them has literally brought about the end of the world."

The warmth of Mercy's smile took some of her pain away. "Oh, child," the goddess said. "You are one node in a very complicated process. This was only one way that events might have played out, and many paths led to this outcome. Let go of your guilt, Desa. It does you no good."

"I can't."

"Yes," Mercy said. "You can. I think it's time you learned the true nature of your enemy."

13

The next morning, Mercy took her into the heart of the pyramid, into the sunlight that fell through the crystal. Clothed in a simple, yellow dress, the goddess stood upon the raised floor. Desa felt her pulse racing. Something about this reminded her of the final tests she had taken at the Academy, tests in which she had been made to demonstrate her proficiency with Field Binding to nearly a dozen instructors. Rael had called her Infusions barely passable. She suspected that nothing she could have done would meet with his approval.

This was it: the reason she had come to this wasteland on the edge of the known world. The secret to defeating *Hanak Tuvar*. For the first time in a very long while, she began to feel a smidge of hope. Maybe when this was over...Well, that could wait.

Climbing the stone steps, Desa planted herself in front of the other woman. She nodded once. "I'm ready."

"Are you?"

"As ready as I can be."

Mercy came forward with her arms folded, a stern expression on her face. Colourful light fell upon her as she approached Desa. "We shall see," she replied. "There is still one final lesson. The most difficult of all."

Desa sighed, shutting her eyes and trying to stifle her frustration. Patience. That was what Mercy expected from her. "I thought we were finished with lessons," she said. "What's this one about?"

"The consequences of your mistakes."

Gaping at the other woman, Desa shook her head. "Wait, wait, wait," she protested. "Last night, you told me that I had to forgive myself. Now, you want me to accept the consequences of my actions?"

"You will see."

Mercy snapped her fingers.

The next thing Desa knew, she was standing on a strange road between ugly, brown buildings. People milled about on the sidewalks, hundreds of them, all wearing fashions she had never seen before. Wool suits and caps for the men, frilly dresses and hats with feathers for the women.

She was so mystified by the sight of it that she barely noticed the car that came sputtering up the street. The driver honked his horn several times, pulling Desa out of her stupor. He was cranking the steering wheel, trying to swerve around her.

Desa threw herself sideways, rolling across the gravel road to the curb. She pushed herself up on two hands. This may have been a fantasy, but the sensations were real. She had scraped her shoulder, and it hurt!

The horn blared a few more times, drowning out the driver's curses as his car rolled past. She saw people watching her with wary expressions. No doubt they were wondering if she was in possession of all her faculties.

What city was this?

Her first thought was that it might be Aladar, but the buildings disabused her of any such notion. Squat structures constructed from brown bricks, each one showing skinny windows on all three floors: this was not Aladri architecture. And Aladar's roads were paved with tar!

This was not Ithanar either. Nothing that she saw made her think of the *Al a Nari*. So, where had Mercy taken her? Across the Caliad to the continent of Rondiri? She had dreamed about going when she was younger just to see what was there, but from what she had heard, the Rondirans had not developed this level of technology.

An old man with a gray beard and silver hair to match stood upon the curb, bending over to offer his hand. "Are you all right, madame?"

Desa let him help her to her feet. She dusted herself off, blinking a few times as she tried to get her bearings. "Thank you, sir," she mumbled. "This may be a silly question, but, where are we?"

Clasping his chin in one hand, the old fellow studied her the way a museum curator might study a painting. "Duster," he noted. "Leather boots. If you don't mind my saying so, ma'am, you look like one of those old bounty hunters?"

"Old bounty hunters?"

"They were legends when I was a boy," he explained. "Men and women who traveled across the country, bringing criminals to justice. One even came through my little village. Got me out of a spot of trouble. Come to think of it, you almost look like... Desa? Desa Kincaid?"

She stumbled backward into the street, squinting at him. "No," she hissed, shaking her head. "It's impossible."

"Desa, it's me!" He took a hesitant step toward her, offering his hand again. She saw no malice in his eyes, no hostility. "You never told me that Ether of yours can stave off old age. If you had, I might have taken Tommy's advice and learned."

"Sebastian?" she breathed.

"Yes!" His smile faded, and he let his arm drop, awkwardly

clearing his throat. "I realize you may not trust me after what happened...But you look like you could use a hot meal. We've got plenty to spare at the boarding house."

"The boarding house?"

He shoved his hands into his coat pockets, blushing hard as he averted his eyes. "Yes," he said. "A lot changed after we parted ways. I try to help those children who...Perhaps it was a foolish idea. Some bridges can never be mended, I suppose."

He turned to go, shuffling up the sidewalk. For a moment, Desa just watched him. Every hard-learned lesson warned her not to trust him. Not after he had betrayed her to Bendarian. But Mercy had sent her here, and she was certain that Mercy would not put her in harm's way. There was something here that the goddess needed her to see.

"Sebastian, wait!" she called out.

He froze.

Desa hurried after him, brushing the remaining dust off her coat. "I would welcome a hot meal," she said. "If you wouldn't mind."

He spun around to face her with a smile that could light up the darkest night. "I would be honoured!" he exclaimed. "It's the least I can do. I never did thank you for saving my life."

SEBASTIAN BROUGHT her to a blue house with black shingles on the slopes of its roof, a homey, little place with a garden in front. Inside, she found a kitchen with a wooden table and two young men standing over a gas stove.

One of them was pale and slim, the other short and broad-shouldered with a dark complexion. They seemed to be checking a pot of stew, stirring it with a wooden spoon.

Sebastian entered the room with his coat draped over one arm, grunting as he inspected their work. "I see supper is coming along," he said. "Well done, lads."

The boys whirled around to face him. "We thought we'd get it started," the short one said with a shrug. "I know it's Lisa's turn to cook, but she has a dreadful headache."

"So, you offered to take her place?"

The two young men shared a fond smile, and then – to Desa's delight – they kissed each other on the lips. "Cody wanted to teach me the recipe," the lanky one explained. "He said you taught him a few years ago."

Seating himself on a wooden stool, Sebastian held his coat against his chest. He chuckled softly. "I did," he admitted. "But Cody makes it better than I ever could. Run along now. It's your free day."

The boys hurried for the door.

"Actually, Cody!" Sebastian called out.

The shorter lad skidded to a stop, twisting around to look over his shoulder. Something about his demeanour made Desa pause. He was happy. If she understood this situation correctly, these two had both lost their parents and yet they were happy here. A rarity for boarding houses.

"Linger a moment," Sebastian said. "There's someone I want you to meet."

After a moment's hesitation, Desa stepped into the kitchen and nodded to the young man. "Hello." It was all she could think to say. She felt ludicrous standing here in clothes that marked her as a relic of a bygone era.

"This," Sebastian said, "is Desa Kincaid."

The boy's face lit up. "No way!" He slammed his hands down on the table, leaning over it to peer at her. You might have thought that he was looking at a character who had leaped out of the pages of a storybook. "It's really her?"

"It's really me," she confirmed.

"Oh, Sebastian told us everything!" Cody exclaimed. "How you fought off the sheriff's men and freed him from that cell. Can you really fly? He said that you can fly! How do you do it?"

Clearing her throat, Desa shot a glance toward Sebastian. "Everything?" she asked. "You told them everything?"

"Everything," he insisted. "Including the part where I betrayed you."

"And...what happened after that?"

"Oh, they know all about my life after I fled Ofalla," he said grimly. "The years I spent wandering, getting involved with the Eradian Army in their campaign against the southern continent, working in the steel mine..."

"I see."

Rising slowly from his stool, Sebastian offered a sad smile and a slight tip of his head. "One lesson that I've learned," he said. "It's no use trying to run from the truth. You have to face it."

He returned his attention to the boys. "Run along," he said. "I need a moment with Desa."

They were much more reluctant to leave now that they knew who had wandered into their kitchen. After a few false starts, they both went for the door, ducking into the backyard.

Sebastian moseyed over to the stove, taking the spoon and stirring the pot. "Dinner will be ready shortly," he informed her. "They did a fine job getting it started."

Ten minutes later, Desa had a hearty bowl of beef stew with carrots, green peas and potatoes sitting before her. And a good thing too! She was famished! "Sebastian," she began as he claimed the stool across from her. "I'm afraid that my memory isn't what it used to be. May I ask a difficult question?"

"Of course."

"What happened that night in Ofalla?"

He closed his eyes, exhaling slowly through his nose, visibly gathering his courage. "You found me in Bendarian's townhouse," he said. "You pointed your gun at me. For a moment there, I thought that you were going to shoot me."

"But I didn't?"

"No," Sebastian replied. "You told me to leave Ofalla and to never come back. You said that if you ever saw me again..."

He shuddered.

Reaching across the table, Desa laid a hand on his forearm. Her touch seemed to calm the poor man. "I'm sorry," she said. "For threatening you. I hated Bendarian, and you...No. There's no excuse."

His answer to that was bitter laughter. "Desa, it's no more than I deserved," he insisted. "You risked your life to save me, and I repaid you with betrayal. It took a long time for me to realize that I hated you for all the wrong reasons."

"Because I'm a woman?"

"There may have been a bit of that," he admitted. "But the truth is I hated you for being all the things I wanted to be. You never hid your attraction to other women. You openly practiced magic – I'm sorry, Field Binding. You lived the kind of life that you wanted to live, making apologies to no one. And I resented you for that.

"One day, about ten years after we parted ways, I realized that if I wanted to be happy, I had to accept myself. After that, I refused to live in shame."

She took a moment to appreciate the home he had created: the sound of laughter from the floor above, the good food, the children who were free to be themselves without fear of judgment. Sebastian had done this. "Well," Desa murmured. "It seems like you've done pretty well for yourself."

He laughed again, but this time, there was no bitterness in it. "Thank you," he said. "I created this place to be a home for people like us. Boys who fall in love with other boys and girls who fall in love with other girls. Some of them are cast out from the homes they knew as children. Others flee. They come here, and they feel safe."

"That's wonderful, Sebastian," she whimpered, unable to hold back her tears. "You should be proud of yourself."

"Thank you."

The vision ended abruptly, the kitchen fading away to darkness. She found herself lying on the raised floor in Mercy's pyramid, curled up on her side and sobbing. And she understood.

At long last, she understood.

TEN MINUTES LATER, Desa sat on the edge of the platform, hunched over and pawing at her face to wipe the tears away. "Thank you," she choked out. "I know why I needed to see that."

"It can't have been easy," Mercy said behind her.

Twisting around, Desa held the other woman's gaze. "No," she said, shaking her head. "It wasn't. But I understand now. That is what he would have become if I had let him live."

Mercy stood there like a teacher whose student had come oh so close to the right answer without actually finding it. "No, I'm afraid you don't understand," she countered. "That is what he *could* have become if you had let him live. The future is not written, Desa. We make it every day."

"What do you mean?"

"There are millions of different paths," Mercy said. "Millions of ways that his life could have unfolded. In some, he becomes a murderer, in others, a healer. We are the sum of our choices, Desa. The point is that Sebastian had potential, potential to become greater than what he was when you knew him. You robbed him of that opportunity."

Desa forced herself to stand, turning around to face the other woman. She couldn't bear to lift her eyes from the floor. "What are you saying?" she whispered. "That I should never take a life again?"

"No," Mercy replied, shaking her head. "It's not that easy. Life cannot be reduced to simple rules. Killing Adele, for instance – if you can manage it – might save millions of lives. I am saying that you must use violence as a last resort."

That made sense. Truth be told, she had never been cavalier about harming other human beings. It was a luxury that Field Binding afforded. You didn't have to shoot first if you could stop bullets. Wait...

Something Mercy had said rattled around in her brain. Something she had glossed over. "What was that?" Desa asked. "About killing Adele?"

The goddess sighed. "It's time for you to learn the truth." Just like that, the world changed. Everything vanished, leaving her alone with Mercy in a void of infinite darkness. And yet, she could still see the other woman. Her first instinct was to panic. If there was no air, she would be unable to breathe. But she felt no pressure on her chest.

Stumbling backward, Desa looked around frantically. "What is this?" she panted. "Where are we?"

Mercy spread her arms wide, gesturing to the infinite nothing all around them. The goddess almost looked eager. As if this were a story that she had wanted to tell for a very long time. "This is called cosmic inflation."

"I don't understand."

"The expansion of space and time."

Confusion settled over Desa. There were scientists in Aladar who believed that the universe was expanding, but she couldn't see what that had to do with *Hanak Tuvar*.

Before she could say a word, Mercy receded into the distance, vanishing into the endless darkness. It happened so quickly that she almost missed it. "Hey!" Desa shouted. "Where did you go?"

"I went nowhere," Mercy said, coming up behind her. The woman's sudden appearance made Desa stiffen and reach for a weapon that she was not carrying. "I was perfectly stationary. The space between us grew."

"Rather quickly, it seems," Desa observed.

The goddess hummed a jolly tune as she strolled through the emptiness. "Yes," she said, twirling around so fast her skirt fanned out. "You might say that this was the cradle of existence. Space expands and expands in perfect uniformity, but then...Look."

Desa examined her surroundings, unsure of what to expect. It took her a moment to find what the goddess was trying to show her. Orange dots appeared, hundreds of them in every direction. There were even more above her and more below as well. These too began to expand.

The space between them grew even faster so that they never collided. Each dot swelled to the size of a pea and then to the size of a marble. And finally, to a ball that she could hold in the palm of her hand.

"What are they?" Desa breathed

Mercy giggled, leaning sideways to peek at her from behind one of the glowing orbs. "Universes," she said. "Millions of them, all taking shape, developing a unique set of properties."

Desa turned slowly on the spot, taking in the sight. "Millions of universes," she whispered. "I never dreamed there could be so many."

"Most are inhospitable to humans."

Desa reached for one. Just before her fingertips brushed it, she heard whispers in her mind. Harsh, discordant. Like thousands of voices all speaking incomprehensible words. Somehow, she understood what it meant; this universe was home to life, but it was completely alien to her.

The next one produced no sound whatsoever. Nor did the one after that. Dead universes then? If what Mercy said was true, some of these might have properties that would preclude the existence of intelligent life.

"Here," Mercy said, standing behind one of the pulsing

spheres. Its flickering light cast shadows over her face. "This is your universe, Desa. Come and see!"

Approaching with caution, Desa reached for the ball of light. Once again, she heard voices in her head, but these were intelligible.

"Friends, we have traveled long and far," a woman boomed. "This island will be our home, a testament to the glory of our matron goddess. We are the *Al a Dri,* the people of Vengeance."

"One hundred ships to sail across the Great Anrael," a man declared. "To settle the savage continent and tame it in the name of the Crown. It shall be called Eradia, the new home of our people."

Desa recoiled, shaking her head in disgust. "That's quite enough of that," she growled. "I know more about my world's history than I would like to."

When she turned around, another universe hung in the infinite blackness, glowing and pulsing like a giant firefly. Maybe she was imagining it, but she almost thought she could feel the warmth. Curiosity made her stretch her hand toward it.

"The snow," a voice whispered in her mind. "The storms have come. Many still pray to the gods, but there is no longer any doubt in my mind. They have forsaken us. The world freezes..."

She left that universe and moved on to another. There was nothing to distinguish one from the next; they all looked the same. But somehow, she could sense which ones contained human life. Those were an extreme minority: dozens out of trillions.

"The imperative is clear," a woman declared. "Expand or die. We will not know stability until the Empire's borders stretch to every corner of the map."

She abandoned that universe, wandering through the blackness. It was a relief to know that her world was not the only one to contain violent, war-like cultures, that her people were not an aberration.

She continued her exploration, passing several more universes before one caught her eye. She wasn't sure what had drawn her to it. Intuition, she supposed. When she reached for it, a man's confident voice spoke in her mind.

"We choose to go to the Moon in this decade and do the other things, not because they are easy, but because they are hard; because that goal will serve to organize and measure the best of our energies and skills."

Well, that was positive, at least.

Letting her arm drop, she turned away from the ball of light and made her way back to Mercy. "All right," she said. "I am humbled by the majesty of creation. But if you will forgive my impertinence, what does any of this have to do with *Hanak Tuvar?*"

Mercy didn't answer her with words; she just pointed into the void above her head. Desa had to strain to see it, but once she did, a lump of fear settled into the pit of her stomach.

Tendrils of darkness slithered through the gaps between universes, blacker than the blackness. Greedy tentacles, slick and oily, they searched for something – anything – to grasp. Desa had encountered many things in her travels, but these filled her with a terror like nothing she had ever experienced before.

"*Hanak Tuvar* does not come from another universe," she mumbled. "It comes from emptiness between universes."

"It is a creature of the void," Mercy confirmed. "Of the primordial emptiness. We have intruded upon its solitude, and it wishes to punish us for our transgression."

Desa would never have believed that such a thing was possible. She knew little of the grander cosmos. If *Hanak Tuvar* predated not just her universe but every other one as well, there was no telling what it might be capable of.

The vision that Mercy had created faded away, leaving them once again inside the pyramid. The air was warm, but Desa still felt as though her blood had been frozen solid. She had no idea how to fight this entity.

"My people discovered that the Unifying Field can bridge two universes," Mercy explained. *"Hanak Tuvar* detected us and followed one of our expeditions back to our world. It came through the gateway, destroying everything in its path, reducing the capital city rubble.

"We counterattacked, but even our most powerful weapons were useless against it. In less than two months, it had rendered over thirty percent of the planet's surface uninhabitable."

Desa felt the blood draining out of her face. "How?" she asked, storming up to the other woman. "It *can't* be that powerful."

Shutting her eyes, Mercy drew in a calming breath. "Do you recall what happened on the day that it took possession of Adele?" she asked. "How the light changed and your metal tools melted?"

Desa nodded.

"In its true form, *Hanak Tuvar* can alter reality itself. It changed the laws of nature, leaving pockets where organic life cannot survive. Nearly a dozen people volunteered to be part of my Transcendentalist Project, hoping to become strong enough to challenge *Hanak Tuvar*. Dri was the first to succeed, and I followed soon after. But even together, we were overmatched.

"I began to search for a compatible universe in the hopes that some of us might escape and live on. We found a pristine world, untouched by human civilization. Dri and I led two million people through the gateway. Two million out of eight billion. We saved as many as we could.

"For a time, we thought we were safe. The survivors divided into three groups: those who would follow Driala, those who would follow me and those who wanted nothing to do with either of us. It was inevitable that conflict would arise.

"Thirty-seven years after we came to this world, *Hanak Tuvar* followed us through the gateway, hoping to finish what it had started. The three tribes united for the last time, making a final stand. But their efforts were for naught. *Hanak Tuvar* cannot be destroyed.

"In a last act of desperation, Dri and I created a pocket within the Unifying Field, and together, we lured *Hanak Tuvar* into our trap. Once we had it contained, we sealed it away in a bubble, floating at the very edge of this universe.

"The decades passed in relative peace, but without a common adversary, the three tribes fractured. Old hatreds began to fester. I built this school to teach the Great Art to anyone who would learn, hoping that the crystal would accelerate the process. This city flourished, and my people regained much of what we had lost.

"Then the first attacks came.

"Driala's people had used the Great Art to create terrible weapons. I was horrified to discover that she had created a school of her own. And that she had used it to teach her students how to kill. And all the while, *Hanak Tuvar* whispered in the minds of those who were susceptible to its evil."

Unsure of what else to do, Desa threw her arms around the other woman. The warmth she felt when Mercy returned her embrace was surprising. It was like being hugged by her mother. "It's not your fault," Desa whispered.

Chuckling, Mercy pulled away from her. "The student becomes the teacher," she said. "No, I suppose it isn't."

"You said that killing Adele might save lives," Desa pressed. "How exactly would that work?"

With a sigh, Mercy looked up at the crystal, colourful light falling on her face. "The prison we created was designed to pull

Hanak Tuvar back in," she said. "Adele is its only anchor to this universe. If her physical form is destroyed…"

"That's it?" Desa spluttered. "All I have to do is kill her?"

"It's no easy task," Mercy admonished. "You have inflicted grievous injuries on her, and yet she survives. *Hanak Tuvar* can repair the damage."

"Then how?"

"There may be a way," Mercy said. "But you will have to lure her here. Come. I will show you."

MERCY LED her to the roof of the pyramid, where the giant crystal glittered in the sun. Desa could feel it pulsing, singing to her in her mind. If what Rojan said was correct, this thing contained some of Mercy's essence.

"Yes," Mercy said, guessing her thoughts. "There is a piece of me Infused into the crystal."

Desa stood with her arms folded, frowning at her distorted reflection. She ran her finger over the crystal's surface. "So, what am I supposed to do with this?" she asked. "Create a thousand Infused bullets?"

"You've learned that you can temporarily disrupt Adele's power by manipulating the Unifying Field."

"Yes."

She saw Mercy's shadow before she felt the woman's hands on her shoulders. "Concentrate," the goddess said. "Reach through the crystal and make yourself one with the Field."

Clearing her mind, Desa did as she was told. It was easy with those pulses lighting the way. She pulled the Ether through the crystal, and the world changed. Particles did their endless dance, but they were insignificant compared to the radiance that drowned out her awareness of everything else. It was as if she stood before a star.

It took her a moment to collect herself, but when she did,

she realized that she could sense...everything. Her awareness extended for miles! Past the edge of the desert and the sparse fields beyond its eastern border. Past the curve of the Vinrella and the tiny village of Thrasa on its northern bank.

She followed the route she had taken a year ago back to Ofalla. The city was abuzz with activity, people hurrying this way and that, going about their daily lives. It was hard to track them – even with the crystal, her mind could not process that much information – but the fact that she could sense them at all from nearly five hundred miles away was remarkable.

She directed her thought southward, over the vast expanse of empty wasteland, beyond the desert to Pikeman's Gorge. A caravan of people and horses was coming north. Once again, it was hard to track any one individual, but she could sense the group.

And she could sense Mercy.

The goddess shone as brightly as the crystal, a warmth that drove away fear and hurt and loss. "Very good," she said. "With this, you can manipulate the Field to greater effect. You will be able to obstruct Adele's power for more than a few seconds. Long enough for her body to die."

Desa severed herself from the Ether.

"So," she said. "Bring her here, and use the crystal to finish her off."

"Essentially."

"Good," Desa whispered. "That, I can do."

14

Tommy walked with a heavy heart down a street lined with gray houses. Tonight was the night; Delarac's party would begin in three hours. The architects of his disgusting war all gathered in one place. Tonight, they would pay for their sins.

Tommy was ready.

He had gone over the plan a hundred times with Miri and Kalia; he knew his role backwards and forwards. Strangely, he didn't feel much apprehension, only sadness. Men would die by his hand. He accepted that necessity, but he could never make himself like it. Perhaps that was a good thing.

Reminding himself that every one of those bastards had condemned hundreds of men to die on foreign shores helped matters. Or maybe it just drowned the guilt in rage. He couldn't tell. All he knew was that tonight, *he* was going to war, and he might not be coming back. A good time to sort out those niggling concerns that he would hate leaving unattended.

He found Dalen shuffling up the sidewalk on his way home from work. Just the sight of the other man made his heart flutter. Tall, lean, tanned with short, brown hair and just a hint of stubble: Dalen was a masterpiece. But it wasn't just a handsome face that drew Tommy's eye. The man had the kindest heart in the world.

Of course, Dalen walked with his head down, lost in his own private reverie. He didn't look up and notice Tommy until they were just about to collide. "Oh," he stammered. "Hi."

"Hi."

"What...What?"

Slipping his hands into his pockets, Tommy smiled down at himself. "I thought I'd join you for the walk home," he said with a shrug. "If you wouldn't mind the company, that is."

"I'd love the company."

They walked in silence for nearly a minute. Tommy kept scanning the tall, gray houses on either side of the road, hoping to catch a face in one of those dark windows. Or perhaps hoping not to. It was just instinct. Spend enough time planning clandestine affairs, and you learned to take stock of your surroundings before you opened your mouth. "How is book-keeping treating you?" he asked at last.

Dalen forced a smile. "Not bad," he said. "Not as exciting as what you-"

Tommy gently touched his arm, quieting him. Some things were best not discussed in the open. Luckily, Dalen sucked in a breath and nodded as if to say that he understood. "My apologies."

"Think nothing of it."

"Jim seems to like the work."

"That's wonderful."

Something was off. He could feel the other man's tension. Dalen wanted to say something, but he was holding back. Well, that simply wouldn't do. If Tommy had learned one thing over this past year, it was that love required honesty.

He took Dalen's hand.

The other man froze, looking over his shoulder with utter shock on his face. "Oh," he mumbled. "I thought...I thought..."

Unable to help himself, Tommy broke out in a fit of laughter. "What can I say?" He pulled Dalen close for a peck on the cheek. "I spent a lot of time worrying about what people might think if they saw me expressing my true feelings. And then I remembered that I'm a Field Binder."

Dalen touched his nose to Tommy's, their foreheads pressed together. "That does make things easier, doesn't it?"

"Much."

"So..."

At a gesture from Tommy, they started up the street again. He was amazed to find that he wasn't afraid. All those people who might have been looking out from any one of those windows? Let them see the truth and say what they would. He might be dead in a few hours; he didn't have time to fret about the opinions of backward-thinking townsfolk.

They walked hand in hand for a little while, but it wasn't long before Dalen grew tense again. "I...I have to tell you something," he began. "And I want you to know that I didn't plan any of this."

When Tommy spun to face the other man, Dalen was breathing hard, mouthing words that he couldn't bring himself to speak. "Jim kissed me," he said at last. "I wasn't expecting it. I didn't ask for it!"

Tommy's eyebrows shot up. "Interesting."

"It is?"

Tommy answered that with a shrug and a sheepish grin. "I already share you with Miri," he said. "I can't see the harm in sharing you with one more person. If you return his feelings, that is."

"I...I honestly don't know."

Resting his hands on the other man's shoulders, Tommy kissed Dalen softly on the lips. "Well, I guess you'll have to figure it out," he said. "But there is one thing I want to tell you."

"What's that?"

"I know I've been spending a lot of time with Miri lately," Tommy murmured. "For obvious reasons. But that doesn't mean I love you any less. It's not a competition. And I need you to know that."

He found relief in Dalen's large, brown eyes. Relief and understanding. "I do. I just wish I could help with…you know."

Backing away, Tommy paused for a moment to regard the other man. "You have!" he insisted. "You think we could have done any of this without you? Paying the bills and doing the research might not be glamorous, but without you, we never would have made it this far."

"I suppose."

"Come on."

It took another twenty minutes to get home. Their open affection earned a few questioning stares from the people they passed, but Tommy was ecstatic to find that his fear was gone. True, there was the possibility of drawing unwanted attention from the City Watch, but he was willing to risk it. This might be his last chance to share an intimate moment with Dalen.

They found Miri and Kalia in the living room upon arriving at the apartment. Both women had donned their black clothing. He could already tell that Miri was carrying the Infused accessories that he had made.

She had her back turned as she laced her boots. Twisting around, she shot a glance in his direction. "Out for a walk?" she asked. "You should be getting ready."

Tommy leaned one shoulder against the wall, cocking his head as he studied her. "We have time yet," he replied. "The sun won't be down for another hour, and we certainly can't risk traveling by daylight."

"I suppose."

"Maybe you might like to have a quiet moment with Dalen," Tommy suggested. "Given that this will be a risky endeavour."

Miri stood up slowly, turning around to face them full on.

At first, Tommy thought she might protest, but her face softened. "You're right," she said. "Come on, my love. We should talk."

They disappeared into the bedroom, leaving Tommy alone with Zoe, Victor and Kalia. The young lovers were sitting on the sofa, murmuring soothing things to one another. Tommy decided to let them have their privacy.

Kalia stood by the window with her arms folded, looking out on the street below. He was confident that he could guess what the poor woman was thinking about. She missed Desa.

It was unfair. He and Miri had been given a chance to say their good-byes to the man they both loved. Kalia had no such opportunity.

Joining her at the window, Tommy chose his words with care. "She knows you love her," he murmured. "She always has."

Kalia looked up, blinking. A smile replaced her puzzled expression in an instant. "I certainly hope so," she replied. "But Desa can be a bit thick when it comes to matters of the heart."

"I haven't known her much longer than you have," Tommy said. "But one thing I learned very quickly is that Desa runs when she feels overwhelmed. Ten minutes after she told me about killing Sebastian, she hopped on Midnight and fled into the desert. It was easier than facing me."

"And you think she's running from me?"

Tommy grinned and shook his head. "No, I think she's running from herself," he said. "From the guilt that is always two steps behind her. She thinks that if she can fix her mistakes-"

"Then she'll finally have peace."

"Yeah." He racked his brain for words, for something to say that might ease Kalia's anxiety. "I don't know what she's gonna find in that desert. But I do know she'll survive it. And she will be coming back to you. So, let's make sure you do the same."

"Thank you, Tommy."

He grunted when the tiny woman threw her arms around him in a fierce hug.

THE NIGHT WAS cool but not painfully so. Tiny stars twinkled over the city. Tommy felt the wind cutting right through his black clothing, but he heard nothing. The Sonic-Sinks that muffled his footsteps silenced everything else as well. He wore a black mask with two eyeholes. And just to be on the safe side, he had shaved.

With his bow in hand and a quiver slung over his right shoulder, he ran along the peak of a gabled roof. A Gravity-Sink in his belt buckle kept him from falling, one of several that he had created over the past week.

At the edge of the roof, Tommy leaped

He sailed effortlessly over a narrow alley, then killed his Sink and somersaulted across the flat top of the next building over. A second later, he was on his feet again and running at full speed.

Miri and Kalia were nearby, following routes that ran parallel to his. He could feel their Infusions even at this distance, especially Miri's. Hers, he sensed all the time. He only detected Kalia's by the stirring in the Ether when she used them.

Fifteen minutes later, he stood silently in the street outside Delarac's mansion. He sensed Miri's approach before he saw her falling out of the sky. She touched down in a dark spot between two lamps, massaging a sore back. Tommy hissed when he imagined the jolt she must have experienced. Using a Gravity-Sink for a controlled fall was no easy task. None of them had Desa's finesse.

Not missing a beat, Miri spun around and strode right

toward him. How she found him was a mystery. She couldn't feel his Infusions the way he felt hers.

She was gesticulating forcefully, glancing about as if searching for something. It took a moment for him to realize that she was trying to speak. The Sonic-Sink that she had failed to deactivate swallowed her every word.

He tapped her second button.

"What?" she snapped. "Oh. Thank you."

"What were you saying?"

Miri turned her head, staring off toward the wall that surrounded Delarac's property. "I was asking if you were ready."

Before he could answer, Kalia dropped out of the sky to land gracefully in the road. She dusted her hands as if she had just finished sweeping her kitchen floor and then joined them in the shadows. "I think I'm getting the hang of this."

"Lovely," Miri growled. "Are we ready?"

Setting his jaw, Tommy nodded once. "Ready," he said.

"Ready," Kalia echoed.

"Then there's no sense in dawdling."

They formed a line with Tommy in the middle and the two women on either side. Together, they began a sprint across the street, each one pulsing their Gravity-Sinks as they leaped.

One by one, they soared over Delarac's wall, dropping to land in the grass of his front yard. And then they ran. Tommy was in the lead at first, but Miri quickly overtook him, scrambling toward the mansion at full speed. Kalia managed to keep pace with him.

They made no effort to hide. If someone saw them, it wouldn't matter. By the time whoever it was warned Delarac, it would be too late.

The house grew larger and larger as Tommy charged through the field. He saw lights in almost every one of its windows. The place was abuzz with activity: that much was certain.

Miri tapped her belt twice and then jumped, hurling herself up to the slanted roof. She landed perched upon the shingles, waiting.

The instant he got within range, Tommy ordered his buckle to feast on gravitational energy. The wind whistled around him as he rose into the air. What a rush! Nothing in this world compared to it. How was it possible that he had never known about the Ether until Desa came along? He let gravity reassert itself for half a second, bringing himself down in a gentle descent.

Kalia was right on his heels.

"Come on," he said.

He took off across the length of the north wing, heading for the main building. His nimble feet barely touched the shingles; the Gravity-Sink lessened his weight without completely freeing him from the Earth's pull. Poor Miri. A physical trigger restricted an Infusion to performing one task and only one task. For her, it was either complete weightlessness or nothing at all. Still, she kept pace.

As he neared the central structure, Tommy jumped and grabbed the lip of its roof. He pulled himself up, then rolled aside to make room for his companions. They were quick to follow.

Wasting no time, Tommy got up and moved toward the back of the mansion. The ballroom had a skylight, a round window framed by metal beams that expanded from the centre.

He crawled closer, peering through it. He found aristocrats in fancy suits dancing a slow waltz while others sat at tables near the walls. There must have been at least fifty guests. Probably more. Tommy fished a small coin out of his pocket, tossing it onto the skylight.

Twisting around, he shared a glance with the two women who followed him. "It's time," he said. "Are we ready?"

They both nodded.

"Stand clear."

They moved to a safe distance, and then Tommy triggered the Force-Source that he had created for this specific purpose. Glass shattered, raining down on frightened guests who screamed in terror.

Tommy loped across the rooftop and then dropped through the opening, using his Gravity-Sink to control his descent. He landed in the middle of the dance floor, bending his knees upon impact.

Gathering his courage, he stood up straight and scanned the room. "What can I say?" he teased. "I like to make an entrance."

Most of the guests were pressed up against the walls, forming a haphazard square around the perimeter of the room. A few were still sitting at their tables. And they all looked like they were ready to faint.

Kalia came down on his right and then Miri on his left, both grunting when they hit the floor. Like him, they wore black masks to hide their faces. The partygoers must have thought they were being robbed.

One man, an older fellow with thick, gray sideburns and curly hair, turned and bolted for the door. He nearly tripped over a fallen chair, but that didn't stop him.

Retrieving an arrow from his quiver, Tommy twisted around and raised his bow. Nock, draw and loose. It was as easy as breathing. The weapon had become an extension of his body.

His arrow zipped past the fleeing man and drove itself into the tiles about three inches away from the door. Tommy triggered the Force-Sink he had Infused into it, and the old fool froze in mid-step.

Several people gasped at the sight.

The cowardly, old codger had one foot lifted off the floor, his arms flung out wildly. But he did not fall. It was as if time had stopped in a small pocket around his body, which – for all intents and purposes – it had.

"I don't recall giving anyone permission to leave," Tommy said. He searched the room and found Timothy Delarac in the corner with a glass of wine in hand. Something was off there. The host of this party should have said something by now. "Now, where is Anthony Phillips?"

The man he had named stood up from a nearby table. Phillips was tall with a bit of a belly. He had the kind of face you'd never forget: square with a thick, gray mustache and matching hair that was much too thick for a man of his age. "What is the meaning of this?"

No cowardice there.

Tommy sauntered up to the man, a wolfish grin revealing his intentions. "You've argued quite passionately for the war in Ithanar," he said. "You arranged the loans that financed this new expansionist policy."

Phillips drew himself up, puffing out his chest. "And quite proudly, sir," he declared. "If you think I'm going to cower before rabble like you."

Tommy was about to reply, but the sound of wood scraping on tile made him turn around. One of the younger guests – a heavyset man with broad shoulders – got out of his chair, slipped through the space between two tables and charged onto the dance floor.

Stretching his hand out, Tommy released a wave of kinetic energy from his ring. The young fool was thrown backward, hurled across the room as if by a powerful wind. He slammed into the wall.

Some of the tables had been displaced as well, their occupants tossed out of their chairs. One woman was down on her belly while her husband knelt at her side, muttering something that Tommy couldn't hear.

He caught the flicker of motion a second too late.

A young man in the corner got up and drew his revolver. He cocked the hammer, pointing the weapon at Tommy.

Before he could fire, a knife sank into his shoulder, causing him to yelp and drop the gun. He stumbled backward, clutching the wound and hissing air through his teeth. Some of the others started shrieking.

Kalia fired several shots through the skylight. The thunder of gunfire drowned out everything else, and when it faded, Delarac's guests were silent. "That's better," she said.

"Let me be perfectly clear!" Tommy boomed. "No one is getting out of this room unless I let them go. So, I suggest you all sit down and enjoy the show. Because, tonight, court is in session."

He rounded on Anthony Phillips, prompting the other man to step back. "You!" he growled, pointing an accusing finger. "You stand accused of carrying out a war of aggression against your neighbours. You have already admitted your guilt."

"I am guilty of nothing!" Phillips spat. "The Empire conquers by divine right. We need not justify ourselves to-"

Tommy's hand was a blur as he pulled an arrow from his quiver. He nocked it, drew back the bowstring and loosed.

The shaft punched right through Anthony Phillips's forehead, protruding from the back of his skull. The old man twitched a few times before keeling over on his side.

Some of the others were weeping.

Why was Delarac silent? The things Desa had said about him indicated a pompous man who did not take kindly to being challenged. Surely, he would have *something* to say about all this! But no. He just stood there, watching.

"Now," Tommy said. "Where is Adam Miller?"

The instant he finished speaking, a spindly man with flecks

of gray in his brown hair got out of his seat and ran. Not for the door. For the window at the back of the room.

Tommy's first instinct was to use a Gravity-Source, but that would be dangerous. Even with directional modifiers, it would pull more than just Miller to him. He wouldn't look very intimidating dodging plates and knives. He was about to reach for an arrow, but he needn't have bothered.

One of Miri's throwing knives landed in the back of Miller's thigh, forcing the man down onto his knees. Tommy could hear him sobbing. Some of the other guests shied away from him, eager to avoid whatever punishment Miller would receive. Wasn't that just way with aristocrats? Rats fleeing a sinking ship, every last one of them.

Grinding his teeth, Tommy felt a wave of heat in his face. He narrowed his eyes as he approached the condemned man. "Mr. Miller," he said. "Last year, a bill came before parliament to formally abolish slavery throughout the empire."

Miller didn't answer.

"You organized a resistance to that bill," Tommy went on. "Convinced several MPs to change their votes from yea to nay. And as a result, slavery is still in practice on the southern coast."

Miller had his back turned, but Tommy could see that he was trembling, weeping bitter tears. "Please," he begged. "Don't."

Tommy stopped dead, unable to believe his ears. Was this fool really pleading for his life? Did he think that he could escape the consequences of his actions. The answer was obvious: of course, he did. Wealthy people always thought they were untouchable. "Why not?" Tommy replied. "You were willing to condemn thousands of innocent people to brutal conditions? Why should we spare you?"

"Please!"

Tommy seized another arrow, nocking it and drawing back

the string. He took aim and let loose before the man could say another word. Miller stiffened when the shaft went through his skull.

Tommy ran his gaze over the crowd, his eyes hard and merciless. "There is nowhere you can hide from us!" he shouted. "Nowhere you can run! Your mansions aren't safe. Your country estates aren't safe.

"War, slavery, the flagrant abuse of the poor for your own profit: do these things, and we will hunt you down like dogs. And just when you think you've escaped us, when you've fled to the one place we can't find, that is when we will come. And the very last thing you will ever see...will be us." Some of the guests started murmuring. Good. He had gotten his point across. "Now, run and tell everyone what you have witnessed here tonight."

Just as they began to rise, the sound of clapping echoed through the ballroom. He looked up to find a black-clad Adele hovering above the dance floor, smiling viciously down at her uncle's horrified guests. "Glorious!" she said. "I was going to kill every last one of these pigs. But this was so much better! What a delightful surprise! I didn't think you had it in you, Thomas!"

Moving by instinct, he fired an arrow up at her, an arrow that streaked toward the ceiling. Adele vanished at the last second, and his shot went through the shattered skylight.

"Now, now," she said, shouldering her way between two men and stepping onto the dance floor. "Is that any way to take a compliment?"

THE INSTANT HE SENSED AN OPPORTUNITY, Arnold Taylor got out of his chair and ran. Not for the door. Old Bill Hendricks was still frozen at the entrance to the ballroom. No, Arnold ran in the opposite direction.

A large window with muntin segmenting the glass into individual panes the size of his palm looked out on the backyard. Safety beckoned. All he had to do was reach it.

Heedless of any danger, Arnold leaped and crashed through the glass, leaving a large hole in the window. Shards cut him. He felt blood trickling down his leg. But that didn't matter. He kept running.

The wall at the edge of the property.

He would scale it, and-

An old man in livery stepped in front of him, blocking his path. One of Delarac's servants. The man was a fossil: skinny and short with deep creases in his leathery face. "My humblest apologies, Mr. Taylor," he said. "But I'm afraid you can't leave yet."

Skidding to a stop, Arnold placed a hand over his heart and gasped for breath. He wasn't used to such exertion. "Get out of my way."

"I'm afraid not."

Only then did Arnold notice the other servants stepping out from behind bushes, emerging from behind trees, closing in on him from all sides. Every single one of them carried a gun.

"No one will be leaving," the old man said. "Not until the party is over."

ADELE GIGGLED as she watched the young man charging through the back window. Something about her laughter sent chills down Tommy's spine. There was more going on here than realized. "Now," she said, flicking her coarse, black hair with a scaly hand. "Where were we?"

Kalia raised her pistol, but Adele disappeared again. The sheriff spun around, searching the room for a target and finding nothing. "We need to get out of here," she said. "This wasn't part of-."

A chair went hurtling toward her.

Lightning quick, Kalia raised her left hand and used her bracelet to drain its kinetic energy, leaving the thing to hover about two feet in front of her. Tommy was about to help, but something else caught his eye.

A woman in red came striding onto the dance floor, carrying a nasty-looking dagger. She was tall and lean, but that was all Tommy could say about her. Every inch of her was swathed in red fabric, including her face, which she hid under a hood. He had no idea who she was, but that didn't matter.

She was working for Adele.

Backing up, Tommy pulled a Heat-Sink arrow from his quiver. With swift, mechanical precision, he fired a shot that would pierce her heart.

She already had her hand thrust out toward him, fingers splayed. The arrow was flung backward. It landed at Tommy's feet half a second before a wave of kinetic energy slammed into him. He stumbled, trying to regain his balance.

Using his momentum, Tommy pulsed his Gravity-Sink and jumped. He back-flipped over a table, landing on the other side.

Clever.

The Woman in Red was a Field Binder and a particularly talented one at that. The most common response to an arrow was to use a Force-Sink, but this lady had anticipated Tommy's next move. She knew that he would trigger the Heat-Sink while the arrow hung in front of her; so, she didn't let it get anywhere near her.

He noticed Adele floating under the skylight, raining streaks of fire down on Miri and Kalia, who leaped out of the way.

The Woman in Red kicked the chair that Kalia had left in the middle of the dance floor, and with a wave of her hand, she sent it flying toward Tommy. He had only half a second to duck before the damn thing went over his head.

And then he heard footsteps.

He looked up to find the hooded woman leaping onto his table, the wicked blade of her knife catching the lamplight. She jumped and kicked him in the face, His vision went dark, dizziness creeping in as he fell to the floor.

He heard a soft squeak when his adversary hopped off the table. In a second, she would be on top of him.

His hand flew up, unleashing a torrent of kinetic energy from his ring, energy that hurled the strange woman up to the ceiling. She cackled, grabbing the frame of the skylight to steady herself.

A Gravity-Sink in her belt buckle kept her aloft. Tommy felt it draining energy into the Ether. "Not bad, boy," she mocked. "Better than I would have expected."

Slipping one hand into her pocket, she pulled out a fistful of something that he couldn't see. Infusions, no doubt. Who in blazes was this woman? He would rather be fighting Adele.

Coins rained down on him.

Triggering his Gravity-Sink, Tommy pressed his hands to the floor and pushed off. Freed from the Earth's tether, he soared upward and flipped upright so that he could see what his enemy had done.

Frost spread across the tiles in a wave, crystalizing with a sharp, crackling sound, snuffing out the fires Adele had started. He could feel the sudden drop in temperature. His breath misted. The frigid air seared his lungs. Those aristocrats who had failed to escape were frozen solid in seconds.

Miri.

He scanned the room for his love and found her taking cover in Kalia's arms. The Sheriff had used a Heat-Source to hold back the cold, creating a small island of safety. Safety that wouldn't last. Adele swooped low with a triumphant grin, moving in for the kill.

Tommy hovered under the ceiling. In the blink of an eye, he had an arrow nocked and the bowstring drawn.

He loosed.

The bolt went straight for Adele, a perfect shot that would pierce her ribcage if it landed. But he didn't let it strike her. Instead, he detonated the Force-Source within the arrowhead just before it punctured her skin.

The blast had Adele careening toward the back wall, tumbling through the air like a log rolling down a hill. What remained of the window shattered as she crashed through it with a blood-curdling scream.

Kalia's Heat-Source died out.

It wasn't strong enough to contend with all those Sinks.

He took two arrows from his quiver and threw them down without even bothering to use the bow. Once they hit the floor, he triggered the Heat-Sources that he had Infused into them

It was a beautiful thing to witness. Energy flowed out of the Ether only to be drawn right back into it. Divine symmetry. A perfect circle that only a Field Binder could appreciate. In the end, the room was just cool. Not cold.

A feral hiss caught his attention.

He twisted around to find the Woman in Red flying at him with her arms outstretched. She grabbed him by the shoulders, shoving him backward.

Tommy went flailing toward the wall. He planted one foot against the plaster, then pushed off and launched himself across the room. His opponent was waiting above the dance floor, giggling with mad glee.

She offered a high punch.

Ducking his head, Tommy barely evaded the hit. He drove his fist into her belly, then popped up to back-hand her cheek with. The woman's head wrenched around, blood flying from her mouth.

Tommy brought his knee up into her abdomen, and then, when she was winded, he yanked down the hood. What he saw froze his blood.

Exploiting his moment of hesitation, the woman flipped over backward and kicked his chin with the toe of a soft, red boot. He was so dazed that he barely even noticed her reorienting herself.

Nor did he sense the surge of kinetic energy that slammed him into the wall with enough force to leave cracks in it. His body ached; his head felt like it was stuffed with cotton. But for all that, he was distinctly aware of a crisp, clear voice ringing throughout the room.

"That," Adele said as she glided through the shattered window. "Was not nice."

15

Lying in bed with her hands folded over her stomach, Desa stared up at the stone roof. A long day with much to think about. She still hadn't sorted out how she felt about everything she had seen. Sebastian. Somehow, knowing that he might have become a good man made her happy even as it stoked her guilt.

She wasn't sure, but she suspected that Mercy's visions had changed her outlook on a great many things. Perhaps the world was not full of greedy, selfish people looking for any excuse to betray you. Perhaps...Perhaps humanity had the potential to be something magnificent. If they had the right support.

The door flew open, Light-Source disks beginning to glow, illuminating a small bedroom with a wooden table and a vase of flowers. "Forgive my intrusion," Mercy said. "But your friends are in trouble."

The goddess wore white, a simple dress with sheer sleeves and frills along the hem. Strings of delicate pearls were threaded through her hair. She looked as though she were on her way to a fancy dinner at a wealthy tycoon's house.

Desa sat up, her mouth stretching open in a yawn. She

clamped a hand over it instinctively. "What do you mean?" she mumbled. "How could you know that my friends are in trouble?"

"I've kept an eye on them for you."

Swinging her legs over the side of the bed, Desa stood. She shook her head to clear away the fog of fatigue. "Well, thank you," she grunted. "What's wrong?"

"They've encountered Adele."

"What?"

"She's in New Beloran."

Sliding her pistol into its belt holster, Desa searched the room for her knife. Ah! There! On the table! She could be there in...Well, that presented a problem didn't it? Why would Mercy tell her about this when there was nothing she could do? "New Beloran is almost five hundred miles from here," she said. "I don't see how we can help."

Mercy stepped into the room, appearing far more calm than Desa would have expected given the situation. "Now that you have restored my power," she began. "I can have you there in a few seconds."

Pausing in the act of lacing her boot, Desa shot a glance over her shoulder. "A few seconds," she muttered. "Can you come with me?"

"I can."

"Then let's go."

The goddess forestalled her with a raised hand. Of course. She should have realized it wouldn't be so easy. "I do not know how strong Adele has become," Mercy explained. "If I confront her in a city of thousands, innocent people may be hurt."

Desa thought about it for a moment, then nodded her agreement. "Good point," she said. "We'll lure her out of the city. To the grasslands near the Vinrella. You and I will face her together."

It took all of two minutes for Desa to get ready, and then

they proceeded down the stairs to the front door. She found Midnight waiting in the street; the stallion had been saddled and bridled. Something in the way he looked at her made Desa feel like he was scolding *her* for taking too long.

Mercy stood by the door with her hands folded over her stomach, smiling as if she could sense the horse's thoughts. "I hope you don't mind," she said. "But given the urgency, I took the liberty..."

Slipping her boot into the stirrup, Desa climbed into the saddle. "Not at all," she said, taking the reins in hand. "We'll herd Adele toward the river. Assuming, of course, that she doesn't just disappear on us."

"I sincerely hope that she does," Mercy replied. "Chances are, she will flee to some remote hideaway. I can track her if she tries to run."

"Wonderful! Then all you have to do is come get me, and-"

Scowling, Mercy shook her head. "No," she said. "Desa, when I brought you here, I was under the impression that I would have to work by proxy. I never dreamed that my power would be restored to me. So, I taught you what you needed to know to defeat *Hanak Tuvar*.

"But the situation has changed. Adele is no match for me now. She can hide from me, but she cannot defeat me. If I attack her, she will put up a fight, but in the end, she will lose. All I need you to do is lure her out of the city so that no one gets hurt. Beyond that, there is no reason to put your life at risk."

Gliding forward with such impeccable grace, Mercy rested a hand on Desa's thigh. She stared up at Desa, and her smile lit up the night. "Besides," she went on. "I shall need someone to teach Field Binding when I reopen the school. I was hoping that you might take the job."

"I accept," Desa said. "Now, if you don't mind-"

"Of course."

Mercy snapped her fingers.

Just like that, Desa and Midnight were in the middle of a street lined with tall flat-roofed buildings. The lamps illuminated gray cobblestones and steps leading up to every front door.

She could sense Field Binding nearby. Quite a bit of it. The Ether was practically quivering with activity. Well, at least she didn't have to guess where to go.

Clutching the reins, Desa set her jaw and nodded. "All right," she said softly. "Let's do this."

Midnight took off at a gallop, charging up the street. Buildings flew by on either side of her. Sometimes, she heard a shout from someone who was wondering what had caused all the commotion.

In less than five minutes, she saw that this road ended in an intersection with a crossing street. A high, stone wall blocked her path. Whoever was Field Binding was behind it.

Leaning low over Midnight's neck, Desa clenched her teeth as she whispered in his ear. "Keep going," she urged. "Don't hold back."

The stallion did as he was told.

Clearing her mind, she triggered her Gravity-Sink, extending the field into a bubble that encompassed her horse. The larger the field, the faster the Sink would fill itself. But it was necessary.

Midnight leaped, easily cresting the wall, and then she killed the Sink so that he could land on the other side. His hooves churned up dirt as he ran toward a mansion with lights in its windows.

A coach had been parked in front, but it had tipped over when the brown horse that pulled it spooked and tried to bolt. The poor animal was lying in the grass, whinnying in terror.

Under other circumstances, she would have stopped to soothe him.

"Whoa!" Desa shouted.

Midnight drew up short, rearing and kicking his legs. He let out a whinny to echo those of the downed horse, then settled.

Dropping out of the saddle, Desa landed in a crouch. She stood up slowly, patting Midnight's neck. "Take care of him," she said. "I'll see what's going on inside."

She pulled her right-hand pistol from its holster, twirled it around her index finger and caught the grip. She cocked the hammer with a distinctive *click* and then proceeded to the front door.

Getting it open required some effort. The damn thing was locked. Working quickly, she took a pin from her pocket and slipped it into the keyhole. She spun around, pressing her back to the wall.

And then she triggered the Force-Source.

The lock exploded, metal flying off into the yard. Midnight gave her a look, and she could guess what he was thinking. *Dear, Desa. Your propensity for smashing things isn't making my job any easier.*

She kicked the door open and stepped into a large foyer where two curved staircases led up to a balcony. Hallways branched off on her left and right, leading into north and south wings.

Her eye was drawn to the set of arch-shaped double doors under the balcony. They opened into a ballroom. She could feel the Ether stirring on the other side, but that wasn't what worried her.

A man stood just inside, frozen in place with his arms outstretched and one foot lifted off the floor. A Force-Sink arrow near his shoe drained all of his kinetic energy. If she got near it, she would be frozen as well.

She found the Ether with no effort, the world transforming

before her eyes. Directing her thoughts into the arrowhead, she examined the Infusion that Tommy had created. Any doubt that this was one of his vanished when traced the shape of the lattice. As she suspected, the Sink was almost filled to capacity. The Ether fled when she released it.

She retrieved her pin from the broken lock. It still had a little energy left. Enough to get the job done. Desa tossed it into the ballroom. Of course, the pin stopped short, floating in the air.

She ordered it to release its final store of energy, and the old man lurched into motion, stumbling into the foyer. "What?" he stammered. "Who?" He didn't wait for an answer. He just pushed past Desa and ran into the night.

Desa strode through the door.

The scene that played out before her was nothing short of stupefying. The window in the back wall had been shattered, as had the skylight. Miri and Kalia were crouching in the middle of the dance floor, surrounded by dead aristocrats. The two women struggled to get back on their feet.

A dazed Tommy went crashing into the wall, kicked by a woman in red who scrambled to pull her hood back up. Desa didn't get a good look at her, but something was wrong there.

And then Adele came through the shattered window, brushing shards of glass off her dress. "That," she said. "Was not nice."

She paused, noticing Desa for the first time, blinking as if she couldn't believe her eyes. "Looks like the fun's over," she grumbled. "I have no time for you."

Without hesitation, Desa pointed her pistol at the treacherous woman. "Oh, please," Adele muttered, flinging her hand out in a dismissive gesture. The gun flew out of Desa's grip before she could squeeze the trigger, landing between two tables.

"Get down here!" Adele barked. "Do your job!"

The hooded woman descended with the aid of a Gravity-Sink, alighting on the tiled floor. "With pleasure," she purred. "How I have ached for the chance to settle this score."

Wrinkling her nose in distaste, Desa shook her head. "Do we know each other?" she asked. "You'll have to forgive me; I've been a little busy."

"Keep her off me," Adele ordered, turning away and heading for the backyard. She halted as she passed through the window, laughing maliciously. "It's time to do what I came here for."

The Woman in Red drew her knife, creeping forward with deadly intent. Even with her face hidden, Desa could tell that she was smiling. "You have no idea how much I've been looking forward to this."

Suddenly, Kalia jumped onto the woman's back, trying to tackle her. "Go!" she screamed at Desa. "Stop Adele! We'll take care of her!"

The woman bent forward, tossing Kalia over her shoulder. Kalia landed with a grunt, sprawled out on the tiles.

Rage flared up, and Desa reacted, extending her hand and projecting a wave of kinetic energy from her ring. The hooded woman went flying backwards like a rock kicked up by a tornado. She sailed right through the window, landing in the backyard. Kalia slid a few feet along the floor, but she had only caught the edge of the blast.

With a groan, she stood up and knuckled her sore back. She winced as she tried to ignore the pain. "Thanks," she muttered. "Now, go get Adele."

"No."

"No?"

An exhausted Tommy came stumbling up to stand beside her, wiping the sweat off his brow. "What do you mean?" he panted. "I thought bringing down Adele was the point of this mission."

"How did you get here?" Miri asked.

Desa answered that with a cheeky grin and a shrug of her shoulders. "Turns out we have friends in high places," she said. "I found Mercy in the desert, and she wants to help us put an end to this nightmare."

"Grand," Kalia said. "So, let's go."

"No," Desa protested. "Mercy has the power to defeat Adele, but she needs us to lure her out of the city. If they fight here, innocent people will get hurt. All three of you have inflicted damage on her. If you confront her together, I'm sure she'll run. And then Mercy will find her."

"What about you?"

"That hooded fiend wants my blood for some reason. I will keep her distracted while the rest of you do what must be done."

Planting herself in front of Desa, Kalia squinted as she tried to figure out what was going on. The poor woman was so confused. "So, you *won't* be going after Adele," she said. "Are you sure you're the same woman I fell in love with?"

Unable to suppress a fit of laughter, Desa kissed her lover's forehead. "Let's just say I had a change of perspective," she replied. "This is a team effort. I'll do my part; you do yours. With any luck, this will all be over by morning."

They all nodded.

And just in time too!

No sooner did they finish their little meeting than the hooded woman came stalking back through the window, brandishing her knife. She was breathing hard, seething with fury. "You're going to regret that."

"You want me?" Desa sneered. "Come and get me."

She turned and ran back into the foyer, listening for the sound of footsteps behind her. She wasn't disappointed. Whoever this stranger was, she had a singular focus, a need to sate her bloodlust.

Such a weakness could be exploited.

TEN SECONDS after the Woman in Red followed Desa out the door, Tommy turned to the others. "Well," he said. "We know what we have to do. Let's get to it."

He adjusted his quiver, hoisted up his bow and began a sombre march to the window. Miri fell in on his left and Kalia on his right, both women drawing pistols and thumbing the hammers. He could see it in their eyes.

Resolve.

One way or another, this would all be over soon. It was almost a relief. Even if he didn't make it, there would be no more running, no more delays. If they survived, he and Dalen and Miri could ride off into the sunset and...do anything! He hadn't really thought that far ahead. Maybe they could get the revolution going again. Somehow, he thought that his performance tonight had been overshadowed by the mayhem that followed.

They stepped into the backyard, onto the small, stone patio.

Delarac's guests were on their knees in the grass, surrounded by liveried servants who held them at gunpoint. Some of them were crying; others begged for mercy. "You can't do this!" one man wailed. "It's murder!"

Tommy felt nothing but disgust for the lot of them. None of these idiots had any compunctions about sending strangers off to die in pointless wars. But when the guns were pointed at them, suddenly human life was sacred.

The servants were all stone-faced, guarding their captives without a flicker of emotion. He suspected that was Adele's doing. Some enchantment that she had placed on them. Those dead stares reminded him of the gray people he had seen in Aladar and Thrasa.

Adele glided through the grass on bare feet, her long, black dress trailing behind her. She looked up with a deep breath and smiled when she saw Tommy. "So, you want to watch? I suppose I do perform better with an audience."

He reached for an arrow.

"Uh uh!" Adele said, waggling her finger. "No need for that! After all, I heard your little speech earlier. You hate these maggots as much as I do. Can't we have a moment together for old time's sake before we go back to trying to kill each other?"

"Hmm," Miri said. "No."

She and Kalia aimed their guns.

A wave of Adele's hand produced a surge of kinetic energy that hit each woman like a punch to the gut. Miri and Kalia fell on their backsides, grunting.

Before he even realized it, Tommy had an arrow out of the quiver. He nocked it, drew back the string and then stumbled when something invisible struck him across the cheek. His head rang as dizziness washed over him.

Dazed, he sank to one knee and raised a hand to touch his smarting face. He hissed as the pain flared bright and hot.

"Really, I don't want to kill you," Adele said. "Not yet anyway. We've made such wonderful memories together!"

Tommy looked up to find her standing over the cowering aristocrats. Her grin was positively demonic. "I'd like to give you one last fond memory," Adele went on. "Don't you want to see these pigs get what they deserve?"

"Not from you."

Adele planted her fists on her hips, tossing her head back and smiling up at the heavens. "Well, you can't say I wasn't diplomatic," she huffed. "Enjoy the show. It's the last one you'll ever see."

Abruptly, she turned and reached for the nearest man, a portly fellow with his gray hair tied back in a short tail. He trembled, moaning when he realized that he was to be the first victim.

Black ooze engulfed Adele's hand, thick oil that flowed up her arm to the elbow. Then her hand melted. A tentacle of liquid onyx stretched forth and stabbed the old man's chest. It spread over his body – his shoulders, his arms, his legs and his head – consuming him. His screams cut off as he disintegrated.

The tentacle retracted, transforming back into Adele's hand. Black veins ran up her arm, her shoulder, her neck and her face. They dipped into her eyes, changing them into pits of darkness. When she spoke, it was with a chorus of voices. "Yum, yum, yum!"

She spun to face Tommy with a beatific smile, giggling softly. Her eyes! They weren't just dark; they were empty. It was like looking into the Abyss itself. "Kalia," the chorus intoned. "I do hate it when people take what is mine."

The tentacle lashed out, streaking toward the sheriff.

Tommy reached for the Ether and surrendered himself to its comforting embrace. The world changed – particles spinning all around him – and Adele became...something he couldn't even begin to describe. An emptiness so profound it made him want to weep. In that stretched-out instant, with death lurking only a few inches away, Tommy filled the emptiness, forcing the Ether into it.

And then he let go.

Adele stumbled, the tentacle snapping back into her. She hunched over, touching fingertips to her forehead. "I should have known you wouldn't make this easy," she said. "Kill them!"

AS SHE FLED into the foyer, Desa spun around to find the Woman in Red in hot pursuit. The stranger leaped over fallen chairs and sprinted through the ballroom with grace that only someone with a Gravity-Sink could manage.

Raising her fists into a fighting stance, Desa backed up to the front door. "Before we do this," she began. "Would you mind sating my curiosity?"

Cruel laughter echoed through the room as the other woman stepped out from underneath the balcony. She seemed to be considering Desa's request. "I suppose that's only fair. What do you want to know?"

"Who are you?"

"I should think you would have figured it out."

Reaching up with two gloved hands, the stranger pulled back the hood to expose an inhuman face. Her skin was pale, her features properly proportioned, but her eyes were yellow with vertical slits. And she was bald.

Her ears had changed as well. No longer round, they now slanted backward with pointed tips. When she smiled, she displayed two pointed fangs. "Don't you recognize me, Desa?"

"Azra..."

"Indeed."

Desa blinked and then gave her head a shake. "No," she said, stepping forward. "No, you died when I threw you off the train."

"Oh, I should have died," Azra agreed. "Tossed off a train at forty miles an hour, bouncing off trees: it's the sort of thing that breaks a human body. I was bleeding out when Adele found me."

"And healed you..."

Azra came forward with a grin that displayed those sharp fangs. "She warned me that the healing came with a price. I was more than willing to pay. It's funny. I never feared death until I felt the life draining out of me."

Grimacing at the thought, Desa turned her face away from the other woman. "I'm sorry," she whispered. "I didn't want to hurt you. But you left me-"

"Please, spare me your inane justifications. I'm uninterested in the lies you tell yourself so that you can sleep at night. We're here now. Slicing you into little pieces will more than make up for what I've lost."

With a pulse from her Gravity-Sink, Azra jumped and back-flipped as she climbed toward the ceiling. She landed on the balcony railing, cackling gleefully. "If I only get to kill you once, I'd like to have some fun with it."

She turned her back on Desa, hopping down onto the balcony and grabbing a pair of sabres that were mounted on the wall. Long swords with thin blades. She tested each for weight and balance.

Desa tested them as well.

Making herself one with the Ether, she probed the swords with her mind and found no Infusions within them. Never touch another Field Binder's weapon. Or anything that a Field Binder gave you, for that matter. It was unlikely that Azra would have set up a trap in advance, but you could never be too careful.

A human-shaped collection of particles leaped from the balcony and snapped back into the form of Azra as she descended. She landed with a grunt and then giggled as she stood up straight. "Here," she said, offering one sword to Desa.

Desa took it, backing off and lifting the blade up in front of her face. "Are you sure that you want to do this?" she asked. "I've had formal training with a wide variety of weapons. I can't imagine that you can say the same."

Azra's response was to come at her with an overhead swing.

Spreading her feet apart, Desa turned her body and raised the blade in a high parry. Steel met steel with a loud *clang*. She kicked her opponent, driving the other woman back toward the ballroom.

Bad idea.

She wanted to keep Azra away from the others.

Spinning on her heel, Desa bolted for the front door. She charged into the cold night, Midnight perking up when he saw her. This might have been an even worse idea. She didn't want Azra getting anywhere near her horse.

The other woman was hot on her heels, huffing and puffing as she surged out of the house. By the sound of her footsteps, she was gaining ground on Desa. Time to change the game.

With a deft hand, Desa pulled a coin from her pocket and dropped it on the ground. She triggered the Gravity-Sink in her belt buckle and then ordered the coin to release a burst of kinetic energy that had her streaking into the starry night.

The ring on her pinky finger pulled the coin into her hand, and then she tossed it out behind herself, triggering it again. This blast of energy sent her hurtling toward the wall that surrounded the mansion. Once again, she recalled the coin.

Azra screamed, unable to keep up.

Desa didn't have to look to know that she was still giving chase. She sensed it when the other woman activated her Gravity-Sink. Azra leaped, trying to fly, but human legs were no match for the raw power of a Force-Source.

Allowing gravity to briefly reassert itself halted Desa's upward motion and put her on a straight, horizontal path that carried her over the wall. She sailed across the road that bordered Delarac's home and over the buildings on the other side.

The sound of gunfire made her flinch.

Azra was using the recoil to gain speed. She had probably shattered a few windows. Delarac would not be pleased. Was it wrong to take pleasure in that?

Flying with her arms stretched out, the sword blade catching the light of nearby lamps, Desa allowed herself a smile. Wind resistance was already reducing her velocity, but that was fine. There was no need to use the coin again.

Buildings slid past beneath her. She noted that each one had a flat roof. *Yes, That will do nicely.*

Using her belt buckle for a gentle descent, Desa landed atop a boarding house. She took a deep breath, then turned around to face her enemy. She had left the Sink active so that Azra could find her.

The other woman bellowed, her legs flailing as she dropped onto the rooftop. She hit hard, stumbling a few steps and nearly falling flat on her face.

"You know," Desa teased. "If you had learned proper flight techniques, you might not have suffered such grievous injuries when I threw you off the train. Shall we do this? Or do you need a moment to catch your breath?"

Azra shrieked.

GUNSHOTS RANG OUT, startling the servants who kept Delarac's guests from running, but they were far off. On the other side of the house. Somehow, Tommy suspected that Desa was involved.

The servants flinched but quickly recovered, turning their attention to the three intruders. Hard, uncompromising eyes fell upon Tommy. Their leader, a spindly man with gaunt cheeks and a leathery face stepped forward.

"Must I repeat myself?" Adele asked, speaking with a thousand different voices. "Kill them!"

The servants raised their pistols.

Instinctively, Tommy and Kalia stepped forward, the sheriff shielding herself with an iron bracelet while he triggered the Force-Sink in his pendant. *CRACK! CRACK! CRACK!* Guns flashed, and bullets stopped dead in front of him. Three, four, five.

Miri retreated through the broken window.

He and Kalia followed, spreading out, taking cover on either side of it. Several shots whizzed past him, streaking through the empty ballroom and out the door on the other side. Over a dozen servants – most of them armed – and all loyal to Adele. This would not be easy.

Miri and Kalia huddled against the wall on the other side of the window. Tommy shared a glance with his love. She wasn't the least bit afraid. He wasn't sure how he knew, but he knew.

Miri aimed around the corner and fired. Thunder split the air, and when it faded, Tommy heard the moans of some poor man who had been hit. Well, that was one down. Only thirteen more to go.

"Incompetent fools!" the chorus snarled. "Kill them! Kill them! Kill them!" Odd. Why wasn't Adele doing the job herself? A few blasts of lightning would be far more effective than bullets. Why not just lash out with her power?

Maybe she can't, Tommy noted.

But what was stopping her? Did it have something to do with the black tentacles? She seemed to be feeding on Delarac's guests. Perhaps that was a process that, once started, could not be stopped. Which meant...

Which meant she was vulnerable.

Fishing a small coin out of his pocket, Tommy tossed it around the corner, into the backyard. He felt it land in the grass, then triggered the Force-Source. Several people cried out as they were thrown back.

Taking the opportunity, Kalia pointed her gun through the window and fired twice. "Got one!" Her face twisted into an ugly scowl. "Missed the other."

"Trigger your Sinks," Tommy growled. There was no need to specify which ones. He drew an arrow from his quiver and nocked it. Sensing his intentions, Miri and Kalia covered him by firing a few shots.

He spun into the open, pulling back the bowstring, and what he saw terrified him. Most of the servants were closing in on the window. Several were down and bleeding out. Others were lying in the grass, victims of his Force-Source. But that wasn't the worst of it.

Adele had a liquid tentacle extending from each arm, black ooze creeping over the bodies of two aristocrats that she consumed. Some of the others were trying to flee now that their guards were otherwise occupied, but they had nowhere to go. The stone wall that surrounded this house stood over ten feet high.

His moment of hesitation nearly got him killed. One of the servants noticed and aimed his pistol.

Tommy released his arrow.

He quickly spun back into cover and triggered the Gravity-Source he had created five days ago. Everyone started screaming. Servants, guests, Adele: they all howled when they felt the arrow's irresistible pull. Maybe it was Tommy's imagination, but he could swear he heard them clawing at the grass as they struggled for purchase.

Protected by their Sinks, Miri and Kalia peeked around the corner and fired into the backyard. Tommy needed no such protection. He had exempted himself from the arrow's effects.

Drawing the pistol on his right hip, Tommy cocked the hammer. His aim wasn't so good with guns, but that didn't matter very much when all of his targets were anchored to the ground.

He stepped into the open and found a pile of bodies in the grass, some in livery, others in fine suits and gowns. They all tried to crawl away, but the arrow held them tightly in its grip.

That would do.

So long as they were trapped, he could focus on Adele without having to harm any of the bystanders. Drive her out of the city, Desa had said. Mercy would do the rest. Well, he was happy to play his part. But where was Adele?

To his shock, she came striding out of the shadows with a peal of vicious laughter, seemingly unaffected by his Gravity-Source. Her eyes were as black as pitch. "Thank you, Tommy," the chorus sang. "That makes things much easier."

Almighty, no!

How could he have been so stupid?

Adele stretched her arms toward the pile of bodies, both transforming into streams of oily sludge. Sludge that flowed over guests and servants alike, devouring them. "No!" Tommy screamed.

He aimed his gun and fired several times, loosing each slug with a clap of thunder. Adele didn't even try to stop him. She just let the bullets rip through her, focused on the task at hand. Bodies liquified under her touch, transforming into a mass of black goo that she greedily sucked up.

Closing her eyes, Adele licked her lips seductively. "Mmm," she said. "Now, that's more like it."

"Almighty forgive me," Tommy whispered.

Adele tossed her head back, laughing as the tentacles retracted. "And now," she said. "I make my debut."

AZRA FLOWED ACROSS THE ROOFTOP, twirling her blade as she moved in close. Her mouth quirked into a smile. Such glee in those yellow eyes! She swung at Desa's neck.

Desa hopped back, barely avoiding the cut, but Azra wasn't done. The other woman came forward with a fierce, downward slice. It took everything Desa had to get her sword up and block the strike.

She retreated, trying to hold back the assault. Whatever Adele had done to Azra's body had made her stronger. Which made sense. Bendarian had also gained strength from his trans-formation.

Growling, she kicked Azra in the stomach, forcing the woman to back off. Desa jumped, spun in the air and kicked out behind herself. A swift blow to Azra's chest made her retreat again.

Whirling around, Desa landed with a grunt and then raised her blade up in front of her face. She advanced on her enemy.

The momentum changed when Azra hammered her with a series of brutal, overhead strikes. Each one landed with the fury of an avalanche. Desa's muscles burned every time she parried.

With a quick, sideways dash, she ran for the front wall of the building. She had to get away from here. Take a moment and formulate a plan. It dawned on her that she did not have to kill Azra; she only had to keep her busy.

That was it!

Once the others confronted Adele, she would flee. Then Mercy could do the rest, and Desa could rejoin her friends. They would regroup and deal with Azra together. She just had to survive a little longer. With a thought, she ordered her belt buckle to drain gravitational energy.

Desa leaped, propelling herself across the road. She flipped over in mid-flight, then killed the Sink for half a second to adjust her vector of descent. Yes, that would do.

She landed on the front wall of a gray building with skinny, rectangular windows, a near-perfect twin to the one she had left behind. She felt the approach of a Gravity-Sink before she saw Azra hurtling across the street.

Of course, the other woman lacked Desa's finesse. She landed about one story down, her arms flailing as she tried to steady herself. It took her a moment to regain her balance, and she nearly dropped her sword in the process.

Desa took one step forward, which meant pushing herself

off the wall. She began a quick descent to her opponent, the distance between her and the building growing.

Azra looked up, sensing her approach.

Clutching her weapon in both hands, Desa bared her teeth and swung hard. Steel bounced off steel with a ring that echoed through the night. The other woman tried to retreat, but the lack of gravity resulted in her flying off the wall as well.

Clang! Clang! Clang!

Their blades collided again and again as Azra floated backwards. She had to feel the ground creeping up behind her, but she didn't seem to care. The kill was all that mattered. Or rather, it would have been all that mattered if she wasn't on the defensive. Fighting in this way kept her at a disadvantage.

Desperate and frantic, Azra stretched her hand out, releasing kinetic energy from her ring. The blast hit Desa like a gale-force wind. The ground receded, Azra giggling when she alighted on the sidewalk.

Curling up into a ball, Desa somersaulted through the air. She killed her Sink and landed atop the roof with her arms spread wide, the sword held tightly in her right hand. "Is that the best you can do?" she hollered.

Snarling, Azra launched herself upward.

Desa waited.

The other woman popped into view, briefly killing her Sink to halt her ascent, and then Desa kicked her. Thrown backward, Azra went soaring across the street.

Desa followed soon after, triggering her Sink and using a powerful leap to close the distance. Winded and dizzy, Azra seemed only half aware of her. Time to end this once and for all.

With a sweeping horizontal cut, Desa tried to behead her opponent. Blade met blade as Azra deftly parried it.

Screeching like an angry cat, she turned belly-up and kicked Desa with both feet. Hard. They flew apart, streaking toward buildings on opposite sides of the road. A wild wind sang in Desa's ears. Somehow, she could sense the impending collision.

Tucking her legs into her chest, she flipped over and pressed her boots against the brick wall. She compressed like a spring, then pushed off with all her might.

Azra was coming at her, raising her sabre for an overhead strike. Blocking that would be difficult. And there was no avoiding it. No way to change course.

Or was there?

At the last second, Desa killed her Sink for an instant. Just enough to let herself fall a few paces. She grabbed Azra's ankle and hung on for dear life. The other woman pulled free, but the change in momentum sent her face-first into a building.

Bending her knees, Desa slammed her feet into a wall and then bounced off of it, flinging herself back the way she had come. She twisted around to find Azra floating near a four-story boarding house. The woman was stunned.

Desa came up behind her, spun Azra around and pinned her against the wall. She pressed the edge of her blade to the other woman's neck. "You've lost," she breathed. "It's over."

The instant she finished speaking, the ground began to shake. The city trembled, buildings groaning as they were jostled by a powerful quake. What was this? She had never heard of tremors in this part of the country.

Azra opened her eyes. "No," she cooed. "You've lost. It's too late."

Too late?

The enormity of Desa's mistake settled onto her. Once again, she had been played. This *had* been a distraction, but not for Azra. For her. But how? Adele fled whenever she was overwhelmed; that was her way. Two Field Binders and Miri, the woman who had killed a Field Binder: that should have been enough.

Exploiting a moment of hesitation, Azra shoved her. Pain surged through Desa as she crashed into the building across the way. She didn't even bother to fight back; right now, she had larger concerns.

She used her Gravity-Sink to lower herself to the ground, nearly falling over when her feet touched the pavement. Leaping from rooftop to rooftop would have been faster, but with the city shaking, that was unwise.

Dropping the sword, she turned and ran for Delarac's home.

Every step was a labour. The earth was a bucking horse, trying to throw her off. She heard people screaming. Somewhere in the distance, a man shouted for everyone to stay calm. Desa wasn't quite sure if she agreed with that. It seemed to her that a little panic was in order.

What was Adele doing?

A sudden jolt made her stumble, arms reeling as she tried to keep her balance. She fell over, barely catching herself, and then pushed herself up again.

Grabbing a nearby lamppost, she used that to steady herself and then pressed on. Were the others all right? Was *Kalia* all right? Desa didn't know what she would do if she lost her love.

Step by painful step, she made her way back to the wall that surrounded Delarac's home. She was almost there when the quake abruptly stopped. She wished she could say that was a good thing.

Wasting no time, she pulsed her Gravity-Sink and leaped over the wall. Then she was scrambling through the grass, bounding for a mansion with shattered windows. The poor brown horse was still tethered to his fallen carriage, but Midnight tried to calm him. She was tempted to stop and free the beast, but something told her that she couldn't spare the time.

She burst through the door, rushed under the balcony and

into the ballroom. She charged across the dance floor and through the shattered window. That was where she found Kalia, Miri and Tommy. Mercy be praised! They were all right.

A woozy Adele stumbled backward through the grass, her face lighting up when she saw Desa. Pulsing, black veins crawled up her arms, slithered over her face and sank into her eyes. "Ah," she said. "I'm so glad you could bear witness."

Her voice.

Desa knew that chorus all too well. She had heard it before, at a farmhouse on the road to Ofalla. It was the voice of *Hanak Tuvar*. "Bear witness to what?" she demanded.

The veins faded from Adele's skin. When they were gone, she looked normal again. Well, normal for her, anyway. She still had a scaly hand and coarse, black hair, but there was no visible change apart from her eyes.

Those were now windows into some infinite nothing. The space between universes. The void that Mercy had shown her. "The culmination," Adele said.

"Of what?"

"Everything we've been through together."

Desa strode forward with her fists clenched, her gaze fixed on the other woman. "What did you do?"

Adele was about to speak, but a jagged crack ran up her neck and over her cheek. The sound it made was like glass crunching. A second crack joined it, intersecting with the first, and then a piece of Adele's face fell away. It was as if she had become a woman made of porcelain. The hole it left behind was another window into that eternal emptiness. "This vessel was nothing but an incubator," *Hanak Tuvar* said. "I grew within it."

Miri raised her gun, but Desa thrust her arm out to the side, forestalling the other woman. Bullets would do no good here.

Cracks spread over Adele's body, a web of them stretching over her face and down her arms. Even her feet began to fracture. A jagged shard fell out of her forehead, leaving only darkness in its place. "I am the void," *Hanak Tuvar* said. "That which existed before the aberration that you call a universe. That which will remain long after you have been extinguished."

More flakes dropped away, leaving holes in Adele's neck, her arms, her face. Even her scaly hand began to disintegrate. "This one craved adulation," *Hanak Tuvar* went on. "Worship. A disgusting human motivation. Easily manipulated. I whispered in her ear through the gaps in my prison. Her and countless others."

Desa stood there with her mouth agape, a ragged breath pulling its way out of her. "How many?" she whispered. "How many did you influence?"

"Thousands," *Hanak Tuvar* boasted. "Adele was the first to discover how to release me. Her last thought before I consumed her was a desire to tell you that she is sorry."

"No, *we* are sorry," Desa countered. "Long ago, our ancestors traveled between universes. In so doing, we trespassed in your domain. We disturbed you. And for that, we are deeply sorry. Let us go, and I promise you it will never happen again."

Adele laughed, shaking her head. "Foolish child. Do you think something as insignificant as you could ever trouble something like me? Your presence in 'my domain' was nothing more than a curiosity. Regardless, I will exterminate your species."

"Why?" Desa whispered. "We are no threat to you."

"Because it would amuse me."

Adele staggered, lifting a hand to her chest. The cracks spread over her at an accelerated rate. She couldn't last much longer.

Grabbing Tommy and Miri by their sleeves, Desa pulled them back onto the patio. Kalia joined them there, the four of them huddling against the house's back wall. Would it do any good? She had no clue what to expect. *Hanak Tuvar* was about to make its first appearance in ten thousand years. For all she knew, its arrival might destroy the city. But if that were the case, trying to run would be pointless.

Adele's body shattered like a vase struck by a hammer.

And darkness exploded from it.

THE END OF PART I

PART II

16

The world trembled.

Stumbling down the stairs, Dalen threw his hands against the wall and grimaced. All this shaking left a queasiness in his belly. He was just grateful that he hadn't fallen over. A man could break his neck in this chaos.

With careful steps, he made his way to the first floor, but another tremor flung him into the wall again. He braced his hands against the plaster. "Hurry!" he called to those behind him. "But be careful!"

Zoe was five stairs up, clinging to the railing with teeth bared. "Easy for you to say," she muttered, descending one more step.

Jim was behind her, trying desperately to stay on his feet, and Victor brought up the rear. The door to the first-floor apartment opened, and Mrs. Carmichael spilled out. She staggered a few steps and nearly crashed into him.

"Goodness!" she gasped, crossing arms in front of herself to hide her robe? Dalen wondered at that. Wasn't the whole purpose of a robe to hide whatever was underneath? This forced modesty seemed a tad redundant.

Her trembling hands cranked the deadbolt, and she pulled the front door open, falling on her backside as the world shook. Zoe reached the foot of the stairs, collapsing into Dalen's arms. He steadied her and urged her to follow their landlady out into the street.

Jim was next.

Dalen reached for him, taking the man's hand and guiding him down. He went with the others out into the night.

Victor was frozen on the fourth stair, clutching the railing. His face was flushed as he shook his head. "The whole place is coming down!"

"Come on!" Dalen urged.

"I...I...can't."

Scrambling up the steps, the quake nearly knocking him off his feet, Dalen seized the other man's shoulder. A few insistent tugs got Victor in motion again. Together, they ran out the front door.

Stone steps shook beneath them as they dashed out onto the cobblestone street. Despite the chill, Dalen saw half a dozen people standing on the road in their nightclothes. No one wanted to be inside during an earthquake.

He turned to the west, staring off to the edge of the city where the others had gone. Somehow, he knew they were mixed up in all this. But how? What kind of Field Binding could unleash such fury?

Not Field Binding, he realized. *This is something else.*

Abruptly, the tremors stopped.

Dalen bent double with his hands on his knees, muscles aching, nerves racked. He gave his head a shake to clear away the dizziness. "All right," he said, forcing himself to stand up straight. "Is anyone hurt?"

He turned around to find a handful of terrified people standing in the street, all staring at him with wide eyes. They weren't sure of what to make of all this. Neither was Dalen. He scanned his memory for some clue as to what might have happened. Was New Beloran on a faultline? Had he ever read anything to that effect? Somehow, he didn't think so.

For many of these people, this might have been their first encounter with a quake. They probably thought their Almighty was lashing out at them in rage. Life was a good deal simpler when you didn't believe in gods.

Then again, the gods that Dalen had been taught to revere were not only real but playing an active role in this struggle against *Hanak Tuvar*. How frustrating! At the age of fourteen, Dalen had acquainted himself with all the arguments for and against belief in a deity. The nays had a much stronger case. It irked him that even with superior rationality, the atheist position was wrong. The world just shouldn't work like that.

A heavyset man with two chins stepped forward, pointing at Dalen. "You!" he growled. "This is your doing!"

Dalen felt creases lining his brow. "My doing?" he stammered, shaking his head. "How could I have caused an earthquake?"

"I saw you this afternoon," the big man said. "Holding hands with that other boy. The Almighty punishes sin."

Some of the others started grumbling, casting dirty looks at Dalen. A spike of fear went through him. How to handle this? He couldn't fight. He had never learned.

Dalen stepped forward with his hands up in a placating gesture, shutting his eyes and breathing slowly. "Friend, that's impossible," he began. "Earthquakes are caused by shifts in tectonic-"

The big man came at Dalen with his fist raised.

Just like that, Jim was there, placing himself between Dalen and his would-be assailant. "That's enough!" he snapped. "We'll gain nothing by turning on each other."

"Out of my way!"

Jim refused to budge.

The big brute threw a punch, but Jim's hands moved with cat-like speed, seizing the other man's wrist. Jim twisted his arm at an odd angle, producing a screech of pain.

With a little pressure on the elbow, Jim forced the oaf down onto his knees. "Now," he said. "I trust we can avoid any further unpleasantness."

"Give over, Gerald!" Mrs. Carmichael snapped, still hiding her robe behind crossed arms. "The lad isn't to blame and you bloody-well know it!"

Tilting his head back, Dalen looked up at the stars. He blinked, running through scenarios in his mind. "We have to leave," he mumbled before he realized what he was saying. "Get out of the city."

Mrs. Carmichael's cold stare fell upon him. "Why on Earth would we do that?"

"Something is wrong," Dalen insisted. "Our friends..."

"Where *are* your friends?" the old woman inquired.

He ignored her, rounding on the others in his group. Zoe and Victor stood on the curb. The girl wore a frilly night-dress. The sun had gone down less than two hours ago, but Zoe had always been inclined to turn in early. In all likelihood, she had been reading when the quake started. She liked to relax with a good book before going to sleep. Dalen approved.

Victor was in his shirtsleeves, still carrying the flask of whisky that he had been drinking in the sitting room. The man was nervous, his hands shaking.

"Get dressed," Dalen barked. "And gather your things. We're leaving the city."

"Good!" Gerald spat.

The man was cradling his sore arm now that Jim had released him, snarling at Dalen like an angry bear. "Take your sin somewhere else," he added.

Spinning to face him, Dalen stepped forward and thrust out

his chin. "I suggest that you do the same," he said coldly. "Something has gone wrong."

"Like I would take advice from a-"

He cut off when Dalen turned away and ran back into the boarding house. Up the stairs and into their small apartment. He was already dressed, thankfully, but there were other concerns.

Dropping to his knees next to a wooden chest, Dalen began retrieving his books and shoving them into a bag. He couldn't bear to leave them behind. Which was foolish, he realized. He should be thinking about food and supplies. Perhaps Mrs. Carmichael would spare them some bread and cheese from her pantry. If not, they would have to buy food.

But where?

The nearest city was Ofalla, and if he recalled correctly, it was nearly three days away on horseback. Could they survive that long without food? Maybe they could hunt. Jim had some skill with a bow, didn't he? He kept loading his bag with books as these thoughts crossed his mind.

Zoe came barreling into the apartment, suddenly aware of her state of undress. She flew into her bedroom and slammed the door behind her.

Jim was the next to appear in the doorway, bracing one hand on the frame and frowning at Dalen. "You're sure about this?"

Shutting his eyes tight, Dalen nodded vigorously. "Yes," he said. "We have to go. With any luck, we'll find Tommy, Miri and Kalia."

"But how could *they* have caused an earthquake?"

Dalen didn't answer. He just spun around and shoved the bag into the other man's hands. Then he began searching for clothes, pulling his shirts and coats out of a nearby closet. He had come here with only two of the former and one of the latter, but a month spent working had provided enough for a few extra garments. A necessity if you wanted to look presentable.

He chose a shirt and a pair of trousers, stuffing them into the bag on top of his books. The coat he put on and buttoned.

Zoe bolted out of the bedroom, now dressed in black pants and a white blouse, the strap of a bag slung over her shoulder. "Mrs. Carmichael," she panted, running to a chest of drawers and pulling one open. "She'll want payment for this week's rent."

"We haven't stayed the full week," Victor protested.

"Then we'll pay her for two days," Zoe panted

Dalen was pleased to see that Victor had an armload of clothes that he tried to stuff into a bag he had left on the couch. Some of those belonged to Jim and Tommy. Did Zoe get Miri and Kalia's things?

Down the stairs, they went, back out to the street where Mrs. Carmichael waited next to a lamppost. She eyed them, curious. "You really mean to go then?" she asked. "You've found good jobs here."

"We all have to get out of the city," Dalen panted. "All of us. You as well. Go get dressed and retrieve some food from the kitchen. Whatever you can carry."

"Now, listen here-"

The wind began to howl.

Dalen spun to the west, listening. At first, he thought that he might be overreacting, but then he heard it. An inhuman shriek. It was like ice crumbling and nails scratching against a rock, cats screeching and hammers striking anvils. All of these things at once. He had never heard anything so terrible.

Dalen felt his jaw drop, sweat beading on his forehead, rolling over his brow. "We have to go," he said again "Now!"

. . .

THE DARKNESS EXPLODED with a wail that felt like knives stabbing into Desa's skull, a mass of tentacles writhing and undulating, slamming down on the grass with a *thump* that rattled her bones. The creature that emerged was almost like a squid, but there were no eyes. Just a perfectly-round mouth with dozens of sharp teeth protruding from its circular lip like stalactites hanging from a cave's ceiling.

She cowered against the wall with her hands over her ears, tears leaking from her eyes, spilling over her cheeks. "We have to kill it!" she bellowed.

Tommy backed up on shaky legs, stumbling through the shattered window, into the ballroom. He reached for an arrow but hesitated.

Hanak Tuvar screamed, pressing its tentacles down on the ground, raising the mass of its round body high into the air. With limbs fully extended, it stood nearly twenty-feet tall, but it didn't advance.

Something changed.

The air around the creature took on a ruddy haze. It was hard to tell in the darkness of night, but she was sure that the lamplight that reflected off its oily body was wrong. Redder, somehow. *Like what happened at the pyramid,* Desa realized. *On the day that it infected Adele's body.*

If Miri noticed the change, she didn't seem to care. She cocked the hammer of her pistol, raised the weapon and fired with a *CRACK! CRACK! CRACK!*

The bullets melted when they crossed into the halo of redness that surrounded *Hanak Tuvar,* collapsing into puddles of liquid metal that landed in the grass. The grass! It was crumbling to ash beneath the creature.

"All right," Desa said. "Let's try something stronger."

She made a fist and thrust it toward the demon, releasing a stream of lightning from the ring on her middle finger, lightning that vanished when it touched the red halo. She increased the flow, draining much of her Electric-Source's stored energy.

It had no effect.

The lightning didn't even touch *Hanak Tuvar.*

The creature rose up, thrusting its face toward them, its circular mouth expanding with a frenzied howl. The inner cheeks vibrated. Desa knew, in that moment, that she was looking upon death itself.

Slinking toward her on twelve slimy tentacles, *Hanak Tuvar* bobbed up and down. The halo expanded before it, grass withering under its touch.

"Let's go!" Miri shouted.

"We can't!" Desa yelled, stumbling back into the mansion. "We have to kill it here! Before it gets out to the city!"

A flash of light appeared at the edge of the patio, solidifying into a crystalline figure who stood with her arms spread wide and her head thrown back. Mercy's scream echoed through the night.

A cylinder of radiance formed around *Hanak Tuvar,* stretching twenty stories into the sky. A barrier of liquid light that kept the creature contained. Black tentacles slammed against the wall of energy, pounding it over and over.

Strained, exhausted, Mercy looked over her shoulder with eyes like glowing gemstones. "Go!" she barked. "I can't hold it forever!"

"We can help!" Desa protested.

"Go!"

Miri's insistent hand tugged on her arm, and then she was spinning around, running through a ballroom with upended tables. Glass crunched under her boots. Tommy and Kalia were right in front of her, breathing hard.

Desa ventured one last glance into the backyard and found Mercy crouching on the patio with her hands stretched toward the glowing prison she had erected. The goddess was losing strength. Like a man trying to hold up a ceiling that had collapsed onto him. So, Desa did the only thing she could do.

She ran.

The four of them charged through the foyer and burst onto the front lawn. That poor, brown horse was still tied to his carriage, but remarkably, he was calm. Midnight had settled him down.

Drawing her belt knife, Desa snarled and walked up to the frightened animal. "Hold still," she said and cut the straps that held him.

The horse tried to bolt, but a nicker from Midnight stilled him. He stood tall, waiting for direction, glancing back to the mansion. The column of light was a spear that stabbed the night sky.

Shutting her eyes as a shiver went through her, Desa took control of herself. "Miri, Tommy," she said. "The two of you are heaviest. You'll ride Midnight. Kalia, you and I will take the other."

Kalia threw her hands up in irritation. "He's spooked," she said. "We can't ride him."

"He won't rear."

"How do you know?"

Rounding on the other woman, Desa jerked her thumb over her shoulder, pointing at Midnight. "Because," she said. "I trust my partner. And we don't have time to debate this. Let's go!"

Tommy climbed into Midnight's saddle, and Miri settled in behind him, wrapping her arms around his waist. Desa removed the brown horse's harness so that she and Kalia could do the same. The animal had no saddle, but now wasn't the time to be picky.

Together, they took off across the lawn, heading for the wall. That left her with another conundrum. Midnight had been trained to work with Field Binders. He would gladly leap over ten feet of stone, trusting her Gravity-Sink to carry him safely to the other side. But the other horse – Desa decided to call him Champ for want of a better name – would never obey a command to charge toward a wall.

Tommy seemed to anticipate her need, urging Midnight toward the metal gate. He pulled an arrow from his quiver, nocked it and let it fly.

A blast of kinetic energy tore the gate right off of its hinges, metal bars landing in the street with a dreadful cacophony. Midnight galloped through the opening, and Champ followed. They turned left, heading north along a cobblestone road.

Glancing back over his shoulder, Tommy hissed air through his teeth. "We have to find the others!" he insisted. "We can't leave them!"

"Lead on!"

Guiding Midnight with his thighs, he turned right onto a street that ran eastward to the heart of the city. The same street where Desa and Azra had clashed only ten minutes ago. Town-houses flew by on either side of her. She searched for any sign that Azra might have lingered, but the woman was long gone.

Kalia squeezed Desa tight, nuzzling the back of her coat. "Whatever happens," she breathed. "I want you to know that I love you!"

Even in the midst of all that chaos, Desa chuckled, an irresistible smile blooming on her face. "I love you too."

Any warmth she might have felt was killed by *Hanak Tuvar's* incessant screams. The creature was still hammering away at its prison, enraged by Mercy's interference. She could hear the blows even from this distance. Would Mercy be able to finish it off? The goddess had been confident that she could handle Adele, but somehow, Desa suspected that the situation had changed.

People stood in the street, having been drawn out by the earthquake. They stared, dumbfounded, at the glowing tower.

"Run!" Desa screamed. "Leave the city!"

No one listened.

A BEAM OF PURE, white light shot into the stratosphere, eliciting gasps from the people who stood in the street. Dalen felt his hands trembling. His fear was like a blade stabbing him through the heart. Was this Adele's doing? Had she been the source of those terrible shrieks?

Mrs. Carmichael stumbled up beside him, slapping a hand over her gaping mouth. "May the Almighty protect us!"

Shooting a glance over his shoulder, Dalen narrowed his eyes. "Still want to stay here?" he asked. "Or are you ready to leave?"

The poor woman started sobbing, falling to her knees in the middle of the road. "What is it?" she blubbered. "What?"

Dalen wanted to yell at her, but that would do no good. These people were terrified. He had to calm them down and get them focused on an orderly evacuation. He did not know what was going on out there, but he was certain that New Beloran was no longer safe. No, he wasn't Miri or Tommy or Marcus, but of all the people here, he had the most experience with this kind of thing.

When he turned, he found over a dozen people standing in the street. Slack-jawed fools who couldn't stop staring at that pillar of light. Whatever it was. More had come out since the earthquake.

Dalen strode toward them, pointing a finger at the man who had almost assaulted him earlier. "You!" he said. "Gerald! Go with Mrs. Carmichael! Get food!"

The man blinked and then turned his attention to Dalen. "Go flay yourself, boy," he spat. "I won't be taking orders from-"

Stuffing his fear down into the pit of his stomach, Dalen stepped up to the big brute and grabbed a handful of his shirt.

He pulled Gerald close, close enough to smell his foul breath. "This isn't a debate," he said through gritted teeth. "You want to survive? You do what I tell you."

"I will not-"

He shoved Gerald to the ground, the big man landing on his ass and shaking his head. "How dare you-"

Dalen ignored the fool, marching past him into the middle of the crowd. "Listen to me!" he yelled. "We can't stay here! The city isn't safe anymore! Go back inside! Get a change of clothes and all the food you can carry!"

Several dozen eyes fell upon him, people wondering whether they should listen to this stranger who was ranting and raving in the middle of the street.

"Now!" Dalen bellowed.

That was all they needed; the crowd scattered, people running back into their houses to carry out his orders. At least, he hoped that's what they were doing. He couldn't afford to stay very long. If they didn't return in five minutes, he would take his companions and go. They could sort out the food situation when they weren't in immediate danger. *And Tommy?* he wondered. *Miri? Will you be able to find them?*

One problem at a time.

To his relief, several people emerged from their houses, fully dressed and carrying bags full of supplies. Should they leave? Was anyone else coming? How long could they remain here?

Mrs. Carmichael hurried out her front door in a simple, black riding dress, carrying two sacks in each hand. "I brought everything I could," she said, trotting down the front steps. "Some carrots, apples. A loaf of bread and some cheese. Hopefully, it'll keep."

"Where do we go now?" a skinny, black-haired man asked.

Dalen did a quick headcount. Over thirty people stood in the street: men, women, children. The good folks who had hopped to obey his commands had brought their families out. They were ready to go.

"Follow me," Dalen said.

REINING IN CHAMP, Desa brought the horse to a stop. Midnight kept going for a few paces but quickly halted, ignoring Tommy's repeated attempts to spur him into motion. The stallion would not leave without her.

Dropping out of the saddle, Desa ran up to a man who stood on the curb, a tall fellow with a round belly and bushy, gray eyebrows. He blinked when he realized that she was standing right in front of him.

"You have to flee the city," Desa said. "All of you do."

The man started. "Why would we do that?" he demanded. "This is our home!"

Without looking, she pointed westward to the glowing pillar that lit up the night. "That is a barrier," she said. "A barrier created by a being far more powerful than either of us to contain something much worse. And when it fails, everyone in this city will die."

The infuriating fool of a man only laughed at her. "You've had too much to drink," he said. "Go home, woman!"

Kalia stepped up beside Desa to offer her support. Her face could have been carved from ice. "Tell me," she said. "Have you ever seen something like that before?"

"Aladri witchcraft," the man said. "I've heard stories."

Tossing her head back, Desa winced. She pressed her fingertips into her temples, groaning in frustration. "This isn't 'Aladri witchcraft,'" she said. "No Field Binder could ever produce that kind of-"

She was cut off by a devastating screech, a horrible, ear-splitting cry that sounded like the death of hope itself. She turned, gazing westward to the distant mansion, and felt her heart sink when the beam of light faded away.

"Mercy," she whispered.

It was too late for all of them.

Hanak Tuvar was loose.

17

The road sloped gently downward, running westward back to Delarac's mansion. From the top of this small hill, Desa could see over the wall that surrounded the man's property. She could just make out the roof of the mansion from half a mile away.

Something dark landed on it, a squid-like creature that let out a menacing wail. Its oily tentacles dug into the shingles, tearing them up. And then it was slinking forward, dropping into the front yard.

The portly man almost fell over, bracing a hand against a lamppost to steady himself. His thick, gray eyebrows tried to climb up his forehead. "What was... What was..."

Desa shook her head in dismay. "That is the thing that will kill you if you stay here," she said. "Gather your neighbours and get them out of here as quickly as you can."

"Hurry, Desa," Miri urged. "We have to find the others."

Starting down the slope, Desa closed her eyes and sighed softly. "It's too late for that now," she said. "The rest of you go. Find your friends and get out of the city."

"Where are you going?" Tommy demanded.

She twisted around, looking back over her shoulder with a

glare that insisted she would suffer no arguments. Tommy and Miri stood side by side, both backing away when they sensed her resolve. "To buy you time."

She opened her mouth to protest when Kalia fell in beside her, but the other woman spoke up before Desa could get a word out. "You are *not* going to face that thing alone. I'm going with you, and that's final."

"Fair enough," Desa said. "Replenish your Infusions."

She made herself one with the Ether, the world transforming into an ocean of writhing molecules. Kalia did the same, light exploding from her body with the fury of a thousand suns. Such power! Shouldn't this have been enough to defeat *Hanak Tuvar*? No, that was foolishness. If Mercy couldn't do it, what chance did two Field Binders have?

She could feel the squid-creature creeping across Delarac's front lawn. And that wrongness that surrounded it, that strange halo that distorted the very laws of nature: she could feel that too. Why so slow? Surely that thing could move faster. Perhaps Mercy had weakened it. In the end, it didn't matter; if *Hanak Tuvar* wanted to give her more time, she would use it.

The denizens of this neighbourhood were fleeing, following Miri and Tommy. She scanned the nearby houses and found that most of the people were gone. A few were cowering in their basements or in closets, but it was the best she could do. If they wouldn't leave, she didn't have time to argue with them. Champ fled as well, choosing to stay with Midnight, the only one who made him feel safe. Good. Better that he got as far away from here as possible.

Desa began with the Gravity-Sink in her belt buckle. As it stood, she would get another twenty minutes of continuous use out of it. Not good enough. If she was going to fight a demon from the void, she wanted every advantage she could get. Directing her thoughts with an ordered focus, she thickened the strands of Ether that formed the Sink's lattice.

Hanak Tuvar crawled over the wall.

Desa moved on to the Electric-Source in her ring, replenishing its supply of energy. The Force-Sink in her bracelet was already as strong as she could hope to make it. She hadn't needed to use it. Kalia was restoring her Infusions as well, working quickly and calmly despite the impending danger.

Hanak Tuvar began scuttling up the street, roaring at them, its tentacles cracking the cobblestones with every step. Desa ignored it, completing her work. After everything she had been through, she would *not* be intimidated by this thing! What did scare her, however, was the halo.

It didn't just surround *Hanak Tuvar.* No, it expanded a short distance in front of the beast and left a trail in its wake. A trail of wrongness stretching back to Delarac's house. Whenever the halo enveloped a lamppost, it melted, the flames puffing out in an instant. Pools of liquid steel dotted the sidewalks. If Desa was caught in that distortion, every piece of metal on her person would melt as well. And who could say what else might happen?

Opening her eyes, she released the Ether. "You want me?" she said. "Well, here I am."

Bending her knees, she triggered her Gravity-Sink and leaped, shooting off the ground like a firework rising into the night sky. Kalia severed her connection to the Ether and did the same, flying high into the air.

"Bullets won't work," Kalia said. "How do we kill it?"

Hissing air through her teeth, Desa stared down at the beast with rage burning a hole in her heart. "We'll have to find another way," she said. "I'm going to draw it away. You get behind it, and we'll see what we can do."

Lessening the flow of gravity into her belt-buckle, Desa slowly lowered herself onto a nearby rooftop and then killed the Sink entirely. She caught a glimpse of Kalia claiming a perch on the other side of the road. This would have to do.

The squid was down in the street, its tentacles pounding the pavement as it closed in on her. Somehow, the halo allowed her to see it despite the lack of lamplight. Any trace of lethargy was gone; the creature now moved with frightening speed. Perhaps it had recovered from whatever Mercy had done.

It scurried up to the base of her building, tilted its monstrous head up and shrieked. That mouth was an abyss threatening to swallow her whole. With surprising agility, it hopped onto the front wall of the boarding house and began climbing.

Cocking her head, Desa smiled down at it. "Impressive," she said. "I wouldn't have thought you could haul that ugly lump of flesh you call a body all the way up a building."

Backing away across the flat rooftop, Desa reached for the pistol on her right hip only to realize that it was lying on the floor of Delarac's ballroom. Not that it would do much good, but she still wished for a second gun. You'd be surprised how many problems could be solved with a well-placed bullet.

Hanak Tuvar crawled onto the roof, standing up on its tentacles. That strange, crimson haze surrounded it, spreading like an infection. "This is how it should be," Desa said. "Just you and me."

Indeed, a voice whispered in her mind. *You have been a worthy opponent. It pleases me to face you in my true form.*

"You..."

The sound of *Hanak Tuvar's* laughter reverberated inside her skull. *Did you think that I was merely a savage beast?* it whispered. *I no longer possess the ability to utilize your primitive, vocal communication, but my ability to comprehend it has not changed.*

Desa stepped forward with her head held high, summoning as much courage as she could muster. "That's good," she said. "Then you'll understand when I tell you that I am going to kill you."

Impossible.

"We'll see."

The creature surged toward her.

Pulsing her Gravity-Sink, Desa jumped and back-flipped over the narrow gap between this building and the one behind it. She landed on the slanted incline of a gabled roof, backing away until she reached the peak.

Townhouses.

She was atop a block of townhouses, each one pressed close to its neighbours without an inch of space between them. She heard the voices of a dozen people in the street behind her, idiotic gawkers who wanted to see what had caused all this commotion. "Get out of here!" she shouted at them.

Hanak Tuvar launched itself from the flat roof and sailed across the gap with ease. It slammed into the back wall of the townhouse, tentacles digging into the bricks, tearing out chunks of rubble. And then it was climbing.

Desa retreated down the front slope of the roof, gasping for breath. She looked about frantically, trying to form a plan. Think! There had to be something she could do. She could feel Kalia's Gravity-Sink. The other woman was getting close, coming in on Desa's left.

The squid-demon came into view, raising two of its oily limbs into the air and wailing. That was enough to convince those idiots in the street to flee. Kalia was hiding behind a chimney, several houses over, on her left.

Turning right, Desa ran along the slanted roof, using her Gravity-Sink to make herself lighter. At a quarter of her normal weight, it was easy to avoid a fall. She didn't dare look back, but she could hear the shingles cracking as *Hanak Tuvar* pursued her.

When she had put another two houses between herself and Kalia, Desa finally turned around. Her heart was pounding. Her lungs burning with more than just exertion. There was no use in denying it; she was afraid.

Hanak Tuvar was further up the roof, crawling along its peak. It had left a trail of holes in its wake along with that ugly, scarlet haze Yes, that would do nicely.

"Force-Sink!" Desa bellowed.

Trusting her partner to understand, she extended her closed fist and projected a blast of lightning from her ring. A jagged lance of electricity struck the chimney that Kalia hid behind, shattering it to rubble. Rubble that seemed to hang in the air, immobilized.

Kalia popped up from behind that pile of floating bricks, and with a scream, she sent them zipping toward *Hanak Tuvar* at incredible speed. Every single one of those projectiles passed easily through the red halo and drove itself into the demon's body.

It screamed, rearing like a horse, its tentacles flailing about. Its weight came down on the roof, leaving a spiderweb of cracks.

Desa turned and jumped, using her Gravity-Sink to propel herself across the street. She landed atop a townhouse that was identical to the one she had left behind, whirling around to find her enemy squirming and writhing.

"So," Desa said. "You can feel pain."

The creature dug its slimy limbs into the roof, ripping out the shingles, holding them in a tight grip. One by one, it flung them at her.

She had just enough time to get her arm up and activate her bracelet, bits of debris hanging suspended in the air. In less than ten seconds, she had quite the collection of floating garbage. "Turnabout, huh?" Desa called out. "Well, I've never been one to play fair."

She thrust her open palm toward the cloud of rubbish, triggering the Force-Source in her ring at the same instant that she killed the Sink in her bracelet. The blast of kinetic energy sent every piece back across the road.

They pelted *Hanak Tuvar,* causing the beast to screech and recoil.

The roof gave way beneath its girth, the massive squid dropping into a third-floor bedroom. And then the screams started. Someone was still in that house! Someone who hadn't fled with the others.

A thick, black tentacle came up through the hole, wrapped tightly around a golden-haired woman in a filmy nightdress. The rest of *Hanak Tuvar* followed, its mouth stretching into a gaping maw that sucked the poor woman in.

"No!"

To her shock and horror, *Hanak Tuvar* grew, its body inflating, its limbs extending. Only a few inches, but the change was noticeable. *How little you understand,* it whispered. *Within my realm, my power is absolute.*

The red halo expanded, spreading down to the sidewalk and then to the curb. It somehow managed to encompass three separate lampposts that ripped themselves out of the ground. They didn't melt! Why didn't they melt? The question was driven from her mind when the three lampposts tilted slightly, angling themselves toward Desa like a volley of arrows ready to fly. The first one streaked toward her.

Desa turned, running along the rooftop, heedless of the unsure footing. Her Gravity-Sink would keep her aloft. The lamppost crashed into the front wall of a house behind her, leaving an enormous hole and rattling the entire block of buildings.

Another one came at her.

This second missile punched through a window, taking a large section of the wall with it. And some of the floor as well. The house was a ruin, chunks of brick and plaster falling to the ground. And still, she ran.

The third lamppost flew across the street.

With a thought, Desa made herself weightless. She bent her

knees and jumped, flinging herself into the sky just before the roof collapsed beneath her. A sharp wind stole the warmth from her body, but she barely even noticed.

Twisting around in mid-flight, she found *Hanak Tuvar* crawling over the townhouses toward Kalia, the red haze expanding to make room for it. Luckily, the other woman was no fool. Desa could track her by her active Gravity-Sink; she was already on the move.

"Oh no, you don't," Desa growled.

She communed with the Ether and directed her thoughts into the townhouse beneath *Hanak Tuvar,* going floor by floor, searching for any innocent bystanders. She found no one within that residence or either of its two neighbours. Mercy be praised.

The Ether fled as she drew her left-hand pistol, the one with Infused ammunition. "Your power is absolute, is it?" Furious, she fired a single shot, a Gravity-Source bullet that melted into a puddle of lead when it got within two feet of *Hanak Tuvar.* That made no difference. An Infusion remained intact no matter what happened to the molecules that it was bound to.

Desa triggered it.

The surge of gravity combined with *Hanak Tuvar's* weight caused the roof to collapse, pulling the squid down into an empty bedroom and anchoring it there. Unable to move, it screeched and feebly waved its tentacles like a man shaking his fist.

With her enemy trapped, Desa fired a second shot.

Her bullet became a drop of metallic goo that landed on *Hanak Tuvar's* bulbous head. At her command, it released a torrent of heat, enough to kill a man and scorch his flesh. *Hanak Tuvar* might not have died, but it certainly didn't enjoy the experience.

Its misery was compounded when the floor gave way, and it

plunged into one of the house's lower levels, taking the Gravity-Source with it. Cries of rage echoed through the night.

Kalia was nearly a block away, leaping from the rooftops to land on the sidewalk and continuing on foot. Excellent. With *Hanak Tuvar* distracted, she'd had the time she'd needed to get away.

Desa gasped when the squid-creature emerged from the ruined townhouse, crawling back onto the roof. Her Gravity-Source was still active, still tugging on the beast with a force twice as strong as the Earth's natural pull, but *Hanak Tuvar* just ignored it.

Within my realm, my power is absolute.

It didn't bother using its tentacles; it just screamed, and the buildings crumbled around it. Bricks, shingles, pieces of wood from inside the house: they all formed a cyclone around a huge, black creature that hovered despite the pull of a Gravity-Source. A storm of rubble came hurtling toward Desa.

She pointed her gun forward and to the right, firing several shots that pushed her backward and to the left. The flying avalanche surged through the space where she had been hanging, streaking off into the starry sky and then falling on buildings several streets over.

The last of her ammunition was gone. She didn't mind; it wouldn't do much good anyway. She killed her Gravity-Sink for half a second and began her slow, steady descent. She twisted around to find the ground rushing up to meet her.

Kalia was running on the sidewalk.

Desa fell in beside her, killing the Sink when her foot touched the ground and sprinting as fast as she could. *Hanak Tuvar's* screams sent chills down her spine.

Unable to resist the temptation, she looked back. The creature was standing in the road, surrounded by that ruddy haze. *Why isn't it chasing us?* she wondered.

Kalia was huffing and puffing, her face flushed, sweat glistening on her skin. "What do we do now?" she asked.

"We regroup," Desa said. "And come up with another plan."

"STAY TOGETHER!" Tommy shouted.

At least three dozen people ran along the cobblestone road between two lines of tall, blocky buildings. Most of them were carrying bundles of clothes or bags full of food. A few had guns. Others held small children. Young and old, men and women: they were a motley bunch. But they all had one thing in common.

Fear.

Hanak Tuvar's inhuman screams pursued them through the night. They had been running for over ten minutes, but Tommy could still hear the creature shrieking in the distance, an endless, cacophonous song, punctuated by the sound of buildings crashing.

Sitting tall in Midnight's saddle with the reins in hand, Tommy frowned as he watched the people running past. He kept the horse at a trot to keep pace with the crowd. Midnight could outrun these folks without breaking a sweat, but he didn't dare leave them behind. Someone had to guide them out of this city.

With Desa and Kalia off fighting the demon, Miri had claimed the brown horse that they had rescued from Delarac's mansion. She moved up beside a man who had stopped to look back at the destruction. "Keep going," she urged.

The good fellow nodded and hastened to join the others.

"They'll be all right," Tommy said. "Won't they?"

Miri looked at him, and he could see the hopelessness in her eyes. She might put on a brave face for the others, but she couldn't hide her feelings from him. "I don't know," she barked. "We have no idea what that thing is or what kind of power it might...Look, if anyone can survive against an enemy like that, it's Desa Kincaid."

The crowd surged into Bowman Plaza, where the Parliament Building stood solemn and silent on the north side of the square. Ten seconds after that, they all dispersed, running in a hundred different directions with nothing resembling a plan.

Nudging Midnight into motion, Tommy rode the stallion into the middle of the square. He stood in the stirrups, scanning back and forth to let his gaze fall upon anyone who might be looking. "Stop!" he called out. "We have to stay together!"

No one listened.

"Stop!"

They just kept running.

Growling in frustration, Tommy retrieved an arrow from his quiver, nocked it and pointed his bow into the sky. He let it fly, the shaft vanishing into the darkness. And then he triggered the Electric-Source he had created.

A spiderweb of lightning streaked across the heavens, jagged, silver bolts expanding in all directions. For a moment, everyone just stopped. And then they started screaming, running even harder, trying desperately to get away.

Hanging his head, Tommy pressed two fingers against his forehead. "Should have seen that coming," he muttered. "For the love of the Almighty..."

He dropped out of Midnight's saddle and climbed onto the rim of the fountain in the middle of the plaza. Triggering his Sonic-Source, he drew in a deep breath and spoke with all the confidence he could muster.

"STOP!"

His booming voice brought everyone to a halt.

One by one, they turned around to see who had addressed them. Nearly a hundred people, many of them dressed in bedclothes, all staring at the idiot who stood in the spray, heedless of the night's chill.

"I know you're afraid," Tommy began. "But we have to stay together."

"That thing!" one man shouted, pointing westward. The poor fellow looked like he was about ready to faint. "It'll come for us."

Pressing his lips together, Tommy nodded slowly in agreement. "Yes, it will," he said, jumping down from the fountain and striding toward the man. "Which is why we need a plan. If we're going to flee the city, we need supplies."

A young, pale-skinned woman with her hair hanging loose clutched a bag of food to her chest. "You can't have mine!" she declared as if she expected everyone to fall on her like a pack of wolves. Which only brought her the attention that she had been hoping to avoid.

"We're going to make for Ofalla," Tommy said. "It's the nearest settlement, the safest place we can go right now. We stay together as a group, share our resources. No one gets left behind. Is that clear?"

"But there's not enough for everyone!" someone shouted.

Cold and wet, Tommy drew himself up to full height. He let his gaze fall upon the speaker, silencing any further dissent. "If necessary, we'll resort to hunting," he replied. "These lands are full of rabbits. We can cook them over a fire if we need to."

He hoped to the Almighty that no one realized he was improvising. He had no idea how plentiful rabbits were. Or any other animal for that matter. In the end, it was irrelevant. Staying here meant certain death. So, they would just have to take their chances in the wilderness.

"Tommy!"

Dalen led a procession of disheveled people out of a side street. At least fifty of them. Most were properly dressed, thank the Almighty. Tommy couldn't imagine traveling through the wilderness in bedclothes. But for those who had fled the west end of the city, there was no going back. *Hanak Tuvar* was still out there.

Tommy sauntered up to the other man, grinning and shaking his head. "You beautiful bastard!" He seized Dalen by the shoulders and kissed him on the lips. "I knew you'd be able to find us!"

The other man pulled away. "All I did was follow the lightning," he said. "It wasn't hard."

Tommy stepped aside so that Miri could throw her arms around Dalen's neck and kiss him. That drew a few stares from the people who had gathered in the plaza. He heard angry mutters from several of them.

"All right," Tommy said. "Now that we're all here, it's time to get organized."

"We should head down the south road," Dalen said as Miri rained kisses over his face. "Swing west and make for Ofalla."

"We can't leave yet," Tommy insisted.

"Why not?"

He gestured to the buildings all around them, sweeping his hand back and forth in wide arcs. "There are people in those houses," he said. "Frightened people who heard the commotion and decided that hiding was their best option. If we leave them, *Hanak Tuvar* will get them."

Mrs. Carmichael approached him with a bag of food held to her chest. "But what are we supposed to do?" she asked. "We can't save them all."

"We'll divide into teams of five," Tommy said. "Spread out through the neighbourhoods and knock on every door. Tell anyone you find that we're evacuating the city. They're to bring as much food as they can carry and join us here in Bowman Plaza."

"And if they won't come?" a young woman asked.

"Then we leave without them," Tommy said. "If someone doesn't want to join us, respect their wishes and move on to the next house. Do not get into a fight over it! If you're wounded in the process, it will only slow you down.

"Miri, take a team of twenty with you. Go to the stables. Bring back horses and wagons. Dalen, I want you here in the plaza. Keep a count of the supplies that everyone brings in. We need to know what we're working with so that we can properly ration the food.

"The rest of you, spread out and start knocking on doors. Whenever you collect five more people, split them off into a new team and send them in a different direction. I want to cover as much ground as possible. We leave the city at dawn. Anyone who hasn't joined us by then gets left behind."

A portly fellow with a double-chin pushed his way through the crowd, planting himself in front of Tommy. "Why should we listen to you?" he demanded. "A bloody degenerate! Just who are you anyway?"

Tommy stretched his hand into the air, releasing a thin bolt of lightning from his ring. A demonstration that produced more than a few screams. When it was over, they were all watching him in wide-eyed horror. "I'm the one who's going to keep you alive," he said coldly. "Now, get moving!"

GASPING FOR BREATH, Desa fell back against the wall of an alley. She placed a hand over her heart as she tried to fight off her fatigue. "Is it still out there?" she whispered. "Sweet Mercy, doesn't that thing ever quit?"

Kalia was at the mouth of the alley, peering around the corner. "It seems to have stopped for now," she murmured. "I don't know…"

They had been running for over two hours, trying to get back to Tommy. Twice now, they had encountered one of his teams, townsfolk who had instructed them to go to the central plaza and join the evacuation. Desa would like nothing better than to reunite with her friends and flee this wretched city in haste. Unfortunately, that wasn't an option.

Hanak Tuvar was spreading its infection, distorting the very laws of nature everywhere it went. It seemed to be expanding its territory in fits and bursts, moving into a new neighbourhood and then resting to regain its strength. The one thing that diverted it from its ghastly purpose was Desa. When it saw her, it focused all of its energy on capturing her. She was quite sure that if it ever managed to trap her inside that red haze, it would kill her with a thought.

That seemed to be its only weakness. Its power *was* absolute – or nearly so – within the red halo, but it had very little influence in the areas that it had not yet changed.

Hunched over with a hand on her chest, Desa shut her eyes and trembled. "All right," she said. "We can't stay here. Let's get moving."

Kalia rounded on her, striding into the alley and laying a hand on Desa's shoulder. That look of concern in her eyes. Desa knew that she was in for a lecture. "You're much too tired," Kalia said. "If you go back out there, you're going to get yourself killed."

"We have to keep it distracted."

"At the cost of your life?"

Overwhelmed, Desa threw her arms around the other woman, resting her chin on Kalia's shoulder. "I'm just one person. If my death saves a hundred others, I'll pay that price."

"And you wonder why I love you."

Tears leaked from Desa's eyes. She nuzzled her partner's shoulder, trembling. "I don't wonder," she said. "Not anymore."

Unwilling to waste another second, she crept to the sidewalk and peered up the street. The red haze started about two blocks away. As she took in the sight, Desa realized that "haze" was the wrong word. It wasn't fog or vapour; the colours simply changed as if the light passing through that spot had been refracted.

Hanak Tuvar landed atop a church with a high steeple, its bulbous head thrown back, its tentacles digging into the stone. The entire building collapsed under its weight. And then it began tossing the rubble aside.

At first, she didn't know why, but the answer became clear when *Hanak Tuvar* moved a large, stone block to expose a battered man lying underneath. The poor fellow was still alive. Barely. He yelped as a tentacle slithered around him and stuffed him into the creature's mouth.

The demon began to grow after it swallowed him. Desa had seen it do that several times. Whenever it fed on someone, its bloated body swelled by several inches. Several inches for each victim. If it consumed most of the city...

"Hey!" Desa shouted.

Hanak Tuvar whirled around, focusing its attention on her. It scrambled up the street, stopping at the edge of the red halo, refusing to move beyond that point. Why it didn't just expand its reach, she couldn't say. Perhaps it was too tired.

Hanak Tuvar raised its two front tentacles and brought them down on the cobblestones, smashing them. Dozens and dozens of small rocks floated into the air and then shot toward Desa like a hailstorm.

She had just enough time to duck back into the alley before a hundred projectiles went flying past. Going back out there would not be wise. She had the beast's attention. That was all she needed.

"Come on," Desa said, running deeper into the alley.

"Where are we going?" Kalia panted.

"Anywhere but here."

. . .

TOMMY INSPECTED a wagon full of food. Sacks of apples, pears, carrots, bread, cheese and jerky filled the wagon bed. Enough to last for months if he were still traveling in a small group. Sadly, that was no longer the case.

Over four thousand people had gathered in the square when the first traces of sunlight crept into the eastern sky. Four thousand lost souls, most of them frightened and talking quietly with one another. The few snippets of conversation that he overheard were centred on the most inane topics. These people could stand here while a monster ravaged their city and argue about whether a marriage betrothal between two of their neighbours would go forward. It must have been an attempt to keep their minds occupied, and he was more than willing to leave them to it. Anything that kept them from panicking was all right with him.

Four thousand people. A few years ago, Tommy would have been unable to conceive of it, but according to Dalen, it was less than a quarter of the city's population. The teams who returned to the plaza all had stories about cantankerous citizens who refused to leave their homes.

Well, he had expected as much. Some folks were just too stubborn to do what was sensible. At least no one had gotten into a fight. He'd heard several tales of men brandishing firearms when someone suggested that they should evacuate, but no one had been hurt, thank the Almighty.

Miri had done her job well, bringing back thirty wagons and enough horses to pull them. He had expected recalcitrance from the stablemen, but most of them were quite willing to evacuate. He suspected that Miri had persuaded them with her usual charm. Most of the wagons she had brought back were stuffed to the brim with food, but even with the feast laid out before him, he feared it wouldn't be enough. Not for four thousand mouths.

It had started as a trickle: three or four people wandering

into the plaza, saying they had been told to come. Then three or four became ten or twelve. By the wee hours of the night, dozens of people were showing up every few minutes. He worried about gathering them all in one place – a big crowd was easy prey for *Hanak Tuvar* – but he could think of no other way to organize them. And Desa seemed to be keeping the demon busy.

Tommy had gone up to the roof of a tall building at the edge of the plaza, hoping to get a sense of what was going on. His biggest clue came from the lamplight, or rather the lack thereof. Large patches of the city had gone dark. He was certain those were the areas that had been visited by *Hanak Tuvar*. Lampposts melted and flames were snuffed out everywhere it went.

A few hours ago, Kalia had shown up to give him a report. She and Desa were keeping the demon contained in the west end of the city. Every ten or fifteen minutes, they would come out of hiding to taunt the creature and distract it from whatever it was doing.

According to Kalia, *Hanak Tuvar* never left the confines of the strange, red halo that it had created. Whenever it saw Desa or Kalia, the demon flew into a rage, directing all of its efforts toward catching them, a hunt that was impeded by its limited mobility. Why on Earth it would be so single-minded, he couldn't begin to guess – perhaps some remnant of Adele remained – but the plan seemed to be working. Energy that could have been put to use expanding its territory was instead focused on capturing Desa. Or killing her. Tommy wasn't sure what it wanted. He was just grateful for the opportunity his friends had provided, an opportunity to gather people.

Still dressed in black, Tommy stood near the fountain with his hands in his pockets. He had removed the bandana; there was no point in hiding his face now. Anxiety clawed at his insides. He had told Kalia to be here at dawn, but there was no sign of her or Desa.

Zoe came plodding up to him, the wind teasing thin strands of her red hair. Her eyes were downcast. Whether from exhaustion or emotional stress, he couldn't say. "The sun is coming up," she said. "Some of the people are starting to wonder why we haven't left the city."

He said nothing.

"Do you want to wait for Desa?" Zoe asked.

"We can't afford to do that," he said. "Spread the word. We're leaving."

Zoe offered a curt nod and then ran off to follow his instructions. He had put himself in charge. That came with certain responsibilities.

Hopping onto a bench, Tommy triggered his Sonic-Source. "Everyone, please listen!" Silence fell over the plaza. "It's time for us to leave the city."

He saw many people nodding in agreement.

"We will proceed south on Main Street until we reach the outskirts of town. From there, we will turn west toward Ofalla. Wagon teams will go first, and the rest of us will follow. I want an orderly procession. Stay together. No shoving, no hollering. We will move as quickly as we can.

"I know that many of you are hungry and tired, but we must put at least twenty miles between us and this city before we stop to rest. Now, let's move."

It startled him when the wagons lurched into motion, rolling out of the plaza and down the wide thoroughfare. He had expected some resistance – fears, misgivings, *something* – but the people listened to him. They had made up their minds that his plan offered the best chance of survival, and once that decision was made, there was no point in quibbling.

So, they began their journey.

· · ·

WITH DAWN'S light painting the sky a deep blue, Desa landed on the slanted roof of a small house. She looked back over her shoulder.

The distortion was more visible in the daylight. Not a cloud or mist, it was just a patch of the city where the colours were *wrong.* As if everything but red had been stripped away. *Hanak Tuvar's* gruesome head poked up over the rim of the building.

Kalia landed beside her, crouching on the rooftop with a hand on the shingles. She was exhausted. "I was hoping it would flee when the sun came up."

"I don't think we're that lucky."

"So, what now?"

Wiping sweat off her brow with the back of one hand, Desa exhaled roughly. "Tommy will be leading the citizens away down the south road," she panted. "We meet up with him and get out of here."

Their conversation was cut short when *Hanak Tuvar* ripped the chimney off its mountings and flung it at them.

Twisting around, Desa raised her left hand to shield herself and activated the Force-Sink in her bracelet. The chimney came to an abrupt halt, hanging five feet above the lip of the rooftop, allowing Kalia to take position behind it.

Inwardly, Desa whispered a prayer to Mercy. It had been sheer luck that saved her. Her Sink was almost filled to capacity. She had replenished its hunger for energy twice, but *Hanak Tuvar* rarely gave them enough time to craft proper Infusions. Everything was a hasty touch-up while they hid from the beast.

Desa killed her Sink while Kalia released a blast of kinetic force that sent the chimney back toward the demon. Not enough force. The damn thing barely closed half the distance before falling to the ground.

"Come on!" Desa growled.

Together, they sprinted to the peak of the roof and then down the other side, triggering their nearly-depleted Gravity-

Sinks as they jumped off the edge. They drifted gently down to the sidewalk, killed their Infusions and ran.

Hanak Tuvar wasn't following.

Maybe it was too tired; it seemed to grow weary every time it expanded the red halo. Desa had witnessed it on several occasions. *Hanak Tuvar* would give up the chase and start searching for something to eat. Devouring humans seemed to restore its energy.

She and Kalia had landed on a road lined with small houses, all of which seemed to be empty. There was no way to be certain without embracing the Ether, and she was too fatigued for that. She toyed with the idea of knocking on doors but quickly dismissed it. Tommy's crews would have passed through almost every neighbourhood. She had encountered them half a dozen times throughout the night. Anyone who was willing to evacuate would have already left. She didn't have time to stand here arguing about it.

Less than half a block away, a crossing street ran southward to the edge of the city. That was the way to go.

Ignoring her aches and pains, Desa half ran, half stumbled along the road, Kalia at her side. They rounded a corner onto another street. This one had tall, gray buildings that would have served as offices for the city's various businesses. All were empty at the moment.

"We're not gonna make it, are we?" Kalia muttered.

"Of course, we are."

"It's five miles to the edge of the city."

Desa stiffened, a new wave of determination washing over her. "I don't care," she growled. "I'm not letting that thing win!"

Kalia heaved out a breath and then forced herself to press on. "You're right," she whispered. "To the bitter end!"

And it would be bitter. The thought of what *Hanak Tuvar* might do when it got its slimy tentacles on them turned Desa's stomach. But at least she kept fighting. If nothing else, she could face death with the knowledge that she had not given up.

Just as the despair settled over her, Midnight emerged from a nearby street, stopping in the middle of the road. He snorted as if to say it was about time that Desa and Kalia showed up. He had probably been wandering for hours, searching for them.

Grinning triumphantly, Desa stumbled up to her horse. "There you are," she murmured, caressing Midnight's face. "Good boy."

She climbed into the saddle, Kalia snuggling up behind her, and Midnight took off. The buildings flew past, the morning sunlight driving away the night's chill. She searched for any stragglers – people who might have failed to reach the central plaza in time – but found nobody. If anyone remained in this neighbourhood, they had hunkered down in their houses.

Hanak Tuvar screamed in the distance.

Another horse might have spooked, but Midnight remained calm, galloping down the street at full speed. How many times had he saved her life now? She was losing count. "This," Desa said, "deserves a carrot."

Midnight neighed his agreement.

They encountered no one else on their way out of the city.

18

The morning sun, shining bright in a beautiful, blue sky, was almost enough to make Kalia forget about everything that had happened the night before. A procession of thousands followed a dirt road on the southern outskirts of New Beloran, making their way westward.

Mothers carried young children; boys just shy of manhood walked with their heads down. Some wore fine clothing of silk or cotton. Others wore overalls and work shirts. *Some* were still in their bedclothes. They were young and old, dark and light, people from all walks of life. And they plodded along like condemned criminals on their way to the headsman.

Life was starting to creep into the fields on either side of the road, yellow grass turning green with the onset of spring. Birds fluttered about; squirrels carried nuts back to their nests. You would never guess that a demon lurked just a few miles away.

On her right, the city stood silent under the harsh sunlight. The road was about a mile away from the outermost buildings. Sometimes, she caught a glimpse of redness, a place where *Hanak Tuvar* had spread its infection. The creature had not made its presence felt since her last encounter with it. Perhaps it was recuperating.

Desa was rigid in Midnight's saddle, clutching the reins in a firm grip. She hadn't said a word since they left the city. That worried Kalia to no end. She knew her partner well. Desa was probably blaming herself for all of this.

The caravan of lost souls continued its mournful journey.

After about an hour, they came to a bridge of white bricks that ran over the train tracks. It was wide enough for ten people to walk abreast, but that still slowed things down more than she would have liked. Where were Miri and the others? At the front of this procession, no doubt. Kalia suspected that she and Desa were somewhere near the back. It was hard to be sure. But she needed to speak with them.

Midnight walked slowly over the bridge, giving her plenty of time to take in the scenery. Four parallel tracks ran southward to the distant horizon, but she saw no trains. That presented a new problem. Sooner or later, a train would pull into New Beloran station, bringing dozens – if not hundreds – of passengers with it. Fresh meat for *Hanak Tuvar*.

"It will destroy the world," Desa mumbled.

Kalia pursed her lips, considering that, and then leaned in close to whisper in her lover's ear. "Surely, it can't be that powerful," she insisted. "A few well-placed cannons might be able to kill it. Assuming we can make them fire rocks."

"Mercy," Desa said, her hands tightening around the reins. "Her people came from another universe, a realm similar to this one. She told me that in less than two months, *Hanak Tuvar* had rendered almost a third of her world uninhabitable."

Kalia shuddered. "It takes our finest sailing ships the better part of two years to circumnavigate this globe," she said. "How could that thing make the entire world uninhabitable in just a few months?"

"That distortion."

"What?"

"The redness," Desa growled, stiffening in Kalia's arms. "Didn't you see the grass in Delarac's backyard? It crumbled away. Somehow, *Hanak Tuvar* changed the structure of reality. And I suspect that one consequence is that plants won't grow."

Changed the structure of reality?

Yesterday, Kalia would have insisted that such a thing was impossible. The world was what it was. But she couldn't deny what she had seen with her own eyes. This was all a bit over her head.

Shutting her eyes, she touched her nose to the side of Desa's neck. "Whatever it is," she whispered. "You'll find a way to stop it."

Her partner said nothing.

She found more green fields on the other side of the bridge, a vast expanse of grassland that stretched all the way to the southern bank of the Vinrella. The river was too far off to be seen, but it was there. Maybe they could catch a ship. No, that wouldn't do. No captain would take on four thousand passengers.

It occurred to her that this might be the same road Desa and Tommy had traveled a year ago, a road that would take her back to the desert. Did she want to go back? Her deputies would have plenty of questions. Harl was probably sheriff by now.

With the danger passed and the terror fading away, Kalia became painfully aware of her hunger. Her stomach rumbled. One glance at the people walking beside Midnight, and she was certain they felt the same way. Tired, hungry, hopeless.

Kalia squinted against the sunlight, her hair fluttering in the breeze. "What if we could contain it somehow?" she mused. "Trap in a cave or something?"

"Last time," Desa replied. "Mercy and Vengeance had to

work together to contain it. To trap it within a pocket of the Ether. Now one of them is gone, and the other one is dead."

"We don't know that Mercy is dead."

Once again, Desa fell silent.

Onward, the sombre procession continued, through the endless grasslands, over rolling hills. No one said much of anything; people just shuffled along with their heads down. Kalia wanted to engage her love in conversation, to say something that might ease the sting of loss, but she could tell that Desa needed quiet. So, she kept her thoughts to herself.

Morning blossomed into afternoon, the warm sunlight of a spring day offering a respite from her gloomy thoughts. It was almost pleasant. Almost. Every time she started to enjoy the scenery, cold, hard reality hit her like a splash of water in the face.

By late afternoon, she was starting to feel the weight of her fatigue. How long would this death march continue? If *Hanak Tuvar* was going to pounce on them, surely it would have done so by now.

Those thoughts crystalized in her mind only moments before the people in front of her came to a halt. Desa reined in Midnight; the horse was more than willing to pause for a break. Kalia caught the stallion eying the grass on either side of the path. She wasn't the only one trying to ignore an empty stomach.

A man in ratty clothing pushed his way through the crowd, moving toward the back of the procession. "We're stopping!" he announced. "We're stopping! Move into the field! We'll be eating shortly!"

Head hanging, Kalia shut her eyes tight and pressed the heel of her hand to her brow. "Thank the Almighty," she whispered.

"The Almighty had nothing to do with it," Desa muttered.

. . .

IT TOOK the refugees less than ten minutes to get ready. Really, there wasn't much for them to do: just move off the road and into the field. Tommy looked out on a sea of bodies. Thousands of dejected people staring dumbly at nothing at all.

He hesitated.

Refugees?

When had he started to think of them in such terms? The word was appropriate, he realized. These people had no homes. It was all too likely that they would be unwelcome almost anywhere they went. One thing he had learned, traveling this wide world, was that people were seldom accepting of strangers.

He leaned against the side of a wagon with his arms folded, a toothpick waggling in his mouth as he grumbled to himself. He was tired. Every muscle in his body ached.

Dalen came around the front side of the wagon, heaving out a sigh and massaging his forehead. "I did the calculations," he said. "We should have enough food to last three days. Assuming no spoilage and light rations."

Shutting his eyes, Tommy nodded slowly. "Start passing it out." He paused. That sounded too much like a command. Well, he *was* in command, but a leader should take part in the hard work. "I'll help."

People lined up at each wagon, forming thirty parallel queues. One by one, they received a small meal and then stalked off to eat it, most of them grumbling about how little he had to offer. Well, there was no getting around that. He couldn't conjure food out of thin air.

It took the better part of an hour to get them all served. He kept a smile on his face the whole time. His people needed to see optimism even if he didn't really feel it.

When it was over, he sat against the base of a wagon with his legs stretched out and pulled the brim of his hat down over his face. He was happy to have it. Dalen had been kind enough to pack some of his things when they fled Mrs. Carmichael's boarding house. Come to think of it, where was Mrs. Carmichael? She should be somewhere in this crowd. Tommy put the question out of his mind. It was so bright. He just wanted to rest for a while.

Dalen sat down on his right, snuggling up with his head on Tommy's shoulder. "You should eat something," the other man grumbled.

Before he could protest, Miri cuddled up on his left, lightly kissing his cheek. "He's right," she said. "You need to eat."

"In a few minutes," Tommy promised.

"You're worried."

Sitting up, Tommy pulled the hat off his face and blinked a few times. "You mean you aren't?" he muttered. "Aren't we all?"

Blushing, Miri brushed a strand of hair off her cheek. "Of course, I'm worried," she said. "That was an invitation to talk about it, Lommy, you idiot."

"She's right, Thomas," Dalen put it. "No one should bear such weight alone."

He tossed his head back, rolling his eyes. These two! What was he going to do with them? Despite his exasperation, a slow smile came on. "All right," he said. "I'm worried about what will happen when we get to Ofalla."

"You think they won't take us in?" Miri asked.

"I think they're going to need some convincing."

Miri was grinning, staring out on the field where thousands of people had gathered, most kneeling in the grass and sharing meals with their families. "Just put on one of your displays. That'll convince them."

"One of my displays?"

"You know," Dalen said. "The big, booming voice. The grand theatrics. 'Weep oh peoples of the world, your saviour has come.' That sort of thing."

"I do *not* do that!"

Miri sat up straight and hit him with one of her disapproving stares. "Lommy," she said. "Last night, you literally projected a bolt of lightning into the air and told these people you were the one who would keep them alive."

Tommy felt a flash of heat in his face. Overwhelmed by chagrin, he stared into his lap. "All right," he muttered. "You have a point."

Leaning back against the wagon with hands folded behind his head, Dalen smiled. "So," he said. "Just put on a display."

Tommy stood up with a grunt, stretching his fists above his head as his mouth fell open in a yawn. He stalked off through the field.

"Where are you going?" Dalen asked.

Tommy spun around, walking backwards. "To renew my Infusions," he said. "I'll need them if I'm going to put on a display."

WORN DOWN AND WRUNG OUT, Desa sat on a large rock in the middle of the field. Her muscles were stiff, her stomach growling. And whenever she let her guard down, she felt sleep coming on.

The sound of footsteps made her look up to find Kalia approaching with some food. The other woman looked just as bone-weary as Desa felt. But she managed to keep her chin up. That was something.

"Dinner," Kalia said softly,

It wasn't much – just a slice of bread, a hunk of cheese and half an apple – but Desa was famished. Weeks spent enjoying the delicacies that Mercy conjured with a wave of her hand had spoiled her. Still, good food took the edge off her fatigue. Her head was less foggy, thoughts forming with vivid clarity.

Mercy...

The thought of never seeing Mercy again twisted her up in

knots. She had come to think of the goddess as...as what? A surrogate mother? No, not quite that. No one could ever take Leean's place. As a friend.

Kalia sat down in the grass, curling up her legs as she munched on her slice of bread. "You should get some sleep after," she said despite the abundance of sunlight. Night was still a few hours off.

Touching fingertips to her temples, Desa closed her eyes and massaged away a headache. Or tried to, anyway. "Too early," she said. "I sleep now, and I'll be up all night. Besides, I don't think I'll get much rest lying in a field. I don't suppose you still have that tent Rojan gave us, the one you took when we parted ways."

Kalia sucked the apple juice off her finger. "We sold it for train tickets," she muttered. "And the bedrolls too."

Desa barked a laugh. "Just as well," she said. "I still have mine."

"And we only ever needed one." Kalia's smile was entirely genuine, as was the slight flush that reddened her cheeks. She leaned in to kiss Desa on the forehead.

Nearby, a bald man shot a glance in their direction and muttered under his breath. He was wise enough to look away when he caught Desa glaring at him. Quite wise indeed. She was in no mood to deal with Eradians and their backward attitudes.

Desa sighed.

Kneeling in the grass with one hand on the ground, Kalia studied her with inquisitive eyes. "So," she began. "I suppose you're telling yourself that this is all your fault. That you're responsible for what happened."

"No."

Kalia raised an eyebrow.

It was all too much. Desa started laughing again, prompting the other woman to give her one of those concerned looks. But what else could she do? Mercy had shown her the truth. At long last, Desa understood. But it was too late.

"No, this is much bigger than me," Desa explained. "I'm only one player in a story that stretches back to the dawn of our civilization. One way or another, we were always going to end up here."

"That's very...enlightened of you."

A frown tightened Desa's mouth. Dismayed, she shook her head slowly. "It was inevitable," she said. "Mercy's people. They started it. They put us on this path. Now, we have to figure out how to change course."

She hugged herself, rubbing her arms as chills raced through her body. For the first time in a very long while, Desa Kincaid was terrified. "Mercy," she mumbled. "She was our best chance of getting through this, and now she's gone."

Tilting her chin up with two fingers, Kalia kissed Desa's nose. "You're wrong," she whispered. "You were always our best chance of getting through this."

They just held each other as the sun went down. Even after everything they had been through over the last twenty-four hours, Desa still felt a seed of joy growing within her. She had found Kalia again, and that fact alone made it seem as though she might get through this. Those weeks they had spent apart left Desa feeling as if a piece of her soul had been carved out. Now, she was whole again.

Kalia rested her head in Desa's lap, and Desa gently stroked her hair. Within moments, the other woman was starting to drift off, falling into a sweet, peaceful sleep. Desa was content to just let her stay like that.

A lanky fellow with dark, brown skin and flecks of gray in his black hair paused to give them a dirty look. He said nothing, but the contempt was hard to ignore.

"Something I can do for you?" Desa asked.

"Just thinking."

"About what?"

The man turned his back on her, gazing out on the people who had gathered in the field. "Our city is attacked by a demon," he said. "And I see sin all around me. It's hard not to imagine that the two are connected."

Pinching the bridge of her nose, Desa groaned in frustration. "I can assure you that what happened to New Beloran had nothing to do with me or my partner." She looked up at him. "In Ithanar, men marry other men, and women marry other women. They've been doing it for centuries without drawing the attention of any demons."

The angry fellow looked back over his shoulder. "Ithanar," he said. "A land ruled by savages."

"If you only knew..."

Kalia sat up with a mumbled curse, brushing the hair out of her face. "If you don't mind," she said. "Some of us are trying to get some sleep."

The idiot stormed off.

"I think that sleep is still a ways off," Desa lamented. "I need to go find Tommy."

"I'll come with you."

Locating her former protégé wasn't hard. Desa could feel him communing with the Ether a short distance away, somewhere on the north side of the road. She had to wade through the densely-packed crowd, stepping around clusters of people who had gathered together for their evening meal.

She saw families: children giggling as their parents tickled them, young adults sparing a coat or a warm blanket for one of their elders. So many people, all displaced. Good, honest people. This was what *Hanak Tuvar* wanted to destroy? Why? Her first instinct was to search for a rational motivation, but that was folly. The creature had told her its motivation. It wanted to destroy humanity for its own amusement. Simply to relieve its boredom. There could be no peace with an entity like that.

Dalen and Miri were lounging by one of the wagons, talking quietly with one another, occasionally sharing a kiss. It warmed her heart to see them. Desa had thought endlessly about Kalia during their time apart, but she had missed the others as well. They weren't just friends anymore. They were family.

"I'm going to go say hello," Kalia murmured, slipping away to join Miri and Dalen. They greeted her with bright smiles and warm hugs. Jealousy flared up within Desa. It lasted for only a moment but left a bitter taste in her mouth. Kalia had bonded with the others in ways that Desa never had.

It was her own fault, always holding herself apart, running off alone at every opportunity. Maybe, when this was over – if they survived – she would have a chance to correct some mistakes.

She crossed the road, moving through the field toward a small copse of trees. The soft thrumming of the Ether came from that direction. Ducking under the branches of a tall ash, she found Tommy kneeling in the grove with his back turned. The shadows were lengthening with the onset of evening, a soft breeze promising a chilly night.

Tommy severed contact with the Ether.

Crossing her arms with a sigh, Desa cocked her head. She frowned at him. "You know, not so long ago, it was you sneaking up on me doing that."

He chuckled, standing up and turning around to face her. Placing a hand over his heart, he offered a shallow bow. "Mrs. Kincaid."

"Tommy."

"What's on your mind?"

She puckered her lips, turning her face up to the darkening sky as she blew out a breath. "Well, I could make some pretense about wanting to discuss plans with you," she began. "But the truth is I had no specific purpose in coming here. Except to tell you that I am very proud of how far you've come."

He sniffled, a tear sliding down his cheek. "Desa," he mumbled, wiping that tear away. "You're going to ruin my brilliant, stoic leader façade."

"Good!" she teased. "Your earnest streak was always your greatest strength, Tommy. Don't lose it now."

He sighed, leaning back against the ash tree. "You don't need to worry about that," he muttered. "The truth is I have no idea what I'm doing. I'm making it up as I go along."

Desa shuffled into the grove with her hands clasped behind her back, smiling at the ground beneath her feet. "Don't tell anyone," she said. "But so am I."

"What do we do now?"

"I don't know," she admitted. "Mercy was our best bet, but she's gone. While I was training with her, she showed me how to use the crystal on her pyramid. She said it might give me the strength I need to return *Hanak Tuvar* to its prison."

"So, we go back to the abandoned city."

"It's not that simple," Desa said, shaking her head. "I don't think the crystal has unlimited range. We have to trick *Hanak Tuvar* into following us."

Tommy nodded.

Their little tete-a-tete ended when Kalia and the others came to join them in the small grove. Desa felt her heart racing. In the waning, evening light, Kalia was nothing short of breathtaking. Her beautiful eyes, her playful smile.

She listened to them chatting for a moment, unsure of what to offer, and then something caught her eye. The others from Tommy's war camp on Hebar's Hill had come as well. She recognized them – a tall, pale man, a shorter man with tanned skin and a young woman with red hair – but she could not put names to them. Perhaps it was time to change that. She chose the tall man first.

Striding toward him, Desa thrust out her hand. "Desa Kincaid," she said. "Nice to meet you."

He took her hand and gave it a single pump. This one was younger than she would have expected. Younger than Tommy had been when she took him from that sleepy, little village. But not by much. "Jim," he said. "We met before, but we never had a chance to get acquainted."

"So, you're the famous Desa Kincaid," the girl interjected. "Tommy talks about you all the time." She moved as if to offer a curtsy and then realized she was wearing pants. Embarrassed, she averted her eyes. "He says that you taught him everything he knows."

"But not everything *I* know!" Desa said.

"Ha!"

The other young man stepped forward, sizing her up with an inquisitive stare. After a moment, he offered a nod of respect. "Victor," was all he said. And really, what more did you need? After years of listening to the Synod prattle on, Desa had developed an appreciation for brevity.

Shifting his weight from one foot to the other, Jim directed a glance toward Dalen and the others. "Tommy's been teaching us how to Field Bind," he murmured. "With very limited success."

"Don't get discouraged," Desa replied. "For some people, it takes years just to find the Ether. But if you keep practicing, it will come."

"Yes, ma'am."

"And don't call me ma'am."

The girl folded her arms, tapping her pale cheek as she studied Desa. "I'm more interested in how she fights," she said. "Tommy says she could stand up to an entire army if she had to."

"Tommy exaggerates," Desa assured her.

The young woman forced a smile, bowing her head and

running a hand through her hair. "I'm not so sure," she said. "I saw you on Hebar's Hill. You were like a storm made flesh. The name's Zoe, by the way."

Desa stood with hands clasped demurely in front of herself, closing her eyes and nodding to the lass. "I would be happy to teach you," she promised. "All of you. Mercy knows, we'll need it in the days to come."

They all agreed.

"Come," Desa said. "Let's join the others."

DESA FELL ASLEEP AS SOON as her head touched the folded-up coat that she used for a pillow, drifting off into a deep, dreamless slumber. Twilight still lingered, but she was too tired to do anything else. And Kalia's warm body held the night's chill at bay.

She woke up sometime later, feeling as if she had slept for twelve hours. Except, she couldn't have. It was still pitch dark. A soft breeze sighed through the nearby tree branches, nearly drowning out the hooting of an owl.

They had chosen a spot near the grove, far from the other refugees. All of the old crew had come together. Even Midnight was lying in the grass, snoozing after a hard day's work. And a hard night, to boot.

She knew that she should go back to sleep – she needed the rest – but her mind was alert now. There would be no relaxing until she burned off some of that excess energy. And besides, she had work to do.

Making herself one with the Ether, Desa began a series of Infusions. She started with her belt buckle, Reinfusing it with a hunger for gravitational energy. The Sink was all but spent after a night of running from *Hanak Tuvar*, and she had been too tired to replenish it.

It took the better part of ten minutes to thicken the lattice to a point where she would feel confident leaping from rooftop to rooftop. You wanted a Gravity-Sink to survive at least half an hour of continuous use. That way, if you were smart enough to use it sparingly, you would get several hours out of it.

From there, she moved on to her bracelet. Defensive Infusions first; she would make weapons later. She only had one gun and a couple boxes of ammunition. That irked her. To lose her second pistol after all the money she had spent purchasing it...

Well, there was no getting it back. By now, *Hanak Tuvar* would have spread its red halo across the entire city. The gun was probably a puddle on the floor of Timothy Delarac's ballroom. Her mind reeled at the thought of what the people might have endured. She knew that there were many who had refused to flee. With her Force-Sink Reinfused, she moved on to-

Something changed.

Desa felt a disruption, a strange shifting sensation. It wasn't the wrongness that she felt around *Hanak Tuvar*. No, this was something very different. As if matter had been spontaneously generated out of nothing. Or transported from somewhere else.

And just like that, she knew what it was.

Tossing the blankets off of herself, Desa crawled out of her bedroll, prompting Kalia to mumbled something incoherent. No time for that. Desa stood up as a flash of light made her eyes smart.

A crystalline figure stumbled out of the grove, bent double with one hand pressed to her side. Almost as if she had been stabbed with a sword. She groaned, nearly losing her balance, and when she pulled that hand away, Desa gasped.

A network of black veins had spread through Mercy's body like an infection. They had covered half of her stomach and stretched up her side almost to the shoulder. The goddess screamed with a sound like glass shattering, and the infected

part of her tore itself free, breaking into a thousand pieces when it hit the ground.

Inky, black tendrils of ooze slinked through the grass, making their way eastward. Back to *Hanak Tuvar.*

Mercy staggered.

She now had a big hole in her body, like a pastry that someone had taken a bite out of. Moaning, she braced a hand against a tree trunk and tried to stay on her feet. Her legs almost gave out.

Another flash of radiance emanated from her, transforming her into a living star, waking everyone in the nearby field. When it faded away, she was human again: a plump, matronly woman with dark skin and curly hair.

She fell flat on her face.

Desa rushed to her.

With a gentle hand, she turned Mercy over. The goddess was sound asleep in the soft moonlight, almost serene. The hole in her stomach was gone. She had no fever, no obvious signs of illness or injury. She was just unconscious. Unfortunately, Desa had no idea how long she would stay that way.

Kalia sprinted over, gasping, and dropped to one knee in the grass. "What happened?" she breathed.

"I wish I knew."

19

Stretched out in a wagon with her head propped up on Desa's coat, Mercy slept. The warm sunlight fell upon her, causing her to sweat – Desa would have never expected such a human reaction – but she didn't wake no matter how much she was jostled about.

And there was plenty of jostling.

The wagon rumbled along a dirt path that cut through a green field with trees on either side. Elms, poplars, maples: they grew tall and strong, providing sporadic bursts of shade as the caravan of refugees passed beneath them. Desa was grateful for it. It was quite warm for a day in the middle of spring.

She knelt beside her "patient," smoothing the hair off Mercy's forehead. She wasn't sure what else to do. With their food supplies dwindling, Tommy had ordered everything cleared out of this wagon and moved to others that had room to spare. One of their fellow travelers had been a surgeon back in New Beloran; he had spent an hour examining Mercy before they set out this morning, and he swore that he could find nothing wrong with her. She was just asleep.

Kalia rode Midnight as he walked alongside the wagon.

"Well, one thing's for sure," she said with a devilish grin. "I was right."

"About what?"

"I told you Mercy wasn't dead."

Desa's first instinct was to point out that it was a poor time to say, "I told you so," but then she saw the glint in her partner's eye. A joke. Kalia always found a ray of sunshine in the darkest of times. A reason to keep hoping.

Stifling a yawn with her hand, Desa murmured her agreement. "That you did." It came out as an incoherent mess, but Kalia seemed to get the gist of it. "Once again, I bow to your superior wisdom."

Kalia grunted, nodding once as if to say that she was satisfied by that response. "I have to remind you of these things," she insisted. "Otherwise, you'll just take all the credit. And we can't have that."

"Perish the thought."

The wagon driver – a portly fellow named Burt who wore a rumpled hat over his gray hair – glanced back over his shoulder. "Boss man's coming," he said. "Thinking he'd like a word with you, ma'am."

Up ahead, Tommy was lumbering along the path with his head down, making his way back to them. He had gone to make sure they wouldn't find trouble waiting around the next bend. Desa couldn't help but smile. It almost reminded her of Marcus. "How is she?" Tommy asked, patting the dappled gray horse that pulled the wagon.

Desa scowled, scrubbing sweat off her brow with the back of her hand. "The same," she said. "I don't know if there's anything we can do."

"Too bad we don't have any crystals," Kalia said.

"What's that supposed to mean?" Tommy snapped.

Kalia flinched as if someone had just slapped her. "Nothing," she said. "Why? Do you happen to have a crystal?"

"I don't think it would help," Desa said. With the gentlest touch, she used a wet cloth to dab Mercy's face. The goddess never even stirred. "The crystals are calcified fragments of the Ether. They accelerate the body's natural healing process. However, Mercy isn't sick."

Tommy spun around, shoving his hands into his pockets and walking beside the wagon. If the young man was blaming himself for all of this, Desa would have to have words with him. It wouldn't do to let others pick up her bad habits.

"Have we thought about what we're going to do when we get to Ofalla?" Kalia asked. "I can't imagine they'll be willing to take in four thousand refugees."

Lifting a toothpick between two fingers, Tommy slipped it into his mouth as if it were a cigarette. "Miri says we should put on a demonstration," he muttered. "I figure, between the three of us, we can come up with something impressive."

"You want to use Field Binding to *intimidate* the city officials?" Desa exclaimed. "Tommy, the Great Art is not a bludgeon to coerce people into doing what you want."

"Desperate times, Desa."

"He has a point," Kalia chimed in. "Put aside the issue of finding a safe place for all these refugees. You *know* that *Hanak Tuvar* won't be content to remain in New Beloran. Once it's finished there, it will move on. We'll have to rally the people of Ofalla, and we don't have time to play politics with their city council."

"Assuming it comes this way," Desa growled. "For all we know, it could decide to go south, north or east."

Kalia had a sombre expression as she stared off into the distance. "If I were a hungry squid demon," she said, "I would head for the closest settlement. I'm afraid, when we arrive at Ofalla, we'll be bringing a nasty surprise on our heels."

Well, there was no arguing with that. In a way, this was for the best, though Desa hated to admit it. If *Hanak Tuvar* came after her, she could at least exercise some measure of control. She could attack it, slow it down. Maybe even find a way to stop it. But if it went anywhere else, she would be helpless. People would die.

Worst of all, it would blight the ground anywhere it went, twist the laws of nature so that metal melted and plants refused to grow. Even if they found a way to slay the beast, the wounds it left in the countryside might be the end of their civilization. An entire continent left unable to feed itself.

Tommy scrunched up his face. "This one's bigger than us, isn't it?" he mumbled. "Until now, we always had a chance. Bendarian, Adele: we could beat them. But now…"

"Tommy," she said. "It was always bigger than us."

"Then what do we do?"

"The same thing we always did," Desa said. "We fight until we can't fight anymore."

WITH THE SUN hovering above the western horizon, casting its golden glow on the plains, Desa led her new friends into the field north of the road. They stood in a line, Jim on her left, Victor on her right and Zoe between them.

Having discarded her coat, Desa stood before them in tan pants and a sleeveless undershirt, the wind teasing her short, brown hair. "Gentlemen," she said. "I'm told the two of you know how to use a bow. But all three of you would benefit from a little hand-to-hand training. Victor, please attack me."

The young man flinched.

"Don't worry," Desa said. "I know I look small and defenseless, but you won't harm me."

"I'm not worried about you," Victor stammered. "I'm worried about me."

"I promise not to hurt you either."

With a heavy sigh, Victor strode forward until he was right

in front of her. He looked her up and down, perhaps choosing his method of attack. Then he threw a punch, a punch that moved with deliberate slowness.

Desa brought one hand up to strike his wrist and bat his arm away. "Don't try to block the blow," she said. "Simply reidirect it. Use your opponent's momentum against him."

She stepped back, urging him forward and deflected his next blow. "Just like that," she said. "Zoe, Jim, please come closer so that you can see what I'm doing. Victor, one more time, please." He was kind enough to wait for the other two to take their positions.

Another punch came at her.

Once again, her hand came up, striking Victor's wrist and flinging his arm away. The young man muttered and tried again with the other fist, a blow that she easily countered. "Simple muscle memory," Desa said. "We'll practice that maneuver for the next fifteen minutes. Deflect ten punches and then switch roles. Go slow at first, but speed up when you feel you're getting the hang of it. Gentlemen, why don't you pair up? Zoe, you're with me."

The girl planted herself in front of Desa with fists up in a sloppy fighting stance. Her feet were too close together, her elbows pinned to her sides, posture rigid. She was scared. Desa felt a moment of sympathy. Zoe had been taught all her life that she was property. The idea that she might defend herself had probably never occurred to her.

Desa shook her head. "No, child," she said, striding up to the girl. "I will attack, you defend. Loosen up a bit. Don't be afraid, I won't hurt you."

And so, they began.

At first, Desa stuck to simple, slow blows that Zoe deflected with ease. After that, Desa sped up the pace and varied the timing and the target. It took her a few moments to adapt, but

Zoe began to show some enthusiasm. "Is this all we're going to learn?" she asked.

"Of course not," Desa replied.

"What else is there?"

Backing away, Desa covered her mouth with one hand. She was trying to decide if Zoe was ready for the next lesson. Training Tommy had been a learning experience for Desa as well. It wasn't just about the forms and the patterns, the correct way to block, punch and kick. It was about nurturing self-confidence in your students. "All right," she said. "You attack me."

Zoe came forward with a high punch.

Leaning back, Desa clamped one hand onto the girl's wrist and the other onto her elbow. She gave a twist, applying just enough pressure to make Zoe fold up and yelp. Then she immediately released the child.

Straightening, Zoe winced as she rubbed her smarting elbow. "All right," she said. "You have to teach me that."

"In time."

"What if we don't have time?"

Desa turned around, pacing through the grass as the wind caressed her. "Whether we have time or not is beside the point," she said. "With a few days of training, I can teach you some rudimentary skills, but it takes years to become a master."

She was about to begin a new lesson when she heard Tommy's voice calling to her. The young man was jogging toward them, clearly troubled by something. "Desa!" he called out. "She's awake!"

"Mercy?"

He nodded.

"Keep practicing," Desa told her students. "Zoe, join the others. Take turns. I'll be back shortly." And with that, she was charging back to the camp, following Tommy. The wagon was parked on the roadside. In the evening light, she could see a woman sitting up with her hand pressed against her stomach.

Mercy looked as though she were suffering the after-effects of a night of heavy drinking.

The other refugees had set up camp on the south side of the road. Families huddled together for warmth, some of them wrapped in blankets they had brought from New Beloran. Men shuffled about aimlessly, searching for something to do. She noticed a pair of young women talking under the hanging branches of a willow tree.

Massaging her temples with the tips of her fingers, Mercy squeezed her eyes shut. "Desa," she mumbled. "Good. I wanted to speak with you."

"Are you all right?" Desa inquired.

"No."

Desa hopped into the wagon, sitting beside the other woman. She waited for Mercy to say something, but the goddess remained silent. Finally, Desa decided to press the point. "What happened?"

"I tried to contain it," Mercy gasped. "But its power..."

"We saw it pounding against the barrier you had created."

Pressing the heel of her hand to her forehead, Mercy groaned. "No," she muttered. "*Hanak Tuvar's* physical strength is the least of our concerns. It warps the very laws of nature, distorting reality to suit its whims. It was able to overpower me, and when the barrier fell..."

Miri approached the wagon, flanked by Dalen and Kalia. None of them looked particularly happy to see Mercy. "What happened?" Miri demanded. "When the barrier fell."

"It attacked me," Mercy said. "It tried to apply its power to me, to change me as it changed the world. I don't know what would have happened if it had succeeded."

Shoving Miri aside, Kalia stepped forward to glare daggers at the humbled goddess. "Why didn't you tell us?" she demanded. "Desa said that if we destroyed Adele's body, *Hanak*

Tuvar would be sent back to its prison. Why didn't you tell us it could break free?"

"Because I didn't know."

"You didn't know?"

Mercy looked up at her with bloodshot eyes. The haggard stare of a woman who had been worked to exhaustion. "Dri and I designed its prison to pull it back in," she said. "We thought it needed an anchor to remain in our world. We didn't think it could fully escape."

Kalia folded her arms, lifting her chin to stare down her nose at the other woman. "Some goddess you are," she growled. "Poor planning makes for poor outcomes."

"That's enough!" Desa snapped.

"No," Mercy whispered. "She's right."

"Wasting time on assigning blame will get us nowhere," Desa said, fixing each of them with a hard stare. "What matters in that you're back. We can make another attempt to confront *Hanak Tuvar.*"

"No," Mercy said. "We can't."

"What?"

With a grunt, Mercy stood up. She stumbled forward, nearly losing her balance, and Dalen had to help her remain on her feet. "I spent a day trying to excise that thing from my body," she said. "I got rid of it, but the damage was done. I was dying, my body losing molecular cohesion."

Desa's stomach was churning. When Mercy had returned to them, she had begun to feel a measure of hope. Maybe *Hanak Tuvar* wasn't that strong. But that hope was fading. "What are you saying?" she stammered.

"I had only one way to survive," Mercy whispered. "I locked myself into this form. I'm human, Desa. My powers are gone."

"Swell," Miri muttered.

Human?

Desa wasn't sure what to make of that. She knew that Mercy

had once been mortal, but she had thought that the goddess had transcended human limitations. Never in a million years would she have dreamed that the process could be reversed.

Miri stood there with her fists on her hips, smiling and shaking her head. "So, no more powers," she said. "Then what use are you to us?"

"I can still Bind the Field," Mercy said.

"And," Tommy put in from the other side of the wagon. "We're not in the habit of turning people away just because they aren't of use to us." By the eyes of Vengeance, how long had he been standing there? The man could be so quiet sometimes. It was easy to forget his presence.

Spinning around to face Desa, Mercy tapped the side of her head with two fingers. "I may not have the power," she began. "But I still have the knowledge. I can help you to slow down *Hanak Tuvar* and lead it back to the desert."

"And what will we do there?" Desa asked.

"You and I will use the crystal," Mercy explained. "And return *Hanak Tuvar* to its prison."

"You can do that?" Kalia asked.

"With the aid of the crystal, yes."

Tommy stepped out from behind the wagon, nodding to each of them. "Then we have a plan," he said. "But first, we need to get these people to safety. Let's get some rest. We should reach Ofalla by tomorrow afternoon."

NIGHT HAD COME, bathing the whole field in darkness. Desa moved through the grass on the north side of the road, light streaming through the cracks between her fingers. Just enough to avoid an embarrassing fall. She didn't want to tell the whole camp where she was going.

Bit by bit, she made her way northward to the riverbank. She had seen Kalia going that way earlier and had decided to follow. The other woman was upset about something, and Desa wanted to know what it was. She didn't like the thought of turmoil in their relationship. It left her with a queasy feeling that she just couldn't shake.

The uneven ground began to slope downward. It wasn't long before she heard the lapping of water on the shore. She knew, somehow, that she would find Kalia here. She couldn't say what force had guided her to the other woman, but she felt it like an instinct. Kalia hadn't simply gone north in a straight line. Her path had meandered eastward. Desa could have searched the riverbank for hours without finding her partner, and yet, somehow, she knew exactly where to go. Perhaps she should ask Mercy about that.

Kalia was wrapped in a thin blanket, gazing out on the dark waters. "I wanted to be alone," she said.

Desa let her fingers uncurl, revealing a glowing ring in the palm of her hand. Its light spilled over the riverbank, illuminating the grass, sparkling on the water. "Is there some reason you came out here?" she asked.

Kalia said nothing.

Approaching the water's edge, Desa let out a deep breath. "All right," she mumbled. "I guess I'll have to drag it out of you. Why are you so angry with Mercy?"

"She was supposed to protect us."

"So was I," Desa replied. "You're always telling me to stop blaming myself for everything that goes wrong."

Kalia tossed a rock, and it skipped several times before sinking beneath the surface with a loud *plunk*. "That's different."

"How?"

"Because you're not a god!"

"Neither is Mercy," Desa countered. "You saw the images in that crystal. She was human, just like us. She changed herself so that she would have the power to fight *Hanak Tuvar,* but she was never divine. We're all just fallible, flawed creatures, stumbling our way from one decision to the next. She did the best she could."

Kalia just stood there with a blank expression, trying her best to hide her feelings. "That's the other problem!" she muttered under her breath. "You seem to have a special connection with her."

Desa blinked. Was this about jealousy? It had never occurred to her that Kalia might feel threatened by Mercy. The very idea was absurd. She was about to say as much, but something made her hesitate. She had never been very good at maintaining relationships, but she was fairly certain that dismissing her partner's concerns would only deepen the rift between them.

Gently, she laid a hand on Kalia's cheek. The other woman leaned into her touch. "You have nothing to fear, my love," Desa murmured. "I love *you*. Not Mercy."

"You ran off to the desert and left me alone."

Wrapping an arm around the other woman, Desa pulled her close. Kalia snuggled up, resting her head on Desa's shoulder. "I did that to save the world," Desa murmured. "Not to be with Mercy."

Kalia sniffled, brushing a tear away. "Yes, but you came back so different," she said. "More confident. More at peace. Mercy gave you something that I couldn't."

"Perspective," Desa said. "You're right. A powerful being does have a slight advantage in that respect. Mercy showed me the long history of our people, where *Hanak Tuvar* came from. It's easier to stop blaming yourself when you realize that a problem started centuries before you were born. But I love *you*. Just you. No one else."

"Really?"

"Really."

Backing away, Kalia pulled the blanket tighter around

herself. She offered a wan smile, a blush putting some colour in her cheeks. "So, there's nothing between you and Mercy then?"

"Well, I did kiss her once. But only to heal her."

"Are you serious?"

Now, it was Desa's turn to blush. She stood there with her eyes downcast, trying to find the words. "The Ether responds to emotional intent," she said. "Choosing a loving gesture put me in the right frame of mind to heal."

"I suppose that makes sense," Kalia said. They started back to camp, trudging up the gentle hillside. "But wait a second. If all you needed was a loving gesture, couldn't you have just hugged her?"

"I just went with the first thing that came to mind."

"Uh-huh. I think you just wanted to kiss a goddess."

Desa rolled her eyes, trying to contain her exasperation. After all, she *had* earned a little playful ribbing. You couldn't just go around kissing people. Especially if you were involved with someone else. "You're joking right?"

Kalia's playful smile confirmed her suspicions. "Not to worry, my love." She leaned in to smooch Desa's cheek. "Lucky for you, I just so happen to be a woman of infinite patience and understanding."

"Oh, really?"

"Why, yes!" Kalia teased. "How else do you think our relationship lasted this long?"

"Funny."

"Oh, it is!" Kalia said with a bounce in her step. "I'm *hilarious!*"

20

The road sliced cleanly through the green field, following a course parallel to the river. Sunlight sparkled on the dark waters of the Vinrella. In the distance, the buildings of Ofalla stood tall. Some were five-stories high! A year ago, Tommy would have never thought that such a thing could be possible.

Despite their impressive size, most of those buildings were gray with black roofs. Dreary, boring and uniform, but at least the city was clean. Tommy still remembered his visit to Hedrovan, and he had no intention of ever going back there.

The nearest of the four bridges stretched over the river to an identical city on the other side. Each was built low to the ground so that tall ships could not pass underneath. Ofalla was a trading port, a hub where ships coming downriver from High Falls could exchange goods with those coming upriver from New Beloran or the cities along Eradia's eastern coast.

At the head of the caravan, Tommy walked side by side with Mercy, carrying his bow in hand. The easiest job was done; he had seen his people safely to Ofalla. Now, came the difficult part.

"You seem nervous," Mercy observed.

Shrugging his shoulders, Tommy chuckled. "That easy to read, am I?" he asked. "I guess I'll have to learn to hide in better."

Mercy shot a glance in his direction, quirking an eyebrow. "My boy," she said. "I'm over ten thousand years old. At my age, *everyone* is easy to read."

"I'm worried about what the city will do when over four thousand refugees show up on their doorstep." They had passed through two of the outer communities earlier this morning, and the looks the caravan had received from the people living there did not fill him with confidence.

"You will find a way," Mercy promised him.

"You seem awfully sure about that."

Turning her face up to the sun, she smiled. "I led my people to a new universe," she said. "When you've survived that, a short journey to the next town over seems a lot more manageable."

Tommy supposed there was some truth in that. It occurred to him that he should probably be taking advantage of Mercy's vast knowledge, but he didn't even know where to begin. What should he ask about first? The prospect was daunting. Just about anything that came out of his mouth would make him look like an idiot.

"Can you teach me more about Field Binding?"

"Oh yes," she said. "I can reveal many things you have yet to discover."

Reaching up with one hand, Tommy tipped his hat to her. "Much obliged, ma'am," he said. "For your time. And for the patience you will display when I inevitably struggle to master the first thing you show me."

Mercy grinned, shaking her head. "You are much too modest," she said. "But there is much to learn. I believe I know a way to resist *Hanak Tuvar*."

"And what might that be?"

"A special kind of Light-Source," Mercy explained. "A slight modification of the Infusion you already know how to create. I shall explain more when we have a moment to sit down and talk."

"Thank you...Ma'am."

"Call me 'Nari.'"

"If you say so."

It took another half hour to reach the outermost buildings, and the dirt road became a cobblestone street well before that. When they arrived, a group of twelve men in blue uniforms stood in a line, blocking their path. Members of the City Watch. Someone must have warned the local precinct captain about a massive caravan coming his way.

Every one of those officers had a hand on the grip of his holstered pistol, ready to draw in an instant. Their leader was a barrel-chested man with pale skin and gray hair poking out from under his cap. A yellow band around his right arm marked him as a sergeant. "That's far enough," he said. "State your business here."

Tommy strode forward, still carrying his bow, and held the man's gaze. "We're refugees from New Beloran," he said. "The city was attacked by a powerful creature."

The watch sergeant took one look at Tommy and his brow furrowed in confusion. "So, you thought you'd slay it with arrows?"

"You must believe me-"

The sergeant raised a hand to cut him off. "You don't have to convince me," he said. "We've spoken with postmen who passed by New Beloran. They told us all about the devastation."

That made sense. A lone rider could cover the distance between the two cities much faster than a caravan of tired, beaten-down refugees. If they were aware of the danger, Tommy's job would be a little easier.

He turned, gesturing to the line of people behind him.

"These folks need shelter," he said. "And you must rally the Watch. Ofalla will soon be under attack. The creature is coming here."

"Following your trail, no doubt."

Tommy grimaced, shaking his head in dismay. "No," he said. "It would have come anyway. This creature wants nothing less than the utter destruction of humankind. We *must* stand together and face it."

Several men chuckled.

A smile broke out on the sergeant's face. "'The utter destruction of humankind,' you say," he scoffed. "I see you're prone to exaggeration."

Nari came forward to stand beside Tommy, projecting a regal serenity that said she expected to be obeyed. One look at her, and Tommy could easily believe that people had worshipped her as a goddess. Even in a rumpled, green riding dress, she was a queen. "It is no laughing matter," she said. "*Hanak Tuvar* is a threat to every living being on this planet."

"I firmly believe that something attacked New Beloran," the watch sergeant replied. "Two postmen arrived yesterday, practically trembling as they told us of the destruction they had seen. We thought they were just spinning tall tales. But then a family of four showed up and confirmed everything they said.

"The city was attacked by some kind of creature. Most likely something that came out of the Vinrella. A squid that swam upriver and then dragged itself onto dry land. A ghastly beast, I'm sure, but nothing that can't be handled with a few bullets."

Nari lifted her hand to reveal a penny pinched between her thumb and forefinger. "For your trouble, sir." She flicked it toward the sergeant, who caught it and then gasped when the coin burst alight with a fierce, red glow.

"How..."

Nari tossed a second penny to one of the other watchmen. When that fellow caught it, the coin emitted orange light. The next man in line received a yellow coin. And then a green, a blue and a violet.

They were just Light-Sources, of course, but Tommy was still amazed. So far as he knew, Light-Sources only gave off pure, white light. The notion that he would be able to select the colour had never occurred to him.

Placing her hands on her hips, Nari smiled for the sergeant. "There are forces in this world that cannot even begin to comprehend," she said. "Believe me when I tell you that *Hanak Tuvar* is one such."

"But..."

Nari turned around, extending her hand toward the troop of disheveled men, women and children who waited patiently behind Tommy. "Desa, would you please bring me the object that you carry in your saddlebags?"

A moment later, Desa trotted up, proffering the strangest thing that Tommy had ever seen. A blue crystal in some kind of brass cage. It was beautiful, but Tommy could not fathom how it would be of any use in persuading these men to grant them admittance to the city. Was she planning to trade it?

Nari set the crystal down in the middle of the cobblestone street and then backed away. "Do not be alarmed," she said. "All will be well."

The Ether stirred when somebody triggered an Electric-Source, and then the crystal began to glow. Blue lines shot out of it, sweeping back and forth. The startled watchmen gasped, several of them pointing their guns at the spectral images that appeared from out of nowhere.

Tommy couldn't blame them for their fear; in truth, he shared it, and he had some inkling of what was going on. To someone who had never heard of the Ether, this must have looked like magic.

Ghostly buildings sprang up all around him, towering structures that pierced the sky. He chose the tallest one and tried to determine its height by counting the lines of windows on each floor. He had to give up after twelve. Remarkable. How could any man-made structure stand so tall without collapsing under its own weight? And to think, he had been impressed by Ofalla's five-story buildings!

"This was my home," Nari said.

She was crouching next to the crystal, manipulating it somehow with a series of gestures. Pictographs appeared before her, symbols made of nothing but light, but they responded to her touch.

The ghostly city vanished as the blue lines drew another image. This time, they seemed to be sketching a bulbous creature with thick, black tentacles, a squid with a mouth full of sharp, pointed teeth.

"*Hanak Tuvar,*" Nari said. "It ravaged my city, destroyed it in a matter of days and blighted the land. It swept across the surface of my planet like a plague, and everywhere it went, the world changed. Plants would not grow, electricity failed."

The watchmen were ashen-faced, staring at the squid demon with gaping mouths. Tommy wouldn't be surprised if they soiled themselves. Poor men. Nothing they had ever experienced had prepared them for this.

"Please," Nari said. "We must speak to your city council."

OVER TWO HOURS LATER, Tommy stood in a room with a long table of polished wood. Three rectangular windows, each segmented with white muntin, looked out on a garden that had not yet come into bloom. The leaves on the tall elm tree were not yet fully formed.

Tommy stood by the window with one hand clasping his chin, idly musing on what he might say when the mayor came in to talk to him. The other members of his inner circle were all here.

Desa, Miri and Kalia stood in the corner, talking quietly with one another. Zoe sat primly in a chair that she had turned away from the table. Like Tommy, she was gazing out on the garden, perhaps wishing that she was out there instead of in here.

Victor was at her side with one hand on her shoulder. That warm smile on his face...Tommy had never seen a man so in love.

And then there was Dalen.

He had taken Nari to the far side of the room so that he could ask her a thousand questions. The former goddess – or whatever she was – didn't seem to mind. On the contrary, Nari was amused by his thirst for knowledge. Dalen was downright adorable when curiosity got the better of him. Truth be told, Tommy would be over there with them if he wasn't so busy worrying about what he would do if the city turned the refugees away.

The door swung open, allowing a woman in a green dress to come storming into the room. She was short, almost skeletal, with cold, blue eyes and sliver hair that she kept pinned up. "All right," she said. "We've deliberated."

Tommy spun to face her, folding hands behind his back and flashing a smile. "And what have you decided, Madame Mayor?" he asked. "Will you be able to find room for my people?"

"For four thousand people?" she said, wincing and shaking her head. "No, I'm afraid there's just no way."

Crossing his arms, Tommy sat down on the windowsill. He nodded slowly, choosing his words with care. "I understand your predicament, Mayor Dobrin," he began. "But the fact is you're going to need those extra bodies."

"Because your monster is coming here?" She sniffed, shooting a dirty look toward Nari, who was still speaking softly with Dalen. It had taken quite a bit of arm-twisting to gain a meeting with the City Council; having several men of the Watch vouch for them certainly helped matters.

Nari had used that strange, blue crystal to show the council images of *Hanak Tuvar*. By the end of her little demonstration, everyone in that room had looked as if they were about ready to sick up. Except Zerena Dobrin. Ofalla's new mayor had endured the whole thing with a cold, calculating focus. "Surely you don't doubt what you've seen with your own eyes," Tommy said.

"Oh, your parlour tricks are quite impressive," Mayor Dobrin replied. "And I have no doubt that something nasty is coming this way. But you showed up on my doorstep with four thousand tired, hungry people. Do you really think they'll be able to lend a hand when the time comes?"

"We're all in this together," Tommy said.

Zerana Dobrin rolled her eyes. "Thank you for the platitude," she said. "Anyone who can afford to rent a room is welcome to stay in the city. Otherwise, I'm afraid I must ask you and your followers to leave."

Miri stood behind the mayor, sneering at the back of her head. "That simple, huh?" she countered. "Just send thousands of people off into the wilderness with no food, water or supplies?"

Rounding on her, Zerena shoved a finger in her face. "I don't know what you imagined you would find here," she said. "But this city isn't exactly overflowing with food. Many of our winter preserves went toward the war effort."

"A pointless war," Desa muttered.

The mayor spared her a glance. "You're entitled to your opinion," she said. "But the reality is what it is."

This wasn't working. Clearly, another demonstration was in order. Unfortunately, Tommy had surrendered his bow, quiver and pistol before coming in here. And it was much the same for the others. So, he would have to find another way. "You have guards out in that hallway, yes?"

"A reasonable precaution," the mayor said. "Wouldn't you agree?"

"Send one in here."

He had to repeat himself twice before the mayor sighed and poked her head out the door. A man in a brown uniform came shuffling in, eying Tommy suspiciously. This one was young, twenty years old at the absolute most. Which would still make him Tommy's senior by several months. But it certainly didn't feel that way.

Tommy stood at the head of the table, tapping his foot as he examined the young man. "All right," he said. "You'll do. Guardsman, I want you to shoot me."

"Sir?"

"You heard me," Tommy barked. "Take that pistol out of its holster, and put a bullet in my chest."

The poor lad was flustered, shifting his weight from one foot to the other. "Sir," he began. "I'm not inclined to commit murder."

"Trust me. You won't harm me."

"This is ridiculous!" Zerena snapped, shoving the young guard out of the way. She stomped up to Tommy with a sniff of derision. "No one is killing anyone in my city. And it's past time that you were on your way."

Tommy forced a smile, bowing his head to her. "Begging your pardon, Madame Mayor," he said. "But you seem to think you can handle what's coming. Perhaps you should put that assumption to the test."

"By shooting you?"

"Your man won't hit me. I promise it."

He noticed Miri smirking in the corner, and Nari offered a nod of approval when she caught his eye. As usual, Desa was struggling to contain her exasperation. If Tommy had learned one thing about his mentor, it was that she had little patience for politics. People shouldn't have to be convinced to do the right thing; they should just do it. If only it were that simple.

Zerena Dobrin threw her hands up, turning away from him and marching past the nervous guard. "Fine!" she said. "If it's the only way to be rid of you! Though I'd hate to see what your blood will do to the carpet."

The guard reluctantly drew his pistol, lifting it in a shaky hand. Sweat broke out on his forehead as he mouthed several words of protest. "I...I can't do this," he said at last. "I won't kill another human being."

"Be at ease, young man," Nari said. "You will not harm Thomas."

Thunder split the air as the gun went off.

A bullet hung suspended two inches away from Tommy's chest, stopped by the Force-Sink in his pendant. The poor guard dropped his pistol and stumbled backward, trembling. "How...how..."

His reaction was nowhere near as satisfying as the mayor's. Zerena Dobrin gave no sign of her shock beyond a slight widening of her eyes, but Tommy knew that he had gotten her attention.

He killed the Sink and let the bullet fall to the floor, stepping over it as he approached the woman. "You're about to face something a lot worse than what you just saw," he said. "If we work together, we might just be able to contain *Hanak Tuvar*. You try to go it alone, and your city will be rubble before the week is out. You *need* us."

"What do you need us to do?" the mayor whispered.

Miri stepped forward to answer that. "Gather everyone in the Watch and any troops you have garrisoned here," she said. "We have work to do."

· · ·

MIRI WATCHED a tall ship floating at the end of a long, wooden pier. The crew was busy loading it with crates while the captain stood in the marina, signing forms that had been given to him by the head of the dockworkers' guild. They had been at it for the better part of an hour, the only entertainment she'd had while she waited for her "troops" to assemble.

Off to her left, the Huanemon Bridge stretched over the Vinrella. People hurried across in both directions. Factory workers in rumpled clothing, snooty aristocrats in top hats, and everything in between: you'd find them all on the bridge.

She turned around.

Several dozen men in blue uniforms filled a plaza that over-looked the marina. Some were pale, others dark. Some were skinny, others rotund. She saw boys who were barely old enough to shave alongside grizzled graybeards who must have been working this job for at least thirty years. But they all had one thing in common: they all stared at her in wide-eyed confusion.

Jim, Zoe and Victor were present as well. Miri needed every hand she could get. The Field Binders had devised a plan to save this city; it was her job to implement it.

Standing on a wooden crate with her hands on her hips, Miri flashed a toothy grin. They weren't much to look at. "All right, you crusty boot leavings." That sounded like something a drill sergeant would say. "We're going to get you ready for this fight!"

She hopped off the crate, grunting, and then strode toward them with a swagger in her step. "Is this all of you?" she inquired. "Surely, it takes more than a hundred men to protect a city this large."

A boy with rosy cheeks stepped forward. "Each precinct sent two men, ma'am," he said. "The rest are all on duty."

"Two men from each precinct, huh?" Miri muttered. "I suppose it'll have to do. Scribe!"

Dalen came stumbling out from behind the crate, carrying a clipboard. He seemed to be fascinated by whatever he read there. "Yes, yes," he stammered. "I'm here."

"We'll need cannons."

"Yes, well," Dalen sputtered. "According to the quartermaster's report, there are twenty-seven in the city, though most have been moved to buildings in the north-west quarter that the army was using as a staging ground."

"What about ammunition?" an old man in the crowd asked.

"Unnecessary," Miri replied.

A skinny man with dark skin wrinkled his nose. "You want cannons," he said. "But not cannonballs?"

Miri leaned back against the crate, folding her hands behind her head and favouring them with a smile. "Glad you should ask, Charlie."

"My name isn't-"

"Turns out," Miri said, cutting him off. "When you shoot metal into the red haze that surrounds *Hanak Tuvar,* it just melts. Cannonballs are no good. Neither are bullets or arrows."

"Then what good are we?" one of the men demanded.

Reaching into her coat pocket, Miri retrieved a bag of almonds that she had pilfered from one of the food wagons. There were only a few left. She had been munching on them while the others blew hot air in their oh-so-important meetings.

Miri tossed up an almond, tilted her head back and caught it between her teeth. The men just stood there, gawking at her. A few of them even clapped. Good. A commander should always be a little bit inscrutable to her troops.

"We'll be using special weapons. If Nari's plan works, we're only gonna need about twenty cannons." She jerked her thumb over her shoulder toward the river. "Your job is to get them across those bridges and set them up on the south-east barracks. I want them delivered by sunset."

"But that's barely two hours away!"

"Welp, better get crackin' then."

She turned, stalking off toward the bridge and motioning for them to follow. "Come on!" she said. "Mayor says she's got a team of horses and wagons waiting for us. Let's get to work."

Dalen fell in beside her, still fussing with his clipboard. He gave her a sidelong glance. "It's nice to see you this happy," he muttered under his breath. "You were so dour in New Beloran."

Miri shrugged, a smile bursting to life on her face. "I don't know what to say," she replied. "I guess being back here reminds me of simpler times. When all we had to worry about was an insane Field Binder and his unkillable henchman."

"When it was just you and Thomas," Dalen mumbled.

She grabbed a fistful of his coat and pulled him close for a peck on the cheek. "Now, don't go getting jealous, sweetheart," she teased. "You know we both love you."

"It's nice to be reminded."

"Mmm," Miri agreed. "Well, help me get those cannons set up, and I'll remind you again later."

LIFTING a dagger up in front of her face, Desa squinted as she examined the blade. "Not bad." She tossed it up, caught the tip and held it upside-down. The balance was almost perfect. "Not bad at all."

"Feeling satisfied with your purchase?" Kalia asked.

Desa sat upon a wooden table in the corner of a room with beige walls and red carpets. The golden light of early evening came in through the rectangular windows. The mayor had been kind enough to give them a place to work.

Mercy had set up an easel that she used to paint a strange picture. So far as Desa could tell, it was a rainbow, but instead of the usual arch-shape, the colours were stacked side by side. Red on the left, purple on the right.

The goddess had insisted that she wanted to be called by her human name – Nari – but Desa wasn't sure if she could get used to that. At the very least, it would take some time. Still, she would humour the woman. No sense in causing a fuss.

Tommy stood a few paces back from the easel. Desa could tell, by the look on his face, that he was trying to figure out exactly what Mercy was up to. She decided to leave him to it. If he wanted to guess, he could guess, but Desa had no idea what was going on. And Mercy would tell them everything they needed to know in good time.

Kalia stood beside Desa with her arms folded, frowning pensively at the painting. "You really think a pair of knives will make a difference?"

Desa shrugged. "I used to carry a pair with me," she muttered. "They melted when I fought Bendarian in the temple. I don't know what *Hanak Tuvar* will send against us, but I will take any advantage I can get."

She had purchased another pistol as well. Keeping two on her person just made sense: one for normal ammunition and one for her Infused bullets.

With a soft sigh, Mercy returned her paintbrush to the jar of water. She twisted around, looking over her shoulder. "You won't need conventional weapons," she said. "They will be of no use."

Hopping off the table, Desa strode toward the other woman. "So," she said. "What *do* you have planned?"

Mercy clapped her hands, grinning like a scientist who had just made some grand discovery. "We need a weapon that can penetrate *Hanak Tuvar's* distortion field," she said. "As you've seen, most projectile-based weapons are useless."

"So, what should we use?" Tommy asked.

"To stop the darkness, we will call upon the light."

Kalia strode up beside Desa, her face pinched into an

expression of disapproval. "Very poetic," she said. "But perhaps you could offer something more practical."

To answer that, Mercy dabbed her brush in black paint and drew a wave underneath her sideways rainbow. A simple curve that rose up to a peak then down to a trough. She repeated that further down the page, only this wave had the peaks and troughs scrunched closer together. Finally, at the very bottom of the canvas, she drew one that was just a squiggly line.

"Light is a wave," Mercy explained. "And in some ways, it is a particle as well. But we'll keep things simple for now."

"Sure," Tommy cut in. "But how does that help us?"

"Red light," Mercy said, pointing to the first wave, the one with only one peak and one trough. "Has a longer wavelength than violet light." She pointed to the second wave, the one that looked like a series of rolling hills.

"Humans can only see a small portion of the electromagnetic spectrum. The light we can perceive is this narrow band here." She gestured to her rainbow, then slid her hand to the left side of the canvas. "This is called infrared light. The term literally means 'below red.' It is invisible to humans."

Moving to the right side of the easel, she tapped the canvas several times. "This is called ultraviolet light."

"Above violet?" Desa conjectured.

"Precisely," Mercy replied. "The further you go into the ultraviolet spectrum, the more dangerous light becomes to living tissue. I am going to teach you how to create a very special kind of Light-Source. A Gamma-Source."

Desa stepped forward, stroking her chin as she studied the easel. "And you think this can hurt *Hanak Tuvar?*"

"Hurt, yes," Mercy said. "Kill, no. The light will be redshifted by *Hanak Tuvar's* distortion field. But if we choose a frequency well into the ultraviolet range, it should be sufficient. The goal is to divert *Hanak Tuvar* from the city and convince it to chase us into the desert, where we can use the crystal to return it to its prison."

"Isn't there some way we could destroy it?"

A scowl contorted Mercy's face as she shook her head in dismay. "No," she said. "It's much too powerful for that. We must return the beast to its prison. Together, we can seal it in.

"Gamma rays are highly dangerous. We will need to apply directional modifiers to make sure they fire in the precise direction we need them to."

"All right," Desa said. "Show us what we need to do."

NIGHT HAD FALLEN by the time they were ready to test their new weapon. Under Mercy's guidance, Desa had learned the new Infusion in less than half an hour. It wasn't so different from an ordinary Light-Source. A few tweaks here and there. The directional modifiers were much more stringent than what she was used to. If she understood the situation correctly, they would project this "radiation" – that was the word Mercy had used – in a focused straight line about the thickness of her arm.

Infused bricks in the wall of the barracks provided more than enough light to see clearly. Kalia and Tommy had set them up while Desa completed her work. They had pointed a cannon at the wall that surrounded the building. Its tip now contained the new Gamma-Source.

For safety's sake, she had also created a Gamma-Sink in a mirror that Dalen and Miri had set up. According to Mercy, gamma rays would pass easily through most solid objects. She claimed that lead would provide an adequate shield, but there was none to be had around here. Desa had been hesitant to use a mirror, afraid that the radiation would reflect as normal light did, but Mercy had assured her that wasn't a concern. If the Sink failed – unlikely as that may be – the gamma rays would simply pass through the mirror. There was nothing on the other side of the wall except an open field. No one would be hurt if things went awry.

Mercy stood on a platform with her hands folded behind herself, frowning as she watched a pair of men setting up their target. They had placed a block of wood on a pile of stones stacked high enough to bring it in line with the cannon. "Make sure you get clear of the blast zone," she said for the twentieth time. "If that radiation hits you, it will liquify your organs. I want you both at least ten paces behind the cannon."

Having completed their work, the two men rose and cast furtive glances in Mercy's direction. They hopped to obey, rushing off to hide near the entrance to the barrack.

"Are you ready, Desa?"

Stepping forward, Desa nodded once in confirmation but said nothing.

Her friends had joined Mercy on the platform, eager to see the results of this test. Her stomach churned. She was afraid. Not because she thought the test might fail, because she feared it would succeed. If Field Binding could be used to make weapons like this...

"Begin," Mercy said.

Desa triggered the Gamma-Source and Gamma-Sink at the same time. The chunk of wood blackened and then ignited with a gout of flame that made her jump backward. The whole thing lasted all of three seconds before both Infusions burned themselves out.

Desa blinked. "That's it?"

As if to answer her question, the block of burning wood crumbled, pieces of it falling to land in the grass. Mercy threw a pebble into the blast zone, her Heat-Sink snuffing out the flames.

Turning on her heel, Desa marched to the base of the platform. She craned her neck to look up at the other woman. "A good Light-Source might survive hours of continuous use," she began. "This thing didn't even last five seconds."

Mercy nodded absently like a mother listening to her two-year-old explaining that the sky was blue. "Yes," she said. "The same amount of energy in a concentrated burst."

"I see..."

"We must begin Infusing the other cannons," Mercy said. "Positioning them in a perimeter around the city."

Desa felt creases lining her brow. "Now?" she groaned. "Nari, we're all exhausted from the long journey. If we spend the night Field Binding, we'll be useless tomorrow."

"You are most likely correct," Mercy said. "Come. There is one more thing I must teach you."

The barracks were all but deserted, which was why Zerena Dobrin thought it would be the perfect place to house Desa and her friends. For years a regiment of the Eradian Army had been permanently stationed at Ofalla, but they had cleared out ten weeks ago when Delarac sent them to Ithanar. No one had received word from them in all that time. Most likely, they were dead. Or halfway through the long march home. Assuming, of course, that they managed to get through Heldrid's haunted forest. Desa shivered when she remembered that creature.

The soldiers slept in a long room with stone walls. Beds on metal frames were spaced at even intervals. Each one was just large enough to support a single person. Desa chose one in the corner, near the small, square window that looked out on the yard.

Seated on the edge of the mattress, she planted her elbow on her thigh and rested her chin on the knuckles of her fist. "So," she said drowsily. "What is this lesson you have for us?"

Mercy stood in the aisle between beds, smiling beatifically. "Patience, my child," she said. "Let the others gather."

Kalia slipped past the former goddess, her mouth stretching

into a yawn that she didn't bother to hide. "Patience is for people who aren't about to pass out," she mumbled.

"I will only need the three of you," Mercy replied. "Thomas, please join us."

He came trudging over, head hanging, and then sat on the bed across from Desa. The poor lad looked like he was ready to collapse, and it wasn't just physical exhaustion weighing him down. For days, he had been carrying the hopes and fears of all of those refugees on his shoulders.

The mayor had spent most of the afternoon trying to find room for all those people. Some would be billeted here. Others would be sent to the barracks on the north side of the city. Desa had heard reports of townspeople taking in a family. The various hotels and inns throughout the city were probably packed to bursting. And all of it would be for nothing if they didn't survive the next few days.

Mercy chose the bed next to Tommy, folding her hands in her lap. Kalia seated herself beside Desa. The other woman was a comforting presence. She didn't have to do anything; just being there was enough.

"Excellent," Mercy said. "Now, we may begin. Commune with the Field."

Desa did as she was asked, clearing her mind and losing herself in the Ether's soothing embrace. She felt Kalia and Tommy doing the same. Even with her eyes closed, she could sense every contour of the room. Mercy was sitting cross-legged on her bed. "Now," she said. "Follow my lead."

Light erupted from the goddess as she made herself one with the Ether. Desa waited to see what she would do, but Mercy didn't begin an Infusion. Instead, she created a series of pulses, surges in the Ether that emanated from her like ripples spreading across the surface of a pond.

Desa wasn't sure how to duplicate that feat. She concentrated on the Ether, letting herself feel all the things she had grown accustomed to after years of Field Binding, all the things that her mind had learned to tune out. Yes, there it was. The Ether wasn't still. There was a constant thrumming, and ebb and flow. If she could agitate that natural process...

The pulses erupted from Desa, surging out from her across the barracks, washing over Dalen and Miri as they stowed their bags under their beds. How could they not feel it? This was almost like...Like the crystal on top of Mercy's pyramid.

A few moments passed before Tommy learned to imitate Mercy's pulses. Then Kalia was the last to join in. All four of them were like beacons in the night, waves intersecting, crashing over one another.

Suddenly, the pulses around Mercy changed direction. No longer flowing out from her, they moved inward, converging on her body. Could Desa do the same? It should be a simple matter of changing the way she directed the Ether.

Yes!

The pulses began to flow into her. Kalia and Tommy figured it out a moment later, drawing the Ether into themselves.

Mercy severed her connection, the light around her vanishing. "Well done," she said. "Now, instead of pulling it into yourselves, I want all of you to direct the Ether toward me, to a spot that I will indicate."

She began to glow again, creating a new series of pulses that converged over the palm of her hand. Desa followed her example, directing the Ether toward that spot, amplifying the wave that Mercy had created. Then Kalia joined in. And finally, Tommy got the hang of it.

With four minds all focusing on a single wave, the surges were powerful, almost violent. They built upon each other, each one adding to the last until something began to grow in Mercy's hand.

Desa continued her efforts, the Ether washing away some of her fatigue. She could almost feel the others. Their intensity, their focus. Five minutes passed and then ten. Her anticipation grew with every passing second.

Abruptly, Mercy let go of the Ether.

The others did the same an instant later.

Desa was breathing hard, heat suffusing her body. She hadn't realized just how intently she had been focused on this task.

When she opened her eyes, Mercy was sitting on the edge of the bed she had claimed, smiling at something in the palm of her hand. "We did it," she said. "Look."

Desa stood up to see what it was they had created and gasped when she found a shard of glittering crystal. Mercy held it up so that it caught the light, refracting a rainbow of colours.

"That's how we create it?"

"You focused the Field," Mercy explained. "Gave it physical form and shape. It is a skill my people had only begun to manifest before *Hanak Tuvar* destroyed us. This is a task that requires all of us to work in concert. A single Field Binder will find it next to impossible to create even the smallest amount of crystal. Two might be able to make a few grams. But four? The greater our numbers, the more we can produce. Almost as if the Field *wanted* us to work together."

Mercy stood, nodding to each of them. "Tomorrow, we will begin Infusing the cannons," she said. "And we will create as many of these crystals as we can. Together, we will save this city."

21

A ceiling of thick, gray clouds hung over the plains. The vast expanse of grassland seemed to go on forever, trees dotting the landscape here and there. From her perch atop one of the easternmost buildings, Desa kept an eye on the horizon.

Five days.

Five days had passed without incident since their arrival in Ofalla. She was starting to grow restless. What was *Hanak Tuvar* waiting for? Why didn't it just attack? No doubt the creature had lingered in New Beloran, eating its fill of anyone who had not escaped the city. The thought turned Desa's stomach, but she pushed her way through it to focus on the implications.

How long would it take to eat ten thousand people? Fifteen thousand? She had to figure that her group wasn't the only one to escape. There had to have been other people who fled the city when they caught sight of a giant squid smashing the buildings. But where might they have gone?

She had been operating under the assumption that *Hanak Tuvar* would go west. Ofalla was the only other big city in the area, and a larger population meant more food. But what if they had misjudged the creature's intentions? What if it had gone in another direction? If so, the plan to lure it to Mercy's pyramid would be much harder to execute.

Zerena Dobrin had become suspicious of Desa and her companions. Five days with no sign of the monster had given her the idea that this might all be a hoax, a scam to gain free food and comfortable lodgings. Luckily, the ships that came upriver had disabused her of such notions.

The first had arrived three days ago; the second had come in earlier this morning. Both crews carried tales of what they had seen on their journeys. Desa had taken the time to speak with them, and they all told her the same thing.

New Beloran was gone, reduced to a heap of rubble. According to the sailors, there wasn't a single building left standing. She had asked about survivors, but neither ship had gone anywhere near the riverbank. When the captains noticed the strange, red haze that enveloped the city, they thought it best to steer clear.

No one had seen anything that resembled a giant squid demon. *Hanak Tuvar* was gone, but the distortion field it had created remained. That troubled her, though she should have expected as much. The demon had changed Mercy's world, rendering it uninhabitable.

So, where was it? Might it have gone south, following the train tracks? Perhaps it was terrorizing some small, isolated village. If her suspicions were correct, if *Hanak Tuvar* was forced to remain inside the distortion field – and if expanding the field took a great deal of energy – then it might not be able to cross the countryside at great speed. Not yet, anyway.

Maybe she should have been grateful for the extra time. It had given her a chance to create more Infusions and to work with the others to make more crystals. They now had a couple dozen to spare. Miri had suggested that they pass them out to the Watch commanders with instructions to use them on those men who had suffered the most grievous injuries. Desa approved of that plan, though she had kept one crystal for herself, tucking it away in her pocket.

What was that?

Lifting her spyglass, Desa examined the eastern horizon. There, at the line where green grass met gray clouds, something changed. A crimson haze appeared, creeping over the field, standing at least a hundred feet high and advancing like a wall of flame.

She turned to look over the side of the building.

Six men in blue uniforms stood on the cobblestone street below, chatting quietly with one another. The eastern road continued past them, extending into the field for a quarter-mile before it became a wide, dirt path.

"Hate to interrupt your discussion, lads," Desa said. "But it's here. Benson, run to the barracks and tell Nari that it's time. Dispatch a runner to the teams on the other main thoroughfares. Tell them to be prepared in case *Hanak Tuvar* tries to go around the city. The rest of you, get those cannons in place!"

They scrambled to obey her orders.

Desa hopped off the roof, pulsing her Gravity-Sink to slow her descent, and landed in a crouch. She stood up slowly, pacing into the middle of the road.

Midnight waited for her there, gazing off toward the oncoming storm. The stallion flicked an ear toward her and nickered.

Closing her eyes, Desa nodded slowly. "I know," she said, patting his neck. "I'm scared too. But we'll get through this."

That creeping redness was flowing over the distant hills, choking the life out of the grass. At long last, *Hanak Tuvar* scurried onto a hilltop, its massive tentacles digging into the earth. It was huge! Much bigger than she remembered.

The squid was as large as a three-story building, its bulbous head rearing a good thirty feet into the air. Its lips parted, revealing sharp, pointed teeth that ringed its circular mouth. And it howled.

Covering her ears, Desa winced as the dreadful noise pulsed through her. She felt tears welling up, spilling over her cheeks. "By the Eyes of Vengeance…"

Frantic and frightened, a quartet of soldiers wheeled the first two cannons out of the storage house on the south side of the road. They set them up side by side, pointed toward the creature, and then hurried to retrieve the next two.

The city had over two dozen cannons to spare, but with multiple thoroughfares all leading to the centre of town, they had to block every possible route the demon might take. They had expected *Hanak Tuvar* to come from the east – that was why Desa had four to work with instead of just two – but until now, they couldn't be certain.

The demon kept coming.

Tommy hurried along the east road, charging up to the edge of town with his bow in hand. Miri and Kalia were right behind him, the three of them skidding to a stop behind the cannons.

A squadron of uniformed watchmen followed them, each carrying a rifle. Desa counted at least twenty. No one had told her to expect reinforcements – those guns would be useless if the Gamma-Sources failed – but then where else would the Watch be at a time like this?

Their sergeant was a tall, pale man with golden knots on his shoulders. He met Desa's eyes and nodded once.

"Almighty, protect us," Tommy whispered.

The wave of redness swept over the field, closing in on the city. Deep within that distortion, *Hanak Tuvar* continued its relentless advance. Thick tentacles pounded the ground, tossing up dead grass as puffs of ash.

Desa narrowed her eyes. "That's right. Come closer."

"Closer?" one of the watchmen squeaked.

"I want it feeling good and arrogant," Desa murmured. "Be ready to move the second pair of cannons into place."

Maybe she was imagining it, but Desa could swear that the beast was focused on her specifically. It hated her. Everyone else was just food, but Desa Kincaid? Killing her would not be sufficient. The insufferable, little human who had dared to challenge the majesty of *Hanak Tuvar* had to suffer. Anything less would be an affront to its dignity.

Mercy was huffing and puffing as she stumbled up to join them at the edge of the city. Pausing with a hand over her heart, she let out a breath. The woman had not been an athlete before her ascension. "It has come."

Desa nodded.

The beast saw only a pair of cannons, a last, desperate attempt by the humans to fend off the inevitable. It knew that heavy artillery was useless. This pitiful display of resistance was almost amusing. It would laugh as it crushed them all.

The distortion field was barely half a mile away.

It was time.

Desa triggered the Gamma-Sources that she had Infused into the cannons. An ear-piercing screech made her shiver. *Hanak Tuvar* reared, thin trails of smoke rising from its scorched body. It danced backward, trying to escape whatever trap the humans had set.

The outer layer of its flesh melted, thick globs of blackness falling to the ground and boiling. Tentacles waved back and forth as it tried to shield itself. For a moment, Desa dared to dream that they might have frightened it off.

Then the demon stood up on all twelve tentacles and shrieked with a fury that made the earth rumble. Just like that, it was scuttling toward them, trying to push that distortion field forward.

"Switch cannons!" Desa shouted.

The watchmen were already in motion, wheeling the first

set of cannons out of the way and replacing them with the second two. They inclined each gun as if for a wide, arcing shot, but that served her just fine. She would rather hit the beast's head.

Once again, Desa triggered her Gamma-Sources.

And *Hanak Tuvar* screamed.

Its limbs collapsed, slamming its girth down on the ground. It was like a bear that had been speared, roaring with impotent rage. "Not so insignificant now, are we?" Desa whispered. "That's right, you son of a bitch, the hairless apes outsmarted you."

"It's wounded!" the watch sergeant yelled. "Kill it!"

What? No!

Before Desa could protest, the idiot and his men were charging across the field, shouting and carrying their rifles like a bunch of spearmen trying to storm a fortified castle. Their efforts would be just as useless.

Hanak Tuvar writhed, trying to rise.

"Stop them!" Desa panted.

Tommy stepped forward, his face a mask of cold fury, and triggered a Sonic-Source. "Come back!" he shouted in a booming voice. "This will not make a difference!"

The men kept running.

They hoisted up rifles and fired shot after shot. Every bullet melted as it passed into *Hanak Tuvar's* distortion. What were these idiots expecting? Desa had told them what would happen!

"The mayor told them to do it," one of the cannon operators said. "She ordered us to finish the beast off when it went down."

Gritting her teeth, Miri hit him with a ferocious glare. "And she chose not to share those orders with me!" she hissed. "Undermining my authority!"

The sergeant and his men ran into the red haze, their guns

melting along with every button on their uniforms. But that wasn't the worst of it. The instant they crossed into *Hanak Tuvar's* domain, they stiffened as if they had been hit by an electric current.

One by one, they turned around and marched back out, loose clothing hanging off their bodies. And when they emerged from the distortion, they were gray. Completely gray from head to toe. Even their uniforms had been stripped of colour.

They began a mad scramble back to the city, snarling like enraged animals. Their eyes were black from corner to corner, every trace of humanity gone.

"No," Tommy whispered, shaking his head.

"What's going on?" the young cannon operator asked.

Miri drew her pistol, cocking the hammer, and extended her arm to point it at the oncoming men. "Our problems just got a lot worse."

Tommy beat her to the punch, pulling an arrow from his quiver, nocking it and letting it soar. He loosed shaft after shaft, striking one man between the eyes and another through the heart. Bodies fell to land in the field.

Miri's bullets brought down several more.

Desa felt the blood draining out of her face. Her mouth dropped open as she finally comprehended the horror of what had just happened. "'Within my realm, my power is absolute,'" she whispered. "That was what it said."

She rounded on Mercy, causing the other woman to flinch. "If we get caught in that distortion field – even for a second – it can turn us instantly."

"Yes," Mercy agreed.

The watchmen kept running, undaunted by a barrage of arrows and bullets. Behind them, *Hanak Tuvar* rose, stretching its meaty tentacles, raising its bloated body into the air. Its scream rang out like a war horn.

The squid resumed its terrible advance, the red haze expanding to make room for it. She could feel the weight of its malice, its singular focus. "It wants me," Desa murmured. "I have to go."

Tommy shot a glance over his shoulder, scowling at her. "You can't be serious!" he said. "You go out there, and it's death!"

Desa snarled with white-hot rage. "If I don't, it will just keep coming!" she barked. "We need a plan. Kalia, run to the southeast road and make sure those soldiers have their cannons in place, I'm going to bring the demon to you."

Kalia took off in a sprint.

"Tommy," Desa barked. "Once it's gone, Reinfuse these cannons with Gamma-Sources. I may need to bring it back here."

Something was niggling at her, the ever-present sense of some danger that she had failed to account for. She searched for it, running through all the possibilities, but nothing came to mind. So, that left her with no option but to go forward with her plan.

Climbing into Midnight's saddle, she took the reins in hand and stared out on the field. "All right, you bastard," she whispered. "Just you and me."

With a gentle squeeze of her hips, she had Midnight galloping down the road in a headlong charge. She bent low over the stallion's neck, the wind whipping her face and making her short hair flutter.

Hanak Tuvar noticed her approach, rising up and thrusting its hideous face forward. Its mouth opened, sucking in the air along with bits of debris. Yes, she had assessed the situation correctly.

It wanted her.

Midnight turned right, running in a straight line parallel to the red wall, his hooves churning up clumps of dirt. Of course, the demon tried to expand its territory. So, Desa veered her horse back toward the city.

The redness chased her, swooping over the field.

Midnight was always two steps ahead of it. She could feel it on the back of her neck like concentrated evil threatening to scour her soul away. Her efforts had changed the shape of the distortion field.

Instead of a uniform wave that advanced in one direction, it now grew in fits and starts, chasing her. *Hanak Tuvar* was focusing all of its efforts on catching Desa, ignoring the city as a prize that it could claim later.

The squid scurried alongside Midnight, dark tentacles propelling it forward with incredible speed. Desa was easily within arm's reach of that thing – so to speak – but it didn't dare leave its crimson domain.

It screamed.

Hissing air through her teeth, Desa felt sweat rolling over her forehead. Her heart was pounding.

A tendril of redness wrapped around her from behind, encircling Midnight and trapping them both in a pocket of normalcy that was quickly shrinking. With a powerful whinny, the stallion leaped over the crimson haze.

He landed on the other side, free and clear, kicking up a spray of dirt as he galloped toward the south-east road. *Hanak Tuvar* was livid. It slammed a tentacle down with enough force to jostle Desa in the saddle.

She guided Midnight toward the city. Mercy send those idiots had their cannons in place. She could feel the Sources she had created; she knew exactly how far away they were and in what direction, but that said nothing about the surrounding buildings. They could still be in storage for all she knew.

Wait, what was she talking about? Of course, the Watchmen had done their jobs. They weren't *that* stupid.

Hanak Tuvar struggled to keep up. Maybe it was just her, but she was almost certain that the beast was getting tired. All that effort spent expanding its distortion field took a toll.

Squeezing her eyes shut, Desa shuddered. "Just a little further," she panted. "Come on! Come on!"

The redness swelled again, wrapping around her, this time at a height that Midnight couldn't possibly leap. Her island of normalcy kept shrinking and shrinking. In seconds, she would be consumed. And then she would be one of them: a soulless, gray beast. Her friends would have to put her down.

Or maybe not.

A tentacle hovered over her, ready to squash her the instant that she was submerged in the distortion field. Desa sniffled and whispered, "I love you, Kalia." The scarlet wave washed over her. In a last act of desperation, she did the only thing she could think of.

She slammed her fist down on her thigh, crushing the crystal in her pocket. A halo surrounded her and Midnight, a rainbow of colours – red, orange, yellow, green, blue and purple – oscillating in an endless cycle. If the Ether could heal ordinary wounds, perhaps it would undo whatever *Hanak Tuvar* did to transform people into gray monsters.

Desa only wanted a few seconds to escape, but she got more than she had bargained for. The halo expanded, stretching upward to encompass *Hanak Tuvar's* tentacle. When it faded, some of the redness had receded, leaving her in a world of full colour.

And part of *Hanak Tuvar's* slimy limb was now out in the open.

The beast shrieked, pulling back as the end of its tentacle literally fell off. Midnight quickly jumped out of the way. Three hundred pounds of oily, black flesh hit the ground. And it didn't just melt.

It *evaporated.*

The tentacle disintegrated into a cloud of dark smoke.

Hanak Tuvar retreated, waving its amputated limb at her. It slinked away, injured and frightened. "You can't survive outside of your distortion field," Desa whispered.

Suddenly, this war seemed winnable.

She turned Midnight around and set him galloping toward the city, to the east road where she had made her stand with the cannons. *Hanak Tuvar* made no move to attack, but the red haze did not dissipate.

When she arrived, the others were still gathered around the two cannons. Mercy was mystified. "What did you do?" she asked, stepping forward.

Shutting her eyes, Desa drew a breath through her nose. "The crystals," she panted. "They can undo whatever *Hanak Tuvar* did to the land, restore the natural order. The demon can't survive in our world."

Mercy nodded as if that made perfect sense. "Yes," she said. "Its body has a molecular structure that cannot exist within our universe. The laws of nature as they are here would not allow it."

"So, it has to change the laws of nature to make our world hospitable."

"Yes."

Desa leaned forward, squinting at the other woman. "Then what if we changed them back?"

"Um, ladies," Tommy said. "I hate to interrupt your conversation, but I'm afraid we have a new problem."

Desa turned Midnight around and gasped when she saw what Tommy was referring to. People. Hundreds of people deep within the red distortion field, all plodding toward her. She saw farmers in overalls and bankers in fine suits, sailors in striped shirts and at least a hundred lost souls who still wore their bedclothes.

They were an approaching army, all staring at her with lifeless eyes, directed by a singular intent. That niggling fear she had been ignoring came roaring to the forefront of her mind. Why hadn't she put it together before now?

If *Hanak Tuvar* could transform anyone who entered its distortion field, then what might it have done to the citizens of New Beloran? To those who had refused to flee or who had been too slow.

It turned out the beast didn't devour them all.

When the first group emerged from the red haze, Desa was not surprised to discover that they were gray. Stripped of colour from their boots to their scalps. They seemed to notice her for the first time; their plodding footsteps became a frantic scramble for the city and its helpless inhabitants.

"You're right, Tommy," Desa mumbled. "We have a new problem."

22

The gray army ran across the field.

Lifting his bow, Tommy nocked an arrow, drew back the string and loosed. The shaft buried itself in the chest of a portly fellow in a straw hat. And that poor man sank to his knees when Tommy triggered the Electric-Source in the arrowhead. Lightning spread out in a spiderweb, striking anyone who got too close. A dozen gray bodies fell to the ground, but there were hundreds more.

Miri stepped up beside him with her mouth hanging open, blinking as if she could not believe her eyes. "We can't stop that many," she said. "We need to retreat."

"We can't retreat," Desa growled. "If we let them enter this city..."

Shutting his eyes tight, Tommy shook his head. "No, Miri is right," he said. "If we try to make a stand here, we'll be dead in five minutes."

Nari came up beside Desa, resting a hand on her shoulder. The former goddess had a look of anguish on her face. "We cannot defeat so many by conventional means," she said. "We need a new plan."

"I'm open to suggestions!" Miri squeaked.

The lifeless army was still advancing, wave after wave of gray bodies converging on the city. The sight of them made Tommy shiver. Every single one of those bastards wanted to rip him to shreds.

"Hanak Tuvar controls them," Nari said. "If we sever its connection, they will all become inert."

Thinking fast, Tommy retrieved another arrow, nocked it and pointed his bow into the sky. He loosed, and the arrow flew in a wide arc, landing amid the advancing horde. Harmless. Until he triggered the Gravity-Source, that was.

Gray people fell over, sprawled out in the grass. Bodies piled on top of bodies, creating a mass of flesh that served as an obstacle to those who came up from behind. Tommy let out a sigh. From this distance, the pull of the Gravity-Source was incredibly weak. His friends were able to ignore it.

"How are we supposed to sever the connection?" Miri asked.

"With the Unifying Field," Nari replied as if that answered the question. Tommy had no idea what she was planning, but at this moment, he would take any hope, no matter how small. "Let us get to safety."

Men of the City Watch arrived, dropping to one knee and lifting up rifles they had taken from the armoury. They fired with a thunderous roar, bullets ripping through the gray horde, dropping dozens of enemies.

The Ether stirred as Desa triggered her Gravity-Sink. She jumped, rising into the air and then tossed a coin out behind herself, releasing a blast of kinetic energy that seemed to only affect her.

Brilliant! Tommy thought as he watched her fly out over the field, the coin trailing behind her, pulled by a Gravity-Source that only affected it. Now, why hadn't he come up with something like that?

Desa drew her right-hand revolver, pointing it down into the crowd. She fired six shots, producing a spray of black blood with every one. Then, holstering one pistol, she drew the other and fired a single round.

This one was a Heat-Sink that made frost crystallize on a dozen grays, shattering them when they fell over. Desa flung her coin toward the red distortion, and then she was flying backwards, twisting around in midair.

She alighted gently on the cobblestones about ten feet behind the watchmen and then nodded once. "We can't just flee," she said. "We're the only ones who can keep these people alive."

"I cannot challenge *Hanak Tuvar* alone," Nari said. "I need all of you to help me guide the Field."

The watchmen fired another volley.

Desa stepped up to Nari, craning her neck to stare into the other woman's eyes. "It doesn't matter," she said. "You'll be sitting there, in a trance, disconnected from your bodies. Someone has to guard *you*."

The watchmen stood up, turned around and ran along the road, back into the city. "Retreat!" their sergeant shouted. Thankfully, Desa didn't argue. She hopped into Midnight's saddle, offering her hand so that Nari could climb up behind her.

The horse turned around and took off at a trot, moving deeper into the city, the blue-clad watchmen parting to make way. Tommy and Miri followed. They were soon joined by crowds of people from intersecting streets.

Many of Ofalla's roads simply ended abruptly, becoming dirt paths before they even reached the outermost buildings and disappearing entirely soon after. But those gray brutes didn't mind getting a little mud on their shoes. They were flooding into the city on multiple streets.

Kalia came around a corner and fell in beside Tommy. She

was gasping for breath, glancing back over her shoulder, dark hair streaming in the wind. "They're everywhere!" she cried out.

"Nari has a plan."

"Oh? And what's that?"

Red-cheeked and panting, Tommy hissed. Sweat beaded on his forehead and slicked the back of his shirt. "She thinks we can use the Ether to cut them off from *Hanak Tuvar*. They'll all drop dead."

"Works for me!"

The East Road opened into a square of gray buildings with slanted, black rooftops. Most stood two or three stories high, packed so tightly together there wasn't an inch of space between them. He saw an inn, a tavern, a tailor's shop and a bookkeeper's office. On a normal day, this place would be bustling with happy people going about their business. Today, it was filled with frantic people trying their darndest to escape an army of the dead.

Normally, a plaza like this would have something smack-dab in the middle. A statue or a fountain or *something*. But this one offered nothing but cobblestones. Plenty of space to corral the helpless humans.

Narrow byroads branched off on the north and south sides of the square, connecting to larger streets that ran parallel to the East Road. He could see gray bodies rushing past on each of them, moving westward into the city.

"One small problem," Tommy said, turning to Kalia. "Nari needs all of us to help her guide the Ether. There will be no Field Binders to protect the city."

"There will be one," Desa said, pushing her way through a crowd that parted to make room for her. Her face was grim, her eyes as hard as diamonds. "I'm making my stand here."

Kalia rushed to her, throwing her arms around Desa. "Then I'm staying with you."

Desa pulled back, resting her hands on the other woman's shoulders. That look of anguish on her face. Tommy suspected that Kalia wouldn't like whatever came next. "No," Desa replied. "Mercy needs you."

"But-"

"Look, we don't have time to argue about it," Desa snapped. "You, me, Tommy and Mercy. That's all we have to work with. Which of us is most skilled at combat Field Binding?"

"You are," Kalia admitted.

Desa ground her teeth, turning her face away from the other woman. "Then it makes sense for me to guard you while you do what needs to be done," she grumbled. "No arguments now. We need to get to work."

"But I want to help you," Kalia protested.

Desa kissed her nose and then smiled. "You will be," she promised. "Go with Tommy."

Nari came forward, shoving her way between two men in blue uniforms. She nodded to him and then to Kalia. "We must find a safe place to work," she said. "Hurry. We do not have much time."

Tilting his head back, Tommy squinted at a building on the west side of the plaza. "The floors above the bookkeeper's office," he said. "That should do. If these things have any kind of intelligence, they'll probably look to the inn for victims."

"Let's go."

They ran to the bookkeeper's door. Tommy was planning to use a Force-Source pin to break the lock, but jiggling the knob was enough to get the thing open. Inside, they found a small office with wooden desks and a clock on the wall.

The head clerk, a copper-skinned man with a ring of frizzy, gray hair around the back of his head, stood up with a huff. He was rather ostentatious in a purple, three-piece suit, and the pocket watch that he carried on a golden chain didn't help matters. "What is the meaning of this?" he demanded.

"We need your office," Tommy said.

"I beg your pardon."

Tommy licked his lips, shut his eyes and cleared his mind of frustration, irritation and fear. "Forgive the intrusion, sir," he pressed. "But I'm afraid we have no time to argue. And you don't want to remain in this square, believe me."

The man grunted, turning his face toward the large, front window. "Yes, there is some hubbub out there," he muttered. "What is this all about?"

"The city is under attack," Kalia said, stepping up to stand beside Tommy. "Take your staff and leave. Please."

One of the clerks, a young woman in a white blouse who wore her brown hair up in a clip, ventured a glance out the window. "I think they're right, Mr. Carson," she said. "We should probably leave."

Crossing his arms, Carson frowned at Tommy and his friends. "That may be," he said. "But I don't see why we should let you remain here. We have some very sensitive documents in this office."

Nari came forward, tossing up a glowing, green coin and catching it with a deft hand. "Because we have the power to save this city," she said. "Please, sir. We have no interest in your accounts."

"I...Yes, perhaps we should go."

It took barely two minutes for the clerks to file out the door, leaving Tommy, Nari and Kalia alone in the office. Once they were gone, he took charge. Someone had to. "Help me move those desks to block the door." He didn't want gray people getting in here while they were guiding the Ether.

He bent over the nearest desk and shoved it across the room, propping it up against the front door. Kalia and Nari did the same with another, creating a suitable barricade. That only left the window. No way to block that with desks.

Inspiration struck him.

Closing his eyes, Tommy made himself one with the Ether and began an Infusion, a Force-Sink that he placed into the metal latch that held the window shut. He gave it a physical trigger. The Sink would activate if the latch was forced open, and anyone who tried to come through would be frozen in place. Even wrapped in the Ether's embrace, Tommy would feel that, giving him plenty of warning.

It took almost two minutes for the lattice strands to thicken. During that time, Nari touched the Ether as well. She must have been wondering what he was up to. At long last, he broke off contact.

"Clever," Nari said.

He nodded. "Thanks. Let's get to work."

DESA WATCHED the blue-clad watchmen spreading out through the plaza, raising their rifles, ready to take a stand. No, this was no good at all. So many men. They would just get in her way.

The sergeant was practically choking up on his gun. He had his back to her, facing the road that led east out of the plaza. "Stand ready!"

Desa grimaced, shaking her head as she strode up to the man. "I need you to leave," she told him in no uncertain terms. "Take your men and guard the neighbouring streets. I'll hold the square."

Whirling around to face her, the sergeant frowned. He was a tall man, skinny with pale skin and large, brown eyes. "Ma'am, with all due respect," he began. "I've seen what you can do, but even you can't hold this place alone."

"Don't be so sure."

"But-"

She turned, gesturing to the stubby road that led westward out of the plaza, a road that ran for maybe fifty feet before intersecting with a crossing street. "They'll try to come around and catch me from behind," she said. "Keep them off my back."

Before she could say another word, two watchmen aimed their rifles and fired into the East Road, scattering gray men who had tried to rush the plaza. Their bullets hit arms and shoulders, spilling black blood but doing no serious harm.

They did buy her a few moments, though. The half dozen gray beasts who had been trying to charge the plaza ducked into alleys. She saw even more coming, feral men and women who had been stripped of humanity, bloodlust shining in their dead, black eyes.

The sergeant groaned.

Desa stepped past the man, shouldering him out of the way. She retrieved a handful of coins from the pouch on her belt. "We don't have time to debate this!" she growled. "Go! I'll be fine!"

Gesturing to his men, the sergeant set them running down the narrow streets on the north and south sides of the plaza. He was quick to follow, venturing one last glance over his shoulder. He looked like he wanted to say something but thought better of it.

Miri planted herself beside Desa with a revolver in hand, staring down the mass of oncoming enemies. "I'm fighting with you," she said. "If anyone wants to hurt Lommy, they go through me."

"No!" Desa barked. "I fight better alone."

"But-"

"Trust me, Miri," she pleaded. "I can't be as effective if I have to worry about hitting you with the blast from an Electric-Source. Help the watchmen. Take Midnight with you. I don't want him anywhere near this."

The other woman hesitated a moment and then nodded. She gently took hold of Midnight's bridle and guided him to the south side of the plaza. "I will do what I can to guard your back."

"That's all I ask."

The horde kept coming up the East Road. She counted at least twenty. Some of those monsters broke away from the main group, running down side streets, perhaps in an attempt to surround Desa. She heard screams and gunfire to her left and her right.

Half a dozen gray men came charging into the square, lifeless ghouls that moved with eerie synchronicity. One was tall and bald with a scar on his cheek, another short and dark of skin. They paused for a moment, noting her presence, and then advanced.

Desa flung her hand out toward them, fingers uncurling, coins glittering as they tumbled through the air. And then she triggered the Force-Sources that she had Infused into every one, releasing multiple blasts of kinetic energy.

The six oncoming brutes were thrown backward, hurled out of the plaza and into the street. One by one, they landed on the cobblestones.

Footsteps behind her.

Desa drew her daggers.

Pulsing her Gravity-Sink, she jumped and back-flipped over the head of a gangly, gray man. She landed behind him and then stabbed him in the back. Pulling her knives free, she let the dead man fall to his knees.

More footsteps.

Desa twirled her right-hand dagger, catching it in a reverse-grip, the blade pointed downward. She stepped to the left and flung her arm out to the side, plunging the knife into some poor bastard's throat.

She tore it free as the gray man stumbled past her, black ichor fountaining from the wound and spilling onto his shirt.

He lost his footing and landed atop the corpse of his companion.

The first six were back on their feet, hissing and snarling at her. Once again, they ran into the square. She let them come. When they had closed half the distance, Desa triggered her Gravity-Sink.

She leaped, propelling herself over them, sailing across the plaza. Killing her Sink, she landed at the mouth of the street they had come from and then twisted around.

All six men had rounded on her.

They began another mad dash.

Tossing up her left-hand dagger, Desa caught the tip and then hurled it at them. It landed with a clatter in the middle of the plaza. She waited until all six of her enemies were almost on top of it. Then she triggered the Gravity-Source in the blade along with the Sink in her belt buckle.

Bodies fell to the ground, anchored by a force twice as strong as the Earth's natural pull. Even the corpses were dragged across the cobblestones to join the pile. Buildings creaked. Small objects banged against nearby windows.

Sheathing the other knife, Desa drew her right-hand pistol. She cocked the hammer and then jumped, launching herself across the plaza.

As she flew over the pile of enemies, she pointed her gun downward and fired three rounds. Thunder split the air. Bullets ripped through gray flesh.

Killing both Source and Sink, Desa landed with a grunt. She twirled the gun around her index finger and then caught the grip.

A soft growl made her look up to find a gray woman perched on the slanted roof of a bakery. The stranger hissed, baring her teeth, and flung herself at Desa with a powerful leap.

Desa extended her hand, lining up a shot.

CRACK!

A hole appeared in the gray woman's forehead, black goo trailing out from the back of her skull. The corpse landed with a *thump* and skidded across the cobblestones.

The men she had incapacitated with her Gravity-Source were starting to rise. Four of them, anyway. Some had been wounded by her bullets, their broken bodies unable to move. She had no idea why. The gangly man who had taken a blade through each lung was back on his feet. But the one she had stabbed through the throat was still down.

The bald man stepped forward despite a hole in his chest that leaked black fluid onto his shirt. But a smaller man with a shoulder wound refused to budge. There seemed to be no rhyme or reason to it. Some of them reanimated after she put them down. Others didn't. If she could just figure out what distinguished one from the other, she might be able to end this.

Four men stood in a line, each one as gray as a rock. The bald one snarled at her, black spittle flying from his lips. Two others flanked him: one short, the other notably skinny. The fourth was an old man with unruly, white hair. Despite his age, he moved just as nimbly as the others.

In unison, they charged.

Lifting her gun in one hand, Desa squinted as she took aim. *CRACK!* Her first shot pierced the shorter man's chest, shattering his ribcage and dropping him to the ground. *CRACK!* Her next shot hit the skinny man's knee. He fell flat on his face. Only two left. And she was out of bullets.

Desa holstered her pistol.

The bald man was bearing down on her, spreading his arms wide as if to wrap her up in a bear hug. He screamed.

Desa jumped, using her Gravity-Sink for extra height, and turned belly up in the air. She wrapped her legs around his neck, ankles locked. For half a second, she just hung off him like a dangling pendulum. Then she curled up and slammed her elbow down on his fat head.

The brute fell backward, landing with a groan. That gave her a chance to rise and run for the middle of the square. Her knife was still lying on the cobblestones, surrounded by fallen bodies. A blast of kinetic energy from her ring shoved the corpses aside. It also sent the dagger skittering away, costing her precious seconds.

The old man was right behind her.

Desa threw herself into a headlong dive, somersaulting over the pavement. She came up in a crouch, seized the fallen knife and quickly got to her feet.

When she turned, the old man was almost on top of her.

She backed away, pointing her dagger at him, narrowing her eyes to slits. "You do *not* want to do this." Ignoring her warning, he kept coming.

Desa pulsed the Gravity-Source.

The old fool was yanked forward a few steps, and she rammed her blade up through the underside of his chin, into his skull. His eyes widened. Blood fountained from the wound as she withdrew the steel from his flesh.

His body fell to the ground, lying at her feet in a spreading pool of dark ichor. "Trying to reason with the dead," Desa muttered. "I must be going mad."

MIRI STOOD on a narrow street that ran parallel to the East Road, blue-clad watchmen forming a line in front of her. They were all down on one knee, holding rifles, ready to stop the oncoming charge.

Over half a dozen grays were scrambling toward her, hissing and snarling like wolves that had been forced into a cage. They moved with incredible speed, feet pounding the pavement.

The watchmen fired.

Bullets tore through the grays. Bodies dropped to the ground, landing among the corpses of their fallen comrades. Remarkably, some of those poor souls began to rise again.

Miri felt her jaw drop, then shut her eyes and gave her head a shake. "Why?" she wondered aloud. "Why do some rise while others stay down?" She drew her belt knife, holding it in a reverse grip. If anyone got past that line of riflemen, she'd be ready.

A noise from behind.

She turned around to find four grays coming down the street from the west, trying to sneak up on her. Their leader, a short fellow with big, round eyes, launched himself at Miri with a powerful leap.

She stepped aside, moving toward a towering man with thick arms and a mustache. "Enemies behind you!" she called to her allies. If they heard, she couldn't tell. She was too busy. Mr. Mustache swiped at her.

Miri ducked, letting his hand pass over her. She slashed his belly with the knife, then stepped past him and flung her arm out to the side. Her blade punched through the back of his neck, severing his spine.

Down he went.

The next gray to attack was a woman with wavy hair. She spread her arms wide and tried to charge Miri.

Miri kicked her in the stomach, throwing her down onto her backside. She knelt beside Miss Wavy Hair and plunged her knife through the other woman's chest. Right through the heart.

Two down, two to-

A hulking man with dark skin flung himself at Miri, slamming into her, knocking her down. They rolled across the width of the street, each trying to gain dominance.

She ended up on top of him, straddling his chest, but his open palm came up to strike her nose. Silver stars filled her vision. Her head rang like a struck gong. She was barely aware of falling over.

Now, the man was on top of her, his hands trying to grab her neck and squeeze the life out of her. She seized his wrists, holding him back, fighting with all her strength. It was no use. He was just too-

CRACK!

When her vision cleared, she saw a hole in the gray man's forehead. He slumped over, onto his side, lying in the road.

One of the watchmen stood over her with a pistol in hand, smoke rising from the barrel. He nodded once, then turned away without a word.

Groaning, Miri sat up and pressed the heel of her hand to her forehead. That awful throbbing pain behind her eyes... "Well, that was a whole new kind of horrible," she muttered. "Any more coming?"

"Plenty," the man who had saved her replied.

Miri stood up, rolling her shoulder to loosen the joint. "Well," she said. "At least we won't be bored."

THE ETHER SURGED WITHIN TOMMY.

With Kalia and Nari working beside him, focusing his thoughts toward a single purpose, he directed his mind outward. Into the square where Desa struck down gray man after gray man. And beyond.

He felt the next batch of monsters coming up the East Road, each one a bundle of wrongness in the shape of a human. They were like gaps in the fabric of reality, places where the Ether had been taken away. Like Adele. The only difference was that the malevolent force that animated them wasn't nearly as strong as it had been in her.

Which should make this easier.

He chose a gray man at random and shoved the Ether into

the emptiness. That poor fellow keeled over, lying dead on the cobblestones. *No,* Nari whispered in his mind. *We cannot cut them off one by one. We must go to the source.*

How?

Follow, was all she said.

He felt her presence through the Ether, felt her focusing on something. One of the grays who attacked Miri on a nearby side street. Tommy wanted to help, but Nari would only dissuade him.

There was something off about this particular gray man. It was as if the wrongness was not confined to his body. No, it extended in a hair-thin line, running eastward all the way...All the way to *Hanak Tuvar.*

The demon was hiding in its distortion field, fighting through the pain of its severed tentacle. It sensed Tommy's attention and spun on him, screaming. Just like that, he was hurled away like a leaf in a gale, his mind sent flying across the city, right back into his own body. *What just happened.*

We must approach with caution, Nari said. She was a cluster of particles sitting beside him in the parlour of a small apartment above the bookkeeper's office. *We must work together. Hanak Tuvar is too powerful for any one of us to challenge it alone. Only together do we stand a chance.*

We better do something, Kalia thought. *Those gray things are still coming. If we don't stop them soon, we'll be surrounded. Desa...*

She will be fine, Kalia, Nari promised. *Have faith.*

Then what do we do? Tommy asked.

Follow my lead.

JIM BURST out of an alley with his bow in hand, skidding across the cobblestones. Gray buildings on either side of the road, each two stories tall. He saw no one in those windows. Perhaps the residents of this neighbourhood had been wise enough to get out of here.

He forced his eyes shut, heaving out a sigh, and then leaned his shoulder against a brick wall. "Just breathe," he whispered. "Just breathe."

Years of working as a slave had given him quite a bit of endurance, but those years had not been spent running from monsters who wanted to tear his face off. It was terror, not physical strain, that made his heart race.

Two of the gray creatures were prowling the street, scanning this way and that, searching for a victim. One laid eyes on Jim and snarled.

Reacting quickly as Tommy had taught him, Jim took an arrow from his quiver and nocked it. He drew back the string, aimed for his enemy's head and loosed.

His arrow went through the dead man's shoulder, causing him to stumble. When the creature regained its balance, it turned those black eyes on him. Jim had never shared Tommy's proficiency with the bow. A few months of training wouldn't change that.

The gray man broke into a sprint.

Ducking back into the alley, Jim ran for his life, heart pounding, breath rasping from his lungs. He could hear those creatures behind him. Almighty have mercy! They were gaining ground.

He came out the other side, dashing onto a street that looked very much like the one he had left behind. With no concrete plan in mind, he turned eastward. It was a stupid move – yes, let's move *toward* the enemy – but there was no changing his mind now. The two grays were still chasing him. His feeble attack had incensed them.

Frightened people were coming up the street in the opposite direction. When they saw Jim's pursuers, they screamed and ran into nearby buildings. One poor man actually crashed through the front window of a store.

Victor stepped out of an alley, standing tall with his feet apart and raising his pistol in both hands. He lined up a shot and then fired.

Thunder growled in Jim's ear.

A glance over his shoulder proved that Victor's aim was true. One of the grays was lying in a pool of inky blood. The other was still chasing him.

Jim spun around, dropping his bow.

A gray hand tried to claw his eyes out.

Bending his knees, Jim reached up with both hands to seize the other man's wrist. He twisted it in a way that should have brought pain, but his enemy was silent. It didn't matter; Jim had the momentum.

Pulling the dead man close, Jim brought his knee up into the corpse's stomach. That powerful hit threw his opponent to the ground. Just like Miri had taught him.

Victor came forward, gun in hand, and casually put two bullets in the dead man's head. At long last, the corpse stopped thrashing.

"Thank you," Jim panted.

Victor shot a glance in his direction. That hardness behind his eyes. He was enjoying this. "We need to find the others."

"We can't!" Jim moaned. "These things are everywhere."

"What do you want to do?"

Drawing in a shuddering breath, Jim closed his eyes and considered his options. These things were coming from the east, from the direction where Desa and the others had set up their trap. If they had been overrun.

Well, what could Jim do? If four Field Binders weren't enough, then a man who could barely work a bow wasn't going to add anything of value. That was for damn sure. No, if he was going to die, then he wanted to be-

"Back to the barracks!" he snapped.

"What? Why?"

Jim retrieved his bow and broke into a sprint, running west along the street. "Because!" he cried out. "Our people are there!"

He turned south down a side street, then west, then south again. In about five minutes, he arrived at the stone wall that encircled the military compound. Dead people were trying to scale it, trying to get inside.

Emerging from an alley, Zoe stumbled toward them. Her face was flushed, her eyes wide with fright. "What?" she gasped. "What do we do?"

Jim didn't answer her with words.

He strode forward, pulling an arrow from his quiver, and then lined up a shot.

The shaft drove itself into a gray man's back, causing him to fall off the wall and land on the pavement. With any luck, he wouldn't rise again. The others didn't seem to notice or care.

Taking his cue, Victor stepped forward, raised his gun and squeezed the trigger. Another gray fell to the ground, but two more crested the wall and dropped out of sight on the other side.

"Dalen!" Jim shouted.

He ran for the wooden gate that had been shut tight after he and the others had left to find Desa. He threw his shoulder against it, pain flaring through his body, but the gate wouldn't budge. He had to get inside.

"Move!" Victor said behind him.

Hurrying out of the way, Jim watched as the other man pointed his gun at the gate's hinges. Each peel of thunder was accompanied by the screech of shredded metal. Then Victor stepped forward and kicked the gate, knocking it over.

The three of them ran into the yard. Each barrack was a single-story, stone building with a flat roof. To his horror, he found Dalen in front of one. He must have come out to see what all the commotion was about.

Dalen was as pale as a ghost, his eyes bulging out of their sockets. He backed away slowly, moving to the wooden door behind him.

Two grays lunged for him.

Jim didn't bother with his bow; if he missed, he might hit Dalen. He just ran at full speed, bounding over the grass, and hurled himself at one of those monsters. He tackled the gray man to the ground.

The other one swiped at Dalen, fingernails leaving scratches on Dalen's cheek. No, no, no! Jim couldn't deal with both of them! Not together. Someone had to step in.

CRACK!

A bullet hit the remaining gray man, ripped right through his body and went on to pierce Dalen's chest as well. "No!" Jim screamed, watching in horror as the man he had come to love fell to the ground. Red and black blood stained the door.

Lost in a fog of rage, Jim pounded the squirming corpse beneath him, striking its skull again and again. He didn't relent until the dead man stopped writhing.

Then he stood, rounding on victor and striding toward him with a finger pointed. "Idiot!" he screamed. "Don't you ever think before you pull that trigger?"

Victor was backing away, mumbling words that Jim couldn't hear. "I didn't," he managed at last. "I...I...I didn't realize that..."

People were idiots. They always assumed that a bullet stopped when it hit its target. What to do? What to do? There had to be a way to save Dalen! Think, think, think! What was it Mercy had said about-

Jim reached into his pocket, retrieving the shard of crystal he had been carrying. He ran to Dalen, who was now sitting with his back against the door, his legs stretched out before him.

Shallow breath rasped its way out of the other man's lungs. Dalen was fading fast. In a few moments, he would be gone.

Jim pressed the shard into Dalen's palm and closed Dalen's fingers around it. With a forceful squeeze, he shattered the crystal. A rainbow spread over Dalen's body, up his arm, over his chest and head, all the way down to his boots.

The other man drew in a long gasp, blinking several times as lucidity returned to him. "What...What happened?" He pawed at his chest, but the bullet hole was gone, replaced by unblemished skin.

Dalen turned his gaze upon Jim, and his face lit up with a smile. "You saved me," he whispered. "You saved me!"

"I couldn't just let you-"

Before Jim could say another word, Dalen grabbed his shirt and pulled him close. His lips were the softest lips Jim had ever kissed, the warmth of his skin like the sweet caress of sunlight itself.

When it finally passed, Jim cleared his throat, a flush setting his face on fire. "Well," he mumbled. "It's nice to be appreciated."

SILENCE HUNG IN THE AIR, broken only by the occasional distant scream. The bald man, a hulking figure with arms like tree trunks, lumbered across the square toward Desa. He made a fist, drawing his arm back as if he intended to pound her, but then – without warning – he fell to his knees and collapsed on the ground.

Desa blinked.

That was unexpected. It was as if the life had just drained right out of him, leaving him here like a discarded tool. A hush fell over the plaza. She could hear screams in the distance. The battle wasn't going well. She had to-

Footsteps.

Desa whirled around to find a gray man on the East Road. This one wore a military uniform and carried one of those new revolver rifles with a nasty bayonet. His pale face had been drained of colour, but it was his eyes that caught her attention. At first glance, they were no different from any of the others – black from corner to corner – but she saw lucidity behind those eyes. *Hanak Tuvar* had taken direct control of this one.

The man lifted his gun, pointed it at her.

With a thought, Desa triggered the Force-Sink that she had Infused into her shirt buttons. The rifle went off with a flash, and then a bullet hung in the air before her. She let it fall to the ground a second later.

Once again, the dead soldier raised his gun.

Desa thrust her fist out, releasing a hair-thin stream of electricity from her ring, a jagged bolt that struck the rifle and jumped from that to the man's body. He staggered.

Desa ran into the street, closing the distance in seconds, then jumped and kicked the fool in his chest. The man went stumbling backward, struggling to stay on his feet. She advanced on him, raising her knife and bringing it down in a swift, vertical arc.

The soldier lifted his rifle with both hands, parrying her strike by catching her blade on the barrel. He kicked Desa in the stomach, then spun for a hook-kick, his foot whirling around to clip her across the cheek.

Darkness filled her vision as the dizziness set in. She was barely aware of stumbling sideways and crashing into the front wall of a tanner's shop. Sweet Mercy, the pain! It took everything she had to turn and face her enemy.

The soldier hoisted up his rifle, taking aim.

Screaming in ragged desperation, Desa lashed out with a blast of kinetic energy that knocked the man off his feet. He landed on his backside, the rifle going off and firing a bullet into the sky.

Undaunted, he stood up and wiped his mouth with the back of his hand. "Did you know," he began in *Hanak Tuvar's* chorus voice. "That when I take direct control of a body, I can manipulate your world?"

"Really?" Desa asked, striding into the middle of the road.

"Just like Adele."

He stretched a hand toward her, and Desa heard a strange, crumbling sound. Like rocks being crushed with a hammer. Bricks flew out of the wall behind her.

Pulsing her Gravity-Sink, Desa jumped and let them fly past beneath her. She fell to the ground, then thrust out her hand with fingers splayed. Kinetic energy exploded from her ring, accelerating every single one of those bricks until they pelted the soldier like a hailstorm.

Desa charged in.

Recovering his wits, the soldier shook his head and then lifted his rifle for a shot that would take her right between the eyes.

Crouching down, Desa swung her knife up to strike the underside of his weapon, batting it aside before it went off with a roar. She stepped forward and drove her fist into his gut, winding him.

The man recoiled, drawing back his rifle, intending to use it like a spear. That wicked bayonet came at her.

Desa twisted out of the way.

She kicked the side of his leg, forcing him down onto his knees, and then snuck around behind him. Grabbing a handful of his hair, she tilted his head back to expose his neck. Her knife flashed across his throat, spilling black blood onto his clothing.

Planting her boot between his shoulder blades, Desa forced the gray man down onto his belly. "You were saying?" she murmured. "Something about unlimited power?"

"This resistance serves no purpose."

She looked up to find a gray woman in a billowy dress floating over the roof of the tanner's shop. This one was tall and leggy with long, dark hair that fluttered in the wind. Like the soldier, her eyes were black. "Destroy one vessel," she said with *Hanak Tuvar's* voice. "And I will simply claim another."

"Then come down here and fight."

"Foolish child," the woman said. "I grow weary of toying with you."

She snapped her fingers.

The air became smoke, forming a thick cloud around Desa. It burned her lungs as she sucked it down. Within seconds, she was bent double and choking, clamping a hand over her mouth. She couldn't stay here.

She triggered her Gravity-Sink and then jumped, shooting into the air at incredible speed. The cloud dissipated as she rose up to the rooftops. She gulped down fresh air with sharp, heaving gasps.

Her eyes had watered, but she could see her enemy on the other side of the road. The gray woman cast a hand down toward the cloud, projecting a streak of lightning that blasted the cobblestones.

She looked up, snarling at Desa.

Desa reached into her pocket, fished out the special coin and tossed it out the side. She triggered it for a surge of kinetic energy that sent her soaring back into the plaza. The gray woman followed.

Extending her hand, Desa recalled the coin and then killed her Sink. She landed on the slanted roofs on the north side of the square, shingles crunching under her boots. Fear blossomed within her. She had been unable to defeat one Adele. How was she supposed to stop dozens? Sooner or later, she would deplete her Infusions, and then she would be helpless. If only Mercy and Tommy could do their part before that happened. Carefully, she returned her knife to its sheath. It wouldn't do her much good

The gray woman floated into the middle of the plaza, hovering about thirty feet off the ground. She spread her arms wide, threw her head back and cackled.

"Why are you dragging this out?" Desa shouted. "Why not just turn me to stone? Or snap my neck with a wave of your hand?"

"Now there's an idea!"

Once again, the woman snapped her fingers.

Desa felt something that she could only describe as a tugging sensation. It was as if her molecules were trying to rearrange themselves into a new configuration. It lasted for only a moment and then faded; so far as she could tell, nothing had happened.

The woman screeched, snapping her fingers again.

Desa felt the tugging sensation, but once again, it faded without having any effect on her. Enraged, the other woman thrust her hand out with fingers curled as if she meant to choke the life out of Desa.

Desa felt those fingers as a gentle pressure on her neck, barely noticeable. Was this the best that *Hanak Tuvar* could do? She was beginning to wonder why she had ever feared this creature.

Grinning triumphantly, Desa shook her head. "You can't do it, can you?" she said. "You couldn't transform Marcus either. I remember that day when you first took control of Adele's body. You tried to turn him into a frog."

The gray woman screamed, thrashing about in her impotent fury. Cobblestones ripped themselves out of the ground, surging up to surround her. A hundred tiny meteors, ready to fly at her command.

"But why can't you use your power on me?" Desa mused. "You healed Azra, which means you *can* manipulate living tissue. So, what makes me different? Why don't you just squish me like a bug?"

The woman howled.

"The Ether!" Desa exclaimed. "That's it, isn't it? You can't use your powers on those who have communed with the Ether! Not without permission! They have to *invite* you like Bendarian and Adele!"

With a soul-piercing bellow, the woman tossed her head back and sent every one of those floating cobblestones hurtling toward Desa. Desa moved by instinct, raising her left hand and triggering the Force-Sink in her bracelet.

A dozen rocks jerked to a halt right in front of her. Others flew past on either side, some striking the roof. She let those she had captured fall to the ground with a dreadful cacophony.

The dead woman climbed higher into the air, a fireball igniting above her upturned palm. "I don't need the full extent of my powers to kill you!" she yelled. "Die in agony, Desa Kincaid!"

She hurled the fireball.

Desa turned, running along the rooftop, hopping over chunks of debris. The fireball struck the shingles behind her, blasting a hole in the building. And just when the roar died down, another one came her way.

Desa leaped, easily crossing over the narrow gap between this block of buildings and the next one over. She landed with a jolt of pain that raced up her leg but forced herself to keep running. *Have to end this.*

Twisting on the spot, Desa thrust her fist toward the floating woman. She unleashed a torrent of lightning from her ring, a silver lance that pounded her opponent. The woman raised her hands, gathering the electricity between her palms.

Just like in Ithanar.

Lifting the ball of flickering lightning above her head, the woman cackled. "You never do learn, do you?"

Desa let her arm drop and then thrust out her other hand, fingers splayed. Kinetic energy surged across the square, slamming into the gray woman and sending her into a tumble. She lost control of the electricity.

The crackling ball went speeding into the clouds.

Tumbling head over heels, the dead woman screamed as she tried to regain her balance. She managed to right herself at last, hovering over the square with teeth bared. "That was uncalled-"

Desa already had her left-hand pistol drawn, her arm extended to point the gun at her enemy. *CRACK!* A bullet erupted from her weapon, Heat-Sink activating, leaving a trail of crystalized frost in its wake.

It tore through the gray woman's chest, her body flash-freezing in an instant. For the briefest fraction of a second, she just hung there, covered in ice from head to toe. Then she dropped to the ground and shattered on impact.

"Actually," Desa said. "I've always considered myself to be rather observant."

Any thought she had of celebrating vanished when she glanced eastward. Another swarm of gray bodies flooded into the city. Dozens of them on each of the parallel streets. Her heart sank as despair crept over her. There was no way she could fight so many.

23

Tommy threw his will against *Hanak Tuvar*. Backed by his two companions, he should have made some headway, but the beast only laughed at him. He tried and tried to sever its connection to the horde of dead soldiers that surged into the city, but it was no use. Three people just weren't enough. Even with Desa, they would have had a hard time defeating this creature. It might have been impossible.

He sensed her in the plaza outside the bookkeeper's office, a tiny figure made of trillions of particles who leaped from a rooftop. He felt Desa's Gravity-Sink draining energy into the Ether, cushioning her fall so that she landed gently on the cobblestones.

And he felt the swarm of enemies coming to kill her.

So many.

Did they know that Tommy was here in this little apartment, that he and Nari and Kalia were waging a futile war against their master? No, he suspected they didn't know much of anything. But they would storm this building if *Hanak Tuvar* directed them to do so. And then it would be over.

Nari was beside him, her molecules dancing about. He

could sense the shape of her, the way she slumped with fatigue. Kalia wasn't much better. The woman was as rigid as a statue. They were failing.

Desa was out there alone. Miri and the watchmen were nearly overwhelmed. He had sensed Dalen's pain when a bullet pierced his love. Damn Victor! If they survived this, Tommy would have words with that man.

He had sensed the surge in the Ether when Jim used a crystal to save Dalen. Bless that man! Dalen would start fretting about his moment of passionate indiscretion, kissing Jim. Tommy knew his love all too well. He would have to reassure Dalen once again that he was not the jealous type. Assuming they got through this.

That was looking less and less likely.

He felt Desa's determination, her grim resolve to face down a hundred enemies and die in the attempt. It broke his heart. And Kalia...She was wilting under the weight of her despair. There had to be something they could do! He tried to come up with a new plan! Anything was better than hurling futile attack after futile attack at *Hanak Tuvar*.

But wait.

What was that?

Tommy stretched his mind eastward, over the demon and its distortion field, searching for whatever had distracted him. No...It couldn't be.

STANDING ALONE IN THE SQUARE, Desa lifted bloodstained daggers. Her lips parted as she drew in a breath. Her face was flushed, eyes wild. So, this was how she died. Well, at least she had fought to the bitter end. Whoever was waiting for her on the other side had to take that into account.

Didn't they?

Several dozen grays scrambled up the East Road, rushing

toward her like a flood, ready to sweep her away. She could see the hatred in their black eyes, the unrestrained fury. It was sickening. And yet, this would be the fate of the entire world. Who would stop the demon after she fell here?

They just kept coming. She was ready. Maybe she would take down three or four before they overwhelmed her. One last act of defiance.

The Ether stirred.

Desa lifted her eyes to the eastern sky and saw...something. Dots against the breaking clouds. She couldn't make out whatever it was, but she heard *Hanak Tuvar's* enraged screeching even at this distance, and she knew what she felt. Gravity-Sinks. There must have been a hundred of them.

Men and women in hooded cloaks came soaring over the city, each carrying an odd, crescent-shaped pistol. Desa recognized those weapons. The *Al a Nari!* The *Al a Nari* had come to save Ofalla!

The hooded figures pointed their weapons down into the street, firing jagged bolts of electricity, blasting the gray men who tried to charge the square. Smoldering corpses fell to the ground, smoke rising from their scorched clothing.

One of the newcomers wore the yellow robes of an Elite Guardian. Twirling a metal staff over her head, she landed gently in the road and then turned her back on Desa. She slammed the end of her weapon down, releasing a blast of kinetic energy that sent her enemies flying.

Raising a hand to shield her face, Desa stumbled backward as the wave hit her. She let her arm drop and blinked.

Andriel stood before her with her staff in hand, wavy, red hair fluttering in the wind. She cast a glance back over her shoulder and winked at Desa. "You just going to stand there?"

Grays charged her.

Andriel swung the end of her staff into one man's stomach and then – with a quick pivot – she smashed the other end into a gray woman's head. Both enemies fell, and more took their place.

Twirling the staff like a windmill blade. Andriel backed away. She slammed it down once again, another surge of kinetic energy throwing the horde backward. The front ranks landed in the road, and those behind rushed over them.

With deft fingers, Desa reloaded her right-hand pistol with ordinary ammunition. "Get down!" she shouted to Andriel.

The other woman listened, ducking.

Desa lifted her gun with both hands, choosing her targets with care. She fired all six rounds, striking down grays who tried to surround Andriel. Blood flew, and bodies dropped.

With a powerful jump, Andriel launched herself into the air, her Gravity-Sink letting her soar up to the rooftops. She hovered over the oncoming mob, then tossed a handful of coins down on them.

Gray men froze when she triggered her Heat-Sinks, falling and shattering on the ground. Further down the road, other *Al a Nari* were perched on rooftops, blasting the army of the dead from above.

Rojan landed in the plaza, dusting himself off and striding toward Desa with a winning smile. "How did I know I would find you here?"

"What are *you* doing here?" she demanded.

He answered that with a shrug, directing a furtive glance toward the battle. "We came north to end the war," he explained. "We thought that perhaps taking your capital would convince your politicians to end this pointless aggression. What a shock it was when we arrived and discovered that New Beloran had fallen."

"It's-"

"*Hanak Tuvar,*" he said. "Yes, we saw the beast. I take it you are responsible for its injuries."

"I had help," she growled. "How many of you are there? Can we make a stand here?"

Rojan stepped up to stand beside her, lifting his crescent-pistol in both hands. He faced his enemy with cold focus, ready for anything. "There are over a hundred of us," he said. "But I fear it will be a desperate fight."

Desa let her head hang, sweat drenching her dark hair. "Mercy has a plan," she said. "To stop them all at once."

"Mercy?"

"I found her," Desa said, drawing her knives again, readying herself for the next wave of enemies. She's here."

"Then we may have a chance."

A dozen grays came charging into the square. The one in front, a dark-skinned fellow with his hair in a short tail and his shirt unbuttoned, came right for her, ready to rip her throat out when he got his hands on her. "Can you handle him?" Desa asked.

"I can."

Pulsing her Gravity-Sink, Desa jumped and flipped over the man's head. She landed behind him, ready for her next opponent. A pale, bare-chested man came for her, swiping at her face like a cat trying to swat her.

Desa brought one knife up to slash the underside of his wrist, causing his arm to recoil. She kicked him in the stomach, sending the big oaf lurching backward into the trio of grays behind him.

Motion on her left.

Rounding on this new adversary, Desa tossed her left-hand dagger up and thrust her hand out. A wave of kinetic energy sent a plump woman flying backward until she hit the front wall of a cobbler's shop.

Desa caught the knife as it fell, then spun and immediately slashed the throat of a man with a goatee. Black blood fountained from the wound as he landed face-down on the pavement.

An old, leather-skinned woman attacked, brandishing a rolling pin of all things. With a furious growl, she lunged for Desa.

Desa extended her left hand, pulsing the Gravity-Source in her dagger, pulling her enemy close. The old woman stumbled, nearly losing her balance. Good enough. Desa rammed both knives into the crone's chest.

The body collapsed as she pulled her blades free.

She turned to her right, where she found herself confronted by the bare-chested man once again. He curled his fingers into a meaty fist and tried to bring it down on Desa's head.

Leaning to her left, Desa barely evaded the hit. She sliced his belly with the right-hand dagger, pulsing the Electric-Source and sending blue sparks flashing over his flesh. He dropped, and she searched for her next target.

She was surprised to find that there weren't any. Every enemy within a hundred feet of her had been put down. Some had fallen to blasts of electricity from Rojan's gun. Exhausted, Desa took a moment to catch her breath.

Further down the street, the *Al a Nari* were engaging the dead army, holding back the tide. Andriel stood in the road, twirling her staff and facing down three of the beasts. She dispatched them easily, and Desa felt a swell of pride. Whatever problems her homeland may possess, nothing rivaled Aladri training.

She turned, rushing back into the square, gasping and bending double in front of Rojan. Forcing herself to stand up straight, she met his eyes. "Mercy needs more Field Binders," she said. "You and I should join her."

Rojan's eyebrows climbed up. "I don't know what we can do there that we can't do here," he muttered. "But all right."

Desa led him to the bookkeeper's shop where Kalia and the

others conducted their attack. She tried the door, but it was blocked. Her friends had been wise enough to barricade the entrance. Perhaps the window? She could see into the shop; there were no obvious obstructions. But no. Tommy was too smart for that.

"Come on," Desa said.

She focused and triggered her Gravity-Sink. A quick jump sent her flying to the building's upper levels. There were windows that looked in on what seemed to be an apartment, but it was too dark to say for certain.

She halted her upward momentum by killing her Gravity-Sink for only a fraction of a second. That done, she hovered about fifteen feet off the ground. A distant scream sent shivers down her spine.

Rojan joined her, floating effortlessly at her side. Desa had to admit that she was impressed. Precision flight was no easy feat. You had to learn to control your velocity, when to trigger and kill your Infusions and for how long.

Thrusting her hand out, Desa triggered the Force-Source in her ring. The window collapsed – not just the glass but the wooden frame as well – and debris flew into the bedroom.

Desa grabbed the sill and pulled herself through the opening, killing her Sink once she was inside. She stood up, glass crunching under her boots, and scanned her surroundings. A neatly-made bed with red sheets was propped against the wall. A mirror with a brass frame reflected the sunlight.

This was probably the bookkeeper's apartment.

She paced across the room and opened the door to the parlour. There, she found Kalia, Tommy and Mercy sitting crosslegged on the hardwood floor. Rojan followed a moment later.

He stopped dead beside Desa, his brows drawn together as he studied the trio. "This is Mercy?" he asked. "She looks so...ordinary."

Crossing her arms with a sigh, Desa shook her head. "She's human now," she explained. "It's a long story."

Mercy severed contact with the Ether and then cracked an eye, smiling when she saw who had come to help her. "Ah, Rojan," she said. "I've wanted to meet you for some time now. I would make a proper introduction, but I'm afraid we must make haste. Please make yourself one with the Field."

"The Field?" Rojan stammered.

Desa knelt on the floor, folding her hands in her lap and closing her eyes. "The Ether," she clarified. "Hurry."

The Ether came the moment she reached for it, the world transforming into a sea of molecules that flitted about like fireflies on a summer night. Her friends were all glowing. Except Rojan. He took a seat on the floor, concentrating, but nothing happened.

Desa's heart went out to him. He had never come into contact with one of those enormous crystals. He had never felt the steady thrum of pulses that guided him to the Ether, that opened his mind.

It had been much the same for Desa before her first trip to the desert. On a bad day, it might have taken her several minutes to find the Ether. She used to lose herself in the forms while training with the Elite Guardians, letting her mind drift.

Unfortunately, they didn't have a few minutes. This city was crawling with grays. Every second they wasted cost lives. She needed Rojan to focus, but pressuring him would only make the task more difficult. What to do?

Pulses began to emanate from Mercy, a steady rhythm that flowed over Rojan like waves crashing on a sandy beach. He felt them instantly, flinching as if someone had splashed him with cold water. It wasn't long before he too was glowing, wrapped in the Ether's embrace.

Now, Mercy said. *Together...*

. . .

DALEN COULDN'T RESIST the urge to prod his chest with two fingers. The bullet hole was gone, and he felt fine. Better than fine. He felt as if he had just woken up from a good night's sleep. Even knowing about the crystals' strange powers, he was still amazed by that.

Jim stood up, clearing his throat, and then turned his back. He seemed to be staring off toward the wall that surrounded the barracks. "Are you all right?"

"Fine," Dalen mumbled.

"Good. Because we've got trouble on the way."

Scrambling to his feet – and bracing himself for a surge of pain that didn't come – Dalen examined his surroundings. Another troop of grays was coming over the wall. He counted six.

Zoe backed up until she stood beside him, glancing this way and that like a rabbit searching for a way to escape a predator. Her face was even paler than usual, and that was saying something. "What do we do?"

"We fight!" Victor declared.

Jim hesitantly took an arrow from his quiver and nocked it. "I'm not sure I want you anywhere near a firearm," he muttered. "I don't have any more crystals."

"I think there are some in the barrack," Dalen mumbled. He grimaced as soon as the words were out of his mouth. Why had he said that? What good were the crystals that Miri hid under her bed? It wasn't as if he could get at them in a pinch.

The gray goons landed just inside the wall, each bending his or her knees to cushion the impact of a ten-foot drop. One by one, they straightened and then began a slow shamble toward Dalen and his friends. It was as if they knew they had cornered helpless prey.

Jim sent an arrow streaking toward them.

It scraped a gray man's shoulder as it zipped past and then struck the wall behind him, falling uselessly to the ground. The fellow didn't even seem to notice that he had been wounded. He just kept coming.

"Inside!" Dalen yelled.

Zoe and Jim bolted for the nearest barrack. Victor lingered a moment, reloading his pistol with fresh ammunition and slapping the cylinder into place. He lifted the weapon, taking aim, and narrowed his eyes.

CRACK!

His first shot struck a gray woman, leaving a hole in her forehead. She toppled over, landing in the grass. And then the others started running.

Dalen took Victor by the arm and dragged him to the nearest building. He kicked the door open, pulling the other man inside, ignoring the string of muttered curses and the glare he received for his trouble.

Once they were clear, Jim leaped into motion, slamming the door shut and locking the deadbolt. That would do for now. Even the strongest foe wouldn't be able to force his way inside.

The small foyer was lit only by two narrow windows on either side of the entrance. Neither one was large enough for a person to squeeze through. Which meant they should be safe within these stone walls.

His confidence faltered when something pounded on the door. By the Eyes of Vengeance! Did those monsters have a battering ram?

Dalen gasped, stumbling backward to the hallway that led to the sleeping section. He braced one hand on the wall.

Another blow came and then another, each one rattling the wood. It held. Mercy be praised, it held. His heart rate slowed, his sense of panic fading away. If they could just hang on long enough for Desa to do whatever she had to do. Dalen was beginning to feel a smidgen of optimism. Just a smidgen.

He should have known better.

The sound of glass shattering told him that he had miscalculated. The captain's office was right next to the foyer, and it had a big, beautiful window for plenty of warm, healthy sunlight.

The door on his left flew open, and two gray men with large, thick arms came storming in. Zoe screamed, backing away from them until she was pressed against the opposite wall.

Victor moved to defend her.

Showing no fear, he strode toward his enemies with his pistol gripped in one hand. He fired two shots that punched through the nearest man's chest, but the big fellow didn't even notice.

The gray man moved across the room with alarming speed, grabbing Victor's wrist and twisting until the gun fell out of his hand. With a casual shove, he flung Victor into the front door, cracking the wood.

Zoe screamed again.

Standing inside the hallway, Jim nocked an arrow and drew back the bowstring. He loosed, and the shaft went straight through the gray man's head, fletchings poking out from the side of his skull.

One down.

The second gray ignored Jim entirely. Zoe's shrieks had enraged him. It was as if he could think of nothing else until he quieted that awful noise. He lumbered up to Zoe, drawing back his fist.

Dalen tackled him from behind, wrapping his arms around the other man's neck. The big brute writhed like a bucking horse, trying to throw Dalen off. He held on. Sweet Mercy, he held on!

For ten seconds.

A sudden undulation sent Dalen flying sideways until his shoulder hit the front wall of the foyer. He fell to the floor, landing next to Victor, pain surging through his body. He knew that he should get up, that he should keep fighting, but his muscles resisted.

Jim attacked the gray man with his belt knife.

Zoe kept howling. The poor girl was huddled against the wall, terrified. She could run, use the opportunity to slip away, but her brain was addled by fear. Dalen could see it in her. This child was no warrior. She didn't have Desa's battle-hardened instincts. She was just a scared kid in over her head.

The gray man tossed Jim to the floor as easily as he had Dalen, and then he rounded on Zoe. A fist to the belly made her fold up and wheeze, but the gray man wasn't finished with her.

He spun Zoe around, pulling her hard against his body. He seized her head with both hands and then – with a quick, wrenching motion – he snapped her neck.

Her body hit the floor with a *thump*.

Suddenly, there were no more screams.

"No!" Victor moaned. He forced himself to rise, clamping a hand onto his wounded arm. Tears leaked from his eyes. With shaky steps, he shuffled toward the gray man, then lost his balance and fell to his knees.

It's over, Dalen thought. *This thing is going to kill us.*

TOGETHER WITH HER FRIENDS, Desa directed her will toward *Hanak Tuvar*. Her mind swept over the city, over townhouses and cobblestone streets with frightened people, over plazas filled to bursting with gray monsters. She felt the others with her, Kalia and Tommy, Mercy and Rojan.

Their thoughts drifted over the East Road and the field beyond the city's edge. And there, in a pocket of pure, undiluted *wrongness*, she found the squid demon nursing its wounds. It sensed her immediately, turning its hideous face toward her. That gaping mouth let out a scream.

The beast was angry, enraged by this sudden twist of fate, by the notion that these lowly humans could resist. When it recovered, it would lash out again, smash their city and punish their arrogance.

Desa wouldn't allow it.

Under Mercy's direction, she searched for the tendrils of wrongness that connected *Hanak Tuvar* to its monochrome minions. She found them as hair-thin cracks, gaps where the Ether should be. So small they were almost imperceptible, and yet when she let her mind drift into them, they were as vast as the space between universes.

Fill them, Mercy said. *With the essence of the Field.*

Three minds working together had not been enough to overpower *Hanak Tuvar,* but perhaps five could do the trick. Desa took the lead, gathering the Ether, directing into those horrible cracks.

They resisted, pushing her out.

Hanak Tuvar squealed.

She tried again, throwing her will against the creature. She felt Rojan and Tommy and Mercy adding their strength to hers. And Kalia. Kalia most of all. The others were a light in the darkness, but with Kalia lending her strength, Desa felt as though she could lift mountains.

The Ether bent to her will, flowing into those cracks.

Hanak Tuvar pushed back, trying to widen the fissures. They strained. Like fault lines in an earthquake. Tremors reverberated through Desa, shaking her to her core. She held on, refusing to relent.

Elsewhere in the city, gray monsters were scrambling over walls, knocking down doors and terrorizing helpless people. *Al a Nari* Field Binders fought back against the darkness, saving those they could.

Desa felt something.

A cry of pain and alarm.

Her thoughts slid back to the barracks where Dalen, Jim and the others fought a hulking gray man. Four others surrounded the building, pounding on doors, smashing through windows. In moments, her friends would be overwhelmed.

And Zoe.

Desa sensed her lying on the floor, the life draining out her broken body. She hadn't known the young woman for very long, but this still felt like a knife through the chest. She had to do something! She couldn't just leave her friends to die!

No.

At first, she thought it was Mercy whispering in her thoughts, but that wasn't Mercy's voice. No, it was Kalia's. Sympathy and love as vast as an ocean washed over Desa. *The best way to help them,* Kalia said. *Is to stop all of those gray creatures. Now. Together.*

Once again, Desa rallied her strength and directed her will into the Ether. It surged at her command, flowing into the cracks, filling them. *Hanak Tuvar* fought back. Its will was like a boulder pressing down on her.

Desa reached out to her friend. Tommy added his will to hers. Like another set of hands holding up the boulder. And then Mercy. Rojan. And finally, Kalia. Together, they directed the Ether.

It sealed the cracks with a flash of light, severing *Hanak Tuvar's* connection to its minions. All over the city, gray corpses dropped to the ground, the life stripped away from them.

Sensing its defeat, *Hanak Tuvar* recoiled and retreated into the distortion field it had created. In that blessed moment, Desa sensed something she would never have expected. The demon was afraid of her.

Yes, it was afraid.

She had won the day. At great cost.

· · ·

THE GRAY MAN COLLAPSED, falling flat on his face, stretched out on the floor of the foyer. Dalen forced himself to rise, the pain in his shoulder spiking, sending shockwaves through his body. He wanted to rest, but there was no time for that.

Shambling over to the gray corpse, he kicked the body and rolled it onto its back. The darkness that seemed to fill its skull receded, leaving ordinary eyes. Colourless but ordinary. The thing was dead.

"The crystal!" Dalen panted.

He stumbled through the narrow hallway that led to the sleeping area, stepping into a long, rectangular room with beds in neat rows along each wall. Miri's was the third one on his left. Wasting no time, he ran to it and dropped to his knees.

He pawed underneath the bed, searching, searching. Finally, his hand fell upon a wooden box that he slid out with considerable effort. Opening it revealed exactly what he had been looking for.

Crystals.

Thin, glittering shards reflected the lamplight, each one casting a rainbow on the walls. He chose one that was about the size of his palm, carrying it in a delicate grip, staggering back to the foyer.

Victor was crouching by the door, holding Zoe in his arms, her head resting on his shoulder. He kept murmuring soft words of reassurance and gently stroking her hair. "Save her," he pleaded when he saw Dalen. "Save her."

Rushing over to the girl, Dalen took one of her hands in his. Her skin was still warm! That had to count for something, didn't it? He pressed the shard into Zoe's palm, closed her fingers around it and squeezed hard. The distinctive *crunch* told him that he had shattered the crystal.

But nothing happened.

No rainbow.

Zoe's fingers uncurled when he released her hand, fragments of crystal falling to the floor. She was perfectly still in Victor's arms, her dull eyes staring at the wall. Gone. Dalen wanted to weep. He had liked the girl.

"No," Jim murmured, shaking his head.

"Try again," Victor demanded.

"It's too late."

"Again!"

Taking one of the slivers off the floor, Dalen crushed it in his palm. The rainbow surrounded him, flowing up his arm, over his body and his face. He closed his eyes, tilting his head back, breathing deeply as his pain faded away.

His eyes snapped open, fixed upon Victor. "It's too late," he insisted. "She's gone, Victor. We need to...We need to find the others."

"I won't accept that!" Victor snarled, tears streaming over his cheeks. He sniffled and touched his nose to Zoe's forehead. "I won't! I won't!"

Dalen left him to mourn, taking Jim and stepping out into the yard. The other grays were scattered around the building, lying dead in the grass. He heard people moaning in the distance. The city had suffered a tragedy. He had to find Miri. She would know what to do. "Come on," Dalen muttered. "We're needed."

24

Evening sunlight streamed over the city, leaving the buildings of Ofalla as shadows against the glare. Zerena Dobrin stood upon a stone balcony, her hands braced on the balustrade as she watched her people.

In the plaza below, men loaded bodies into a wagon bound for a mass grave. They were burying the dead a few miles southwest of the city. Some of those corpses were gray. Others were just ordinary people who had fallen during the attack.

"These are the fruits of your labour," Zerena muttered. "You promised us help, and this is what you brought us."

Dressed in tan pants and a blue shirt under her leather coat, Desa stood in the shadows. Her bob of short, brown hair was an absolute mess, thin strands falling into her eyes. "If not for us," she began. "Your city would have been destroyed."

Zerena gripped the railing, stiffening as she peered down at the people below. "You will forgive me if I take little comfort in that," she whispered. "Such carnage...Now that you've fought your little battle, will you help us clean up the mess?"

Desa strode forward to stand beside the other woman, clasping her hands behind her back. "We can't stay," she said softly. "As much as I wish we could. We have to lead the demon away from here."

"How convenient."

Though it took some effort, Desa ignored that comment. Convenient? Hardly. She had nearly died a dozen times during the battle, to say nothing of what she had endured in the days leading up to it. The constant fear, the sense of impending doom nipping at her heels: it wore her down.

Sweet Mercy, she had lost one of her people in the fighting! Zoe's death would haunt her for a good, long while. She had barely known the girl, but she could already feel the grief weighing her down like a stone. Desa might have learned to stop blaming herself for everything, but that didn't mean she had stopped caring.

She wanted to stay, to help these people rebuild – she felt she owed it to them – but the urge to leave was an itch she couldn't scratch, growing more insistent with every passing second. The longer she stayed here, the greater the risk to the citizens of Ofalla. *Hanak Tuvar would* return. Her only hope was if its hatred for her was stronger than its desire to crush the city. If so, she might be able to coax it away and lure it into the desert.

"Rojan will be leaving a contingent of Field Binders here," she said. "They can help you rebuild and protect you against future attacks."

"I suppose that will have to be enough."

Desa nodded.

She hopped over the railing and used her Gravity-Sink for a gentle descent to the plaza, producing a gasp from Zerena. She landed in a crouch, then rose slowly and let out a sigh.

Kalia joined her as she started down a narrow street lined with gray townhouses. At first, they walked in silence, content to just enjoy each other's company. Desa caught a glimpse of a man in a nearby window, a tall fellow in his middle years who sneered at her and pulled the curtains shut. Maybe she was just imagining it, but she couldn't help but think the citizens of Ofalla agreed with their mayor. This was all Desa Kincaid's fault. It was pure foolishness, and she knew it. But people were often looking for a scapegoat.

"Are you all right?" Kalia asked.

Shutting her eyes tight, Desa shook her head. "No," she whispered. "I went to the desert. I found enlightenment. I'm supposed to be past this."

"But…"

Desa stopped dead, standing there with her mouth agape, the enormity of her grief bursting through her pitiful defenses. "But I look at these good people, and I can't help but think that I should have been able to do more."

Kalia was staring straight ahead, nodding slowly as she considered Desa's words. "Maybe there's no such thing as enlightenment," she said. "Maybe we can't overcome our deepest anxieties by spending a few weeks in the desert."

"Then the trip was a waste of time."

"I don't think so."

"No?"

Kalia took her hands, pulling Desa close for a kiss on the lips. "Darling," she said. "Overcoming our fears is a lifelong process. You *have* made progress. But you are still Desa Nin Leean."

"I suppose I am."

"And that's how I know we're going to get through this," Kalia murmured. "Because we have you."

WHEN NIGHT FELL, Dalen found himself pacing in the yard outside the barracks. He had never understood how Miri and Tommy could throw themselves into physical danger so easily.

His battleground was the written word. But after today, he thought he might have a vague idea.

When you were scrambling to stay alive, you didn't have time to fret about all those pesky emotions. It was all just instinct. But once the heat of battle faded, all the things you had been ignoring came roaring back.

He hadn't known Zoe all that well, but he remembered when she first arrived on Hebar's Hill. Those first few weeks had been rough. She would barely speak. But after a little while, she started to come out of her shell. She could be downright jovial at times. It wasn't fair! She had only just gotten her life back, and then it was snatched away from her in the blink of an eye.

Grief warred with confusion in his head. He had kissed Jim, but now he had to decide what he wanted to do about that.

The broken, wooden gate swung inward, and Tommy came trudging up the shallow hill with his head down. His duster was ripped, and his wide-brimmed hat looked as if it had seen better days. Miri was right behind him, walking with a slight limp. She must have taken a few bruises during the fighting.

"I have something to tell you," Dalen began. "Something-"

Tommy looked up, bleary-eyed and exhausted. Without warning, a playful grin spread across the other man's face. "You kissed Jim again."

Dalen froze.

Miri snorted and limped past him, lightly patting him on the shoulder. "About time," she muttered.

A sudden blush set Dalen's face on fire. He just stood there, dumbfounded, unsure of what to say. "You...You know?" he managed at last.

Tommy reached up to remove his hat, exhaling slowly through his nose. "I was communing with the Ether at the time," he explained. "It was kind of hard to miss. Like a great, big bonfire."

Dalen licked his lips, working up the courage to ask the question that he had been dreading. "So," he began, turning to Miri. "How does this affect us?"

She stood in the light that spilled out from the barrack's windows, scrutinizing him as if he had just asked why water was wet. "Do you still love me and Lommy?"

"Of course."

"Then I don't see why it should affect us at all," she said. "Go tell Jim how you feel."

"Just like that?"

"Just like that."

Tommy slapped him on the back and then followed Miri to the barrack. "Have fun."

"Wait, wait!" Dalen stammered. "Is Jim part of our relationship now? Are we a quartet?"

Tommy shrugged as he pushed open the door. "Don't think I really feel that way about him," he said. "No, I think you have Jim all to yourself."

Dalen wandered off into the night. He was bone-tired, but there was no way that he could sleep. Not with all these thoughts racing through his head. Damn it all! The end of the world was no time to be starting a new relationship. And he had no idea if Jim would want to be with a man who had not one but *two* other lovers. One thing was damn sure. There was no way that Dalen was giving up Tommy and Miri.

He followed the wall around the compound. Not for any specific reason. He just needed to walk, and that was as good a path as any. Sometimes Dalen wished that he had learned the art of Field Binding. A Light-Source would be quite useful on a moonless night. Each of the barracks had a lamp next to its front door, but their range was limited. What he wouldn't give for one of Desa's glowing rings.

It wasn't too late – Tommy had indicated more than once that he would be willing to share what he had learned – but all that time spent sitting still, meditating for hours on end? How could anyone stand it?

Dalen's mother had taken him to the Academy when he was just nine years old. The instructors there had tried to teach him the basic lessons about clearing his mind and putting himself in a relaxed state. They said it was the only way to sense the Ether. Sadly, it didn't work out for him.

Dalen's mind was always full of thoughts, always chugging along with the momentum of a freight train. He needed that noise, that constant buzz of questions and ideas. Meditation was just too damn *boring*.

The sound of whimpering drew him out of his reverie.

He found Victor crouching in the corner where the south wall met the west wall. The man had his face in his hands, his body shaking as sobs racked him.

"Victor?" Dalen mumbled.

The other man looked up. It was too dark to see Victor's expression, but Dalen could feel the hostility radiating from him. "Go away."

"I cared about her too," Dalen said. "She was-"

"I don't want to talk."

Dalen opened his mouth to protest, but what could he say? Sometimes, the best thing you could do was leave a man alone to sort out his own problems. He turned away, stalking off through the grass.

"Hey!" Victor called out behind him.

Dalen paused.

"It's not fair, you know."

Shoving his hands into his pockets, Dalen shut his eyes turned back to the other man. "No, it isn't," he agreed. "It's never fair when someone so young dies."

Victor stormed out of the shadows, the light of the distant lamps falling on his face. He looked haggard, his cheeks flushed, his eyes puffy and red. "That's not what I mean," he snapped. "You freaks go about flaunting your sins in front of the whole world. But *Zoe* is the one who dies?"

"You don't mean that."

Stepping forward with teeth bared, Victor growled like a chained dog. "Oh, don't I?" he spat. "Maybe you don't know me that well."

"Look, just try to get some sleep."

"I don't want sleep!" Victor bellowed. He started laughing... or crying. Dalen couldn't tell which. Maybe it was both at the same time. "They carted her off. Wrapped her in a sack and just *threw* her away with all the others!"

"Victor, they had to take the bodies."

It was the wrong thing to say, and Dalen knew it as soon as the words were out of his mouth. The other man grabbed his shirt with both hands and shoved him backward. Dalen landed on his backside, damp grass squishing beneath him.

He should have been terrified, but his fear evaporated when a shadowy figure fell out of the sky and landed atop the wall. "That's enough!" Desa's voice cracked like a whip. "Leave him alone!"

Victor hesitated.

He twisted around, staring at her, and then the fight just drained out of him. Deflated, he shuffled away, muttering under his breath.

Desa hopped down from the wall, landing with a grunt, and then strode out of the shadows. At first glance, she didn't seem all that menacing – just an ordinary woman in well-worn clothing – but Dalen saw a glint in her eye when she looked at Victor.

She came back to herself, shaking her head to dispel whatever thoughts had been troubling her, and then offered Dalen her hand. "Are you all right?"

He let Desa pull him to his feet.

Dusting himself off, Dalen looked around for the crowd of

gawkers that always seemed to gather in moments like this. Of course, there was no one, but he wouldn't have been surprised if a hundred people started laughing at him. His luck was just that rotten. "I'll be fine," he said. "He's just...He's angry, and he doesn't know what to do with all that rage."

"Well, there's no reason he should direct it at you."

"Agreed."

"Get some rest," Desa said. "I'll sort this out."

"Why you?"

Desa was ten steps away when she froze and answered him with a shrug. "Who else is going to do it?"

THE RING on Desa's finger was far brighter than any oil lamp, casting a soft, white glow over the grass. She found Victor standing with his back turned, staring at the wall. He sensed her coming by the light reflecting off the stone. "What do you want?"

Desa tossed a wad of bills at him.

The man crouched down, retrieving them, and then stiffened when he saw what she had given him. "There must be fifty dollars here." He spun around to face her. "Why?"

Sauntering toward him with lips pursed, Desa held his gaze for a very long time. "To help you start a new life," she said at last. "You're going to take that and be gone by the time I wake up tomorrow."

"Look, I'm sorry for what I said to-"

"Oh no," Desa cut in. "It goes far beyond a little misplaced anger, and we both know it. I saw Jim on my way back from the mayor's house. He told me about how you almost got Dalen killed."

Victor shuddered, turning his face away from her. He backed up and grunted when he hit the wall. "I'm sorry," he mumbled. "I was only trying to help."

"I know you, Victor."

"Is that a fact?"

Rolling her eyes, Desa heaved out a breath. "By the Eyes of Vengeance," she said. "I *was* you. About a year ago, I met an angry young man who had been mistreated by the people of his village. He betrayed me to my most bitter enemy. And I shot him for it."

"Sounds like he had it coming."

Desa answered that with bitter laughter, shaking her head as she strode toward him. "Be glad that I am no longer that person," she said. "Because if she were here, she might just shoot *you.*"

Victor went pale.

"I promised myself," Desa went on, "that I would never make that mistake again. That if I found a young person who was going down the wrong path, I would offer them guidance instead of condemnation. I wish I could do that for you, Victor. But the stakes are just too high.

"The things you believe make you a threat to my friends. And the way you behave makes you an even bigger threat to my friends. I can't fight *Hanak Tuvar* if I have to worry about you starting a brawl with Tommy or shooting someone because you're too stupid to look before you pull the trigger. So, I do the only thing I can. Take the money and leave, Victor. Try to find a little spec of happiness."

She turned to go, stomping through the grass toward the barracks, sighing softly. Hopefully, Victor would avoid getting into any more trouble. Maybe things would turn out differently for him than they had for so many others.

"I don't really believe it!" he called out to her.

She spun around.

Victor was leaning against the wall, his eyes downcast as he drew in a rasping breath. "What I said to Dalen," he clarified. "I don't really believe it. That's not me. That's not who I am."

"Perhaps," Desa replied. "But that didn't stop you from using it as a bludgeon when you needed a target for your anger. Casual bigotry or outright hatred: does it make a difference when the result is the same? Take your money, Victor. Find some happiness. Maybe if we survive this, we'll meet again."

"The plan is simple," Rojan said.

He paced a line in front of the narrow, rectangular windows in the sidewall of the barrack, shaking a finger at his audience. "It's not enough to simply get to the desert," he said. "We need to provoke *Hanak Tuvar* into following us."

Desa agreed.

She had discussed this with him before turning in last night. Things would be much easier with Rojan and his forces backing her up. Which only meant that the plan had gone from impossible to not quite impossible, but she would take any advantage she could get.

Tommy sat on the edge of his mattress frowning at the other man. "So, how exactly do we do that?"

The barrack was filled with *Al a Nari* Field Binders, all wrapped in gray cloaks. Andriel had come as well. The former Guardian seemed to have benefitted from her time with Rojan and his people. At the very least, she was less hostile.

Miri had her shoulder pressed against the wall, her long, brown coat showing signs of wear and tear. "It's a good question," she said. "You got any ideas about how we're supposed to herd that monster toward one of the most desolate regions on this continent?"

Kalia stood in the aisle between the beds, shaking her head in exasperation. "Desolate," she muttered. "You know, my people have been living there for centuries, and we get along just fine, thank you very much."

"Me," Desa said.

Tommy twisted around to stare at her. "What?"

With a great deal of reluctance, Desa marched down the aisle and joined Rojan on his improvised stage. "Me," she said again, turning to face the lot of them. Sweet Mercy, she hated speaking in front of a crowd. "I'm the bait."

"You want to use yourself as bait," Miri grumbled.

"We know that it will chase me," Desa insisted. "We know that when it sees me, it flies into a rage. So, let's use that."

Rojan stepped up beside her, laying a hand on her shoulder. His stern expression reminded everyone that this mission was going forward whether they liked it or not. "It won't be just Desa," he assured the others. "Some of us will be going with her."

Tommy stood up, opening his mouth to say something. He thought better of it and forcefully shook his head. "There is one small flaw with this plan," he began. "It'll take the better part of two weeks to reach the desert. How do we make sure the monster doesn't lose interest and go somewhere else?"

"We'll have to keep provoking it," Desa said.

"And the pace?" Tommy asked. "We don't know how much ground that thing can cover in a day. We may have to run our horses to exhaustion. How do you expect to deal with that?"

"*Hanak Tuvar* seems to be limited by its ability to spread the strange distortion field it lives in," Rojan said. "We won't be following the route you took last year, the slight northward curve of the river. Instead, we will go directly south-west, cross the plains and then Ander's Woods. That should shave a few days off the journey, but it will be a long, difficult ride."

STEPPING FORWARD, Desa let out a breath. Her head sank as she contemplated the enormity of what she was proposing. "We may be able to slow it down," she said. "We've seen that our crystals can make its distortion field recede. If it has to waste energy covering the same area twice, we'll gain some ground."

Rojan was at her side, stroking his chin with the tips of his fingers. "We're going to need a lot of crystals," he cautioned. "Which is why our Field Binders will be producing more as they ride."

Tommy barked a laugh. "Forgive me," he said. "But communing with the Ether in the saddle? That's no easy task."

"We don't have good options, Tommy," Desa replied. "It's this or let the demon rampage across the land. One last adventure. What do you say?"

"I'm in."

"Excellent!" Rojan exclaimed. "I want all of our Field Binders to spend the day making crystals and Infusions. We leave tomorrow morning."

25

The redness was like a wall that stood a hundred feet high, a curved wall that flowed in an almost wave-like pattern, expanding here, contracting there. Blue sky above, green grass below, and in front of her? Nothing but red.

Desa stood on the field in tan pants and her long, brown duster, a wide-brimmed hat sitting squarely on her head. Midnight was next to her, saddled and bridled and ready to run at a moment's notice.

They were a mile out from the city, far enough that there was little chance of any innocent bystander getting hurt. Unless, of course, *Hanak Tuvar* decided to ignore her and go for a more tempting target. But that would be a break in its pattern of behaviour.

Rojan stepped up to her, leading his brown gelding by the bridle. The animal nickered, unwilling to get too close to that red haze. Desa couldn't blame him. Only an idiot would walk willingly into *that.*

So, what did that make her?

Pressing his lips together, Rojan examined the distortion for a moment. "You're sure about this," he said, shooting her a sidelong glance. "We could try something else. I think we might have luck just breaking a crystal.

Craning her neck, Desa took in the sight of the crimson wall. "We have to get its attention," she said, stepping closer. "And I'm the one it hates."

"You'll be on your own."

"I'm used to it." She heaved out a breath, then checked her pockets once again. She had five crystals, exactly the same amount as the last time she had checked. But she was nervous. Everything had to go just right, or...Well, that didn't bear thinking about. "You shouldn't be here. I want you at least a mile away before we start."

"The others have begun their journey westward," he said. "Are you certain that you can catch up? You'll be pushing your horse hard."

"Midnight isn't like other horses."

Rojan nodded. "Very well." He turned his gelding around and led it away from the redness. The animal was more than happy to go. "I wish you luck, Desa Nin Leean. I will see you when you rendezvous with the group."

She waited a good, long while, giving Rojan time to get away. Most horses couldn't run like Midnight. Yet another reason why Desa should be the one to do this. When she was sure that he was gone, she retrieved a crystal from her pocket.

It was time to begin.

Desa poked the tip of her finger into the redness. It felt like touching a teapot that was seconds away from boiling. When she pulled her hand away, her finger was gray.

A monstrous creature appeared before her, just inside the distortion field. It rose up on slimy tentacles and let out a soul-splitting cry.

Desa shattered the crystal.

The rainbow engulfed her, taking the pain from her hand, and then expanded into the distortion field, nearly capturing

Hanak Tuvar. The demon vanished just before it was consumed by the Ether's power.

Desa lifted her hand and wiggled her fingers, pleased to find that the colour had returned to her skin. She rather liked her olive complexion. "Almost caught the damn thing." She climbed into Midnight's saddle, spun the horse around and set him running westward.

It wasn't long before she heard another menacing screech, distant but no less threatening. A quick glance revealed the massive body of *Hanak Tuvar* standing three-stories high, about a mile into the distortion field. The creature started slinking toward her, moving like a predator.

Desa bent low in the saddle.

Baring her teeth with a hiss, she whispered in Midnight's ear. "Keep running. That bastard isn't going to catch us."

Her horse galloped over lush, green fields where the land was almost perfectly flat. The sky was clear, the air fresh with the scents of spring. It was a beautiful morning if you ignored what was happening behind her.

Half a dozen villages were clustered around Ofalla in a haphazard semicircle, concentrated mostly on the southern and western sides of the city. She turned Midnight southward, following a course that would take her between two of them, guided by one of her Force-Sources. Tommy had placed it in the grass several hours ago when he and the others had passed through this area.

They had planned this out ahead of time. Members of the Watch had visited the neighbouring towns last night, urging the citizens to evacuate. Mercy send those people were wise enough to take the suggestion. If not, *Hanak Tuvar* might turn aside and gobble them up.

The demon was still coming. Its distortion field crept ahead of it, sweeping over the grass, killing everything it touched. It managed to keep pace with Midnight, but it wasn't gaining ground on him.

Squeezing her eyes shut, Desa sucked in ragged breath after ragged breath. Why was her heart racing? Midnight was the one doing all the work. "You can do this," she murmured. "Keep going."

Behind her, the beast screamed in impotent fury.

Twisting to look over her shoulder, Desa flashed a cheeky grin. "What's the matter?" she called out. "You getting tired already?"

Midnight's hooves pounded the earth. He was like the wind itself, refusing to slow down, refusing to let *Hanak Tuvar* gain even an inch on him. The poor boy couldn't keep that up forever.

"It's time," Desa muttered.

She urged Midnight slightly to the right, guiding him around the hidden Force-Source. It sat there in the grass: a small rock about the size of her baby finger, tied to a shard of crystal almost three times as large.

Hanak Tuvar continued its deadly pursuit.

A line of redness cut through the grasslands, a narrow corridor just large enough to encompass the squid demon. The creature wasn't bothering to expand its territory in any other way. It had focused all of its energy on one task: catching Desa.

"Slow down," she urged Midnight. "Let it think you're tired."

Her horse was eager to obey, losing speed. She could almost feel *Hanak Tuvar's* anticipation. She ventured a glance and saw a horrifying vision. The crimson corridor stretched toward her, the massive demon moving within it. Thick tentacles sliding over the ground as it closed in on her. It passed over the rock that Tommy had left behind.

Desa triggered the Force-Source.

The crystal shattered, and a rainbow surged up over *Hanak*

Tuvar, causing the beast to scream and scuttle away. It vanished in an instant. Since the corridor was so narrow, the rainbow was able to spread further along it, healing the distortion field for almost half a mile. When it faded, full colour had returned to the world. The grass on that narrow strip of land had been reduced to ash, but the redness was gone.

Somewhere in the distance, *Hanak Tuvar* screeched. Rather than gaining on Desa, it had lost ground. And possibly suffered a few wounds in the process. Now, it would have to expend even more energy to catch up, and she could already tell that it was tired.

Sadly, Midnight wasn't doing much better.

"Come on," she said, urging him forward at a quick trot. "We've got to get out of here before it comes after us again."

THE SUN LEFT a fringe of silver on every cloud that dotted the blue sky. It was just past noon on their second day of travel. The horses were grazing in the field, and Desa's companions? They were eating as well.

Rojan had brought twenty Field Binders with them, leaving the rest in Ofalla with orders to spread out to the neighbouring communities and offer whatever assistance they could. Most of his people wore their simple, gray cloaks, though they usually kept the hoods down. Desa recognized a few from her time in Ithanar. Jensia, Tara, Novalo. Men and women fought together in Rojan's army.

Hanak Tuvar had chased them well into the evening. They had been forced to keep going after sunset, using glowing rings, coins and pendants for illumination. Rojan hadn't called a halt until midnight, and then, it was a fitful sleep.

Two people were put on watch at all times. Their instructions were simple: if they saw redness approaching from the east, rouse the others. Of course, that was a lot harder to do at night, when a subtle change in colour might be unnoticeable; so, they had placed Infused pebbles a few miles away from the camp. Each one projected a beam of light into the sky. If those beams turned red, they would know that *Hanak Tuvar* was nearby.

Desa had not been assigned to watch duty. Everyone seemed to think that since she had been the one to provoke the demon, she deserved a little rest. She appreciated the thought, but sleep had been hard to find. The enemy might sneak up on them at any time. She had to be ready to pack up her gear and leave at a moment's notice. It was hard to relax under those circumstances.

Mercy came toward her in an orange riding dress with short sleeves, a garment that she had purchased in Ofalla. The former goddess carried a bag with a strap over one shoulder. "Here," she said, retrieving an apple and tossing it to Desa. "Eat something."-

Desa caught it, held it up and squinted. "You know, you're not my mother, right?" she muttered. "You don't have to feed me."

"You will need your strength when we arrive at the pyramid. I will need you to help me return the demon to its prison."

Desa stood up, pressing her lips together as she studied the other woman. "You're sure that's the way to go," she said, eyebrows rising. "Isn't there some way that we could destroy it?"

Mercy winced, shaking her head. "Don't you think we've tried?" she snapped. "Dri and I threw everything we had at it. Nothing worked."

"Have you tried using the crystals?"

Heaving out a sigh, Mercy spun around to stand beside Desa. For a moment, she just stared out on the endless expanse of grassland, saying nothing. "Yes, we tried that too," she muttered at last. "You saw what happens. It simply disappears."

Desa crossed her arms, nodding slowly as she considered

that. "What if there was some way we could trap it?" she asked. "It can't seem to manipulate anything outside of its distortion field. So, if we heal a large enough section-"

"It will simply recreate it," Mercy cut in. "Where do you think that distortion field comes from? *Hanak Tuvar* twists the fabric of reality. There was no field in place when it hatched from Adele. It created the distortion while constructing its own body molecule by molecule. It is *too powerful,* Desa. You cannot beat it. You can only contain it."

"All right," Desa said. "All right, you win."

"I hardly consider this a victory."

Castrian – a hefty man with dark, bronze skin – was gasping as he came running through their camp. "Trouble!" he said, pointing to the eastern horizon. "Look!"

Desa noticed a band of redness at the line where green fields met the blue sky. *Hanak Tuvar* had found them. "Time to go!" she barked.

Rojan was two steps ahead of her. "Everyone, gather your things!" he shouted, doing up the saddlebags on his brown gelding. "We're leaving! Now!"

THE SUN WAS SINKING at the end of their third day of travel, golden light streaming over tallgrass that swayed in the wind. It was cool, but not unpleasantly so. A welcome change after a day spent in the saddle.

Desa stomped through their camp, scrubbing at her eyes with the back of her hand. "Remember when I said this would be a good idea?" she growled. "Well, why did you ever listen to me?"

Tommy was down on one knee with his back turned, relacing one of his boots. Miri stood over him, smiling fondly. It warmed Desa's heart to see it. One look at Miri, and you could tell that she was in love with both of her young partners. And they with her. "Because you're forceful and insistent?" Miri said. "Yes, that must be it."

"I am *not* forceful and insistent."

"Darling," Miri grumbled. "Handle this one. I'm too tired."

Tommy stood up, grumbling as he stretched his fists above his head and arched his back. He spun around to face her. "No offense, Mrs. Kincaid," he said. "But you're pretty damn forceful."

"When have I ever been forceful?"

"The night we met," Tommy said, "You busted into the sheriff's office, beat up one of his deputies and demanded that I be set free."

"And then there was the time you threatened to kill me if I didn't tell you who I was and what I was planning," Miri added.

Desa's face was on fire. Sweet Mercy, had she really done that? It pained her to realize that yes, she had. A lot had changed in the last year. "All right," she said. "So, I can be forceful on occasion, but-"

"Oh!" Tommy cut in. "And then there was the time that she pestered a *goddess* until she got what she wanted!"

"All right!" Desa said. "You win. I-"

"Trouble!" someone shouted.

She twisted around and found a purple sky over an endless field of swaying tallgrass, a purple sky that was turning red. By the Eyes of Vengeance, that demon was relentless.

Rojan's Field Binders began packing up their things and readying the horses. Dalen paused with a bowl of stew in one hand, a spoon raised halfway to his mouth. "Again?" he moaned. "Will it ever stop?"

Striding toward her at a brisk pace, Rojan glared daggers at anyone who crossed his path. "We need to slow it down," he said. "Send flyers out. Hit it with a couple crystals."

"I'll go," Desa volunteered.

One glance from Rojan put paid to that idea. "No," he said.

"Sorry, but you're too important. Mercy says she will need you when we arrive at the pyramid. Donas, Temiel, fly out with a few crystals! Try to slow that thing down!"

The two men he had named triggered their Gravity-Sinks and launched themselves into the sky. Using the technique that Desa had developed during her time in Ithanr, they each tossed small objects out behind themselves. A rock for one, a coin for the other.

The blast of kinetic energy they unleashed sent them hurtling toward *Hanak Tuvar*. That patch of redness in the distance was growing larger. She almost thought she could hear the squid's inhuman cries.

"Come on!" Rojan said. "We have to get moving."

BY THE END of their fourth day of travel, Desa was beyond tired. Every night brought fitful sleep at best, outright insomnia at worst. The ever-present fear that the enemy might sneak up on them at any moment made it impossible for her to relax.

She was hungry. Zerena Dobrin had been kind enough to furnish their expedition with plenty of food, but those supplies were dwindling. But she suspected that it was the stress that made acid churn in her stomach. Keep moving. Never stop, never slow down. Or the demon would catch up.

She had taken watch duty for the second shift. She wasn't going to get much sleep anyway; so, she may as well put her time to good use. The sky was black and dotted with tiny stars as a wind whistled over the open plains.

In the distance, three pillars of light stabbed the night sky, each one about as thick as her index finger, but bright enough for her to see them from miles away. It had taken an hour to Infuse coins with enough light energy to last the night. She had made one herself. Maintaining contact with the Ether while Midnight plodded along beneath her was a challenge in and of itself. She couldn't move her body while she was creating an Infusion. And she was always tempted to let go so that she could adjust her posture or shift her weight. Only the instant she got back to work, the temptation returned. Still, she would have plenty of warning if *Hanak Tuvar* got too close.

Desa sat on a rock with her hands on her knees. She stared into the distance, thinking.

What would she do if they actually survived this, if Mercy returned *Hanak Tuvar* to its prison? Measures would have to be put in place to ensure that the demon never escaped again. She couldn't even imagine what those might be. Was there a way to heal the land it had blighted? If not, the country might endure food shortages.

Even now, a voice whispered in her thoughts, *you're still alone.*

Desa sat up straight, blinking. "You!" she hissed. "What do you want?"

I thought we should talk.

"I have nothing to say to you."

Then just listen. For I have much to say to you. This quest of yours is futile. Do you think that I am unaware of your plan? You hope to lure me to the desert so that you may use the crystal to return me to my prison.

A chill went down Desa's spine. Taking control of herself, she kept her voice even. Confidence. She had to project confidence. "If you know, why are you following us?"

Because your plan will fail. You lack the strength to complete it. Driala and Nari were enhanced, changed so that they could directly access the power that you call the Ether. Even working together, they were barely able to contain me. Now, Driala is gone. And Nari has lost her power. You cannot hope to succeed.

Desa stood up, pacing quickly to the edge of the camp. Something about this didn't feel right. Those pillars of light were still bright and pure. No redness. So, if this wasn't an attempt to distract her, then what was *Hanak Tuvar's* purpose? "If that's the case," she began cautiously. "Then what are you doing here? Did you just come to gloat?"

You amuse me.

"You'll forgive me if I don't take that as a compliment."

Humans flee from me, break before me like the pitiful creatures they are. A wasted form of life, unworthy of existence. But not you. You persist in your defiance even when you know your efforts are fruitless. And I must know why.

Desa shuffled through the grass with her head down. "I'm not so sure they *are* fruitless." She turned on her heel and went back in the opposite direction. "You didn't take Ofalla."

A minor delay.

"We'll see."

Something occurred to Desa, and she reached for the Ether before she realized what she was doing. The ground became a vast expanse of particles packed tightly into a rigid structure. The air became a sea of loose particles swirling around. Her friends, her horse, the equipment: nothing but collections of molecules.

She stretched out with her thoughts, searching, searching. Unaided, her range of perception wasn't much more than a mile. Perhaps she should wake the others? Was there time? She strained and strained, letting her mind slip over the land, looking for-

Emptiness.

An emptiness as profound as the void that surrounded her tiny planet. She had found *Hanak Tuvar's* distortion field. And worse yet, she had found it in the *wrong* place. It was further west of here, ahead of them. Which meant...

Desa let go of the Ether.

"Wake up!" she screamed, running to her friends. She nudged Maladon with her boot, and when he groaned, she moved onto Jesina. Then Andriel, Donas and Tommy. "Wake up! It's coming for us!"

Rojan stumbled toward her with bleary eyes. "They're unchanged," he said, pointing to the distant lights. "The demon isn't out there."

"It's coming from the *wrong* direction."

"What?"

"From the *west*, Rojan," she snarled. "It went around us so that it could sneak up on us from behind!"

The colour drained out of his face as he stood there with his mouth hanging open. Quickly, he took control of himself and began barking orders. "Everyone up! Get ready to move! We'll head north to get away from the demon!"

Desa strode up to him. "That won't work!" she snapped. "We have to confront it, clear the way and keep moving forward!"

"What?"

She pushed past him and ran to the bag where they kept the crystals they had been making over the last few days. Dropping to her knees, she reached inside and retrieved five of the larger ones.

"Desa," Rojan said, coming up behind her. "You can't just go out there. If you try to confront *Hanak Tuvar...*"

She ignored him.

Standing up, she triggered her Gravity-Sink and then jumped. Untethered, she soared into the sky, the open plains dropping away beneath her, the campfire shrinking to an orange speck.

Desa closed her eyes, the wind caressing her face, blowing her hair back. "Sorry," she whispered. "But we can't afford to wait."

She stuffed the crystals into her coat pocket and then pulled out her small coin. Tossing it into the distance, she triggered the Force-Source and rode a wave of kinetic energy toward her enemy.

The ring on her pinky finger called the coin back to her hand. She clutched it tightly. It was the only way to slow herself down or change direction.

The ground slid past beneath her: open fields illuminated by silver moonlight. She saw no sign of life or civilization, nothing to indicate the presence of another living soul. Or of her enemy for that matter. But she knew the beast was out here.

She felt it.

Pinning her arms to her sides, she flew belly-down over the fields. The harsh wind assaulted her, threatening to strip away her speed. That didn't matter. She would use the coin again if she had to, but she was fairly certain she wouldn't have to.

When her eyes adjusted, she found what she was looking for. A patch of land that was darker somehow, where the pale moonlight took on a ruddy hue. *Hanak Tuvar* was in there. She could feel the demon's hatred. "All right, you piece of cow dung!" she hissed. "Let's end this!"

She killed her Sink for an instant.

That put her into a quick descent. The patch of darkness was drawing near, growing larger and larger until it dominated her field of view. She retrieved the crystals from her pocket.

The instant she entered the distortion field, Desa shattered a few, creating a rainbow of light that protected her. She was wrapped in a halo of oscillating colours. Purple, then red, then orange. Yellow, then green, then blue. She streaked toward her enemy like a comet, causing the beast to retreat. Dark tentacles waved back and forth as *Hanak Tuvar* tried to shield itself.

She landed in a crouch, unconcerned by the *snap* of her leg bones breaking. The rainbow healed them in an instant. She crushed another crystal, and the halo expanded, driving the demon backward.

Hanak Tuvar vanished.

The rainbow faded, and when it was gone, she stood under an ordinary patch of land under the crescent moon. The grass beneath her feet had withered, but the distortion field was gone. Part of it anyway.

She turned to her left and found another patch of darkness a short distance away. *Hanak Tuvar* appeared there, towering over her. A boulder rose up behind the demon, flew over its head and rushed toward Desa, threatening to flatten her.

Bending her knees, she triggered her Gravity-Sink and jumped. She rose into the air, passed over the falling boulder, then briefly killed the Sink and dropped gracefully to the ground.

She landed in a crouch, one hand flying up to toss a glittering crystal into the air. As the shard fell, Desa splayed her fingers and released a surge of kinetic energy from her ring, sending the fragment zipping toward her enemy.

Hanak Tuvar shrieked as the crystal pierced its flesh.

Desa rose, drawing her left-hand pistol and cocking the hammer. She extended her hand and fired several shots toward the beast, each round melting into a glob of liquid metal when it entered the distortion field.

It didn't matter.

The third bullet was a Force-Source.

She triggered it, releasing another surge of kinetic energy that shattered the crystal. *Hanak Tuvar* roared as the rainbow spread over its oily skin. Dancing backwards, it tried to get away. But it was like trying to escape sunlight in the desert. Sizzling steam rose from the demon. And then it vanished.

"That's right," Desa whispered. "Keep running."

A short time later – ten minutes, maybe fifteen – she heard the footsteps of horses and saw the approach of distant lights. Rojan marched up to her, scowling. "That," he said, "was entirely reckless."

Desa stood up, exhaustion hitting her like a tidal wave. She pressed the heel of her hand to her forehead. "Unavoidable," she replied. "We had to subdue it or it would have overpowered us. I think I bought us some time."

Folding his arms with a sigh, Rojan tilted his head to one side. "And how did you do that?"

"I wounded it."

"Fine," he said. "Let's put as much distance between us and this place as possible. We'll march another two hours."

CLOUDS FILLED the sky on their fifth day of travel, bringing with them a dreary, sombre mood. Everyone plodded along with heavy footsteps. They had spent the morning riding at a good pace to gain even more ground, but after lunch, Rojan had decided that it was best to walk and let the horses rest.

Walking, however, made it impossible to grow new crystals. They still had plenty to spare, and there had been no sign of the demon since their encounter the night before, but Desa still worried. If she had her way, they would spend every waking second creating as many crystals as possible. But such plans weren't feasible.

Tommy walked at her side, leading his white mare by the bridle. "Mighty brave what you did last night," he said. "Brave and maybe just a little bit stupid."

Desa gave him a sidelong glance, her mouth twisting in distaste. "What happened to the uncertain boy that I rescued from a sleepy village a year ago?" she asked. "The one who went along with everything I said without question?"

"He grew up."

Grinning, Desa felt a touch of heat singeing her cheeks. "Yes," she said, nodding. "He did. So, Thomas, what would you have done?"

"Probably the same thing you did."

"But you just said it was stupid."

He chuckled and replied with a halfhearted shrug. "It *was* stupid," he insisted. "But I never said I was a smart man."

"Smarter than most, in my experience."

Lifting a toothpick with two fingers, Tommy slipped it into his mouth. He gnawed on it for a few seconds before working up the nerve to speak. "So, is it true?" he asked. "What you told Rojan? Is *Hanak Tuvar* aware of our plan?"

"Have you known me to lie?"

"No, I suppose not," he muttered. "But then why are we going through with it? If we know it isn't going to work..."

Stomping through the damp grass and leading Midnight by his bridle, Desa lowered her eyes to stare down at her feet. "Do you have any better ideas?" she asked. "Maybe the demon is overconfident. Maybe we will be able to trap it. I would rather try and fail than do nothing."

"Suppose that's all we can do."

As the day wore on, Desa noticed a strip of green on the western horizon. They had reached Ander's Woods. If the maps were correct, they would spend three days crossing the forest, and when they emerged on the other side, they would quickly find themselves on the desert's eastern border.

The final leg of their trip would prove to be the most difficult. The desert was uniform in all directions. It was easy to get lost if you deviated from the established trade routes. And Mercy's abandoned city was nowhere near those routes. Luckily it wasn't far from the eastern border. A day's ride at most. With over twenty Field-Binders in their company, someone was bound to sense the crystal's pulses.

You hope, Desa noted.

She said very little as they approached the forest. At one point, Dalen came up to walk beside Tommy, and the pair fell into a quiet conversation. Desa felt a twinge of anxiety upon seeing the former librarian. Back in Ofalla, she had been prepared to insist that Dalen and Miri should stay behind –

there was little that either one of them could do on this trip, and she saw no reason why they should put themselves in danger – but Miri had shot down that idea before Desa opened her mouth.

Then again, having them along felt right. After so many journeys together, they had become a family. It was fitting that they should face this final challenge together.

In the late afternoon, Rojan called a halt so they could rest. It seemed wise given that they had not seen any sign of *Hanak Tuvar*. She worried about that. The demon had been on their heels for the entirety of this trip. Perhaps it was lagging behind because she had wounded it. Or perhaps it had lost interest. Why attack the people who could hurt you when there was easier prey over the next hill?

She wasn't sure what she would do if *Hanak Tuvar* stopped pursuing them. Desa wasn't entirely clear on the plan, but Mercy seemed to think that the demon had to be near the crystal for this to work.

She sought out the Ether, scanning her surroundings for any sign of trouble. She found nothing within a mile. Only... What was that? She sensed motion on the very edge of her awareness, people coming in from the east. When she tried to brush them with her thoughts, she felt a wrongness, and she knew exactly what it was she was dealing with.

Desa severed contact with the Ether.

She ran through the camp, huffing and puffing, her heart thundering in her chest. "Rojan!" she called out. "Rojan, we've got trouble!"

He was standing next to a dappled gray, lightly patting the horse. When he heard her shouting, he gave a start and turned around. "What is it?"

Desa pointed into the distance behind him.

They came over a hill that Desa and her friends had crossed maybe ten minutes ago, climbing to the top and scrambling down the other side: a hundred gray bodies, each one stripped of colour from head to toe. When they saw her, they paused for half a second and then broke into a furious sprint, bounding across the land.

"Into the forest!" Rojan shouted. "Move!"

26

They fled into the woods.

The nearest path was only wide enough for two horses to run side by side, forcing them into a bottleneck. Tommy observed his surroundings from atop his white mare. Tall trees with leaves in full flower stood on either side of the meandering path. This forest wasn't as dense as those he had seen in Ithanar, but there was no way they could get the horses over that uneven ground.

Clutching the reins, Tommy bent low to whisper to his mount. "You can do this." The mare didn't seem to notice his encouragement; she wasn't smart like Midnight, but she was a good horse.

Gray shapes rushed past him on both sides of the path, enemies moving through the forest. By the Almighty! Those things were fast! They moved with a speed no ordinary person could match. He suspected that *Hanak Tuvar* was pushing them too hard, running them ragged until their bones snapped and their muscles tore.

More grays surged past above him, leaping from branch to

branch. Why didn't they attack? Was this just about intimidation or-

One of the creatures dropped down from a hanging branch, landing behind him on the mare's back, causing the horse to whinny. A gray arm wrapped around Tommy, bony fingers grabbing his throat.

He squeezed his eyes shut and threw his head backward, smashing the creature's nose with the back of his skull. That gave him some breathing room – literally – though he would pay for it with a headache later.

Leaning sideways, Tommy flung his elbow out behind himself, smashing the other man's nose a second time. That, coupled with the mare taking a particularly sharp turn, was enough to shake the beast loose.

The gray man fell to the ground.

Two seconds later, it was trampled to death by Temiel's horse, bones crunching under the gelding's powerful hooves. But there were more of them! Tommy saw them trying to close in on the caravan from both sides.

Bouncing in the saddle, Tommy retrieved his pistol and cocked the hammer. He pointed the gun into the woods on his right and fired.

His shot took a gray woman in the shoulder, causing her to stumble and fall on her backside. Three others hopped over her, moving toward the path. Those snarling faces. There wasn't a trace of intelligence left in those black eyes.

Adjusting his aim, Tommy fired again.

This bullet went into the ground, and he triggered a Force-Source that sent gray bodies flying along with a spray of dirt and dried leaves. The kinetic wave slammed into the horses that were coming up behind him, causing them to neigh and dance sideways.

"Watch yourself, Eradian!" one of the other Field Binders shouted.

Tommy blushed.

This would be much easier if he could use his bow. Unfortunately, he had started restringing it this morning only to have Rojan order them to get moving before he could finish his work.

Scrunching up his face, Tommy shivered at the thought of those grubby, colourless hands pawing at him. "We have to regroup!" he bellowed. "Use the Ether to sever their connection to *Hanak Tuvar!*"

"Brilliant!" Andriel spat. She was right in front of him, riding a golden palomino with a shaggy, white mane. "We'll just join hands in a circle and ask if they would mind sitting still while we cut them off from their master!"

A gray man leaped out of the treetops, trying to tackle her.

Andriel's hand came up, and she released kinetic energy from her ring. The blast sent her would-be assailant flying away with enough force to crash through a branch. He dropped out of sight somewhere on Tommy's left.

Tommy had to resist the urge to reply with a biting comment. He still wasn't sure how he felt about Andriel coming along for this journey. Ill will from their skirmish last year still lingered within him.

"It's the only way to stop them!" Tommy insisted.

"And it's not an option!" Andriel shot back.

Red-faced and fuming, Tommy squinted at her. "You'll do anything to undermine me," he muttered under his breath. "Bloody Aladri. Think you're so much smarter than everyone else."

The man riding next to Andriel pointed one of those crescent-shaped pistols into the treetops. A hair-thin bolt of electricity erupted from his gun, striking a gray woman who stood upon a branch.

She trembled, falling backward into the forest.

Up ahead, the caravan came to an abrupt halt. Tommy's horse reared, throwing her head back with a fearsome whinny before her hooves slammed down in the dirt. Men and women in gray cloaks flew past above him, dropping into the forest and engaging the grays there.

Tommy narrowed his eyes. "We need to be out there too." He slipped off the mare, landing in the dirt, and then gave her a gentle pat. Drawing his pistol, he turned right and stalked off into the forest.

Miri joined him, carrying a rifle that she had taken from one of the wagons. Her jaw was set, her eyes as hard as granite. "Jim's guarding Dalen," she said. "And I will be guarding you."

Cocking his head, Tommy raised an eyebrow. "You sure it's not the other way around?" The dirty look he received told him not to press that point.

They moved between the trees, over the uneven ground where roots slithered beneath the surface, occasionally poking up. Leaves fluttered in the soft wind. Twigs snapped underfoot.

Tommy stayed low with his pistol clutched in both hands, scanning this way and that. "I don't see them," he whispered. "Funny, they were more than willing to make a scene two minutes ago, but now they hide."

"Tactics," Miri hissed behind him.

They made their way toward a fat oak tree with drooping branches, its trunk gnarled and weathered from who knows how many winters. As they drew near, an old man with wispy hair stepped out into the open, carrying an axe. He was as gray as a stone with black eyes that seemed to glisten.

And he charged for them.

Extending his hand, Tommy pointed his pistol down at the ground. He fired a single round that landed two feet in front of the old codger, releasing a blast of kinetic energy that sent the man flying backward into the tree. More grays surrounded them, moving toward them in a ring.

Tommy dropped to a crouch, extending a closed fist toward one and projecting a stream of crackling electricity that struck the gray fellow's chest. The poor fool was thrown to the ground.

Miri spun to face one, worked the lever of her rifle and fired, her barrel flashing as thunder split the air. Her shot ripped through the chest of a woman in a bonnet, dropping her. A dark-skinned man stepped over her corpse as he shambled toward Miri. She ran to fight with him.

Tommy trotted toward a group of three with his pistol held up beside his head. He slid to a stop, aimed his gun and fired.

His bullet whizzed through the narrow gap between two gray men, and when it passed them, Tommy pulsed the Gravity-Source. All three grays were yanked backward, landing in the dirt.

"Watch it!" Miri snarled.

With the trio down and momentarily incapacitated, Tommy let loose another stream of lightning, bathing them in so much electricity it scorched them black. They stopped squirming a few seconds later.

"WATCH MY BACK," Desa said.

She stood in the woods on the south side of the path, a dagger in each hand. Perhaps a dozen grays were trying to surround her. Would *Hanak Tuvar* possess one as it had last time? Or was it too wounded for that?

Kalia was right behind her, standing back to back. The other woman shot a glance over her shoulder and then nodded. "You got it."

One of the grays – a hollow-cheeked man with a broken nose – stumbled toward her. Without warning, he broke into a sprint. Desa ran to meet him.

She leaped, pulsing her Gravity-Sink, and flipped over his head. Dropping to the ground behind him, she landed in a crouch. With a twist of her body, she slashed the back of his knee, severing the tendon.

The man fell over before he got near Kalia. Desa heard her lover's gun going off and the thump of men hitting the dirt. She dispatched the one she had just immobilized, plunging a blade into his back and releasing enough heat to roast him.

Three more came at her: one in front, two flanking him.

Desa ran for them.

She jumped with another quick pulse of her Gravity-Sink, twirling in the air for a roundhouse kick that struck the lead man's jaw. His head wrenched sideways, a tooth flying out of his mouth.

Spinning around, Desa landed with her back to him. She twirled her dagger into a reverse grip, backed up and rammed it into his stomach. The Heat-Sink drained the warmth from his flesh. Frost covered him from head to toe. When she pulled the blade free, he fell over and shattered.

The other two came up behind her.

Pulsing her Sink, Desa jumped a good ten feet into the air and let them stumble past beneath her. She landed with a grunt, daggers ready. She slashed one man with her left-hand dagger – scorching him to ash – and the other with her right-hand dagger, freezing him solid.

Two more down.

A GRAY MAN hopped between two trees.

Hoisting up her rifle, Miri stepped forward with a growl and fired. Her bullet ripped through the bearded brute's chest, producing a spray of black blood. The old man fell on his backside, thrashing in the dirt, the darkness slowly fading from his eyes. *Hanak Tuvar* had let him go. How many was that now? She had lost count.

Miri turned and ran.

She dropped to her knees, sliding through the mud, narrowly evading a spindly man who tried to grab her. That one stumbled past, having over-extended himself, and fell on his face behind her.

Her slide brought her to a tall, heavyset man without an ounce of colour anywhere on his body. That one almost seemed to smile when he looked upon her. His fat hands trembled with anticipation.

He reached for her.

Miri stood, raising her rifle horizontally, striking his arms and knocking them upward. She swung the stock into his belly, making him flinch, then twisted and slammed the end of the barrel into his cheek. The man stumbled.

She kicked him in the gut, forcing him down onto his knees. Then, with another quick pivot, she brought the stock around to smash his forehead. The poor fool made almost no noise as he fell over to land on his side.

Sweat rolled over Miri's face. She blinked a few times, catching her breath. "It doesn't make sense."

Tommy was off to her left, fending off a pair of youths who had lost every trace of colour. He stretched a hand toward them, and they both flew away, propelled by some unseen force. "What doesn't?"

"*Hanak Tuvar,*" she shouted. "It's smart enough to spend ten millennia plotting its escape, subtly manipulating people with false promises of infinite power, tricking them into writing its narrative into religious texts."

"And?"

"And then it throws the same useless tactics at us?"

Tommy went pale, turning his head to stare at her with wide eyes. "You think we're missing something?" he gasped. "Something important."

Miri backed away from a copse of trees, working the lever of her rifle to eject a spent shell. "I think all of this is a diversion," she said. "An attempt to distract us. From what, I can't say."

A gray man in rags dropped from the nearest tree, landing right in front of her. He must have been a beggar before he was changed, but now he moved with a skill that rivaled one of her teachers, beginning a high kick.

Miri ducked, allowing his foot to pass over her. She backed away to get a little space, but the gray fellow pressed his attack, coming in for a palm-strike.

With a quick pivot, Miri slammed the rifle into his arm, knocking it away. She poked him in the chest with the barrel, then snapped that up to strike the underside of his chin. The one nice thing about these creatures: they seemed to share human weaknesses.

Miri spun, twirling like a whirlwind, her foot wheeling around to strike the goon across his cheek. He was thrown sideways, left to squirm on the ground. And then, when he was immobilized, she put a bullet through him.

All around her, gray people fell as Field Binders struck them down. Rojan's troops were swift and efficient. An entire army of Desas. This was no way this attack could work. Coming at them when they were on horseback and trapped in a bottleneck was one thing, but this? This was just pointless.

What were they missing? There had to be something. Some reason why *Hanak Tuvar* was wasting its energy on these futile attacks. *If I were* Hanak Tuvar, *what would I be trying to accomplish?*

The answer came to her in an instant.

KALIA FOUGHT WITH PRECISE FOCUS. That was a thing you learned after five years as a sheriff to a backwater town that treated laws as polite suggestions. Field Binding offered all sorts of useful tricks, but at the end of the day, it was all just theatrics. A steady aim and a pair of six-shooters were a sheriff's best friends.

A gray man came out of the thicket on her right.

Extending her right hand, Kalia pointed her gun at him and fired a single shot that went right through his chest. The man staggered a few steps and dropped to the ground, black blood spreading around his body.

Movement to her left.

With a quick turn, Kalia aimed her left-hand pistol and fired. *CRACK!* A bullet went through some poor woman's belly, and her corpse dropped to the ground. So many. Was this what *Hanak Tuvar* would do to the world?

A rustling above her.

Kalia looked up just in time to see a gray figure descending from the treetops. A boot landed on her chest, and then she was thrown backward, down to the ground. She hit hard, grunting.

The gray man stood over her with a gap-toothed smile, bloodlust shining in those dead, black eyes. He raised a foot to stomp on her.

Kalia rolled aside.

Coming up on one knee, she brushed her long, brown hair out of her face. "Oh no!" She realized that she had dropped her guns when she fell. The gray man strode toward her with a high snap-kick.

By instinct, she brought up her left hand and triggered her Force-Sink bracelet. The man froze, his foot hanging in the air an inch away from her. Kalia killed the Sink, and the gray brute stumbled, trying to recover his balance.

That gave her a chance to rise.

Another one tackled her from behind, arms wrapped around her, hands pawing at her. She heard him hiss and imagined the horrifying possibility of him sinking his teeth into her neck.

Kalia bent forward, throwing the man over her shoulder.

He landed right in front of her, grunting, startling the other one who had only just regained his footing. That one growled, his lips parting, forcing her to look at that awful, rictus grin.

Stumbling backward, Kalia fished a coin out of her pocket and tossed it toward them. Their eyes latched onto the glittering metal. Like a pair of cavemen gazing upon a pulley system for the first time, wondering what it was.

Kalia triggered the Force-Source.

The kinetic shockwave sent one man flying backward while the other one slid along the ground, leaving tracks in the mud. Mr. Gap-tooth landed atop his companion, the pair of them rolling in a tangle of limbs.

Kalia saw Desa in the corner of her eye. Her partner moved like a ribbon on the wind, dancing from one target to the next, striking down enemies with effortless grace. It was beautiful. And terrifying.

But what was that?

A flash of red in the forest.

A hooded figure stepped out from behind a tree, lifting a rifle that she pointed at a very distracted Desa. Azra lined up a shot through the sights.

"No!" Kalia screamed.

She thrust a hand out, emptying her Force-Source ring of every last drop of kinetic energy in the very moment that the rifle went off with a *CRACK!* Pushed sideways by the blast of energy, the bullet went askew and missed Desa's head by inches.

Desa spun around, her eyes flaring when she realized how close she had come to her own demise. She sheathed one of her knives, reaching for a pistol instead, but it was too late.

Azra didn't stay to fight.

She turned and ran deeper into the forest, hopping over roots and fallen logs. Every single gray got the same idea, retreating the instant their master realized that the plan had failed. Only they went in a different direction, heading east while Azra fled south.

Kalia growled.

Desa stumbled up to her, heaving out a breath. "That was the plan," she whispered, watching Azra go. "Distract me and then kill me?"

Kalia nodded.

"I thought she would challenge me," Desa mumbled. "Another contest to prove that she's the better fighter."

Kalia crouched next to a fallen branch, retrieving one of her pistols and shoving it back into its holster. "Azra can't beat you in a straight-up fight," she said. "So, she resorts to cunning."

"I didn't think she had that kind of cunning."

"It probably wasn't her idea," Kalia said. *"Hanak Tuvar* is getting desperate."

WHEN TWILIGHT CAME, they gathered in the narrow corridor that cut through the forest. The horses needed a rest after that harrowing chase, especially the poor beast who had been forced to pull the wagon. Sadly, there wasn't much for them to graze on. They had brought some hay from Ofalla, but it would have to last for the two and a half days it would take to cross this forest and their trip through the desert as well.

Rojan's Field Binders were clustered together in little groups, each gathered around a glowing ring or coin while they ate their dinner. Their Infusions provided enough light to see the path and the surrounding woodland, but Desa still felt a sense of foreboding when she looked into those shadows. Her most-deadly enemy was out there somewhere, just waiting to take a shot.

Azra might be hidden in the darkness at this very moment, watching her through the sight of a rifle. A terrifying thought.

Desa had taken to reaching out to the Ether and scanning her surroundings every few minutes. She just didn't know what else to do. She had been able to contain Azra when the other woman had been dead set on besting her in a straight fight. But Azra wasn't interested in *winning* anymore. She just wanted to kill Desa. And she was still working with *Hanak Tuvar*. Even knowing that the demon would bring about the end of humanity and leave this world a lifeless husk, Azra still chose to give it her allegiance.

A strange thought occurred to her? When had Azra become her most-deadly enemy? Once upon a time, that had been Bendarian.

Tommy was a silhouette to her eyes, leaning against the side of the wagon and fiddling with a toothpick. "I'm sorry," he said as she passed. "I should have figured that *Hanak Tuvar* would try something new."

Desa stopped in front of him, allowing herself a small smile. "Tommy, I've been doing this for over a decade," she said. "And I didn't anticipate the change. There's no reason why you should have."

He grimaced, turning his face away from her. "Miri did," he muttered. "But only after the battle had started. The squid outwitted us."

"How long has it been since we left New Beloran?"

"Fifteen days."

Desa sighed, folding her arms as she watched the *Al a Nari* talking quietly with one another. "And we've been running ourselves ragged for most of that time," she replied. "Living in that way limits your capacity for long-term thinking."

He grinned, bowing his head and running his fingers through his hair. "Even now, you're still teaching me, Mrs. Kincaid."

"Someone has to."

"Hey!"

The sound of footsteps made her look up, and she saw Rojan coming toward her. The man looked as if he had been the one pulling the wagon all this way. He spared a glance for Tommy. "Well, it seems things have changed."

Pursing her lips, Desa held his gaze and then nodded once. "I would have to agree with that assessment," she said. *"Hanak Tuvar* is resorting to new tactics."

"It seems to have made killing you a priority."

"Oh, it always wanted me dead," she said. "But I thought it wanted to do the deed itself. Crush me in its tentacles. It seemed so angry. All I had to do to provoke it was let it see me."

Cocking his head, Rojan studied her for a moment, deep creases forming in his brow. "Are you sure it was anger that motivated the beast?" he asked. "Perhaps it was always looking for the most efficient way to kill you."

"Why?"

"Because you can hurt it," Mercy said, coming around the wagon. Her dress was rumpled, her curly hair tangled, and she looked as if she had been walking for several days without rest, which wasn't far from the truth. "It fears you, Desa."

Rojan put a hand over his heart, bowing low. "My lady." He had started calling her that when Mercy...when *Nari* had insisted that she was not a goddess and that she did not want his devotion. That seemed to be as far as he would go, however. Desa supposed she couldn't blame him. After all, she was also having a hard time accepting that Nari was not divine.

"Why would it fear me?" Desa asked.

Nari gave her an exasperated glare that said the answer should be obvious. "I have lived for over ten millennia," she said. "And I have met only a handful of individuals who can manipulate the Field as you can."

"We've got twenty Field Binders here-"

"And none of them have your skill," Rojan cut in.

"Directly challenging *Hanak Tuvar* as you did last night was reckless," Mercy said. "If we had lost you, it would have been disastrous."

Desa turned away from the other woman, stomping along the path as she tried to collect herself. She paused after a moment and looked back over her shoulder. "I am very grateful for your confidence in me. But I refuse to do nothing while that thing kills my friends!"

Nari sniffed. "Someone else could have challenged the beast."

"No," Tommy said. "They couldn't."

Everyone looked at him, and Dese felt a wave of relief. It was nice to have someone support her in these ridiculous discussions. Tommy leaned against the wagon, rolling the toothpick between his thumb and forefinger. "She's not just an expert at creating Infusions and manipulating the Ether," he explained. "She also knows how to use those Infusions creatively. How to analyze a situation and devise a winning strategy. If someone else had gone up against *Hanak Tuvar,* the demon would have crushed them, and we probably wouldn't be here right now."

Desa blushed.

"Perhaps," Nari conceded. "But, Desa, I *will* need your help to return the creature to its prison. Please do not put yourself at unnecessary risk."

"I will try," Desa muttered.

ABOUT AN HOUR LATER, full darkness had come. Many of the others were turning in for the night. Tommy sat on a rock, wrapped in the Ether's embrace and scanning the land with his mind. He found trees and stones, twigs and dried leaves but no sign of *Hanak Tuvar.*

It was Tommy's turn to take watch, which meant several hours spent sitting here and doing very little of anything. The range of his awareness had grown in the months since he had first learned to commune with the Ether. He could sense everything for about a mile. Not perfectly. He had to focus on an object to get details like size, shape and position, but he would know if anyone planned to sneak up on the camp.

With nothing better to do, he decided to try creating crystals. It would be incredibly difficult with no one to help him, but what did he have to lose? He directed pulses into his own hand, trying to concentrate the Ether in one spot as Nari had shown him.

He was well aware of Andriel long before he heard her footsteps. She shuffled around people who were curled up in their bedrolls, making her way to Tommy's rock. And then she sat down beside him. "You would have made a good Guardian."

He severed contact with the Ether.

Opening his eyes, Tommy drew a slow breath through his nose. "I'm surprised to hear you say that," he admitted. "Kind of thought you hated me."

"Because of our scuffle last year?" she asked. "Let's just say that living among the *Al a Nari* has given me a new perspective."

Tommy said nothing, choosing to return his attention to watch duty. He found the Ether with little difficulty and let his mind drift over the land. Trees, roots, and dirt in all directions. No threats that he could detect.

"You find it quickly, don't you?" Andriel remarked. Tommy saw her as a cloud of dancing molecules in the shape of a human, but he didn't need the Ether to feel her eyes upon him. "Rojan told me that those crystals increase one's affinity, but I didn't believe him until...Well, that's not important. Actually, our scuffle is *why* I think you would have made a good guardian."

With a monumental effort of will, Tommy turned his head ever so slightly. He often wondered why it was so hard to move while communing with the Ether. He was starting to think it might have something to do with disconnection. As if his mind had been separated from his body.

Andriel sensed that she had piqued his interest. "I'm one of the best," she clarified. "And you beat me. You've got a talent for improvising."

"I...learned...from...the...best." The words came out slurred. He couldn't make his tongue work properly, but she understood.

Sitting forward with hands on her knees, Andriel stared at the trees on the other side of the path. "It's funny," she said. "Back home, Desa Nin Leean is a disgrace."

Unable to help himself, Tommy let go of the Ether and sucked in a breath when he regained full control of his body. "Your people have accomplished much," he said. "But with such success comes arrogance."

Andriel answered him with a small smile. "Yes," she agreed. "I see that now."

"Desa is a good person."

Twirling a ringlet of red hair around her index finger, Andriel chuckled. "Yes," she said. "I see that too. The world looks different when you travel it and see all the ways that people suffer."

"Careful," Tommy said. "I might start to like you."

"Would that be so bad?"

Tommy opened his mouth, but he had no words. He gave his head a shake, trying to centre himself. This was a silly discussion, and he had a job to do. Once again, he found the Ether, checked his surroundings and found nothing amiss. That done, he returned his attention to Andriel.

"Shame Miri got to you first," she said, staring wistfully up at the stars. "I think you and I might have had some fun."

"Weren't you with Marcus?"

"Yes," she replied. "So, you can imagine how I can appreciate the value of a man who knows how to have fun."

Tommy's face was on fire. "I hate to be rude," he began. "But I really should be paying attention to the land. *Hanak Tuvar* might sneak up on us again."

She just sat there, smiling into her lap. "Yes," she said. "Watch duty is usually shared by two people, is it not?"

"Yes. Why?"

She tapped her chest with one finger, her shy smile becoming an outright grin. "Guess who volunteered to take this shift."

Great.

"Come on," she said. "If we work together, maybe we can extend the range of our awareness."

THEY SAW no sign of *Hanak Tuvar* the next day. No creeping wall of redness washing over the forest. No army of colourless corpses attacking from all sides. It was just a quiet ride in the drizzle.

The clouds that had gathered the day before finally delivered on that rain they had been promising. The water soaked through Tommy's poncho, leaving him with a constant shiver that wouldn't let up. How he wished that he had one of those Aladri contraptions he had seen last year. What were they called again? Oh, right! Umbrellas!

The path meandered this way and that, slowly making its way westward. The horse's hooves sank into the mud as they plodded along. Tommy spent the morning in the mare's saddle, wrapped in the Ether's embrace and making crystals with three of Rojan's Field Binders. Colayos was a likable fellow. A bit quiet but friendly enough. Most of the *Al a Nari* were easygoing, but for some reason, Shari seemed a little standoffish. Tommy supposed she was just a tad closed off. It didn't really matter. They didn't have to be friends; they just had to make crystals.

You needed at least four people if you wanted to complete

the task at anything more than a snail's pace. A single person working for several hours could create a crystal the size of Tommy's fingernail. Four working together could make one the size of his palm in about twenty minutes.

After lunch, the humans walked so that the horses could rest. Mud squished under Tommy's boots. He was tired and cold and sore. And this forest seemed to go on forever. He kept wondering what *Hanak Tuvar* would throw at them next.

They reached the western edge of the forest late the following afternoon. Tommy was glad to be out in the open again. Even if it did mean another stretch of grassland. At least the horses had plenty to eat.

They traveled for another two days before arriving at a small village of thatch-roof houses. The people were friendly and willing to trade some of their food in exchange for Infused trinkets and whatever money Desa and Miri could spare. And a good thing too! Their supplies were running low.

Tommy couldn't help but notice something that did not sit well with him. It seemed the further you got from the centre of Eradian power, the less dedicated people were to their prejudice against Field Binding. No one called Desa a witch here! They marveled at her talents and wondered whether they could learn to do the same. Perhaps, when this was all over, Tommy could return and begin teaching them.

No one had inquired about lodgings, but the villagers were still apologetic. Their inn was small; they didn't have enough rooms for twenty people. Rojan assured them that it was no trouble. His party wouldn't be remaining in any event. Their presence would only attract *Hanak Tuvar*.

The villagers took his warning about the squid demon very seriously. Tommy had expected skepticism but when Rojan finished his story, the crowd began making plans to evacuate the instant they saw a creeping line of redness on the eastern horizon. Tommy's heart broke for them.

Though he knew it was irrational, he felt responsible for their plight. Here he was, leading *Hanak Tuvar* right to them. If he had tried harder, if he had stopped Adele before the demon had escaped, maybe none of this would have happened. He talked to Desa about it when he found her with Midnight in the stable.

She stood there with her back turned, chuckling softly as she ran a brush over the stallion's black body. "You sound like me."

Tommy blinked.

Crossing his arms, he leaned one shoulder against a wooden pole that supported the ceiling. "Is that such a bad thing?" he asked, grinning.

Desa spun to face him. Something in the way she scrutinized him made him feel like this had all been a dream and he was still the naïve boy she had rescued from a village that wouldn't be labeled on most maps. "No," she said. "But blaming yourself for failing accomplishes nothing. What matters is that you tried."

"I suppose that's true."

"Tommy, take it from someone who knows," she said. "If you sit here and wallow in your regrets, the only thing you'll get for your trouble is an unhealthy obsession with your own shortcomings."

They stayed just long enough to purchase what they needed and set out again while there was still plenty of daylight in the sky, moving slowly westward. Long days and hard nights: that was what this journey offered.

The next day, he began to notice a change in the landscape. Patches of yellow grass crept in among the green. Just a few here and there, at first, but it very wasn't long before those patches grew larger. He saw fewer trees and more thorny bushes.

Two days after that, the grass was gone entirely. They had

entered the scrubland that surrounded the desert, an endless stretch of dirt baking under a sun that beat down from a cloudless sky.

Summer was at least two months away, but that harsh glare made him feel as if he were roasting in an oven. And to think he had been complaining about the cold! Right then, he would give anything for a cool drizzle.

If making crystals in the rain was hard, then doing it in the scorching heat was…roughly equal in terms of difficulty, now that he thought about it. There was no such thing as good weather when you were bouncing on a horse's back, manipulating the Ether while simultaneously trying not to fall out of the saddle.

At one point, he found himself walking beside Kalia. The former sheriff was happy for some reason that he couldn't comprehend. When he inquired, she looked at him as if he had just asked why dogs bark. "This is my home," she said. "I wouldn't trade this last year for anything, but it's good to be back."

He kept looking to the east, expecting to see a line of redness on the horizon, but it never came. They set a watch every night, but they never saw any signs of trouble. Where was *Hanak Tuvar*? Had the demon given up its chase? Tommy wasn't sure if he liked the implications of that.

The next morning, Desa stood in the stirrups and stared off to the horizon. Tommy saw nothing but a field of red clay under the blue sky, but Desa pointed at a spot slightly to the north. "That way!"

"You're sure?" Rojan asked.

"Reach for the Ether," she replied. "Sense the pulses."

Tommy did as she suggested, the world changing all around him. He strained for the pulses and felt nothing.

The people all around him began to glow as they found the Ether. He reached out for them with his thoughts, and together, they searched for the pulses. *There!* He felt them like the softest whisper of wind on his skin. Desa was right. She knew the way to the abandoned city.

Those pulses became stronger as they pressed on. Soon, Tommy didn't need the Ether to feel them. They were insistent, drawing him in. Like a song in his mind that he could not resist.

The final leg of their journey was the hardest.

Tommy saw very little in the way of plant life. A cactus here or there, but not much beyond that. The horses were exhausted, and their riders weren't doing much better. Most of the Field Binders had given up on making new crystals. They already had several dozen of them. That would have to do for now.

Miri and Dalen muttered their misgivings about whether they were going in the right direction. Neither one of them could feel the pulses. If they had, they would know. Luckily, the city wasn't too far from the desert's eastern border.

It came into view when the sun was an orange ball on the distant horizon, but it wasn't at all what Tommy had been expecting. He had heard stories about dilapidated buildings, structures that had collapsed to rubble centuries ago. There was none of that. Instead, he saw cute, little homes that looked as if they had been finished less than a year ago, homes that were surrounded by blooming gardens and tall trees.

The pyramid towered over the surrounding buildings. But instead of rising to a point, its top half had been hacked off, leaving a flat roof that supported an enormous crystal in the shape of a teardrop. Sunlight glinted off its smooth surface in a rainbow of colours.

Nari smiled as she looked upon the place that she had called home for the last ten thousand years. Much of that time had been spent in isolation, trapped in a ghostly form that haunted the ruins. But the pride in her eyes...You could tell with one look that she was responsible for the improvements.

"We're here," Tommy mumbled.

Desa nodded. "We're here."

Rojan called a halt just outside the city. "All right," he said, turning to look upon his troops. "First, we stable the horses, and then we all find a place to sleep. Eat a quick meal, and get some rest. I want everyone up by dawn."

"And why is that?" Andriel asked.

"Because," he replied. "We're going to ready this place for battle."

27

Desa found her bedroom much as she had left it. Four stone walls with a window that looked out on a small garden in the backyard. Her bed had a wooden frame and a fluffy pillow. Other than that, there were no furnishings except for a small table and one chair in the corner.

Kalia stood with the strap of her bag slung over one shoulder, pursing her lips as she examined the room. "So, this is where you would sleep?" she asked. "I guess I hadn't pictured anything quite so homey."

Desa leaned against the wall with her arms folded, nodding slowly in response to the other woman's question. "This is it," she said. "Nari rebuilt this house and remade the furniture with her powers."

"I see," Kalia said. "And what would she do while you were sleeping?"

"She would fly around the city, rebuilding houses with her powers."

Kalia heaved out a breath, sitting on the edge of the bed with her hands gripping the edge of the mattress. "Your time here changed you," she muttered under her breath.

Pacing across the room, Desa stopped in front of the other woman. "Please tell me that you're not still feeling jealous of Nari," she said. "Darling, you are the only one I want."

When Kalia looked up, her brown eyes reflected the light of a glowing metal plate in the ceiling. The residents of this ancient city had built their homes with the intention of making Field Binding a part of their lives, using it for the most mundane tasks. Aladar had been much the same before the advent of electricity. "It's not that I'm jealous," Kalia said. "But you became a new person. And I wasn't here to see it."

Desa bent low, pressing her lips to the other woman's forehead. She offered the softest kiss and then pulled away. "We are always becoming new people," she said. "You will be with me as I become a hundred new versions of Desa Kincaid."

"You see?" Kalia protested. "Now, you spout off wisdom like that without even thinking about it." Desa was about to insist that nothing had changed between them, but Kalia started laughing and poking her in the belly.

"Stop it!" Desa squealed, flinching and scooting away. "I wish you had never found out that I'm ticklish."

"Well, everyone needs a weakness."

"Bah! Heresy!"

Kalia was on her feet in an instant, surging forward to throw her arms around Desa's neck, offering a kiss that silenced any further arguments.

A GIBBOUS MOON hung low in the starry sky, casting silver light over the ancient city. For all the sun's fury, nights in the desert were chilly. Tommy barely noticed. He was fascinated by the houses on either side of this circular street.

They weren't anything fancy – just little, blocky homes with flat rooftops – but there was something about them. About the little gardens, the large windows. This place had been built by the hand of someone who wanted to care for her people. It made him feel at home. Safe.

Miri walked beside him, frowning as she inspected her surroundings with the eye of a tactician. "Defending the city will be difficult," she grumbled. "We don't know which direction they will come from. Rojan is thinking that we could set up watchers on the outermost buildings."

He nodded absently.

What would it have been like to live here all those centuries ago? To learn Field Binding under the tutelage of a goddess? Well, Nari wasn't really a goddess – he was beginning to wonder whether there was any such thing – but she was as close to one as anybody would ever get. At least, that was how he saw it.

How could there be a God or an Almighty? What sort of being would create something like *Hanak Tuvar*? It just didn't make any sense. Tommy had never been the sort of person who found much comfort in religion, but he was unnerved by the prospect of living in a godless universe. What did that mean for morality? For a man's purpose in this world?

Miri swatted his shoulder. "You listening to me, Lommy?"

He blushed, shutting his eyes as he shuffled along beside her. "Sorry," he muttered. "I guess I've had a lot of thoughts on my mind."

She linked arms with him and then leaned her head against his shoulder. "So, about the same as usual then," she murmured. "What are you thinking about now?"

"Our place in the universe."

"No. See, that's entirely wrong," Miri teased. "You're supposed to say that you're thinking about my beautiful eyes."

Tommy spun to face her, taking her hands in his, and then he bent to kiss her lips. "Yes," he said. "You've figured it out. I am helpless under your spell."

"Much better."

"Though I do have a question. Why, of all the nicknames you could have chosen for me, did you settle on 'Lommy?'"

His heart raced when she smiled at him. Her face was so beautiful in the moonlight. "Because it makes you squirm," she said. "And you're so cute when you squirm."

"Do you think we're going to survive this?"

"I think so."

They walked in silence for a time, continuing their circuit of the city. It wasn't very big. You could walk around the outermost street in about an hour. More of a village, really. Or a small town. But as he thought about it, those words didn't seem to fit either. They were just too quaint.

Now and then, he would venture a glance toward the crystal. You could see it rising over the top of every structure, glittering even in the starlight. How many lives could they save with that thing? How many people could they heal?

From what Nari had told him, this place had once been a school. She had reminded him several times that he would find a place here if he wanted one. She needed people who could teach the Great Art to her next crop of students. The prospect was tempting, but something within him resisted the thought of settling down. Almighty help him, he wasn't even twenty years old yet. There was still so much of the world to see.

And so much good to do.

Much of what he *had* seen in the past year painted the picture of a world in need of fixing. Injustice, cruelty, oppression: they dominated his continent from one end to the other. But he had also seen the opposite. He knew that a better way was possible. "Have you given any thought to after?" he asked Miri.

"After?" she replied.

"What we'll do when this is all over."

She halted in mid-step, eying him suspiciously. Finally, she shrugged. "Honestly, I haven't," she said. "It's always been about surviving from one day to the next."

"Our work in Hedrovan isn't done."

"Yes, because that went so very well."

Tommy pulled away from her. "Just because the first attempt fails," he said. "Doesn't mean you give up. Those people down there need us."

Miri was watching him from the corner of her eye. He had learned to recognize that dangerous look, the one that said they might be headed for an argument. "You're not going to let that one go, are you?"

"Should I?"

She heaved out a sigh, deflating. "No, I suppose not," she mumbled. "I was just hoping we might get a break from the ever-present danger. Silly me."

GRAVITY-SINKS ALLOWED Desa and Kalia to jump to the roof of a small house where they found Rojan waiting for them. The sun was less than halfway to its zenith, shining down from a clear sky, but it was already quite warm.

Rojan stood at the southern edge of the rooftop, gazing out on the field of red clay that surrounded the city. As Desa approached him from behind, she noticed several of his Field Binders at work down below. She could feel the Ether stirring around them, which meant they must have been creating Infusions.

"A difficult position to hold," Rojan said.

"With any luck, you won't have to hold it long."

"You've spoken with Nari."

Desa stood with her hands behind her back, a frown tugging at the corners of her mouth. She nodded slowly. "She still thinks returning the demon to its prison is our best bet."

Rubbing his chin with the back of his hand, Rojan squinted

against the glare of the sun. "She's probably right," he muttered. "Does she know how long that will take?"

"Minutes," Desa said. "Hours. It's hard to say."

"Great."

Kalia sauntered up to stand beside Rojan, sparing him a glance before directing her attention to the people working below. "Desa will be working with Nari to reform *Hanak Tuvar's* prison," she said. "That means we'll be without our best fighter. The rest of us will have to prevent the creature from getting anywhere near her."

"My people are Infusing every rock they find," Rojan said. "If an army of grays descends upon this city, we'll have a few nasty surprises waiting for them. As for *Hanak Tuvar,* I've got a few others making crystals."

"Don't we have plenty of those?" Kalia asked.

Rojan nodded. "Several dozen, at least. But you can never have too many. So far, they're the only weapon that has proven effective against the demon."

He turned to Kalia, lightly patting her on the shoulder. "When the fight begins, you and Thomas Von Gerald will protect Desa and Nari," he said. "No matter what else might happen, you don't let anything get near them."

"You have my word."

"So, that's it then?" Desa asked. "We just make our preparations and wait?"

"That's it."

THE NEXT FEW days passed without incident. The Field Binders made Infusions in a ring around the city. Desa, Kalia, Nari and Tommy made crystals. As many crystals as they could manage, working from sunup to sundown and only stopping for meals. By the time they were finished, they had over a hundred.

Rojan began passing them out among his people. If anyone

was seriously injured in the fight to come, they would have a way to heal. And if all else failed, they might use the crystals in a last-ditch attack against *Hanak Tuvar.*

Before turning in each night, Desa spent some time with her friends. They laughed together, shared memories of old times and hopes for the future. In the quiet moments, she almost forgot about the impending doom that waited for them.

Sometimes, she wondered if *Hanak Tuvar* had simply lost interest in them. If so, that might prove to be a problem. Their food supplies would not last forever. If the beast didn't come within the next few days, someone might have to make a run to Fool's Edge. The town was less than a day's ride from here.

Desa was growing restless. At first, she had been grateful for the extra time to set up their defenses. But there were only so many Heat-Sinks and Electric-Sources they could make. They were as ready as they would ever be.

Kalia started talking about the possibility of staying here, of teaching at Nari's new school. It sounded like a brilliant idea. Sharing the wonder of Field Binding with the world: it was what she had always wanted. And Desa was *tired* of the vagabond's life. Eleven damn years running from place to place to place. She was ready to settle down.

The thought gave her a little peace when she felt the dread creeping up on her. She was just starting to relax when one of Tommy's Sonic-Sources sounded an alarm.

Desa ran out of her small house, slinging her coat over her shoulders. She skidded to a stop in the road, letting out a breath.

When she turned, Kalia was right behind her, charging out of the house and hastily checking the guns that she wore on her hips.

"In the middle of the afternoon?" she asked, noting the sun's position in the sky. "I thought it would wait until nightfall."

"I don't think it cares to wait," Desa muttered. "It wants this whole thing over with. And so do I."

She bent her knees, then triggered her Gravity-Sink and jumped. Weightless, she flew up to the roof of the house before killing her Sink and running across the hard stone. Kalia uttered a string of curses as she followed. Manipulating gravity had never been easy for her.

Desa leaped from the rooftop, freeing herself from the earth's pull, and sailed over the tiny backyard to a building on the next street over. From there, she jumped across the road to a three-story home on the city's perimeter.

Rojan was waiting for her there, down on one knee near the ledge and holding one of those crescent-pistols in his hand. He shot a glance in her direction and nodded with approval. "It's time."

"You're sure?"

Kalia grumbled when she landed on the roof, dusting herself off. She glared at Desa as if to say that this was all her fault. "What's happening?"

"They're coming," Rojan answered.

Cautiously, Desa approached the ledge and stared out on the vast expanse of clay on the north side of the city. At first, she saw nothing – just cracked earth and blue sky – but the Field Binders who had taken position on neighbouring rooftops were readying themselves for battle.

Desa strained and strained until she noticed the thing that had caused all of this commotion. A crimson patch in the distance, growing larger and larger as it drew near. *Hanak Tuvar* was coming.

Maybe it was just her imagination, but she could swear she saw people marching out of that haze, gray bodies like the ones that she had fought in Ofalla. Was the demon getting desperate? Surely, it wouldn't resort to the same tired tactics a third time.

Crouching next to Rojan, Desa let out a grunt of disapproval. She narrowed her eyes as she watched the approaching horde. "If that's all they've got, this'll be over in time for dinner."

"Don't get cocky," Rojan muttered.

A few minutes later, the enormous squid came into view, standing over four stories tall and pounding the ground with its tentacles as it crept toward the city. Its gaping maw produced a howl that reverberated off the land.

The redness was spreading.

Desa saw tendrils of it stretching to her left and her right, forming a ring around the ancient city. "They're surrounding us," she whispered. "That's the plan."

"One way or another," Rojan said. "It ends here."

Desa was about to reassure him, to insist that they would emerge victorious – after all, they had faced these creatures several times now – but then she noticed the corpses ambling out of that crimson haze. Those weren't villagers. Those were *soldiers* in gray uniforms, carrying gray rifles.

Men wheeled small cannons into position. She counted at least a dozen of them and several wagons full of ammunition pulled by gray horses. Now, she knew what *Hanak Tuvar* had been doing in the days since their last encounter.

It had been gathering an army.

"Get to the pyramid," Rojan growled. "Tell Nari it's time. We'll hold out here as long as we can."

28

Miri soared up to the rooftop with a rifle in hand, then double-tapped her belt buckle to let gravity reassert itself. Her aim was slightly off. She had been intending to land near the ledge but had overshot by a few feet. Her legs gave out when she touched down, and she landed on her knees.

Rising slowly, she dusted herself off and grunted at the pain. Sweet Mercy, how did any Field Binder perform such stunts without breaking every bone in their body? Desa made it look so easy.

Rojan stood on the far side of the roof with his feet apart and his back turned, staring out at the enemies that advanced on them. Even from here, Miri could see the crimson ring that surrounded the city. "Still not used to that, huh?"

A grimace contorted Miri's face, and she shook her head in dismay. "Not planning on getting used to it," she said, striding over to join him. "Once this is over, I plan to go back to my simple, Ether-free life."

He offered a small smile. "If you insist," he murmured. "I'm sure you can see that Field Binding has its advantages."

He gestured to the expanse of clay outside the city, and Miri gasped when she saw what was coming their way. An army. A bloody *army!* If she had to guess, she would say there were at least five hundred gray soldiers out there, all marching in orderly ranks. She noted the teams of men wheeling small cannons into place. They moved with precision, as if some vestige of who they had been remained. The soul was gone, but the skills imprinted on the brain through years of training lingered. Or maybe she was just imagining it. Maybe *Hanak Tuvar* was capable of directing an entire army on its own.

She saw the demon looming in the distance. It had grown since their last encounter. Now, it would dwarf most buildings in Ofalla and many in Aladar as well. Those slimy, writhing tentacles propelled the beast forward.

Sweat broke out on Miri's forehead, a thick bead rolling down the bridge of her nose. "Should we attack?" she asked.

"Not yet," Rojan said. "They're not in range."

The front rank of soldiers continued their relentless advance, hoisting up rifles and pointing them at the people on the rooftops. "Steady now!" Rojan called out, his voice amplified by a Sonic-Source. "Nobody panic!"

"Whatever you're gonna do, Desa," Miri whispered. "Make it quick."

Rojan stood tall with his head held high, his face a mask of resolve. "Now!" he called out. "Trigger the outer defenses!"

Out in the field, gray soldiers dropped to their knees, trapped by some unseen force. Lightning flashed over their colourless bodies, scorching flesh and setting clothes on fire. Miri did a quick count and discovered that at least fifty of those creatures had been incapacitated. Maybe more.

She felt the slight tug of the Gravity-Sources that Rojan's Field Binders had Infused into rocks and chunks of clay, but at half a mile away, it was more of a nuisance than anything else, overpowered by the earth's natural pull. Still, she backed away from the ledge. She really hated heights.

"Get down!" Rojan shouted.

Miri didn't need to ask why.

She threw herself down on her belly, hissing as bullets zipped through the air above her. With a string of muttered curses, she crawled back to the ledge. Some of those distant soldiers were struggling to rise, struggling to lift their weapons. But they still managed to fire another volley.

She scanned the enemy forces and noticed teams of men inclining the cannons for a long-range shot. They loaded balls the size of watermelons and then lit the fuses. "Rojan, we have a problem!"

"Force-Sinks!" he bellowed.

The first cannon erupted with an orange flash – strange that the fire should still have colour – and spat a ball that flew over the heads of all those marching soldiers. It descended toward a nearby building, then stopped dead in midair, stilled by three Field Binders who stood on the roof with hands raised in a warding gesture.

Another cannon went off, this one firing at a lower trajectory. The ball sped toward one of the neighbouring buildings and crashed through its back wall, narrowly evading the Force-Sinks, which were limited by directional modifiers.

The three Field Binders atop that building leaped, Gravity-Sinks carrying them into the sky. They drew crescent-shaped pistols and scorched the enemy soldiers with streaks of lighting.

The roar of cannon fire filled Miri's ears.

"Cover me!" she shouted to Rojan.

Getting up on one knee, Miri lifted her rifle and looked through the sight. She settled the crosshairs onto a trio of men, two of whom were adjusting the cannon while the third picked up what must have been a twelve-pound ball. She chose the latter as her target and put him down with a single shot. "Hurry up, Desa!" she whispered. "Please!"

. . .

KILLING HER GRAVITY-SINK, Desa alighted on the pyramid's roof, the enormous crystal towering over her and glittering in the sunlight. She found Nari waiting for her with a look of impatience. "They're here," Desa croaked.

"Obviously," the former goddess replied. "Quickly, there isn't much time. Just like we practiced."

They each pressed a palm against the crystal. It was warm to the touch. Clearing her mind of everything – fear, anger, anticipation – Desa made herself one with the Ether. The world transformed, the pyramid becoming a collection of tightly-knit particles in a roiling sea of billowing particles. Strangely, she could still make out the contours of each individual object. Nari began to glow with pure radiance, a comforting light that blazed like a beacon. *Hanak Tuvar* knew what they were planning, and it had come anyway.

Desa made herself one with the crystal as well, feeling its sturdiness, its stability. This shimmering mass of calcified Ether had been sitting right here for over a hundred centuries, weathering dust storms, scouring winds and the sun's relentless glare. It gave her comfort.

Together with Nari, she manipulated the Ether, softening it, making it malleable, bending it into a shell around *Hanak Tuvar*. The demon screamed, resisting their attempts to Bind it. It thrashed, tentacles flailing, and lashed out with its dark power. The prison shattered before it even formed.

Desa felt crushing despair. How could she defeat a creature like this? What had she been thinking? The melancholy passed, replaced by a renewed resolve, and for an instant, she locked eyes with Nari.

Gathering their will, they began again.

. . .

Miri fell upon her belly, bullets whistling through the air. They had seen her. They knew she was targeting their cannons, preventing them from using the heavy artillery. Or trying to, anyway. A thought occurred to her in the midst of all that chaos.

Wasn't metal supposed to melt in that strange distortion field? Desa had said that *Hanak Tuvar* could prevent it – that it had used street lamps as projectiles – but Miri had assumed it had taken conscious effort to do so. They had never anticipated a fight like this. Surely, the demon wouldn't be able to preserve an army's worth of guns and ammo. Well, they had been wrong.

When she ventured another glance, she saw that the enemy soldiers were trying to stay ahead of the crimson wave. Teams of men wheeled those cannons forward while the others marched toward the city. That seemed to confirm her suspicion. *Hanak Tuvar* had to concentrate to preserve any piece of metal within its distortion field. Maybe that would slow it down.

Rojan was lying prone and gasping, frantically scanning the battlefield. "Second wave of defenses!" His voice boomed in Miri's ears, the Sonic-Source carrying his words to everyone within a mile.

She risked another peek and found the gray soldiers falling, their uniforms igniting as smoke rose from their scorched flesh. Once again, the flames had a natural, orange hue even though they consumed the bodies of men who had been stripped of colour.

One of the wagons got within range of a Heat-Source, and the sacks of gunpowder it carried exploded with a devastating roar, creating a plume of fire that climbed into the air. The blast sent chunks of wood flying.

All that heat! Maybe Miri was imagining it, but she was pretty sure the ambient temperature had gone up a few degrees.

A bullet grazed the ledge of the rooftop, whizzing past her

left ear. She scooted backward to deny her enemies a tempting target. Damn it! She was useless up here! But going down there was suicide.

The building rattled when something pounded it. Most likely a cannonball. A few more shots like that, and the roof would collapse. There had to be something she could do! Something that wouldn't get her killed in less than ten seconds.

Rojan retreated from the ledge, raising a hand to shield himself. Bullets jerked to a halt in front of him, drained of kinetic energy. They fell to land at his feet as he backed up to crouch beside Miri. "We have a new problem."

She arched an eyebrow. "You don't say!"

With a great deal of reluctance, she rose just enough to see over the lip of the roof. That crimson haze had completely surrounded the city, standing two hundred feet tall and slowly closing in on them. A definite problem, but she wouldn't call it a new one. She was about to say as much when she realized that Rojan was talking about something else entirely.

A gray man in a drab uniform floated up to hover over the advancing army, hanging in the air about fifty feet away from the building. Lightning crackled between his fingers. "Die!" he screamed, thrusting his hands out and hurling two jagged bolts of electricity that struck the small house and sent pieces of debris flying.

Discarding her rifle, Miri forced herself to stand.

The flying soldier cackled.

Ignoring good sense, Miri began a furious sprint toward him, double-tapping her belt when she neared the hole in the roof. She leaped and shot toward him like an arrow loosed from a bow.

Coming out of his gleeful reverie, the man noticed her at the last second. His black eyes widened.

Miri slammed into him, and they tumbled through the air, vertigo setting in as she lost the ability to distinguish up from down. It was all she could just to hang on. The man snarled at her.

She pulled a throwing knife from her belt.

He raised a crackling hand.

Miri was faster, jamming the blade into his throat. But not before he landed a kick to the belly that sent her careening to the ground. The Gravity-Sink prevented her from accelerating, but she was already falling at a terrifying speed. Maybe this wasn't such a-

She hit hard, shattering bones on impact, and then bounced off the clay. The next thing she knew, she was racing back into the sky. What? That wasn't supposed to happen! *The Gravity-Sink,* she realized too late.

She double-tapped her belt without thinking and dropped like a stone. Her bones snapped. She was fairly certain that she had broken every one on the left side of her body. And...Her legs. Her legs wouldn't move. A spinal wound? The panic started to well up inside her. One stupid move, and she was paralyzed for the rest of her life? No! Not her! She would rather go out fighting! She would-

The grays were crowding around her, slowly moving in.

It seemed she was about to get her wish. This couldn't get any worse. But what was that she saw? A figure in red streaking through the sky? Miri sighed and whimpered as a flash of pain went through her body.

She had spoken too soon.

AZRA LANDED in the narrow gap between two gray buildings, killing her Gravity-Sink when her booted feet touched the ground. She drew herself up to full height – a woman in a red hood with the hilt of a sword poking over her right shoulder – and flowed out of the alley. One last task and then her work was complete.

She stepped onto a curving street lined with small, stone houses on both sides, very much aware of the sounds all around her. Every scuff of shoes on the pavement, every whisper of wind, every growl of gunfire. The changes that Adele had forced upon her had sharpened her ears among other things.

That was why it was no surprise to her when gray-clad Field Binders emerged from neighbouring alleys. One to her left and one to her right. So predictable. They both had those strange *Al a Nari* pistols.

She spun on the one to her left.

Thrusting out her open hand, she loosed a surge of kinetic energy that hit the poor man square in the chest. He went flying backward down the street, legs kicking, and then fell to the ground.

She rounded on the other man, a tall fellow with golden hair and tanned, olive skin. That one cried out in alarm.

Azra leaped with a pulse of her Gravity-Sink, drawing her sword as she passed over his head. It was an elegant weapon, slightly-curved with a single-edged blade. Twirling it, she turned around to face him.

The man pointed his gun at her.

Azra lifted the sword up in front of herself, the Electric-Sink in its blade dissipating the lightning that he sent her way. With her free hand, she retrieved a little rock dust from her pocket and threw it at him.

She triggered the Light-Sources that she had Infused into every grain, a series of tiny fireworks flashing before his eyes. Blinded by the glare, the man stumbled backward and looked away.

She jumped, kicking him in the chest.

The sudden, ferocious blow knocked the wind out of him, cracking one of his ribs. He wheezed, hunching over and pawing at his body.

Azra spun, her blade whistling through the air in a swift, horizontal arc, slicing right through his neck. His severed head dropped to the ground, the body following a second later.

The second man was half a block away, standing with the lightning gun clutched in one hand, pointing it at her. Such delicious horror in his eyes. The poor fool didn't dare fire when his friend stood in the way – that had been part of Azra's plan – and now, it was too late.

Sauntering toward him with the tip of her blade leaving a furrow in the dirt, Azra smiled within the depths of her hood. "I'm not here for you," she said. "Step aside, and I will spare your life."

The man jumped, triggering a Gravity-Sink and climbing to the rooftops. He pulled a handful of coins from his pouch and let them rain down on Azra.

She jumped, back-flipping with a growl. When she landed, instinct took over, and she retreated further. Circles of frost expanded from the coins, spreading and intersecting with each other, leaving a thin sheet of ice on the road. And it was *cold!* Even with the harsh sun beating down, it felt like a morning in late autumn.

The Field Binder aimed his strange pistol.

Azra leaped to the side seconds before lightning struck the ground where she had been standing. She maneuvered into an alley, taking refuge in the shadows. The element of surprise had given her an edge over that first man. Now, she'd have to be careful.

Triggering her Gravity-Sink, she jumped and rose grace-fully to the rooftops, landing on the nearest building. Her enemy was floating above the road, watching her with wary eyes. "Why?" he asked.

"Why what?"

The man cocked his head, studying Azra for a long moment. "You're trying to kill Desa before she can return

Hanak Tuvar to its prison," he said. "Why? What do you get out of the deal?"

"Amusement."

"Don't you understand? That demon will destroy the world."

"Yes," Azra agreed. "Should be quite a show."

The idiot raised his gun again.

Her sword snapped up, the blade absorbing the stream of electricity before it got anywhere near her. She killed the Sink, ran across the rooftop and leaped from the edge. Once she was airbourne, she triggered the Sink again.

Azra twirled in the air for a kick that hit his jaw with enough force to shatter bone. The poor fool was dazed.

She extended her free hand again, releasing a torrent of kinetic energy. Blown backward with incredible force, the enemy Field Binder soared across the street. He collided with a stone wall and then hung there, kept aloft by his Gravity-Sink. He would float until the Sink gave out.

She turned her attention to the pyramid.

The massive crystal was glowing with a powerful light, as if someone had captured a star within it. Azra could feel a thrumming in the Ether. Somewhere in the distance, *Hanak Tuvar* screamed.

It was time to do what she had come here to do.

DESA WAS LOST in the Ether's caress, riding tidal waves of energy that crashed over her enemy. *Hanak Tuvar* screeched, its tentacles flailing as it struggled against them. The Ether coalesced around the demon, guided by Desa and Nari working in concert, forming a gigantic cocoon.

With the gentlest touch, they trapped the creature inside a new prison, a pocket of reality from which it could not escape. She understood, at last, the brilliance of Nari's plan. They had created a micro-universe around *Hanak Tuvar*, cutting it off from the rest of space and time. Now, all they had to do was force that tiny universe into the void.

It would affix itself to the edge of a larger universe like a boil growing out of healthy tissue. There was no avoiding that. Most likely, it would be Desa's universe as that was closer than any other. *Hanak Tuvar* would be able to whisper in the thoughts of greedy and vicious people, manipulating them into setting it free once again. But if the knowledge of what it was could be preserved, that danger would be contained.

Desa and Nari gathered their will.

The Ether flexed.

The bubble that surrounded *Hanak Tuvar* drifted out of phase with the rest of her universe. It was working! Just a little further! Just a little further! The demon redoubled its efforts to break free, but together, Desa and Nari held it in a tight grip.

PAIN RACED through Miri's body like a fire burning out of control. She couldn't move her left arm or her left leg. She had broken bones in the fall; she knew that. Sweet Mercy, it was so hard to focus! The grays were surrounding her. She had the briefest glimpse of one man lifting a rifle, ready to finish her off.

In a moment of desperation, Miri reached into her coat pocket and closed her hand around the first thing she found. She squeezed hard, the crystal shattering into a thousand tiny fragments that all vanished a second later.

The rainbow spread over her, consuming her from head to toe, colours oscillating in an endless cycle. Lucidity returned to her mind as she drew in a ragged breath. Her bones reknit themselves, and her pain evaporated like dew on a hot, summer morning. Startled by the sudden flash of light, the grays recoiled, backing away from her.

Curling up into a ball, Miri slapped her hands down on the ground and sprang off with core strength. She landed on her feet, flinging her coat open and retrieving another pair of throwing knives. The rainbow slowly faded.

Scanning the enemies that surrounded her, Miri flashed a smile. "Well, come on then," she said. "What are you waiting for?"

The grays surged.

She threw one knife and then the other, glittering metal tumbling through the air. One sank into the shoulder of a bald man with a neat goatee, causing him to drop his rifle. The other stung the arm of a skinny fellow with a scar on his cheek.

A hulking brute came up behind her, trapping Miri in a bear hup.

She squeezed her eyes shut, then flung her head backward, striking his nose with the back of her skull. That momentary distraction earned her a little wiggle room. She elbowed the brute in his belly.

Too many.

She saw dozens of bodies crowding around her, all trying to grab her. If they got their hands on her, they would throw her down and trample her to death. No way out! She was trapped! If only she could go up.

You can, she realized.

With a deft hand, Miri double-tapped her belt and felt a sense of weightlessness settling onto her. She jumped, shooting into the air just in time to avoid a dozen grasping hands. The freedom! She had never wanted to learn Field Binding, but she was beginning to see the appeal.

The ground dropped away beneath her, gray faces staring up in dismay. Her new-found confidence fizzled away when she realized that she had no way to slow down or change direction. And that wasn't the worst of her problems.

Miri looked over her shoulder and gasped when she saw

the red haze creeping over the ground, slowly moving toward the city. It enveloped the cannons at the back of the army, and those melted. *Hanak Tuvar* had no further need of them.

The demon was flickering! At first, she thought there was something wrong with her eyes, but no. It was real. The humongous squid would vanish for half a second only to reappear and then vanish again. What could be causing that?

The crimson wall was nearly upon her.

"Oh no..." she whispered.

Thinking fast, she twisted around in midair and drew her pistol. She pointed it at the oncoming distortion – angled slightly upward – and fired several times. That put her on a downward trajectory, headed back to the city.

Miri turned her body, swooping low over the outer buildings, rushing toward those on the other side of the street. She double-tapped her belt buckle and fell the last few feet, somersaulting over the rooftop.

Gasping for breath, she stood up and looked around. Where was Rojan? She got her answer when she looked into the street below. The Field Binders were fighting an army of grays that had surged into the city. They were going for the pyramid, trying to reach Desa while she was vulnerable. Well, that settled it. There was nothing for Miri to do but join the fight.

DESA HEAVED with every ounce of willpower she could muster, trying to shove *Hanak Tuvar* out of this reality. Every time she gained an inch – so to speak – the beast fought back twice as hard.

It was just too damn powerful!

The cocoon of Ether that held it stretched as *Hanak Tuvar* struggled against its prison. She kept having to reinforce it before the demon ripped through the barrier. Four times now, she had almost lost control.

And she was *so* tired.

Her body was a distant thing, a lump of aches and fatigue at the edge of awareness, but that distance would not help if the exhaustion overwhelmed her. If her physical form collapsed, Desa would lose contact with the Ether. And then it would all be over.

She had to keep fighting.

TOMMY SAT with Kalia on the steps that led up to the pyramid's main entrance. Wrapped in the Ether's embrace, he felt the series of pulses that Desa and Nari created. They were ten times as powerful as those produced by the crystal, each crashing over *Hanak Tuvar* with the force of a hurricane.

The demon writhed under their persistent onslaught. Tommy could sense the shell that surrounded it. He had no other word for it. Somehow, Desa and Nari had wrapped a pocket of the Ether around the towering squid creature.

"Focus," Kalia said, her speech slurred.

Seated beside him with her hands folded in her lap, she blazed like the sun, white light forming a nimbus around her body. That one word was enough to draw Tommy out of his reverie. He had let himself become distracted. They were supposed to be keeping watch on the pyramid, not observing the cosmic battle between Desa and *Hanak Tuvar*. But in his defense, cosmic battles were hard to ignore.

Tommy knew his job, and he knew why it was necessary. He let his mind drift over the pyramid, searching it from one end to the other, and found nothing amiss. He sensed no one on the far side of the building, no one climbing the back wall to sneak up on Desa from behind.

The outer streets on the north side of the city were overflowing with grays. Field Binders struck them down – the Ether surging as they triggered their Infusions – but they just kept coming. Dead men in drab, colourless uniforms, all carrying rifles. The whole place was abuzz with gunfire like the constant thunder of a furious storm that would not let up.

His mind recoiled when he peeked into those streets. He couldn't bear to watch. He didn't know what he would do if he witnessed Miri's death.

Dalen and Jim were taking refuge inside the pyramid. It was the safest place for them. Both had insisted on going out to fight, but Rojan had been firm in his refusal to accept their help, and Tommy agreed with the man's decision. Dalen and Jim had no business going out there. Neither one of them could touch the Ether, and between them, they had only a few weeks of training with a bow. Jim wasn't a terrible shot, but a few extra arrows would not turn the tide of this battle.

Tommy scanned his surroundings again.

The battle raged to the north, but he felt nothing to the east, west and south. Not a soul for miles and miles. Sadly, that did nothing to ease his anxiety. There was no doubt in his mind that *Hanak Tuvar* would try something devious; the demon had demonstrated its ability to improvise on several occasions.

"What...that?" Kalia slurred.

He felt the approach of an active Gravity-Sink an instant before he sensed a human-shaped mass of particles flying through the space between two buildings. A tall woman in a red hood landed in front of the pyramid, twenty feet away from the bottom step.

Tommy let go of the Ether.

As his consciousness snapped back into his body, he felt the dull ache in his back that came from sitting on stone for too long. With a grunt, he stood up and started down the stairs.

Kalia fell in beside him.

Baring his teeth with a growl, Tommy shook his head.

"Should have known it'd be you," he said. "Get out of here, Azra. This isn't a fight you can win."

She paused on the bottom step, reaching up to caress the hilt of a sword that she wore on her back. "I just took down two of your friends, boy," she mocked. "Like a wolf in the sheep pen. It was...mildly diverting."

Kalia stood beside Tommy with one hand on the grip of her holstered pistol, her eyes fixed on the other woman. "You won't get past us," she promised.

Azra began her slow ascent, chuckling maliciously as she lifted a beringed hand and wiggled her fingers. A not-so-subtle reminder that she carried many Infused weapons on her person. Tommy wasn't intimidated. He had just as many waiting in his quiver. "How many times have you tried to stop me, Sheriff?"

"Oh, good!" Kalia spat. "More boasting!"

"How many times have I eluded your grasp?" Azra's face was hidden under that hood, but Tommy could still feel the menace of her smile. "Sometimes, a cat will leave a mouse alive. To toy with it. Up until now, I've been content to do that with you. But you've gone and put yourself in an unenviable position. Desa loves you. And when she feels the life draining out of your body, it might just distract her long enough for *Hanak Tuvar* to break free."

Azra leaped for them.

Stepping forward, Kalia raised her hand and triggered the Force-Source in her ring. Kinetic energy slammed into Azra, throwing her backward, but the woman simply used her change in momentum. She back-flipped, landing further down the stairs.

With a growl, Azra thrust out a closed fist. Lightning erupted from her ring, a jagged lance that tried to scorch Kalia. The former sheriff squeezed her eyes shut, turning her face away as the Electric-Sink in her pendant absorbed the energy.

The lightning winked out.

Tommy seized the opportunity.

Stepping forward, he pulled an arrow from his quiver, nocked it and drew back the string. He let it fly, but Azra dodged with inhuman speed, the shaft zipping past her right ear. "Green!" Tommy shouted, triggering the Gravity-Source. Kalia triggered her Sink. They had worked out a code based on colours to signal what they wanted to do without giving the plan away to the enemy.

Azra was yanked backward, stumbling several steps until she too used a Sink to free herself from the arrow's power. That momentary distraction was all Tommy needed. He loosed another arrow.

This one stopped dead right in front of Azra, stilled by a Force-Sink that she kept under her tunic.

Kalia snarled, drawing her pistol in a blur, stepping forward and pointing it at the other woman. *CRACK! CRACK! CRACK!* Bullets hovered in the air mere inches away from Azra's chest.

Azra screamed, then jumped and soared into the sky. Her hand flew out, and the next thing Tommy knew, glittering coins were raining down on him and Kalia, Each one began to emit heat as they landed on the stone steps.

He and Kalia turned, jumping in different directions, desperately trying to avoid the deadly heat. In seconds, those steps were an oven. He felt burns on his body, the wind's soft caress bringing with it a sharp sting.

Killing his Sink, he landed on the plateau near the pyramid's main entrance. He didn't see where Kalia had gone. Hopefully, she was all right. Desa and Nari were still on the roof. He could feel them manipulating the Ether.

Ignoring him, Azra chose to focus on her primary target. She tossed a coin out behind herself and used a surge of kinetic energy to propel herself toward Desa.

Craning his neck to track her, Tommy narrowed his eyes.

"Oh, no you don't!" He pulled an arrow from his quiver, nocked it and sent it into the sky.

As the shaft streaked past Azra, he triggered a Force-Source that knocked her off course. She screamed as she was thrown sideways on a trajectory that took her toward Tommy.

Rather than letting herself get near him, she chose to kill her Sink and end her flight prematurely. She landed on the plateau, right in front of the tunnel that led down into the pyramid.

Standing up in one smooth motion, she drew her strange sword as she marched toward him. "I should have killed you in New Beloran," she said. "No! I should have done it back in Aladar. You have become a nuisance, boy!"

He dropped the bow. It would do him no good in a close fight.

Azra twirled the sword in one hand, the curved blade catching the sunlight. Her soft laughter sent shivers down Tommy's spine. Even after what Desa had told him, he knew he didn't want to see what was under that hood.

She swung at his neck.

Tommy hopped back, the tip of her blade almost cutting his throat and hitting the wall of the pyramid instead. Enraged, she advanced on him, lifted her sword over her head and brought it down in an overhand swing.

Crouching, Tommy raised his hands as if to catch the blade but triggered the Force-Source in his ring instead. The blast of kinetic energy tore the weapon right out of her grip and sent it tumbling through the air.

Azra shrieked and lunged for him.

Tommy kicked her in the stomach, delivering a blow that made her wheeze and bend double. He stepped forward for a punch, but her hands snapped up to catch his wrist, and then she twisted his arm to an odd angle.

Before he could react, he was being shoved face-first into

the wall. Pain. Terrible pain. His head was swimming. His vision blurred, and then he was lying on his back. How had that happened? He didn't remember falling.

Azra drew her belt knife, dropped to a crouch and then rammed it down through Tommy's chest. "You see?" She pulled the crimson blade out of his flesh, blood dripping from its pointed tip. "Easily defeated."

Azra turned and walked away.

Tommy couldn't breathe. The life was draining out of him, slipping away bit by bit. In a few moments, he would lose consciousness. He had to act before that. Summoning every last scrap of willpower, he slipped his hands into his pocket and closed his fingers around a crystal.

The rainbow welcomed him into its warm embrace, a cocoon of light that covered him from head to toe. He felt his pain fading away, felt lucidity returning to his mind. Azra stopped in her tracks, turning around.

Tommy stood up and greeted her with a cheeky grin. "You were saying?"

DESA COULD FEEL the battle raging nearby. Her protégé and the love of her life locked in a desperate struggle with the most dangerous woman she had ever met. A part of her was screaming to abandon this useless plan and go help her friends before Azra cut them to pieces. But she didn't dare. Not when the fate of the world itself hung in the balance. She and Nari worked together, offering one final push, and *Hanak Tuvar* started to slide out of their reality.

I HATE FLYING! *I hate flying!*

Kalia descended to the pyramid, her limbs flailing as she tried to steady herself. She landed on the plateau just outside the main entrance, grunting and killing the Gravity-Sink in her belt buckle.

Azra stood with her back turned, slowly advancing on Tommy, forcing him to retreat to the very edge of the platform. She had him cornered. Not that it would matter very much. If she knocked him off, he would just make himself weightless.

Drawing her pistol, Kalia moved forward at a steady pace. She tried to keep her footfalls as light as possible to avoid making too much noise. A well-placed bullet would end this here and now. She just had to-

Azra rounded on her.

Enough sunlight penetrated the hood for her to see the other woman's face. Deep, yellow eyes stared back at her. "Hello, Sheriff," Azra purred.

Kalia tried to shove her pistol into the other woman's stomach.

Moving like a striking snake, Azra grabbed her wrist and adjusted her aim to point the gun at nothing at all. *CRACK!* A bullet went speeding harmlessly toward the distant buildings.

With her free hand, Azra punched Kalia in the face. Tears blurred Kalia's vision. Her head felt like a rock that had been struck by a very big hammer. She was barely even aware of the boot that landed in her chest, sending her backward across the plateau. She let herself fall.

And Tommy drew his revolver, pointing it at Azra's back.

Reacting with incredible speed, the hooded woman twisted and stretched a hand toward him, hitting him with a blast of kinetic energy that hurled him off the plateau before he could pull the trigger.

Azra stepped forward, looming over Kalia. Her soft laughter was nothing short of demonic, as if she carried a small piece of *Hanak Tuvar* inside her. Which very well might be the case. She certainly wasn't human anymore.

Kalia used a move Desa had taught her.

She trapped the other woman's leg between both of hers, and with a quick tug, she pulled Azra off her feet. The hooded fiend toppled over, landing on her backside.

Kalia was on top of her in an instant, forcing Azra down onto her back, pinning her. If she could just draw her belt knife. They could end this. Desa would complete her work. The nightmare would finally be over.

A pale hand reached up and seized Kalia's throat. Bony fingers dug into her skin, choking her. Such raw power! Kalia's vision began to darken. A thick fog settled into her mind, making it hard to think. She almost failed to notice the shadowy figure who landed on the plateau.

Tommy.

Azra screamed in frustration. With inhuman strength, she flung Kalia sideways into the wall. Pain shot through her body as her shoulder slammed into the stone.

In a heartbeat, Azra was on her feet and rounding on Tommy. She strode toward him like a predator on the hunt. "Come on, boy!" she snarled. "Do your worst!"

Azra jumped, twirling in the air for a spinning kick.

Tommy ducked, a booted foot passing over his head. He backed away, but Azra landed in front of him. She kicked him in the belly, forcing him to bend double and groan in pain.

Retreating to the edge of the plateau, Tommy pressed a hand to his stomach. His face was red, tears glistening on his cheeks. The poor lad was winded. Who wouldn't be after a hit like that?

Azra knelt to retrieve the pistol that Kalia must have dropped at some point. Funny, she didn't even remember losing it. "I don't even need Field Binding to kill the two of you!" Azra said. "I am stronger! Faster! The gifts Adele gave me overshadow everything she took away. Her power courses through my veins!"

Pulsing her Gravity-Sink, Azra threw herself into a powerful leap that had her coming down on top of Tommy.

Frightened and frantic, the poor kid did the first thing that popped into his mind. He stretched out his hand and triggered the Force-Source in his ring, unleashing a tempest of kinetic energy that hit Azra like a freight train.

"Don't!" Kalia shouted.

But it was too late.

The blast hurled Azra backward and up...up to the very top of the pyramid. Cackling with mad glee, she pointed Kalia's gun out to the side and fired blindly at the crystal. Somewhere up there, a woman screamed.

Azra giggled as she floated away. "And so, the world ends!"

29

Bullets flattened themselves against the enormous crystal, bouncing off without leaving a scratch. Lost within the Ether's embrace, Desa gasped, but it shouldn't have surprised her when the crystal survived. The smaller ones were thin and brittle. This thing was as tall as a watchtower and solid all the way through.

Her few seconds of elation ended when Nari's scream filled her ears. One of those bullets had pierced the other woman's back. Nari fell over, stretched out on the roof of the pyramid in a pool of her own blood.

And the light around her went out.

Half a mile away, *Hanak Tuvar* screamed as it tore through the cocoon that they had used to imprison it. Without Nari's strength, Desa couldn't maintain it. The demon rematerialized, standing four stories high, tentacles writhing as it crept toward the city. Its distortion field swept over the outer buildings.

Desa let go of the Ether.

Kneeling beside her friend, she smoothed a lock of hair off Nari's forehead. The other woman was dying, her every breath a ragged gasp. In a few moments, she would be gone. No. It couldn't end like this.

What to do? Think, Desa!

She searched desperately for all the plans that she had abandoned, for the strategies that Nari had called reckless and untenable. Better to try something – even something that would fail – than to sit here until the demon consumed her.

Memories flitted through her mind, half-formed ideas that coalesced into something unexpected. She was riding Midnight while the red haze closed in on her, *Hanak Tuvar's* meaty tentacle hovering over her, ready to squash her. The distortion swallowed her up, and then she shattered a crystal, unleashing a rainbow.

Other memories bubbled up.

She was standing in a forest of skeletal trees, cringing before a creature with an odious grin that sent shivers down her spine. Heldrid leaned in close to whisper in her ear. "It will try to impose its will upon the world. You must not let it."

Its will.

The distortion field.

"'Within my realm, my power is absolute,'" Desa mumbled. She was back on that rooftop in New Beloran, watching as *Hanak Tuvar* ripped streetlamps out of the ground and sent them hurtling toward her.

She blinked, coming back to reality, and bent to run her fingers through Nari's hair. Retrieving a shard of crystal from her pocket, she pressed it into the other woman's palm. "I'm sorry," Desa said softly. "We tried it your way. Now, we have to go with my plan."

She stood and then turned to face the gigantic crystal, pressing her hand against it with fingers splayed. A thought was all it took to trigger the Force-Source in her ring. She emptied it of every last ounce of kinetic energy.

Cracks spread across the surface of the crystal, hair-thin

fissures from which light spilled forth. They snaked around it in tight circles, rising up to the very peak. The whole thing started to vibrate.

And then it shattered.

Desa threw her head back, waiting for the rainbow to wash over her. But no rainbow came. Not at first, anyway. Just as she was starting to wonder – as confusion set in and her hope began to fade – a single tendril of light struck her in the chest. And she was cast into another world.

ROJAN CHARGED through the gap between two buildings, looking back over his shoulder. Dozens of grays followed him like a pack of ravenous wolves. Most had lost their weapons at some point, though a few still carried rifles or pistols. Even so, they were out of ammunition.

Panting as sweat rolled over his face, Rojan forced his eyes shut. "What's going on up there?" he shouted.

Belan, one of his Field Binders, ventured a glance toward the pyramid and then shook his head. "I don't know!" he replied. "She seems to be trying to destroy the crystal! I have no idea why!"

"What?"

The other man's assessment was confirmed when Rojan stepped onto an open street that gave him a view of the pyramid. Cracks spread over the crystal, each spraying light. But why? Why would Desa do such a thing? It was their only weapon against...

Rojan turned around, no longer troubled by the feral, gray creatures that chased him. Something much worse was on the way. The red distortion field engulfed the outer buildings, consuming the city inch by inch.

So, that was Desa's plan. One last desperate attempt to stay alive for another day. Maybe they could come up with something else. Maybe there was some other option they had not considered. It didn't matter. If you were alive, you could fight another day. If you were dead…Well, that was pretty much the end, wasn't it?

He turned, running for the pyramid, holding his breath as he watched the crystal shatter into a million tiny fragments that all disintegrated. The rainbow would come any second now. A brief reprieve from the demon's onslaught.

But nothing happened.

Rojan's heart sank when he realized that they had come to the end.

WARM SUNLIGHT FELL upon Desa as her eyes fluttered open. She was lying in a grassy field, surrounded by trees that she couldn't name. The sky was clear with only a few thin clouds; the air was sweet with the scent of spring.

She sat up slowly, blinking as she tried to get her bearings. Where was this place? The last thing she remembered, she had been atop the pyramid. The crystal had shattered and then…this.

Her exhaustion was gone, wiped away. She felt as if she had just woken up from a blissful night's sleep. Was this Paradise? Tommy's people had legends about the place where the souls of the virtuous went when they died. Was she dead then?

She had a hard time believing that whatever gods ruled this place would admit her. Not if they knew about her laundry list of sins. So, how could this have happened? And how did she get back to her friends before it was too late?

Desa stood up, brushing a lock of hair out of her face. She looked up to the sky, searching for some sign of whoever – or whatever – had brought her to this place. "All right!" she yelled. "I'm here! Whatever this is about, let's get on with it!"

No one answered.

There was nothing to do but explore this strange place. She picked a direction and started walking. Based on the position of the sun, she deduced that she was heading west. The trees all around her were tall with oddly shaped leaves. Some of them reminded her of those she had seen in the Borathorin. But this was no forest. More like a meadow teeming with vegetation.

She soon came to a rocky hill that she climbed with a few muttered curses. With a thought, she triggered her Gravity-Sink, ordering it to take only a trickle of energy. That made her lighter without completely freeing her from the Earth's pull. It was only then that she realized she had all her accoutrements. Guns, daggers, Infused rings on each hand: she was ready to fight if the need arose.

Halfway up the hill, she noticed a strange whooshing sound that she associated with running water. Her suspicions were confirmed when she reached the top and found a bridge that spanned a river at least half a mile across.

On the other side, a pillar of light rose into the heavens, a rainbow of colours shifting in an endless cycle. Was that what she had come for? The power of the Ether? Why hadn't it surged forth when she shattered the crystal.

"Beautiful, isn't it?"

The sound of a familiar voice made her turn and gasp as a young man emerged from the space between two trees. He was tall and lanky, exceptionally pale with black hair that he wore parted in the middle. The brand on his cheek was gone, but she knew that face. It haunted her in her nightmares.

Stumbling backward onto the bridge, Desa grabbed one of the ropes that held it suspended. "Sebastian!" she gasped. "Is this...Are we dead?"

"One of us is."

Desa narrowed her eyes as she studied him. "Why are you here?" she asked. "Is this another illusion like the one Vengeance created?"

Sebastian chuckled as he trudged up the hill, shaking his head in dismay. "Oh no," he said. "It's really me."

"And I assume you want an explanation."

Cocking his head, the young man raised a thick, dark eyebrow. "Why would I want that?" he muttered. "I should think the reasons behind your decision were fairly obvious. I *did* betray you."

"Yes," she said, nodding. "But I still shouldn't have killed you."

"A bit late for remorse, don't you think?"

"Sebastian, under any other circumstances, I would sit here and endure whatever harsh words you have for me. But my friends are in trouble. *Tommy* is in trouble. If you care for him, please help me."

"That's what I'm here to do!" He gestured across the bridge to the colour-shifting light on the other side. "Everything you need is right there."

"The Ether?"

"It awaits you."

Desa turned to go, starting across the wobbly bridge, holding the ropes so hard her knuckles whitened. She managed only three steps before she felt a rush of air above her and the distinct pulsing of a Gravity-Sink.

Sebastian landed right in front of her and turned around to face her with a mocking smile. "Not so fast!" he chided. "Our business is not concluded!"

"I don't have time-"

He stepped forward, forcing her to retreat. She recoiled from the cold fury in his eyes. It was the merciless stare of a judge who had just sentenced a condemned man to death. "If you want the power," he said, "you must prove yourself worthy of it. Face me in single combat."

. . .

"INTO THE PYRAMID!" Miri screamed.

She scrambled up the steps alongside half a dozen Field Binders who ran as fast as their legs could carry them. Their Infusions were depleted, and now, there was nothing left to do but trap the enemy in a bottleneck and hold out as long as they could.

The grays weren't far behind, flooding into the open field that surrounded the pyramid like a swarm of angry insects. The distortion field tightened its grip on the city, spreading over the buildings, closing in on the centre.

When Miri ventured a glance, she saw *Hanak Tuvar* looming in the distance. The humongous squid bellowed, lifted a tentacle and then slammed it down on a tiny house, crushing it to rubble.

We can't survive this.

Miri stifled the urge to sit down and give up. She would not relent, not for an instant. So long as she could draw breath, there was hope. Even if it was fading fast.

When she reached the plateau outside the pyramid's entrance, she found Tommy and Kalia waiting. The pair of them were battered and bruised. Tommy kept pawing at his chest.

Kalia rubbed a sore shoulder with the opposite hand, hissing air through her teeth. "It's our fault," she panted. "We let her get past us."

Miri paused to lock eyes with the other woman. Any anger she might have felt vanished like fog dissipating under the sun's touch. "No time to worry about that now," she said. "Quickly! Get inside!"

Together, they ran down the sloping tunnel that led to the central chamber. If they could trap the grays in that narrow corridor, they might be able to survive for a few more minutes. A few minutes in which Nari might be able to think of a strategy. Or maybe Tommy could-

No!

Focus on the next task. Always the next task. Get everyone inside, fortify the position, and *then* they could talk strategy. Yes, if they could just hold out for a little while longer, maybe-

Her hopes were dashed the instant she entered the central chamber. A raised floor stood almost ten feet tall, and above it, a round hole in the ceiling let sunlight spill into the room. The crystal was gone, and her plan was useless.

Trapping the grays in a bottleneck would be useless if they could just climb up to the roof and drop down from above. She was low on ammo anyway. And the Field Binders had nothing to offer.

She found Dalen, Jim and Nari sitting on the edge of the raised floor, all looking despondent. She could see it in the way their shoulders slumped, in the way they stared dejectedly at the walls: they were out of ideas.

It was over.

Dropping to her knees, Miri covered her face with both hands. Sobs ripped their way out of her, tears leaking from her eyes. "I tried," she whimpered. "Mama, I tried."

Harsh, guttural voices echoed through the tunnel.

The gray men were coming for her.

DESA STUMBLED BACKWARD, stepping off the bridge and retreating down the hillside. "No," she whispered, shaking her head. "No. There has to be some other way."

Sebastian laughed.

He strode toward her with his arms spread wide, a mocking grin on his face. "What's the matter, Desa?" he shouted. "Afraid to face me in a fair fight?"

He made a fist, pointed it at a nearby tree and triggered the Electric-Source in his ring. Lightning blasted the trunk, sending chunks of wood flying, and flames consumed what was left of it.

Standing on the hilltop, Sebastian placed a hand over his heart and bowed like a circus performer thanking his audience for their applause. "Turns out being dead gives you plenty of time to learn all sorts of useful skills."

"I don't want to fight you!" Desa protested.

Turning slightly, Sebastian gestured to the pillar of light behind him. "Don't you want the power?" he asked. "Don't you want to save your friends?"

"Not like this."

"We can't just *give* the power away, Desa!" he bellowed. "Only someone who is worthy can wield it. A test was prepared for you, a challenge that was tailor-made for a woman of your temperament. You're a warrior, aren't you? Face your enemy, and take the power! Or watch your friends die!"

Yes. Desa understood. This wasn't about proving her skills in combat. This was about demonstrating that she had the strength to make the hard choices. That she could live with the guilt if it meant saving the world. Her path was clear.

She reached for her pistol, but something made her hesitate. Sebastian wasn't a demon or a monster or a killer. He was a youth who had been denied the chance to make amends for his mistakes. From the moment he started speaking, he had been taught to hate himself. All because he was the sort of boy who fell in love with other boys.

Desa remembered the vision Mercy had shown her, the man Sebastian could have been – a kind soul who dedicated his life to helping others like him. *She* had robbed him of that chance by acting in haste. "No," she croaked. "No, I won't hurt you again!"

"It's the only way to save your friends!"

Desa started up the hill.

Tears streamed over her face, but she held his gaze, refusing to look away. "Does it have to be?" she asked. "Can't you just step aside? Haven't we inflicted enough pain for one lifetime? What good will come from inflicting more?"

Sebastian hung his head, exhaling roughly. When he looked up, the anger was gone from his eyes. "Congratulations, Desa," he said. "You passed the test. The Ether accepts you."

"Sebastian," she whispered. "I'm sorry."

He threw his arms around her, and she returned the embrace, holding him as he trembled. "It's all right," he murmured. "It's all right. I forgive you."

Desa pulled back, resting her hands on his shoulders, and looked up into his eyes. She nodded slowly. "Thank you."

"Go," he urged. "Save Tommy."

CLUTCHING HIS STOMACH, Tommy sat down with his back against the side of the raised floor. He shut his eyes, resting his head against the stone. "Well," he muttered. "At least, I won't die alone."

No. Never alone. That voice whispering in his mind. Something about it sounded familiar. Why, if he didn't know better, he would swear that it was...

"Sebastian?"

It's me.

Trembling in fear, Tommy drew in a rasping breath. He hunched over, hugging himself. "You're with me?" he whispered. "You're with me at the end?"

I'm with you. But I'm not the one who's going to save you.

"I don't understand."

Look up, Tommy. Look up.

He did so, peering through the huge hole in the ceiling. He saw nothing but blue sky. And the red haze was closing in. It formed an ever-shrinking cylinder around the pyramid. The distortion field came through the walls, frightening the people who gathered in the middle of the room.

And then, in a burst of glory, a figure appeared, floating a hundred feet above the hole. A tiny woman wrapped in a nimbus of rainbow light, the colours changing in a cycle.

Desa.

She was back.

The light intensified, growing brighter and brighter until Desa was submerged in a pure, white glow. She became a new star in the sky, her radiance dwarfing that of the sun. And somehow, Tommy's eyes didn't hurt when he looked at her.

Despite his terror, he felt a smile coming on. "Well, I'll be..."

THE DISTORTION FIELD raged around Desa, twisting the very laws of nature to create an environment where *Hanak Tuvar* could survive. An environment where human life would wither and die. She wasn't afraid. Not after everything that she had experienced. Within her, she carried the power of creation itself.

She was one with the Ether.

Rising up on thick, black tentacles, *Hanak Tuvar* thrust its hideous face toward her. Its gaping mouth emitting a devastating scream, teeth eager to rend her flesh. The force of its roar hit her like a furious wind.

Desa smiled.

This creature couldn't begin to comprehend what she had become. At long last, she understood. She would not defeat the demon by overpowering it. Brute force was never the answer.

The crystal was not just a mass of calcified Ether. Nari had spent centuries building it bit by bit, imprinting her very soul upon it. Desa carried the mantle of Mercy herself, and with it, she would heal the wounds inflicted on this world.

She let herself fall like a meteor dropping out of the sky,

landing gracefully atop the pyramid. And then she slammed her fist down on the stone.

The light expanded from her in a ring that stretched into the heavens. A rainbow of oscillating colours. It flowed over *Hanak Tuvar,* causing the beast to recoil in fear, and then swept across the desert. When it passed, the distortion vanished, leaving a healthy world in full colour. Gray soldiers puffed away under the rainbow's touch, their bodies collapsing to clouds of fog that dissipated in seconds.

Naked, exposed to the Earth in its natural state, *Hanak Tuvar* screeched as its body began to disintegrate. Smoke rose from its sizzling tentacles. Dark flesh streamed off its body in rivulets. Writhing in pain, the demon let its girth fall to the ground with a mighty crash. "You never should have come here," Desa said.

She floated up to the thrashing squid, still cloaked in a thin halo of rainbow light. "You should have gone back to your void," she went on. "You should have stayed there, content to coexist with us."

The beast opened its mouth, sharp teeth flaking away to ash. It let out a pitiful whimper of pain.

Crossing her arms as she hovered in the air, Desa frowned at the revolting creature. "Instead, you wanted to destroy us," she grated. "Now, witness the consequences of your hubris!"

Hanak Tuvar began making a new distortion field, a haze of redness that enveloped its body. "No," Desa said, dispelling the wrongness with a wave of her hand. Another rainbow streamed over the demon, returning the laws of nature to their proper state. "This world is not yours."

The monster strained, trying to lift its body, but its tentacles evaporated in trails of smoke. Its bulbous head crumbled into a cloud of black ash, slowly expanding until a strong wind blew it away.

At long last, *Hanak Tuvar* was gone.

Desa eased herself down, grunting when her feet touched the ground. The last of her light faded away. "Thank you," she whispered to the Ether. The one friend who had always been there for her.

THE RAINBOW EXPANDED IN A RING, surging over the desert and further beyond that, rushing across the face of the continent. It passed over the great plains, where the grass had died, choked by *Hanak Tuvar's* red haze. When it was gone, the plants were still dead, but the land had been restored to health. In time, things would grow there again.

The rainbow passed through Ofalla, rippling through every house, every shop, every garden. Those it touched felt their pains drifting away. An old man flexed his fingers after years of living with arthritis. A woman with a bad knee managed to stand on her own for the first time in weeks.

Onward, the rainbow went, flowing over the land. Eastward to the ruins of New Beloran, where it cleansed the taint that *Hanak Tuvar* had left behind. The city had fallen, its majesty destroyed. But humans were industrious creatures. They could rebuild.

The people of Aladar rejoiced when the rainbow found them. They knew it for what it was, the power of the Ether. It did not change them, did not force them to see the world in a new light – the Ether would not impose its will on anyone – but somehow, just knowing that such a thing was possible gave many of them a new outlook. The world was a brighter place, the future a promise worth believing in.

Scowling through her office window, Daresina Nin Drialla gasped when the wave of light welcomed her into its warm embrace. That dull ache in her back disappeared. She had been living with it so long that she had almost forgotten it was there. Sadly, the absence of pain did little to improve her disposition. She returned to her quiet brooding, dreaming of the day when her people would conquer the mainland with Infused weapons.

And still, the glowing ring expanded. Across the Eradian continent and into the ocean. Over the length of Ithanar. Trees within the Borathorin forest swayed under its gentle caress. The jagged crystal atop the Temple of Vengeance vanished, adding its strength to the wave.

The ring swept over both poles and then began to shrink, converging at the antipode of Mercy's Temple, a point in the middle of the Dramiel Ocean. Its power dissipated, at last, leaving behind a better world.

30

Kalia ran out of the pyramid, raising a hand to shield her eyes from the light. "Desa?" She let her arm fall, taking in the sight. A beautiful world waited for her. As beautiful as any desert could be. The blue sky stretched from horizon to horizon with only a few clouds drifting past overhead. Some of the homes on the north side of the city had been damaged, but the others were still intact. But most important of all: there was no sign of *Hanak Tuvar.* "Desa?"

Her love stood on the field of clay outside the pyramid, staring off into the distance. Panic welled up inside of Kalia. Was Desa all right?

Before she knew it, she was running down the stairs, taking them two at a time. She reached the bottom step and sprinted across the hard-packed clay.

Desa turned around, and for one desperate moment, Kalia wondered if her partner was aware of what had transpired here. She seemed to be lost in some private reverie. Like a soldier who had been shocked by the fury of battle. It lasted only heartbeats. And then a smile broke out on Desa's face. Just like that, she was herself again. "It's over," she whispered. "Sweet Mercy, it's over!"

"It's over?"

Taking Kalia by the shoulders, Desa pulled her close for a kiss on the lips. "Yes, my love!" The touched noses, foreheads pressed together. "It's over."

Emotions swirled within Kalia: relief mixed with hope and love as strong as mountains. She found herself laughing as hot tears streamed over her cheeks. Their long nightmare was finally over!

The others emerged from the pyramid: Miri and Tommy, Dalen and Jim, Nari, Rojan and the rest of his Field Binders. Each paused to feel the warm sunlight, to breathe the sweet air. Kalia didn't mind the wait. Anything that gave her a few moments alone with Desa was all right with her.

At last, they joined her, nearly two dozen people standing in a tight cluster, waiting patiently for some indication of what they ought to do next. Kalia was willing to bet that most of them had not planned on surviving this ordeal. "So," Rojan said after a stretched-out silence. "What do we do now?"

"We live," Desa replied.

"I suppose we should be heading home," Rojan muttered. He turned around, gazing southward over the top of the pyramid. "The Council will want to know what happened to us."

Desa stood with one hand on her hip, appraising him with a critical eye. Finally, she nodded. "You could do that," she agreed. "Or you could send a letter and ask them for permission to stay here."

Rojan rounded on her, his brow furrowing at the suggestion. "To stay here?" he spluttered. "In this land where my people are hated and feared?"

"Nari wanted to turn this place into a school," Desa said. "I think it's a grand idea, but if we're going to do it, we'll need as many Field Binders as we can get."

"A school in the desert," Tommy muttered, scratching at his beard. "No offense, Miss Nari, but you chose a rather terrible location."

She stepped up beside him, patting him on the shoulder. Her laughter was like the tinkling of bells. "This place wasn't always a desert," Nari explained. "Perhaps, in time, it will bloom again."

Kalia folded her arms and sniffed as she shot a glare at Tommy. "Besides," she added. "*Some* of us have been living in this desert all our lives. And we get along just fine. I keep telling you that."

"Come on," Desa said. "We have work to do."

"Work?" Miri inquired.

"A few more loose ends to tie up."

She led them into the city, back to the curving streets lined with small, gray houses. The bright sunlight brought with it a dry heat that left Kalia feeling rather uncomfortable. She was grateful for the fat cloud that drifted past. Even if it did bring only a few minutes of shade.

Slowly, they made their way down one of the inner roads, following its circular path to the west side of the city. There, Desa turned down one of the connecting streets, heading for the outer buildings.

Kalia was beginning to wonder where her love was taking them. What task would require some twenty-odd Field Binders, plus Miri, Jim and Dalen? She didn't mind, however; she was more than content to just enjoy the quiet conversation. Tommy was quite exuberant about the prospect of teaching at Desa's new school.

After half an hour of walking, Desa gestured to a narrow alley between two small buildings. And there, they found a woman in a bright, red hood lying on the ground. Azra groaned when she heard their approach. "It's you."

Desa stood at the mouth of the alley, nodding slowly. "It's

us," she replied. "Get up, Azra. I won't have you wasting away in the dirt."

The other woman grunted, refusing to obey. She was content to just lie there until a sharp glance from Desa persuaded her to change her mind. With a great deal of cursing, Azra stood up on shaky legs and braced one hand against the wall.

"Take off the hood," Desa said.

"Jump into the Abyss!"

"Azra, this is no time for one of your tantrums."

A growl rumbled in Azra's throat. She reached over her shoulder, searching for the hilt of a sword, and found only an empty scabbard. Deflated, she sighed and pulled back the hood.

Kalia gasped.

The snake-like features were gone. Azra was once again a beautiful woman with large, brown eyes and thick curls framing her round face. She seemed to have only just noticed the change herself, pawing at her mouth, nose and ears. "But..."

"No more super strength," Desa said. "No more inhuman reflexes. You are once again an ordinary woman."

"I don't need them!" Azra spat.

She made a fist and thrust it toward Desa. Nothing happened. Whatever Infusions she had placed within her rings didn't work. Flustered, Azra retreated into the alley and thrust her fist out again. "What?"

Triggering her Gravity-Sink, Desa jumped and then killed it just long enough to halt her upward momentum. She hovered a few feet above the ground. "I had a little chat with the Ether," she explained. "We both agree that you've been abusing your powers for too long. Congratulations, Azra. You are now the only person on this planet who cannot Field Bind."

"No!" Azra whimpered. "No!"

Crossing her arms, Desa lifted her chin as she studied the

other woman. "Perhaps those powers will be restored to you one day," she said. "If you prove yourself worthy of them. Until then, you can repay your debt to society."

"I know a jail cell that is just waiting to make your acquaintance," Kalia growled.

Desa alighted on the ground, sighing softly as she peered into the alley. "Come," she said. "I won't allow you to starve while you're in my care. You'll have a good meal and a good night's sleep – under guard, of course. We'll set out for Dry Gulch tomorrow morning."

"NOOOO!" Azra wailed.

Stepping up beside Desa, Rojan nodded with approval. "That's one loose end tied up," he said. "What about the others?"

"Those will take a little longer."

They were halfway back to the pyramid when Kalia noticed the ceiling of clouds that had formed while they had been dealing with Azra. So many! She had lived in the desert all her life, and while overcast days weren't unheard of, they *were* rare. Five minutes later, those clouds let loose with a sudden downpour.

Rain pelted Rojan, drenching his hair and splashing his face. He spat a little water out of his mouth and then turned his gaze upon Desa. "You want to tell me what's going on here?"

"Well," she said, blushing. "I may have requested a few other small changes."

THE CRIMSON SUN hovered over the horizon, leaving the sky a deep, twilight blue. The air was warm and muggy with the lingering heat of late summer. After a long day of riding, Desa was ready for sleep. Sadly, that wasn't an option.

She sat atop her white mare, lightly patting the animal's neck. Starlight wasn't as vocal as her predecessor, but Desa could tell when she was feeling skittish. The poor girl didn't like this place, and who could blame her?

Desa sighed.

Thinking of Midnight felt like being punched in the gut. She suspected that her grief would be with her for a very long time. Her noble steed had guided the other horses to safety during *Hanak Tuvar's* attack on the pyramid, leading them out of the city before it was surrounded by the distortion field.

Most of the herd had narrowly escaped, but Midnight had lingered behind so that the slowest among them would not be abandoned. He didn't make it. Desa had felt his passing while she was connected to the Ether. If not for her desperate struggle against the demon, she would have broken down and sobbed.

The Ether's rainbow wave had calmed the other horses, urging them to come back to the city. She suspected that it might have expanded their minds as well. Not as much as Midnight's had but enough to let them form a special bond with their riders.

Starlight had been the one to carry Tommy through Ander's Woods. The young man now sat beside her on a dappled gray that he had named Hank of all things. Hank! Well, it was the sort of name Tommy would think of.

On her left, Kalia waited atop her golden palomino. Sunset nickered, backing up instinctively. None of the horses wanted to be here. They knew that a predator lurked in this place.

"No more stalling," Desa said. "Let's get this done."

Another forest stood before them, ancient trees standing tall with leaves fluttering in the evening breeze. She saw no pathway through the thicket, but then she really wasn't expecting one.

"It's time!" Desa shouted.

Green eyes appeared between two of those twisted trees, staring out at her from the darkness. She held that unearthly gaze, refusing to blink or look away. At long last, the eyes darkened, receding into the forest.

A moment later, Heldrid emerged from the thicket, perhaps a hundred feet to her left. She had never figured out exactly what was going on here. Was Heldrid the man-bat, or did it serve him in some way?

He stepped into the light of Kalia's glowing ring, cocking his head and greeting them with that hideous, unwavering grin. "Curious," he murmured. "I'm quite certain that I warned you about disturbing me again. Time for what, Desa Kincaid?"

"Time for you to go back to your own world," she said coldly. "This one is under my protection."

"Is that so?"

Starlight danced backward as the creature drew near, but that was all right. A gentle pat stilled her. "I would be more than happy to let you stay," Desa said. "But the legends say that those who cross the Halitha to Ithanar never return. And I suspect that you are the root of many of those tales. I can't have you killing innocent people. Or doing whatever it is you do to them."

"Mmm," Heldrid said. "Very noble of you."

"I don't want a fight, Heldrid."

He slithered up to them, undulating as he inspected their horses. That rictus smile sent shivers down Desa's spine. "Do forgive my bluntness," he purred. "But I think I can handle three Field Binders."

Resting a hand on the grip of her pistol, Desa set her jaw as she studied him. "We are but the first of many," she assured him. "It's a new day, Heldrid. Humanity will flourish on this world. And we have grown weary of outsiders preying on us."

He chuckled, covering his mouth with one hand. "Perhaps." And then, of all things, he bowed to her. "Until we meet again, Desa Kincaid."

He faded away, growing more and more transparent until

he was gone. The forest went with him, leaving a clear, unobstructed path across the grasslands of the Halitha. She hadn't expected such a drastic change.

Kalia let out a breath that she had been holding for some time, blinking several times in confusion. "So, what does that mean?"

"I think it means we won," Tommy mumbled. "Right?"

"Don't jinx it," Desa said.

Rain pattered against the window as Daresina Nin Drialla stepped into her office. She was about to reach for the light switch, but the door slammed shut behind her, and she nearly leaped out of her skin.

"Don't scream," someone said.

Daresina stumbled into the middle of the dark room, one hand over her heart as she tried to catch her breath. "Who are you?" she demanded, scanning her surroundings for shifting shadows. Her eyes weren't what they used to be, but the huge window looked out on a street lined with electric lamps. Maybe she would catch something.

A sudden light appeared in the corner, a glowing ring in the palm of a young man with a thick, golden beard. Daresina thought she recognized him. Yes...Wasn't he one of Desa's companions? A mainlander boy who had come to the city last year.

Just as she was starting to put a name to that face, another light appeared, this one emanating in from a coin. Its bearer was a short woman with tilted eyes and long, brown hair. Two of them? How could they have gotten past the guards?

A third light revealed the face of a matronly woman with dark skin and curly hair. That one was unfamiliar to Daresina, though she bore a striking resemblance to the statues of Mercy outside the Hall of the Synod.

The final light came from a woman who sat upon Daresina's desk, a tiny woman in tan pants and a leather coat. Her olive-skinned face was framed by a bob of short, brown hair. And her eyes! Daresina could not endure the condemnation she saw in those eyes.

Any question she had about how these people had managed to slip into her office vanished. She should have expected nothing less! After all this time, Desa Nin Leean had come back to Aladar.

The four Light-Sources provided ample illumination, allowing Miri Nin Valia to walk out of the shadows. The young librarian was with her – Daresina could not recall his name – and someone else as well. Another foreign boy.

"Hello, Prelate," Desa said softly.

Taking control of herself, Daresina claimed the chair in front of her desk. If these people wanted to kill her, they would have done so already. She crossed one leg over the other, placed her hands on the armrests and faced Desa with as much dignity as she could summon. "So, you've finally come back."

"Just a short visit," Desa promised. "I have a message for you, and I wanted to deliver it myself."

Daresina sniffed. "What message?"

Desa stood up, playfully tossing a coin that glowed like a firefly. "Just this," she said. "We know that you've been planning an assault on the mainland, that you wanted the Spear of Vengeance for that purpose."

So, they had figured it out. Well, that was to be expected. Daresina had concluded that something must have gone wrong when Marcus failed to report back to her. She had thought – had hoped – that all of them might have died in Ithanar. That certainly would have made things easier.

Desa planted herself in front of the chair, leaning forward until she was nose to nose with Daresina. "We strongly urge you to reconsider."

"And if I don't?"

"Well, then you'll find yourself in a most unenviable position," Desa replied. "You see, our cousins are coming north from Ithanar. They've negotiated a treaty with the Eradian Parliament. In exchange for a lasting peace, they will share the secrets of Field Binding and other technologies they have developed."

Daresina went pale, sweat breaking out on her forehead. Her mouth worked silently for a moment before she found the words. "You can't!" she panted. "The mainlanders will use the knowledge that you share with them to make weapons."

"You mean they'll do what you were planning to do?"

"Desa, please!" Daresina whimpered. "The mainlanders are savage and vicious. If you teach them the secrets of the Great Art, they *will* abuse that knowledge."

Turning on her heel, Desa marched back to the desk. She stood there with her hands clasped behind her back, staring out the window. "I'm sure they will," she said at last. "Which is why we've founded the Order of Mercy, a group of Field Binders from all nations, dedicated to preserving the knowledge and ensuring that it is not abused If any government decides it wants to use its new-found power for warfare, we'll be there to stop them."

She turned, looking over her shoulder with a sly smile. "The *Al a Nari* will be sending an envoy to visit you, Prelate," she said. "I suggest you welcome them. Our people could learn a lot from them."

With nothing more than a simple nod, she had her six companions walking to the door. "Oh, and one more thing," Desa said on her way out of the room. "Tell your people that anyone who wants to learn can come to Bekala. We'll teach them more than just Field Binding."

EPILOGUE

A golden sun peeked over the horizon, smiling on a world that rose to face a new day. A single ray of light rushed over green fields under the clear, summer sky. Past the trees of Ander's Woods, where a small party of deer hunters shared breakfast over the remnants of their campfire.

Onward, the light went, swooping over the grasslands, past trees that sprouted here and there. It passed over a small village where farmers shuffled out of their small homes to inspect their fields. A group of washwomen was already carrying wicker baskets to a nearby stream. They turned their eyes westward, watching the light as it passed.

They had heard the legends about a new city in what had once been a sun-scorched desert. They had even met some of the strangers who came through town several times each year, trading their magical devices in exchange for a little extra food. Men and women who called themselves Field Binders. They promised to teach the secrets of their art to anyone who wanted to learn. "Come to Bekala," they said. "And we will show you."

One of those washwomen – a girl named Daisy who wore her brown hair in a bonnet – lingered a few moments longer, dreaming of what might be. Would she ever make the journey? Would she see Bekala with her own eyes?

The light flew by, streaking over vast fields where the tall grass swayed, over the gentle curve of a newly-formed river that flowed southward, passing through Pikeman's Gorge on its way to the Emerald Sea.

It continued past a series of windmills with blades turning lazily in the wind, each transmitting its power through a new device called a Double-Binding. Small flowers grew around them, white petals bursting from a yellow centre. If young Daisy could see them, she might consider it a good sign. It might even be the nudge she needed to take a chance and set out westward.

The light came to a city with buildings of wood and stone forming concentric rings around a pyramid. Small vehicles rumbled along the circular roads, powered by Electric-Sources that were replenished by the glittering crystal atop the new Academy.

It wasn't as large as its predecessor – not yet, anyway – but many Field Binders had laboured on it over the years. In time, it would be able to renew Infusions throughout the city. On the south side of town, construction workers used a vehicle with a large scoop to dig up dirt. With any luck, they will have expanded the network of pipes by summer's end. The urban planners had proposed a new block of homes that they hoped to finish next spring.

Finally, the light passed through a small window and landed on the cheek of Desa Kincaid. She was seven years older, a few strands of gray showing in her short, brown hair, a few wrinkles having formed around her eyes.

She turned around as Kalia came into their living room, carrying Brendan in her arms and gently bouncing him to soothe his whimpers. The baby's face was red, his thin, black hair a mess. "He's fussy this morning," Kalia said.

"Well, he wants his mama," Desa said, offering to take the child. Sure enough, he settled down the instant she picked him up, closing his eyes and resting his head on her shoulder.

"Oh, but his mum isn't good enough?" Kalia protested.

"Of course, you are."

Sighing, Kalia turned around and shuffled into the kitchen. "Suppose it's for the best," she said with a shrug. "I'm supposed to meet with Tommy this morning."

"Oh, they're back?"

Five months ago, Tommy, Jim, Miri and Dalen had left to visit the new Eradian capital in the hopes of opening up a dialogue, developing goodwill that may lead to an eventual treaty. It was the latest of their many adventures. Those four went everywhere together. "They just got in last night," Kalia said from the other room. "I got the message over the Double-Sonic. You were asleep."

Desa stepped into the kitchen to find her love standing over the stove and using a Heat-Source plate to boil a kettle of water. "The two of you are brilliant, you know that?"

Kalia looked over her shoulder, a shy smile blossoming on her face. "Come on," she said. "Everyone knows you're the Field Binding genius."

"The Double-Bindings weren't *my* invention."

Tommy and Kalia had discovered the secret in those first few months when they were still trying to make the city self-sufficient. Sinks and Sources of the same type could be paired, one transferring energy to the other. Since they were always in balance, they never had to be renewed.

The windmills fed their energy to Electric-Sinks that transferred it to Sources in the city's power grid. The electricity flowed perfectly without the need for underground cables. Distance was no issue. Conjoined Infusions could be taken to opposites sides of the planet, and they would transfer energy without any attenuation.

Field Binders used Double-Sonics to communicate over long distances. When Tommy spoke into his Sink, his voice came through the Source that sat on Desa's shelf. It was a remarkable discovery!

Little Brendan was snoring softly.

Desa kissed his forehead. "You going to sleep?" she asked, rocking him. "Hmm? Mama needs to teach a class this morning."

"Zaela should be here in half an hour," Kalia said, cracking an egg that she dropped into a frying pan. She grabbed a wooden spoon from the counter and began scrambling it. "She'll watch him until you get back."

"Or I could just call the school," Desa muttered. "And tell them that the baby needs me."

Kalia spun around, pointing the spoon at her. "No!" she barked, shaking her head. "You've already canceled class *three times* this month. You can't keep doing this, my love. The kids will start to complain."

Tilting her head back, Desa winced at the thought of what her students might do when she permitted them to activate their Infusions. "But it's precision flight!" she protested. "They're going to crash into the walls!"

"Well, it's your job to make sure they don't."

"Why is it that every time we start a new term, I'm the one who gets assigned to teach Advanced Gravity Manipulation?"

Leaning against the counter with her arms folded, Kalia grinned and chuckled. "Because you're so good at it."

"Oh, very well!"

Zaela was more than punctual, arriving fifteen minutes early. That gave Desa some extra time; so, she decided to walk with Kalia on her way to meet with Tommy. It was roughly the direction she had to go anyway.

The streets were busy this morning. She saw shopkeepers opening for business and electric cars rolling down the road with a slight humming sound. Many of the city's residents had adopted *Al a Nari* fashions, particularly their fondness for bright colours. Most of the women wore orange or yellow – light dresses with short sleeves or tan pants with loose-fitting shirts. The men were a little more subdued, opting for blues or forest green.

They followed the circular street for about ten minutes before they found Tommy waiting on a corner. He had changed so much from the young man that Desa had rescued all those years ago. He was still tall but not quite as lanky, his body and face having filled out. And he had shaved off most of the beard, opting instead for a neatly-trimmed goatee.

The instant he saw her, his face lit up with a grin. "Hello!" he shouted, running over to join Desa and Kalia on the opposite corner. "I didn't think I would see you until later today!"

Desa hugged him so hard he squeaked.

She pulled back with her hands on his arms, smiling up at him. "Look at you!" she exclaimed. "You grew up!"

A flush painted his face red. Just like that, he was the Tommy that she remembered. "I'd have thought you might have noticed before now."

"How can I when you're never here?"

Kalia gestured to a neighbouring road that led to the city's interior, and together, they made their way toward the pyramid. The crystal was glittering in the early-morning sunlight. After six years of Field Binders labouring on it for days on end, it was bigger than a house. She could feel its faint pulses in the back of her mind. Those extended almost to the edge of the city.

"So, how are the negotiations going?" Kalia asked.

Tommy slapped a hand over his face, groaning into his palm. "Don't ask." He pulled that hand down, blinking. "The new Eradian Parliament has agreed to send an envoy, but they're still scared of our magic."

Pursing her lips, Desa stared straight ahead, different

scenarios running through her head. If the Eradians decided to attack, it could be disastrous. Bekala would be forced to defend itself, and that would only serve to convince the Eradians that Field Binders were a danger they couldn't tolerate. "We should have expected as much."

"I don't want to talk about that," Tommy said. "I just heard last night that two of my dearest friends have a brand-new baby boy."

"His mother came to us a year ago," Kalia explained. "Fleeing an abusive husband. We gave her a home in the city, but she was not well. She...She took her own life a few months ago. Brendan had nowhere to go."

"So, we took him in," Desa added.

Tommy shrugged as he walked along the sidewalk, grinning down at his own feet. "Well," he said. "He couldn't ask for better parents."

"Thank you," Desa said, patting his arm.

When she arrived at the Academy, she found a group of young students out front, all sitting crosslegged in the grass. Nari stood over them with a glowing coin in her hand. She was teaching them the basic Infusions for Light-Sources.

She met Desa'a eyes and then smiled, offering a curt nod of respect. "Glad you made it," she said. "Your students are eager for their next lesson."

Crossing her arms, Desa shut her eyes and drew in a deep breath. "They're going to crash into the wall again, aren't they?" She sighed. "I'll make sure that I have a few spare crystals on hand."

The pyramid had changed so much from the tomb it had been when Desa first came here eight years ago. The city had constructed a dozen smaller buildings in the field surrounding the main structure. Within them, the students took lessons on mathematics, science, literature and any number of useful subjects.

Climbing the steps at a brisk pace, Desa paused when she noticed a young man kneeling outside the pyramid's main entrance. He was trying to meditate, but she could tell by his stiff posture that he wasn't having much success.

"No luck, Victor?"

He opened his eyes and answered her with a smile. "Not yet," he lamented. "Still haven't found the Ether."

"You'll get there," Desa assured him. "Just give it some time."

Victor fished a slip of paper out of his pocket, offering it to her. When she unfolded it, she found a beautiful pencil sketch of Zoe. The young woman had such a sweet smile. It was easy to see why Victor had fancied her. "Dalen made it for me," he explained. "Did you know he could draw?"

"Actually, I did."

She returned the paper to Victor and left him to resume his studies. Just as she was entering the tunnel that led down to the pyramid's central chamber, he called out to her. "Um, Desa?"

She paused with one hand on the wall, glancing back over her shoulder. "What is it, Victor?"

He blushed, closing his eyes as he tried to work up the courage to say something difficult. "I wanted to thank you for vouching for me," he began. "For convincing the Academy to take me in."

"We all deserve a second chance," Desa murmured. "I know that better than anyone."

She left him and began her trek through the tunnel. If her recent experience was any guide, she would find several of her students waiting for her beneath the crystal, afraid to trigger their Gravity-Sinks without her direct supervision. Glowing bricks in the wall provided ample light. The place was almost cheery. Not at all like what she had experienced on her first visit.

"He seems to be coming along," Sebastian said, suddenly

appearing at her side. He bit his lip, thinking it over, and then nodded his approval. "You'll make a Field Binder out of him yet."

"Of that, I have no doubt," Desa replied. "How are you?"

Pausing halfway through the tunnel, Sebastian turned to face her, and his smile warmed her heart. "Wonderful," he said. "I'm wonderful. I can't tell you what to expect when you get here – there are rules – but let's just say I'm looking forward to being reunited with all of you."

He cut off at the sound of a grumbling Miri who stomped through the narrow corridor with a piece of paper in her hand. She looked up and grimaced when she saw Desa. "Basic self-defense," she said. "They want me to teach basic self-defense. I'm not back in the city for twelve hours, and they're already trying to put me to work."

Desa leaned against the wall, tossing her head back to smile up at the ceiling. "They have me teaching gravity manipula-tion," she said. "So, what can I say? I guess they know talent when they see it."

Miri heaved out an exaggerated sigh and walked right through Sebastian on her way to the exit. She shivered and then halted in mid-step. "Wait. Who were you talking to a moment ago?"

"No one," Desa said. "Sometimes, I just speak my thoughts aloud."

Turning abruptly, Miri frowned at her for a very long moment. She shook her head slowly. "You sure all this teaching isn't wearing you out?" she asked. "Maybe you need a vacation."

"That's what I've been telling everyone," Desa said. "And nobody listens."

"Well, you've convinced me," Miri grumbled. "Take a day off, would you?"

When she was gone, Sebastian cleared his throat and then stepped forward with his eyes downcast. "I suppose I shouldn't just drop by like this," he said. "I don't want them to start thinking you're..."

"Crazy?" Desa asked, quirking an eyebrow. "People have been saying that about me for decades. I'm not going to start fretting about it now. Though I *do* wonder why I'm the only one who can see you."

"Nari can see me," Sebastian insisted. "At least, I think she can. She's just kind enough not to make a fuss about it. You carried the mantle of Mercy, Desa. Even if only for a little while. Are you really surprised that it expanded your mind?"

"No," she said through a burst of laughter. "I suppose not. Come, walk me to class. You can share all sorts of criticisms of me, and I won't be able to say a thing."

THE END OF THE DESA KINCAID TRILOGY

Dear reader,

We hope you enjoyed reading *Face of the Void*. Please take a moment to leave a review, even if it's a short one. Your opinion is important to us.

Discover more books by R.S. Penney at https://www.nextchapter.pub/authors/rs-penney

Want to know when one of our books is free or discounted? Join the newsletter at http://eepurl.com/bqqB3H

Best regards,

R.S. Penney and the Next Chapter Team

Face Of The Void
ISBN: 978-4-86747-604-8

Published by
Next Chapter
1-60-20 Minami-Otsuka
170-0005 Toshima-Ku, Tokyo
+818035793528

21st May 2021